RAMMING SPEED

Sorenson lowered his binoculars. "Right. It's the Seawolf."

Then a flash erupted on the forecastle, blinding Sorenson. The concussion drove air into his ears and squeezed his chest. Acrid gases burned his nose. A lucky hit had exploded at the base of the gun.

(Sonar contact was made again.)

"She's hurt badly!" Steel said. "Blowing ballast! Look out!"

The *O'Leary*'s 4-inch guns boomed. An explosion rocked the conning tower, and many rounds ricocheted off the thick pressure hull. The *O'Leary*'s 20-millimeter guns chattered.

A 4.1-inch projectile blasted the *O'Leary* amidships, and steam jetted out the starboard side from one of the firerooms.

"Fire torpedoes!" Sorenson ordered. MacIntosh repeated the order over his telephones.

"Nobody answers!" the man shouted.

Sorenson knew he had one certain weapon left, and he decided to use it. "Left full rudder, Alvarado, ram the bastard!"

Bantam Books by William P. Mack

SOUTH TO JAVA (with William P. Mack, Jr.)
PURSUIT OF THE SEAWOLF

PURSUIT
OF THE
SEAWOLF

WILLIAM P. MACK
Vice Admiral, U.S. Navy (Ret.)

BANTAM BOOKS
NEW YORK • TORONTO • LONDON • SYDNEY • AUCKLAND

This edition contains the complete text
of the original hardcover edition.
NOT ONE WORD HAS BEEN OMITTED.

PURSUIT OF THE SEAWOLF

A Bantam Falcon Book / published by arrangement with
The Nautical & Aviation Publishing Company of America, Inc.

PUBLISHING HISTORY
Nautical & Aviation Publishing Company edition published 1991
Bantam edition / December 1992

ISBN 0-553-29902-6

Published simultaneously in the United States and Canada

PRINTED IN THE UNITED STATES OF AMERICA

RAD   0 9 8 7 6 5 4 3 2 1

PURSUIT
—— OF THE ——
SEAWOLF

Chapter One

Early in 1942, the American destroyer *Berry* rolled to port 35 degrees, hung there for a few seconds, then came back to an even keel as a mountainous North Atlantic sea passed under her. Twenty feet above the bridge in the 5-inch gun director, Lieutenant Alden Sorenson braced himself against the cold damp steel inside the box-like enclosure.

In the dusk he could see the conning tower of the U-boat ahead of the screening ships as it rose on the waves. "Can you get a range on it?" he asked the radar operator.

"Four six double oh!" shouted the radar operator.

Sorenson turned to the director pointer. "Commence firing!"

"Can't see it except when we're on top of a wave."

"Shoot when you see it."

In a few seconds the *Berry* began to rise, and the director pointer and trainer cranked their wheels furiously. Over the roar of the wind, Sorenson could hear the whine of the hydraulic motors on the forecastle guns as they tried to keep up with the director's orders.

"Fire!" the director pointer yelled. The two 5-inch guns on the forecastle thundered, and the growing darkness was lit up by the explosions.

Sorenson could not see the salvo land, but when the ship rose again just after the second salvo went out, he could see twin patches of bubbles from the first salvo just short of the submarine. Foam spewed from its superstructure vents as it rose and fell with the seas. The *Berry* fell slowly into the depths between the next two waves. When the *Berry* reached the top of the next swell, Sorenson searched anxiously, but the submarine had submerged.

"Damn!" Sorenson said. "She's down."

He pushed down the button on his telephone and reported to the bridge, "Submarine submerged. Four rounds expended. No apparent damage."

As the bridge talker was acknowledging his report, Sorenson could hear the Captain swear and give the order to increase speed.

The large seas held down their speed, and by the time they reached the area of submergence, sonar was unable to locate the U-boat.

Sorenson stood up in the director, poked his head out of the hatch above him, and looked aft. The large convoy astern was slowly overtaking the *Berry*. There was barely enough light to make out the eight columns of six ships bearing down on them. Sorenson shuddered, sat down quickly, and mashed down the transmitter button on his telephone headset. "Bridge, there's a helluva lot of ships headed this way from behind us. Can't the convoy maneuver to one side?"

There were a few seconds of silence after the bridge talker acknowledged his transmission. Then the talker said, "The Captain says there's a submarine contact on each bow, and the convoy commodore has decided to stay on course. We're supposed to hold the submarine down until the convoy passes over it."

Sorenson stood up and looked aft again, trying to fix the positions of the merchant hulks bearing down on them, but now it was so dark he could only see half of the convoy.

In a few minutes darkness was complete, the completeness of a dark night with an overhanging mist that shut out the moon and stars. Only the occasional phosphorescence of a breaking wave top broke the blackness.

Sorenson turned toward the last position of the submarine with his binoculars. He searched through the open director port, because the motion of the ship made using the director optics difficult.

The fire control radar operator said, "Sir, I can't get anything even if there is a submarine out there. Too much wave tops and flying spray."

"Keep trying," Sorenson said.

For a moment he thought he had the submarine, but in the dark every wind-tossed wave top looked like a submarine conning tower. For half an hour they searched for the submarine, hoping that it would broach accidently as it came up to high periscope depth trying to get through the screen to attack the ships of the convoy behind them.

From down on the bridge Sorenson could hear the faint pinging of the sonar; the volume was turned up high so that the Captain, who was on the wing of the bridge, could hear it over the rushing wind. Occasionally the sonar operator would report a contact, but most of them turned out to be non-submarine. One or two were probably the submarine, but the operator was unable to track it long enough for an attack to be made. Sorenson sympathized with the sonar operators, shut up in a small cubicle with the ship rolling and pitching and the rancid air fogging their eyes. Cold as it was, he liked being out in the open better.

Sorenson thought the U-boat captain was skilled and tenacious and he wondered if it was the same one they had been battling for three days. Maybe not, for there were others in the German group. Contacts now on each flank were being attacked by other escorts.

"Goddam bastards are having a field day," muttered the pointer.

"Helluva war!" said another voice. "We'll run out of ships at this rate."

Sorenson knew the Germans couldn't sink all of their ships, but they could sink enough to hamper the war effort.

Now, as the *Berry* and her quarry circled and sidestepped, the convoy astern was getting closer. The contacts on the flanks would still prevent the convoy commander from turning to avoid the contact ahead. Sorenson stirred on his hard metal seat. He knew the bridge watch and the air search radar were tracking the oncoming convoy, and he hoped the Captain would be able to avoid it. The *Berry* did not have a surface search radar, and using the air search radar was a clumsy substitute.

Then, as the first line of merchantmen passed by them, the director talker reported, "Bridge says the air search radar is out of commission. We're supposed to keep a sharp lookout for merchantmen."

"Where?" asked the trainer. "They're all around us!"

Sorenson shook his head in frustration. "Just keep looking!" he shouted.

"Right full rudder! All back emergency!" the Captain shouted on the wing below.

Sorenson knew the captain was trying to turn the ship to parallel the convoy course, but it was too late. A giant hull loomed out of the blackness, apparently out of station. The next seconds stretched into years. Below them the *Berry* shuddered as the engines strained to kill her way and take her out of danger. The bow began to swing, but a towering sea pushed it back. The merchantman's bow knifed into the *Berry*'s side amidships. Sorenson heard a terrible screech of rending metal, and the ship shuddered and rolled over under the oncoming bulk of the huge bow.

Sorenson gripped his director controls to steady himself as the director started to roll too, whipped by the motions of the hull below.

Sorenson knew the *Berry* was doomed. "Get out of the director!" he shouted. "Make sure your life jackets are secured!"

The director crew scrambled out of the hatches and clung to the ladder on the side of the director. By the time they were all out, the director was only feet above the black water. Sorenson yelled, "Jump!" When he was sure all of his men were in the water, he followed them. The coldness of the water almost stopped his breathing, but he started swimming as hard as he could. The action of his muscles helped to overcome the near-paralysis in his body.

He could hear the director crew splashing around him and calling to each other. "Keep together!" he shouted. "We'll make it!" But he knew he might be wrong. Then he remembered that on his last bridge watch he had logged the water temperature at 35 degrees. They would have a chance, even if a slim one, if they were picked up soon. In this frigid water they would last about 10 minutes before the coldness killed them. They would either have to be picked up or find something to cling to soon.

He could see very little at first, because of the darkness and the spray filling his eyes, but then the merchantman turned a searchlight on the *Berry*'s hulk. She was lying on her side, and in the reflected light, Sorenson knew her keel was broken. He shouted to his men, "Swim around the bow and try to get to the merchantman's side!"

Now even his bones felt frozen, and he tried to swim faster to generate warmth. Some of his crew began to fall behind, and he shouted, "Don't stop! The faster you swim the warmer you'll be!"

"Bull shit, Mister Sorenson," the trainer gasped. "I'll never get warm again!"

"Do it," Sorenson said, "or I'll take away your life jacket."

Gradually the group pulled around the *Berry*'s bow. Sorenson gasped and swallowed the cold spray filling his mouth. Strangely, he found the mountainous waves little trouble, as he bobbed to the tops of succeeding waves. When he had almost reached the limit of his endurance, the wind fell off, and he realized they were in the lee of the merchantman. Now he thought they might make it.

There were shouts above, and lines dropped into the water around them. Sorenson grabbed one and tied it through the arm holes of the life jacket of the director trainer who was fast slipping into unconsciousness. Sorenson could barely close his numb fingers, and the pain was intense. "Haul away!" he yelled. The line tautened, and the limp form of the trainer disappeared above.

As his last man vanished into the darkness up the long rope ladder, Sorenson grabbed the lowest rung and began to pull himself up. At first his hands would not close. He tried using his wrists and even his elbows to hold on to the rungs. For a moment he thought he would have to fall back in the frigid water and wait for someone to come down the ladder and help him, but he gritted his teeth and tried another rung. He made it. Then another. Slowly, one by one, he crept up the endless ladder. Halfway up he had to stop. Even his arms were like spaghetti, and his stomach was churning. He heaved up salt water until he thought his stomach would burst, but after a few seconds, his arms felt stronger, and there was a little feeling coming back into his hands. He began climbing slowly again, and soon he could see the top of the ladder.

Strong hands reached down, gripped his life jacket, and hauled him over the side. He tried to stand, but his legs buckled, and he slid down to the deck among the other *Berry* survivors into blackness.

Chapter Two

In May 1942, three months after his rescue, Sorenson stood by the bow of the four-stack destroyer the USS *O'Leary* in the Mare Island Ship Yard. He was waiting for the Captain to join him for a pier-side inspection of the ship. The two new gold stripes on Sorenson's shoulder boards glinted in the sun. All his uniforms had gone down with the *Berry*, and he had to buy new ones during his thirty-day survivor's leave in San Francisco.

The leave had restored him physically, but he still had nightmares of the bow of the merchantman bearing down on the *Berry*. He had tried to compensate for the dreams with alcohol. It had not helped, and he felt he might have more of a problem with stopping the alcohol than in stopping his dreams. Then he had tried to help his problem by working hard in his new job as executive officer of the *O'Leary*.

The long hours of bringing the old destroyer back to a state of reasonable readiness and installing a lot of new equipment in a short six-week period had tired him so much that he could sleep at night now. He bent his knees to ease the fatigue in them, took off his cap, and ruffled his short, blond hair. He rubbed the long scar that started at his hairline on the left side of his face and ended at his firm jaw line.

Sorenson put his cap on, straightened it carefully, and looked up at the white bow numbers of the *O'Leary*. Two deck hands, perched on a stage, were outlining the edges of the small white numbers, 200, bright against the dark gray paint of the bow of the ship.

A few welders' electrical lines spanned the narrow gap between the ship's side and the pier. Sparks showered from last minute jobs of her overhaul and conversion. Deck hands scurried about the topside, stowing gear and preparing the ship for sea.

Sorenson knew the overhaul had not cured all of the engineering department's ills. The twenty-two-year-old *O'Leary* had been in the Philippines at the start of the war and about to enter the shipyard at Cavite for a major overhaul. He had heard that the Japanese attack had forced her to leave Manila Bay and fight her way south to Java and on to Australia. A trip around southern Australia and back across the Pacific Ocean had brought her to Mare Island Naval Ship Yard. Since then the engineering plant had been overhauled, the gunnery wiring replaced, and new equipment installed, but it had been impossible for the yard crew, even working around the clock, to do well in six weeks what normally took four months.

The executive officer figured the ship would steam, but there would be troubles left over from almost twenty years in the tropics and three months of battle.

He bent over and picked up a discarded cigarette package. It said "Lucky Strike." He wondered if the *O'Leary*'s luck would hold. Certainly she had used up a lot of it in the battles off Java. He wadded it up and threw it into the nearest trash can.

The lack of experienced officers and petty officers in the engineering department worried Sorenson, and he knew the Captain was also concerned about the crew. Many of the officers and men of the *O'Leary* had left for reassignment to newer destroyers during the yard period. He knew that the veterans of the *O'Leary*'s battles in the Far East would continue to perform well, but as executive officer, his responsibility was to meld the new men with the old and to insure that they could perform as a team. It would be a tough job, and he realized it would take all of his energy and attention.

He shivered slightly. There was no fat on his six-foot frame, and the cold bothered him. There was a hint of coming warmth in the air, but the fog and wetness of April in northern California reminded him of the terrible weeks in the North Atlantic.

Sorenson looked back along the waterline. He liked the long, slim lines of the *O'Leary*, but the Captain had told him that when she was underway, water surged over the lower main deck in the slightest sea. With her tendency to roll in any weather, she would be very uncomfortable. Sorenson had hoped to be ordered to a newer destroyer, but the present job would have to do.

His thoughts were interrupted by approaching footsteps. The Captain, Lieutenant Commander Jack Meredith, and the engineering officer, Lieutenant Bull Durham, were walking down the pier toward him, laughing together. Sorenson envied their easy rapport, but it was more than their personal relationship that bothered him. Durham was supposed to work through Sorenson, but he had already by-passed him on several occasions. That would have to change. Sorenson noted that Durham was a full six inches shorter than Meredith's six feet, but where Meredith was tall and thin, Durham was stocky and muscular.

•   •   •

Meredith finished listening to Durham's account of his previous night's conquest and looked ahead to the area where Sorenson awaited them. Sorenson saluted and said, "Good morning, Captain. Good morning, Bull." Meredith returned his salute and greeting.

Meredith stroked the luxuriant black mustache that seemed to hold up his long nose. The *O'Leary*'s harrowing escape from the Japanese in the Philippines and Java had thinned him, and the wounds he had received in Java had further depleted his reserves. His concerned wife's cooking and six weeks in the yard had brought him back to a slender normal and perhaps a few pounds heavier. All the heavy cooking had put several extra pounds on Meredith's wife.

Meredith looked at the *O'Leary* and grinned. "Looks pretty good, doesn't she?"

"Not bad," Sorenson said.

Durham said, "Captain, may I join you in a walk down the pier so we can all get a good look at her?"

"Sure, Bull. I know the topsides aren't your responsibility, but you engineers like to think that your engines are carrying all this new equipment around. By the way, I just got a letter from Captain Arkwright. He's taking over a 1,630-ton destroyer in San Diego. He's going to have Ross Fraser, Doc Laster, and many others of the *O'Leary* crew ordered to his new ship, the *Harte*."

Meredith looked at Sorenson, who seemed to be puzzled. "Sorry, Tex. Lieutenant Commander Gerald Arkwright commanded the *O'Leary* when we were in the Philippines and Java, and Ross Fraser was the gunnery officer."

"A couple of good guys," Durham said. "The *Harte* will be a good ship."

The three officers started aft. The same obsolete 4-inch gun still crouched on the forecastle, protected by a metal spray shield. Time had not permitted shifting to 3-inch dual purpose guns, and Meredith had asked that the old 3-inch gun on the fantail be left aboard until a modern version could be installed. Two more 4-inch guns on the amidships deck house and a fourth on the after deck house, all without spray shields, would only elevate 45 degrees, so antiaircraft protection would rest with the six new 20-millimeter machine guns and the 3-inch antiaircraft gun aft.

Durham looked up at the bridge structure. "I liked the old bridge windows we had, but I guess these aluminum ports are better. The bridge will be warmer in cold weather. That quarter-inch armor plate around the front of the bridge won't keep out any big stuff, but it should stop some shrapnel."

Meredith said, "Yes, we may appreciate a warm bridge very soon."

Durham's eyes narrowed. "Does that mean we're leaving the Pacific?"

"Keep it quiet until after lunch tomorrow. I'll tell the officers then and the crew later."

"I almost froze when we passed south of Australia on the way home."

"You'll have a while to stay warm. We'll have two weeks off San Diego for refresher training. Then a trip through the Panama Canal and the Caribbean. But this winter we'll probably be in the North Atlantic."

Meredith heard Sorenson suck in his breath.

Sorenson said, "Damned cold up there."

Durham frowned. "I liked the warm weather out in the Asiatic Fleet, but I didn't like all those dammed Jap aircraft."

"We don't have much more antiaircraft protection now," Meredith said. "But at least the German air threat is less in the Atlantic. The Germans use aircraft mostly for search, unless we get close to occupied Europe. Then we'd probably see dive bombers, torpedo planes, and even fighters. Isn't that right, Tex?"

"Right," Sorenson said.

From behind them the loud whine of high performance aircraft engines suddenly rose to a crescendo until they could no longer hear each other. Even the ship and yard noises were blotted out. When they first heard the sound, Meredith froze and seemed to be looking around for the nearest cover. Sorenson put a hand on his arm and said, "Just a couple of Wildcats."

Meredith couldn't hear him but evidently read his lips and calmed down.

Two pale-bellied Navy fighters roared overhead at low altitude and banked to the left, revealing blue top surfaces. The sun glinted off their plastic canopies.

Sorenson raised his hand to shield his eyes and watched them disappear. Gradually the noise of riveting, escaping steam, and the clank of yard cranes returned as the drone of the engines receded.

"What the hell were they doing here?" Meredith asked.

"Probably using the shipyard as a checkpoint for a cross-country navigational flight. They turned south toward Alameda. That wingman stunk," Sorenson said.

"I thought he turned all right," Meredith said.

Sorenson shook his head. "Not enough rudder, and he hit the throttle too late. He lost 50 feet on his leader."

Meredith laughed. "You're still up there flying. I thought you left that some time ago."

Sorenson shook his head. "Guess I never will."

Meredith looked at him closely. "Tex, you've got to

come down to earth. That's all over. You're a destroy-erman now. Start thinking like one."

There was a sharp edge in Meredith's voice, and Sorenson started to say something.

Meredith stopped. "What's that?"

"Nothing. I know you're right, but it's hard to let go when you've flown one of those things."

"You have to. A good executive officer has only enough energy for one thing—his ship. And that means cutting down on your drinking ashore, too."

Durham sighed. "Now you're hitting us both where it hurts."

"No, I don't think so. All that drinking won't help Tex forget the flying or his trouble in the Atlantic." Meredith stopped and looked directly at Sorenson. "We've got over a hundred lives to think about now."

Durham was looking off into the distance, trying not to listen, but Meredith turned to him, too. "And that goes for you, too, Bull. I know we've always been close friends and we've hoisted a few ashore together, but don't push it too far."

"Aw, come on, Jack," Durham said.

Meredith's voice was soft but firm. "I'm the Captain now, Bull. Don't forget that. And don't forget that Sorenson is my executive officer."

"Aye, aye, sir."

They walked aft toward the amidships deckhouse, where a 20-millimeter machine gun poked its snout over the side just forward of the amidships' 4-inch gun on that side. Gunner's mates were oiling the 20-millimeters and working on the sights and loading mechanisms. The weapons looked more business-like than the .50-caliber machine guns they had replaced.

Meredith grinned. "They look good, although I don't know why we have to use foreign-designed guns."

"I do," Sorenson said. "The 1.1 machine gun designed by the Bureau of Ordnance is a dog."

They were interrupted by a bellow from amidships. Meredith winced. "Jesus, they could hear Chief Morton clear over in the officer's club."

Durham laughed. "He's got the best set of balls in the

fleet. Despite his personality, you have to admit he knows his stuff as a chief boatswain's mate."

They listened in awe as Chief Mortland shouted orders to men working high up on the foremast.

Meredith shook his head. "I visited one of the newer destroyers in the yard here yesterday. They had one of these new 1MC interior and exterior speaker systems. It almost drove me nuts. They passed the word about something trivial every few minutes." Meredith pointed to a smartly uniformed petty officer walking aft on the main deck. "I like our old-fashioned system better."

The cheerful twitter of the boatswain's pipe the man was carrying echoed across the pier. The duty boatswain's mate continued aft to the hatch leading down to the after living compartment and leaned over the open hatch. He blew his pipe and shouted, "Clean sweep down, fore and aft."

Meredith said, "I don't like those damned loudspeakers. With our system, only essential messages are passed; if a man is needed, a messenger is sent after him."

Durham took off his uniform cap and ran a hand through his tightly curled hair. "Yes, sir, beats all that racket."

Sorenson said, "I like it, too. At first, after serving on a new destroyer, I thought the *O'Leary* was old-fashioned, but I'm learning to like a lot of things about her."

Durham grinned. "When we go to sea, you'll wish you had some of that new-fangled stuff back."

They paused just forward of the two triple torpedo tubes. Where there had been a fourth stack and below it a fourth boiler, there was now just deck space with a hatch.

Meredith nodded toward the ship. "The additional fuel tank we've got, where the number-four boiler used to be, will be useful. I think we can do without the extra three knots the boiler gave us, and we'll need the fuel in the Atlantic. If the weather is as bad as Tex says it is, we'll never be able to make much speed in those seas anyway. Besides, we need the extra berthing space that has been built above the fuel tank."

"I agree," Sorenson said.

"Those sixteen new men arrive today?" Meredith asked.

"Yes, sir," Sorenson said. "Mostly sonarmen, radarmen, and gunner's mates. Soon we'll have a total of ten officers."

Meredith said, "The men who man the after 20-millimeter guns will have to double as crews for the new K-guns."

Sorenson nodded. "If we're going to the Atlantic, we can also use the extra fifty depth charges that'll be stowed next to the new berthing area."

Durham said, "I wouldn't want to sleep down there with 50 depth charges and a fuel oil tank. A torpedo could blow you a hundred yards in the air."

Meredith laughed. "There's a set of fuel oil tanks and a magazine near both the forward and after berthing areas, and your bunk is right over the forward ones."

"Jesus," Durham said, "I didn't think about that. But a torpedo just about anywhere would be fatal for almost everybody."

"This is a risky business we're in," Meredith said. "We just take our chances and hope for the best."

They were now opposite the new depth charge throwers, known as K-guns because of their distinctive shape. There were three on each side; each consisted of a mortarlike gun that fired an arbor on which was perched a depth charge. Each gun had an open box-like arrangement next to it for storing additional depth charges.

Meredith studied the K-gun battery. "I like this arrangement even if it will be difficult to bring up the extra fifty depth charges in rough weather. I'm glad we've put our new first lieutenant on that job. Ensign Gerlach seems to have muscles on his muscles. If we're going to be chasing submarines from now on, we might as well put our best officers and men where they will do the most good. This K-gun battery and our new sonar installation will give us an antisubmarine capability as good as any of the new destroyers."

Sorenson frowned. "Maybe in equipment, but our new sonar officer hasn't arrived yet, and most of our sonarmen are new."

"When is our sonar officer due?"

"Today."

"Let's hope he makes it. I hear that the German submarine menace in the Atlantic is getting bad, and you've told us of your experiences. I'm going aboard and do a little paper work before lunch." Meredith walked back to the brow and climbed up the slight incline.

     •   •   •

Durham watched him go, followed by Sorenson, and turned and walked back up the pier. He thought about the last two years of his service as first lieutenant in the Asiatic Fleet, his stay in the hospital in Surabaya, and then rejoining with his leg in a cast in time for the escape of the *O'Leary* to Australia. In Australia he had become chief engineer when Meredith moved up to executive officer, and soon the commanding officer had been detached and Meredith had moved up to command. They had been trying times, and he was glad they were over, but the Atlantic and all those submarines might be worse.

     •   •   •

At the top of the brow, Meredith saluted the colors aft and then the petty officer of the watch, whose sleeve bore the rating badge of a radarman. Meredith looked at his serious young face but couldn't remember his name. He knew the man had come aboard recently. The young petty officer's blues hung well from a trim frame, and his gray eyes seemed to dominate his regular features. Meredith racked his memory, but the name escaped him.

Meredith looked up at the rotating air search radar antenna on the foremast. It looked like a bed spring with a bunch of antenna rods fixed in front of it.

Then he remembered the man's name. "Bronte, I see your men have the air search radar lit off. I hope the surface search antenna inside that damn beehive is working."

"Yes, sir, the surface search radar is lit off too."

"How did you get to be a second class radarman?"

"I used to be a third class fire controlman. I was sent

to radar school, and after that, they made me a second class radarman."

"That makes sense. Do you like the job?"

"Oh, yes, sir. Radar is going to revolutionize surface and air warfare."

Meredith raised his eyebrows slightly. "Perhaps you'd better show me the guts of your new installations the next time you have the consoles and stacks open."

"Glad to, sir. I want to see how the new surface search radar works at sea. It checks out okay in port, but it might have some bugs in it."

Meredith grinned. "Speaking of bugs, before you came aboard we had to be isolated and fumigated for cockroaches and rats and other varmints. The ship had a classic collection from almost twenty years in the tropics. But aside from the bugs, the overall situation for the ship is getting better. In the long history of this ship, this will be the first time she has ever had any equipment that is as good as that of a new destroyer."

Bronte grinned, and Meredith noticed how his white teeth stood out from his tanned complexion.

Meredith asked, "How do you get so tanned in the winter time?"

"Some of it I was born with, but most comes from lying up on the fire control platform in the sun and out of the wind on weekends. I know it's been cold, but out of the wind, it's warm enough to sun bathe."

"Don't you go ashore?"

"Not much. I find enlisted men have a pretty tough time ashore. I'd rather read."

"Do you think we're in better shape now than when you came aboard?"

"Yes, sir. This old bucket . . . ah pardon me, sir . . . this ship was sure in sad shape when I reported aboard. I never thought she'd sail again."

"I wasn't sure, either. Our missed overhaul and three months of fighting and battle damage took their toll, but I think she's as ready as six weeks can make her."

"But she needed four months, didn't she?"

Meredith nodded and turned to go below. He looked back at Bronte, who had turned back to the quarterdeck. He remembered with fondness the old hands in the Asiatic Fleet who had brought the *O'Leary* through its ordeal, but he was grateful for the bright young men who would have to understand and take care of the new equipment.

Then he thought about Sorenson. He remembered from reading Sorenson's personnel record that Sorenson had first served in the Navy for a year in the gunnery department of a carrier before he had entered flight training. Then, a week before completing advanced training, he had been terminated and sent to the destroyer *Berry* as gunnery officer. He meant to ask Sorenson why he had failed to complete flight training. Apparently the sinking of the *Berry* had also left a problem, which he suspected Sorenson had been trying to treat with alcohol. He knew he would have to get to the bottom of the situation if Sorenson was to reach his full potential as an executive officer.

There was another problem he would have to work on, too. He knew that there was a special relationship between himself and Durham, and he would have to be careful not to let that relationship undercut Sorenson's authority as executive officer. He was four years senior to Durham and two years senior to Sorenson. He remembered the times in the Asiatic Fleet when he had gone ashore with Durham. He could not forget them, but he knew he had to put them aside. He had made a first effort on the pier a few minutes ago, but more would be needed. He sighed. It wouldn't be easy, and he hated messy relationships.

•   •   •

After the evening meal, Signalman First Class Jaime Alvarado drew a cup of steaming black coffee from the battered signal bridge coffee pot and walked through the pilothouse toward the bridge wing. As he passed the steering wheel, he patted it, remembering all the hours he had spent at the helm. In small ships, a signalman was not only skilled in a signalman's duties, but was also a qualified helmsman and quartermaster. Alvarado took pride in being the best in all of these duties, and as the senior petty officer among the signalmen and quartermasters, could assign himself to the various duties of the signalmen and quartermasters as he saw fit. As the best helmsman aboard, he also steered the ship for fueling and for general quarters.

He stopped for a moment, tested the coffee, and decided that it was as bitter, black, and scalding as he liked it. He went over to the edge of the bridge wing to join Ensign John Jablonski, the navigator. Jablonski, a former chief quartermaster, had been an ensign for only two months. He had served six years on the *O'Leary* in the Asiatic Fleet and had functioned as navigator because the previous executive officer had been incompetent. The war had led to his commissioning, and Meredith trusted him so much that he had made him navigator in spite of his junior rank.

Alvarado stood beside him and thought that Jablonski's rimless glasses accentuated the quiet intelligence in his deep set eyes. Jablonski's thinning hair gave him a high, prominent forehead. Alvarado had often thought that the bookish Jablonski must have had his share of troubles in the school yard. Alvarado remembered his own youth and the slurs he had endured as a young boy of Mexican descent struggling in a white man's school in New Mexico.

He watched as Jablonski carefully wiped soot off the new varnish on the wooden railing at the top of the bulwark before he put the arms of his new khaki shirt on it.

Alvarado glanced aft at the thin stream of haze lofting from number one stack. "The damned snipes are lighting off and testing. Soon you won't be able to see anything but soot and smoke."

Jablonski laughed. "You guys will be back at war with the engineers again. I guess that's been going on ever since steam replaced sails."

Alvarado stole another look at Jablonski's face. He liked him, but there was something about him he couldn't break through. Jablonski had been a hell of a good quartermaster, but he was always reading books. He knew Jablonski had been to college for a year, a rare accomplishment for an Asiatic Fleet sailor, but Jablonski never made a point of it. Although Jablonski sprinkled his conversation with a little slang and an occasional "ain't," it never rang true, and Alvarado suspected that

Jablonski was just trying to fit in with his less-educated shipmates.

Alvarado said, "You spent all day turning in our Pacific charts and drawing Atlantic ones. Does that mean what I think it does?"

"Could be, but I wouldn't say anything about it to anyone until there's an announcement."

"Jesus, I wasn't made for cold weather. The Philippines were always nice and warm."

"If we need it, I'm sure we'll get some good foul weather gear."

"We've already got it. That's what I was helping to stow last week. I'm sure we've got enough for the whole crew. There were a hell of a lot of boxes."

Jablonski grinned. "Well, you know as much as I do then."

Alvarado looked aft. "Who the hell is that?" A young ensign wearing his blue service dress uniform was getting out of a taxi abreast the brow. "Looks like a sea scout and a little one at that."

Jablonski turned and looked aft. "Let's go aft by the signal bags and watch him come aboard."

•   •   •

Bronte was standing his second watch of the day as petty officer of the watch for a friend who had an urgent date ashore. He looked over on the pier and watched a taxi draw up at the base of the brow. The ensign backed out of the taxi and stood up. He looked to be about five feet four.

Bronte turned to the messenger of the watch. "Looks like a new officer about to report aboard. Go tell Ensign Gerlach, the duty officer."

Bronte moved closer to the side of the quarterdeck so that he could hear the conversation on the pier.

The ensign asked the cab driver, "Are you sure this is the *O'Leary*?"

"Yup. The one and only. Don't look like much, but it fought a lot of Japs, so they say. And if you look up at the side of the bridge, you'll see the evidence. Looks like they bagged one surface ship and one aircraft. Not bad."

The ensign shook his head. "Just the same, she's not

what I expected. She's all painted up, but she looks old and tired."

Bronte's lips tightened, and he prepared to dislike the newcomer.

The ensign paid off the taxi driver, left his bags on the pier, and walked up the brow.

Bronte felt mildly amused. The approaching officer seemed small and unprepossessing, and Bronte suspected that the crew would soon put him in his place. But he maintained his respectful attitude.

The officer saluted the colors, the new gold ensign's stripe on his blue sleeve flashing in the last rays of the day of the California sun. He turned to Bronte. "Sir, I request permission to come aboard."

Bronte returned his salute. "Permission granted, sir."

The officer stepped down off of the brow and handed Bronte an envelope. "These are my orders. I'm Ensign Steele, reporting for duty."

Bronte quickly revised his estimate of the new officer. Steele's voice had seemed to come from his feet. It was low-pitched, loud, and penetrating, and it left no doubt in Bronte's mind that Ensign Steele would know how to give a command. Bronte looked a little closer. Behind the steel-rimmed glasses was a pair of penetrating pale blue eyes and below them a slightly crooked nose and a firm mouth and chin.

"Ah, yes, sir. I'll have a mess attendant bring your bags aboard."

A large, thick-shouldered ensign wearing blue service stumbled out of the hatch at the forward end of the quarterdeck and walked over to Steele. He held out a huge hand. "I'm Ensign Hans Gerlach. I've got the day's duty. I hope you're the new sonar officer. The Captain and the Exec have been wondering where you were."

Gerlach was a head taller than Steele. Mutt and Jeff, Bronte thought, as Steele's hand disappeared in Gerlach's meaty paw.

"Sylvester Steele, your new sonar officer."

"We'll be working together closely. I'm the first lieutenant, torpedo officer, and depth charge battery officer. You find 'em; I kill 'em."

"All three jobs?"

"Until the new torpedo officer gets here. He's due any day."

Bronte had always known of the slight accent in Gerlach's voice, and Steele seemed to detect it too. "Do you speak German?"

"Yes, but not as well as I speak Dutch. My family came to this country from Holland several years ago. My mother is German, and I learned my German from her before I learned to speak English."

Steele and Gerlach disappeared down the hatch behind the messenger. Bronte reached up under his white hat and scratched his stubble of brown hair. "Got a feeling that new ensign is a live one," he said quietly to the messenger.

Chapter Three

There was a knock on the door frame of Durham's stateroom. "Come in," Durham said.

The messenger of the watch pulled aside the curtain. "Sir, Ensign Steele is reporting for duty. I brought him to you because the executive officer is ashore."

Steele stepped forward. "Good evening, sir."

Durham looked up at Steele. His eyes widened. "My God, you're shorter than I am." Durham stood up, smiled, and held out his hand. "Now I'm not the shortest man on board."

Steele shook his hand, his lips compressed. "Sir, height doesn't matter. Performance does."

"That's what my lady friends say, too. They always come back for more. Maybe I ought to take you ashore with me."

"I don't think so. I've been married for over a year. My wife makes sure I'm a happy man."

Durham felt a pang of envy. "Well, I guess we can't do any business there. Let's go see the Captain. He's been anxious to get you aboard."

Meredith's cabin opened off the starboard corner of the wardroom. Durham knocked at his door.

Meredith asked them in and stood to greet Steele. "Please sit down."

Durham moved a second chair in from the wardroom. "I brought Steele in because Tex is off the ship. I knew you were anxious to see him."

Meredith nodded. "Steele, we're glad to see you. We have a new mission. We aren't just a destroyer. We're an antisubmarine escort. I hope you learned something in sonar school."

"Thank you, sir, but I was at top of my class in sonar school, and I had expected to be ordered to a bigger destroyer."

Meredith's eyebrows arched and his mustache straightened.

Durham sat up in his chair. "We're not good enough for you?"

"I was first in my class at Yale NROTC and I thought I'd be needed on a newer ship."

Meredith's mustache recovered slowly, and he said, "Other destroyers may be bigger and even newer, but our sonar equipment is just as good as the newer destroyers'. We're important to the Navy, and we'll be doing only antisubmarine escort work, which will give us more time with submarines than any new destroyer. Obviously your responsibility will be very heavy."

"In that case, I'm glad to be aboard, Captain, and I'll do my best."

Durham said, "You have a very strong and low-pitched voice. What's your secret?"

"I built up my volume as coxswain of the Yale varsity crew for three years. The low pitch came after I was punched in the voice box when I was boxing as a 118-pounder for the boxing team."

Durham smirked. "Inter-collegiate champ, no doubt."

Steele's expression eased, and Durham noticed that there was even a hint of a smile. "Only the last two years."

Meredith's hand and his mustache covered most of his smile. "What did you major in at Yale?"

"Business and economics. After graduation, I worked for Merrill Lynch as a stockbroker for a year. Then I got called up from the Reserves."

"He's married," Durham said.

"Good to see not all shorties are carousers. Too bad, Bull, you'll just have to find another playmate."

Meredith stood up. "Glad you're here, Steele, we need

you. Mr. Durham will have someone show you to your quarters. I'll see you tomorrow."

As Durham and Steele were leaving, Meredith said, "I'm attending a morning ASW briefing at the headquarters of the Commandant of the Twelfth Naval District. You'd better come with me. We'll be back well before lunch."

•   •   •

The next day Sorenson, working in his stateroom next to the wardroom, heard silverware rattling as mess attendants set the table for early lunch. The chatter of the mess attendants disturbed him, and he went out to the wardroom to quiet them. When he saw the cheerful faces of the Filipino mess attendants, he changed his mind and sat down in one of the lounge chairs bolted to the deck at the end of the wardroom. He picked up a copy of *Life Magazine* and leafed through it, but it didn't hold his attention, so he tossed it aside and looked around the wardroom.

The *O'Leary*'s wardroom spanned the 30 feet from side to side of the hull. In its center, bolted to the deck, was the dining table, seating ten. Three steel stanchions, running from the deck up to the overhead, supported the overhead and helped keep the wardroom chairs and their occupants from sliding from side to side in a seaway. On the port side was a small settee, flanked by cabinets containing a sterilizer and surgical supplies. A large overhead lamp converted the wardroom table into an operating table at general quarters.

Then he remembered Ensign Steele's arrival, and he went back to his stateroom and sent for him.

Soon Steele knocked. Sorenson said, "Come in."

Steele entered and said, "Sir, I'm Ensign Steele."

"Yes, I know, and I'm glad to meet you. Sit down and tell me what you found out in San Francisco this morning."

Steele said, "The operations officer of the Twelfth Naval District said there haven't been any confirmed reports of Japanese submarine activity off the west coast nor off Panama. Our trip down should be easy."

"What are the conditions in the Atlantic?"

"The German subs are all over the Caribbean and our

Atlantic coast. They're sinking a lot of ships. We don't have enough destroyers in the North Atlantic. We have some escorts down south, mostly old four-stackers we didn't give to the British. There are also many converted yachts and patrol craft, all doing the best they can. Off the east coast, German submarines are showing up in increasing numbers, and they are beating the hell out of our convoys in the Eastern Atlantic. The British are taking an even worse licking.

"The worst I heard is about the future. British intelligence is telling us that the Germans are designing a new class of submarine based on the Type IX U-boat. It will be well over 1,250 tons, fast, and heavily armed."

Sorenson whistled. "We only go 1,200 tons. It will be bigger than we are. What kind of armament will it have?"

"The British aren't sure yet. One version may have two 4.1-inch guns and two 20-millimeter machine guns. Another will have one 4.1-inch gun and eight 20-millimeter machine guns."

"Not only bigger than we are, but almost as heavily armed," Sorenson said. "At least we'll have enough speed to get away from her. What will she be called?"

"Officially just Type IX, A, B, and C. The German Navy doesn't like names. However, the German sailors call her the Seawolf class, unofficially."

Sorenson shook his head. "I hope we won't run into too many Seawolves."

"It would only take one, but as of right now it should be a year or more before any get to sea."

"I take it we're needed over there."

"Very much. They don't want us to waste a day."

Sorenson suppressed a shudder as he remembered what had happened to the *Berry*. "Well, at least we can take a few minutes off for lunch. We'll be having quarters right after lunch. Tell me a little about yourself."

• • •

In a few minutes Sorenson could hear the officers of the ship filtering in for lunch, occupying the available seats and trying to stay out of the way of two mess attendants who were still working on the table.

At noon, Sorenson entered from the passageway nearest his stateroom, followed by Steele.

Sorenson cleared his throat, and the conversation in the wardroom abated. "Gentlemen, this is Ensign Sylvester Steele, late of Yale University, Wall Street, and the Fleet Sonar School. He's our new sonar officer."

Steele smiled and then said in his deep voice, "Pleased to meet you."

Sorenson continued the introductions. "I'll be sitting on the Captain's right. Across from me is Lieutenant Bull Durham, the engineering officer. Then on the other side, Chuck Steiner, the gunnery officer, and next across John Jablonski, the navigator. Then Gerry Chumley, the communications officer and radar officer, and Hans Gerlach, the first lieutenant. You will sit next to him. Then there are vacant seats for the new supply officer and the new torpedo officer who are supposed to report soon, and at the end of the table is our handsome mess treasurer, David Fineman, who is also our doctor. The Captain will be out in a minute. Please carry on."

•   •   •

Fineman looked carefully at Steele. He noticed his small stature and seemingly mild manner, but there seemed to be an underlying strength in him that intrigued his professional judgement. He decided to observe Steele closely, but before he could look at him again, the curtain to the Captain's cabin flew open, and Meredith walked out. "Good morning, gentlemen, please sit down. I'm starved; I hope Morales has something good for us. I see you've all met Ensign Steele."

Fineman noted again the Captain's erect carriage, common to so many Naval Academy graduates. Fineman was a graduate of Brown University and Harvard Medical School. He had completed one year of internship, but the war had interfered with his planned training in psychiatry. The chance to observe the officers of the O'Leary appealed to him. He wondered what made career military officers tick. His limited exposure to psychiatry had revealed some of the well-springs of human behavior, but in the end he wondered if one could really understand people, even oneself.

He had pegged Meredith as both family-oriented and

professional. He guessed he would treat his crew as he would treat his family.

Sorenson he did not yet know well. He judged that Sorenson was unhappy about something fundamental in his life, but he didn't know what it was, and he resolved to find out. An unhappy executive officer meant an unhappy ship.

Durham, now in bantering conversation with Meredith, fascinated him. Some good in Durham lurked below the surface, and he hoped to root it out in the very near future.

Steiner, squarely built and of medium height, he thought of as a good, professional officer. Steady, conscientious, and a little boring.

The others were even newer on board than Fineman, and he looked forward to analyzing them. He found the Navy both fascinating and sometimes dull. There was not enough medical business for him, since the Navy was manned by healthy young men. Any potentially interesting case had to be transferred to the nearest hospital or a larger ship. At least that gave him an excuse to visit the nearest hospital. In the meantime, he tried to fill the intellectual gap with music; he was now mentally inventorying his extensive record collection.

He sighed, and looked up the table. Steele was seated at his left and was looking at him expectantly, and he realized Steele had said something to him in his low and penetrating voice. "What was that?"

Steele looked slightly startled and said again, "Doctor, one of my roommates, my sparring partner, was Jewish. Are you?"

Fineman chuckled. "One of my grandfathers was Jewish but my mother was an Episcopalian. You have to be raised in the Jewish religion by a Jewish mother or convert as an adult to be a real Jew. I have some of the genes, but apart from that I'm as Episcopalian and as English as Chumley, who claims English blood."

"Chumley is of English descent? My wife would like to meet him. She went to school in London."

Fineman pointed to Gerlach across the table. "Now Hans, there, is of German stock. All those muscles are real. He was an all-American fullback at the University of Pittsburgh. Came right out of the coal fields."

Gerlach grinned and reached for the butter. "After college I came right here. I'm looking forward to seeing more of the world." Gerlach's strong, open face was framed by a short haircut and an outhrust jaw, obviously containing some replaced teeth.

Fineman thought Chumley was different from the others. He was lean and rangy, and his face was angular and slightly strained. He was chewing on a roll, eyes staring straight ahead. Fineman thought he would have some business with Chumley.

Steele said, "Chumley, if you don't mind my asking, are you married?"

Chumley looked up from his plate. "Yes, but we're considering a divorce."

The doctor made another mental note. He would have to talk to Chumley sooner than he had thought.

When lunch ended, Meredith pushed back his chair. He took a deep breath. Presiding over a wardroom conference was still new to him. "Morales, clear the table, but leave the coffee cups. You can leave the pantry door open and listen, because the crew is going to be called to quarters at 1300 and told the same thing we'll be talking about."

The officers pushed their chairs back slightly to allow the mess attendants to get at the dishes, but the white table cloth was left on. One of the new mess attendants started to put ash trays on the table. Morales quietly put a hand on his arm. "No, no, never put ash trays on the table. The Captain doesn't allow smoking in the wardroom."

When all the officers had been settled with coffee refills, Meredith cleared his throat. The wardroom stilled in seconds.

"You know we are about to complete our partial overhaul, and the Navy will want to put us back to work soon. It's obvious that we no longer belong in the Pacific without a better antiaircraft battery, but we have other capabilities that have been increased with our new equipment. Our logical employment would be as an escort in the Atlantic, and that's where we're bound."

There was a murmur around the table. Meredith paused to let the news sink in. "We'll leave here day after tomorrow for San Diego, steaming alone. That will give us a chance to make a full power run, test-fire our guns, drop some depth charges, and arrive ready for two weeks of refresher training."

There was a silence. Finally Gerlach raised a hand. "Pardon me, Captain, but what is refresher training?"

Durham answered. "Two weeks of hell, and a lot like war. We'll have drills and inspections day and night conducted by a crew of experts from the training command. They get into everything."

Meredith grinned. "The area off San Diego is safe. Only the craziest Japanese submarine commander would come near it. Isn't that right, Steele?"

"Yes, sir."

"Then we'll have two days in San Diego to load stores, ammunition, fuel, and to recover."

Someone down the table laughed. "Let's hear it for recover."

When the laughter died down, Meredith went on. "Then we head for Panama. Obviously the exact schedule we follow will be secret, but the fact that we're going to be transferred to the Atlantic Ocean can be talked about. Our new home port will be Norfolk, so you can start moving your families as soon as possible."

"Jesus!" Steiner said. "Gas and tire rationing! How the hell will our wives make it?"

Meredith nodded. "All you married men, I'll be glad to give you my road maps and gasoline consumption data. It won't be easy. You get so much gasoline a week, but for travel orders or home port change you get additional coupons for a certain number of tanks of gasoline. If you work it right, your wife can get your car across country by driving it until the tank is nearly empty and then hoping she can get to a gas station. If she can't find a gas station, she'll need a good pair of shoes."

Steiner moaned. "But shoes are rationed, too, and the damned things are made of cardboard. My kids go through a pair every month."

Durham laughed. "For all you bachelors, remember

that although there is a leather and rubber tire shortage, there's no shortage of rubber condoms."

"And be sure you use them," Fineman chimed in.

Meredith said, "That's all. Please get on with your work. Tex, you, Bull, Chuck, and Doctor Fineman please stay for a few minutes."

When the junior officers had cleared, the older officers gathered around Meredith, who looked at them as they settled in their chairs and poured more coffee. Durham and Steiner had come through a tough period in the early days of the war, and Meredith felt a close tie with them. All three *O'Leary* veterans and Sorenson wore Naval Academy rings; the other officers were either Reserves or mustangs, commissioned from enlisted status. Meredith wondered if the inexperienced officers would measure up to the demands of their jobs.

Sorenson was still an unknown quantity. Meredith liked him, but he knew some changes had to be made. There had been problems between Sorenson and Durham, and he felt uneasy about it.

He looked at Durham on his left, who was examining a hangnail. His brown, curly hair was combed forward in Roman style. Meredith suspected it was hiding a receding hair line, and he was secretly glad that his own luxuriant black hair was holding up. Durham's face was strong and dominating, as were his neck and torso, set on short legs. In any event, there was something there that women liked.

Steiner was over six feet and strongly built. He was somewhat slow, but he was dependable. Everything about Steiner was medium, even the shade of his brown hair and eyes. His performance under fire in Java had been steady, but Steiner was not a quick learner. Meredith hoped the demands of his new job as gunnery officer would not overwhelm him.

Doctor Fineman was a little more intellectual, perhaps. Meredith knew that Fineman's background was impressive, but he wondered if a doctor with more surgical experience wouldn't be more valuable.

As the four officers settled, Meredith placed a hand on the white-covered table. Then he looked up at the operating room light overhead. "Bull, do you remember lying on this table with that damned light in your eyes?"

Durham looked up at the light and squinted. "Hell, yes. I still hate that thing. I remember when the stretcher bearers strapped me to a stretcher and lowered me from the fire control platform to the main deck. When I was put on the table, it hurt like hell. I thought I'd never walk again."

Meredith remembered the wounds and burns he had sustained; he shuddered.

Fineman said, "Navy medicine must have done all right. You're both as good as new, whatever that was."

Meredith sighed. "Enough sea stories. Let's get down to business. We need to plan a little personal strategy. Chuck, I understand you are going to send your wife directly to Norfolk."

"Yes, sir. We're going to sell the car, and she'll go by train whenever she can get a ticket. They're tough to come by these days."

Meredith went on. "My wife and children leave tomorrow by car, so we'll all be bachelors for awhile. When we get to Norfolk, I'd like to be able to see my family frequently, and I'm sure Chuck will want to do likewise. This means Tex and Bull will have to stay close to the ship there. In exchange, I propose that Tex and Bull take shore leave after refresher training in San Diego and also time off in Panama City. I plan to stay aboard both times. Chuck, you'll be loading ammunition in San Diego, and I'd appreciate it if you'd limit your time in Panama City to buying souvenirs so that you'll be ready to help me get us through the canal."

Durham assumed an innocent expression. "Why, Captain, souvenirs are all I'm going to look for in Panama."

Meredith shook his head. "Bull, I've been ashore with you in China. I could keep up with you in the beer department, but after you shifted into high gear chasing women, I got left in the dust."

Fineman spoke up. "Where do I come in?"

Meredith grinned. "Make sure Bull doesn't bring back any physical souvenirs. Panama City has one of the worst venereal disease rates in the world. I need to know whenever you think the chief engineer is . . . er . . . not fully fit for duty."

Durham squirmed. "But Captain, I'm always fit for duty."

"It would be better if he took some prophylactics ashore with him," Fineman said.

"Then make sure he has a pocket full of them. I need him hitting on all cylinders. He's got to keep the engineering plant going."

There were footsteps on the deck above. Meredith said, "It's time for the crew to go to quarters so that I can speak to them. Tex, when you have completed the muster, move all the men aft up to the forecastle. Tex and Bull, when quarters is over, I'd like to see you both in my cabin."

•   •   •

After quarters, Meredith sat idly in his cabin sipping a cup of cold coffee. Sorenson and Durham were still on the forecastle with the crew, answering questions. The coffee had cooled while he waited, but the time gave him an opportunity to go over Sorenson's personnel record again and collect his thoughts. Just as he pushed the cup away, there was a knock on his door frame. "Come in," he said.

Sorenson and Durham entered and sat down in two chairs next to Meredith's desk.

Sorenson said, "You wanted to see us?"

"Yes, and I asked to see you together. If at any time you don't want to answer my questions in the presence of the other, just say so, and we'll separate the conference."

Sorenson looked at Durham. "Okay by me."

Durham returned his look. "Shoot, Captain."

Meredith turned to Sorenson. "First, Tex, tell me about this flight training thing. All it says is that you were terminated in the last week of advanced training."

"They don't have to give a reason. They just write your orders, and you leave."

"Yes, but I want to know all about it."

"All of it?"

"Yes, don't leave out a thing. I don't think you've

done anything Bull hasn't done twice. I can guess that you didn't leave flying because you wanted to."

"No, flying was the only thing I ever wanted to do in the Navy. Being kicked out was the worst thing that ever happened to me."

"Kicked out?"

"Yes, I was in my last week and was waiting for orders to the fleet. After a flight in advanced acrobatics, I felt so good that I flew over the farm of a girl I was dating and flat hatted it."

"Flat hatted?"

"Flew low over the barn and snap-rolled."

"What was wrong with that?"

"Two days before our squadron commander had announced that any flat hatting would be cause for dismissal. I was in sick bay and didn't get the word."

"Didn't you appeal?"

"Oh, sure, but he said it was my business to get the word, and no excuses were acceptable."

"But you didn't do any damage."

Sorenson laughed, and he noticed Durham was leaning forward in his chair listening intently. "I was so low I knocked the weather vane off the barn."

"Well, that wasn't so bad."

"I'm afraid it was. The weather vane fell on my girl's father's best cow. The cow panicked and charged into a barbed wire fence. It took over a hundred stitches to put her back together. My girl's father reported an aircraft tail-number to the base, but it wasn't mine. When I found that a friend of mine was about to get the sack, I had to step forward. The next day I was on my way to the *Berry*. I felt bad about the cow. I knew what she went through. When I was a kid on our ranch in Texas, a horse threw me into a barbed wire fence. That's when I got the scar on my face, also another on my arm."

Durham slapped the arm of his chair. "I knew there was something we had in common. I was thrown out of flight training, too."

"For flat hatting?"

Durham paused. "Er, no, more like low balling. I was caught in the sack with my instructor's wife."

Sorenson grinned. "How the hell did that happen?"

"Easy. She wasn't wearing a ring, I didn't know she was my instructor's wife, and he changed his schedule and came home early."

Meredith pushed the cup full of cold coffee toward the edge of his desk. "Well, this is interesting listening to you ex-fly boys telling stories, but let's get down to business. Bull, I know you are a feisty woman chaser and you drink too much, and I don't expect to reform you, but you've got to keep yourself in shape to run the engineering plant.

"You, Tex, have got to stop the booze ashore and do your job. I think you'll make a fine destroyer sailor if you get with it. I look forward to recommending you for command some day, and I hope to recommend Bull for executive officer. But you'll both have to prove to me that you can work together. If we all cooperate maybe we can survive the tough days ahead."

Sorenson said, "It's going to be hell, I can guarantee you that."

"Yes, Tex, I know your experiences there are a part of your problem, and I'll take that into account. Now both of you get out of here and get to work."

Chapter Four

The next day the deck force bustled about the *O'Leary*'s topside, securing loose gear and making preparations for getting underway. At 0830 the boatswain's mate of the watch passed the word to man all stations for getting underway. Meredith left his cabin and made his way up to the bridge through the moving men.

Jablonski caught his attention when he came through the door to the pilothouse and asked if he could show him the chart of the local area. "Should be easy getting out, Captain. I recommend backing straight out to this point on the chart, twisting to starboard, and then heading down the channel. I'll give you an exact course south when we get through the channel."

Steiner, who was officer of the deck for getting underway, was going down the check-off list with the boatswain's mate of the watch. Ensign Steele, the assistant officer of the watch, was looking over the bridge controls and instruments.

Meredith walked over to his elevated bridge chair and sat down. All was going normally until he looked down at the deck of the pilothouse.

"What the hell are those boxes doing here?"

"Sir?" asked Steele.

"Those two boxes of canned salmon sitting under the ports."

"Oh, those," Steele said patiently. "Lieutenant Durham had them sent up. I think he expects me to stand on them so I can get a good view out the ports."

"Do you really need them?"

"I don't, but maybe Lieutenant Durham does."

Meredith laughed. "Maybe they're a good idea because the new ports are so high, but I can't stand looking at all that salmon. We had to eat it for two months off Java. That was all we had except for rice and Vienna sausage."

Steele cleared his throat. "Captain, request permission to test whistle and siren?"

"Permission granted."

Steele reached for the siren handle and pulled it down three times. Three lusty whoops echoed across the yard. Then he yanked the whistle handle down once, and a single blast followed the siren's echo.

Sorenson came in the bridge door. "That was even louder than Chief Mortland. Sounds like she's still got both her balls."

Meredith chuckled. "I'd call that remark a first cousin to a mixed metaphor, if I didn't know better."

Steele said, "Whistle and siren satisfactory, sir. I request permission to take the ship out."

Meredith's eyebrows shot up. "What?"

"I'd like to take the deck and conn and take the ship out, sir."

"My God, you've only been aboard two days."

"Yes, sir, but I conned the sonar school destroyer out and in the harbor at San Diego for six weeks. Never scratched her."

Sorenson said, "How'd you manage that?"

"I just asked, sir, like I'm asking now, and they let me do it."

Sorenson said, "I suppose you're qualified as officer of the deck, too."

Steele said, "Yes, but only in small formations."

Sorenson looked at Meredith. "That's the hardest kind, steaming in big formations is easier. Maybe you ought to let him try. You can always take over."

Meredith scratched his head. "All right, Steele, take the deck and conn. Steiner, you can go to the after deckhouse where you would be normally for getting underway. Send Gerlach up to the forecastle where he belongs. If Steele doesn't pile us up, he'll become the officer of the deck for special sea detail from now on."

Steele formally took over the watch and conn from Steiner, who frowned but departed for the after deckhouse.

At 0855, Steele said, "Sir, request permission to single up all lines?"

Meredith squirmed in his chair, but he had committed himself, so he said in a controlled voice, "Permission granted. Get underway on time."

Steele turned to the talker. "Single up all lines. Engine room stand by to answer all bells."

Men on deck scurried to take in the extra bights of line. Soon the talker reported, "All lines singled up."

Steele walked out on the starboard wing and looked aft. The only connections to the pier were the six single strands of mooring line. Above him the safety valve exhaust from number one boiler hissed quietly, and clear haze rose from all three stacks. He walked to the other wing and noted that the area astern was clear.

Steele walked back to the door to the side of the pilothouse and looked in at the clock. It read 0859. "Take in all lines except two."

The mooring lines snaked aboard from the pier. At exactly 0900 Steele ordered, "Port engine ahead two-thirds. Starboard engine back one-third. Right full rudder." The ship surged ahead slightly against the number two line, and the stern began to swing out. Muddy water boiled up astern.

Steele took a deep breath. "Take in two. All engines back two-thirds. Rudder amidships. Quartermaster, sound one long blast."

The sound of the whistle drowned out the voice of the talker who was reporting back to Steele. Steele nodded acknowledgement. The *O'Leary* gathered sternway rapidly, and the pier seemed to slide away.

Steele noticed that Meredith's hands were gripping the edge of the bridge wing, as he apparently tried to give the impression of coolness by looking over the side at the bits of trash boiling up in the water.

Steele walked to the opposite wing to get a better

view of the channel. It was still clear, and he kept the ship on a steady heading by commands to the helmsman.

Jablonski, who had been plotting a series of navigational fixes on the chart, said, "Recommend twisting to two two zero."

Steele ordered, "Left full rudder. Port engine ahead full. Starboard engine back one-third."

The ship slowed and began to twist to starboard.

When the ship was dead in the water, Steele said, "Shift the rudder."

The ship began to twist rapidly to starboard. As the heading neared two zero zero, Steele ordered, "All engines ahead standard. Steady on two zero zero."

When they were steady, Steele looked at the Captain and reported, "Sir, we're on the first course for the entrance to San Francisco Bay."

Meredith took his hands off the rail, let out his breath, and turned to Sorenson, who had been standing next to him. "I'll be damned, he did it!"

Steele noticed that Sorenson was also breathing more normally.

Meredith said, "And he didn't even have to use the boxes of that damned salmon Bull sent up."

Steele went out on the wing of the bridge. He breathed deeply. Thank God that's over, he thought.

•   •   •

On the signal bridge Alvarado looked up at a four-flag hoist giving the USS *O'Leary*'s call sign. The multicolored flags streamed aft, bellying and snapping in the breeze. Alvarado said to the signalman on watch, "Tighten the halyard. There's slack in it."

The signalman said, "It looks tight to me."

"Do it!" Alvarado said.

The signalman pulled the halyard a little tighter. Alvarado squinted at the yardarm. "That's better."

Bronte was leaning against the after bulkhead of the chart house nursing a cup of coffee. "Alvarado, why the hell does the Navy still use signal flags. My TBS radio is all we need."

Alvarado sneered. "All you young smart-asses think

electronics is the answer to everything. What about the times when the TBS doesn't work?"

"Ah, well, nothing works all the time."

"The signal flags do. And when they can't be seen, a flashing light does the job."

Bronte shook his head and sipped his coffee.

Alvarado said to the signalman on watch, "Execute the hoist. There's nobody to see it now."

The signalman on watch cast the halyard loose and the block on the yardarm squealed as the smooth flax halyard ran through it.

Alvarado said, "Hear that sound? It's like music."

Bronte fished a piece of soot out of his coffee cup. "What do you mean music? I only hear one note."

"Ask Mister Sorenson. He and Mister Steele were up here watching our last signal drill. He told Mister Steele it reminded him of the opening passage of one of Bartok's pieces composed during his impressionistic period."

"What the hell did he mean by that?"

"I don't know. Mister Steele didn't seem to know either. He said he didn't know much about music, but the note had a lot of up doppler. Who's this guy Bartok?"

"An Hungarian composer."

"Oh, yeah."

"Ask Mister Sorenson."

A red spot grew on each of Alvarado's swarthy cheeks. He was reaching the limit of his patience. "I'll take your word for it."

Bronte put his empty coffee cup in a bucket of water under the signal bridge coffee maker. "Would you like to hear one of Bartok's records sometime? Doctor Fineman has some."

"Any maraccas in it?"

"Nah."

"Any Marimbas?"

"Don't think so."

"To hell with it. It can't be any good."

•   •   •

The *O'Leary* steamed down the upper bay for two hours and rounded Point Richmond. Then a lookout reported, "Fog bank ahead."

Meredith lifted his binoculars and searched the area ahead. There was a low-lying bank of dense white fog from Angel Island south to Alcatraz Island. The tops of both islands poked through the fog.

Sorenson returned from a topside inspection to make sure all equipment was secured for sea. He reported to the Captain.

Meredith nodded at his report. "Thanks. Look at that fog ahead."

Jablonski checked the chart and said, "Captain, we're due to change course to two five zero as soon as Angel Island is abeam to starboard."

Meredith frowned. "How can we enter the channel in that damned fog?"

Steele said, "Easy, Captain. It's done all the time now with surface radar. Come take a look at our new radar repeater console. This is just like the new installations on the ships of the sonar school."

Sorenson said, "He's right, Captain. We didn't have a surface search radar on the *Berry*, but other ships navigated with it."

Meredith was not convinced, but he joined Jablonski and Steele around the circular top of the radar repeater, which the yard had installed at the right front of the bridge. Sorenson looked over Meredith's shoulder.

Steele pointed at the center of the display. "This is a PPI, which stands for plan position indicator. We are in the center of the display, and you can see Angel Island and Alcatraz up ahead of us. You can see that there is no traffic in the channel between us and the main channel buoys. Soon you will be able to see all the main channel buoys and any traffic in them. Eventually the Golden Gate Bridge will come on the display."

Meredith said, "I should have paid more attention to this when it was installed. How do you know so much about it, Steele?"

"The sonar school ships all had them. We navigated in and out of San Diego Harbor using radar when it was foggy."

Meredith turned to Sorenson. "What do you think, Tex?"

"It should work fine. I'll keep my eye on the navigational plot."

Jablonski said, "I'll be able to keep a very good navigational plot using radar ranges and bearings. Bronte, at the control console in the charthouse, controls the antenna sweep. When I want a range and bearing, I tell him over the telephone, and he stops the antenna on the target I designate. Then he reads off the range and bearing and sends them to me."

Meredith tweaked his mustache. "Let's go. I want to see how this thing works."

•   •   •

A half hour later when they entered the fog bank, Meredith had a hard time controlling his nerves. He got out of his chair and paced the bridge, alternately looking at the PPI and Jablonski's chart. The radar showed the channel ahead was clear, but he still occasionally peered ahead out the moisture-streaked ports out of habit.

Sorenson said, "After years and years of being told to slow or stop in a fog, steaming ahead at any speed over five knots is an eerie feeling."

Steele said, "Nothing to worry about, sir. The channel is clear this side of the bridge."

In a few minutes Jablonski announced, "Angel Island abeam. Recommend change course to two five zero."

Steele looked inquiringly at Meredith.

Meredith looked at Sorenson. Sorenson nodded.

Meredith said, "Go ahead."

Steele took a last look at the PPI and gave the order.

They steamed at 10 knots until the Golden Gate Bridge pylons were clearly visible on the PPI. Meredith was gaining confidence. "Take her through," he said.

As they passed under the bridge, Sorenson went out to the bridge wing and looked up. "Captain, I can hear the sound of heavy traffic up there, but I can't see anything."

"Must mean the bridge deck is above the fog."

In half an hour, the *O'Leary* poked her bow out of the fog bank. Ahead about 20 miles were the Farallone Islands.

Jablonski looked up from his chart. "Captain, I recommend coming left to course two zero zero, increasing speed to 20 knots, and zigzagging in accordance with plan twelve."

"Very well," Meredith said. "Mr. Steele, make it so."

Meredith sat back in his chair and said to the messenger, "Go down to the wardroom and ask the duty mess attendant to bring me a cup of coffee."

Meredith felt more relaxed now that they were in the clear California sunshine, but he was troubled. He felt that he should have known more about the recently installed surface radar and its capabilities. He knew the rest of the ship intimately, particularly the engineering department, and he knew tactics and how to handle the ship, but the new capabilities offered by the surface search radar were fascinating. He gritted his teeth and swore silently. He would have to do better, and he was ashamed that his executive officer and a young ensign had rescued him.

Ensign Chumley was standing next to Steele, and the two were going through the routine of turning over the watch. Meredith sat up straighter. "Chumley, have the instruction manuals and wiring diagrams for the radars sent up to me right away. I want you and Bronte to give me a tour through the installations tomorrow morning." He added, "And the same goes for the new sonar, Steele. I want to know just as much about it."

Meredith felt better, and he sat back in his chair and took the cup of coffee offered to him by Morales. He sipped it. It wasn't bad, and it was in a china cup and saucer sitting on a silver tray, but somehow it wasn't nearly as good as the black, bitter coffee brewed in the engineroom in a battered aluminum pot and served in a cracked mug. Command had its privileges, but sometimes he yearned for the days of lesser responsibility when he had been chief engineer.

Chapter Five

The next morning Sorenson, Steele, Chumley, and Bronte came to the bridge early to take Meredith on a tour of the radar installations. Meredith was sitting in his bridge chair massaging the back of his neck.

"What's the trouble?" Sorenson asked.

"That damned bunk in the charthouse is too small, and the pinging of the sonar kept me awake all night. I've got to do something."

Steele grinned. "Sorry, sir. Maybe we can fix that." He unfurled a large sketch and spread it out on the bridge chart desk. "This is a layout of the new operations center designed for these old destroyers. I copied this from a set of plans when I was in San Diego. As you can see, your pipe rail bunk goes."

Meredith looked at the sketch. "Where the hell do I sleep?"

"You move down to the commodore's cabin on the main deck, where the doctor now bunks. That way you will only have one cabin. You'll have more room than in your present cabin, and you'll only be one deck below the bridge."

Meredith grinned. "Sounds great, but we may never get another overhaul."

Sorenson cleared his throat. "What the hell. Why not do what we can with the ship's force? No one will ever know about it after we've finished refresher training."

Steele said, "Let's go back to the charthouse. Chumley

will show you what we have and what we'd like to do. That's his territory."

Inside the charthouse it was hard to see, but Meredith's eyes soon got used to the dimmed lights. Meredith said, "I see the old sonar console is still there, but I assume its guts are new."

"Yes," Steele said. "We also have a new streamlined fairing for our sonar dome."

"I saw that being built in drydock. How much will it help us?"

"It will bring our maximum search speed up to 17 knots. We will be able to classify sonar contacts easier because the background noise will be much less."

Meredith looked in the corners of the compartment where men sat in front of consoles with round glass inserts in their fronts. "Are the radars performing satisfactorily?"

Chumley said, "Yes, sir. Most of the circuitry for both radars is in a new compartment just below us."

"I looked at it. I've got some more studying to do before I know exactly how all of it works."

Meredith looked around again. "When I got into my pipe rail bunk last night I almost stepped on the new dead reckoning tracer. It used to be a solid chart desk."

Chumley nodded toward the large plate glass on top of the dead reckoning tracer. "I'm glad you didn't step on it. You would have put us out of business."

"I'm still not sure how it works," Meredith said.

Chumley rested his hand on the glass top. "A navigational chart or plain piece of tracing paper is taped over the glass. That moving light represents the ship."

"I see," Meredith said. "That little bug traces our course and speed and gives us our position."

"Yes, sir. The bug is driven by a series of simple mechanical computers that take in course and speed and put out orders to two worm drives that position the bug. The bug represents our ship and travels across the paper just like the ship crosses the water."

"I'll be damned. I like it."

Sorenson said, "It saves the navigator a lot of trouble."

Chumley smiled. "You'd better like it too, Mister

Sorenson. This is supposed to be your battle station, and it will soon be called the operations center or possibly the combat information center."

"Why don't we call it the combat information center now?" Sorenson asked.

"I'll buy that," Meredith said. "Make it so." He looked at the dead reckoning tracer. "That means this is the DRT in the CIC."

Steele said, "Exactly. Our CIC is small, and the newer destroyers will have larger ones. We can take the Captain's bunk out, move the DRT over to the port bulkhead, and put up an air plot over the air search radar console."

"Air plot?" Meredith asked. "What do we need that for. Our antiaircraft battery is short-ranged. They can see what they'll be shooting at."

"We'll need it," Chumley said. "We have to be able to plot incoming tracks of aircraft. We can also control the movements of antisubmarine aircraft. We may not be able to shoot down many aircraft, but we need to know where they are, both friendly and enemy, and to be able to tell ours where to go."

Meredith said, "What's all this other new stuff in the sketch?"

Chumley said, "We'll make a few of these changes in San Diego. Between the DRT and the Sonar console will be a small communications center for the executive officer or the man in charge of the watch. There is a TBS control box duplicating the one on the bridge, and a transceiver for communicating with aircraft on medium frequencies. Also we are going to put up a surface status board and a communications status board for use in keeping track of other ships, aircraft, and their radio call signs."

"How am I going to do all that?" Sorenson asked.

Chumley laughed. "You'll have a couple of plotters and a radioman to help you at general quarters. At condition III, there'll be an operations watch officer, two radarmen, and a sonarman on watch in here to run the show."

Meredith opened the door and stepped into the sunshine. "Come on, Tex, let's let these young geniuses get to work. I'm going below and start moving into the main deck cabin."

He paused and looked at Chumley. There was something different about him, but the strained look on his face was still there. Meredith said, "Has something changed about you that I don't know about?"

Chumley grinned. "Yes, sir. I guess I'm a little happier. My wife and I have decided to get back together."

"Don't tell me if you don't want to, but how did it happen?"

"It goes back to the time before I was called to active duty. I was home from the job every night, and I liked it, but apparently my wife didn't. She got a little bored. Now that I'm in the Navy and move around a lot, she likes the life. She came down to San Francisco to make the final arrangements for separation, but it turned into a second honeymoon. I brought her out to the ship for dinner just before we left, and she liked all of my shipmates, especially Lieutenant Durham."

"I'd be careful," Meredith advised.

"I'm not worried. The scuttlebutt is that Mr. Durham never bothers married women."

"So she's happy with the Navy life? Many wives can't take the stress and constant travel."

"Yes, that's what I hear, but my wife likes both. She's off in our car for Norfolk. Says she'll have an apartment ready for us, but I don't think we're out of the woods yet. I want to see how we make out when we settle down in Norfolk."

"Good luck," Meredith said. As he went down the ladder, he thought about his early married days and wondered why his wife hadn't left him. He'd been away from her before the start of the war for over a year after all the wives had been evacuated from the Philippines. Then it had taken the *O'Leary* four more months to return to the States.

•　　　•　　　•

Later that morning Steiner came to the bridge to report to the Captain. "Sir, I've checked all of the 4-inch recoil cylinders and all of the firing circuits. The main battery and the 20-millimeter machine guns are ready for test firing."

Meredith said, "You have permission to fire. Ask the officer of the deck to pass the word to go to general quarters about five minutes before you're ready to fire. Many of the new men have never seen or heard a gun fired."

When they tested the guns, the 4-inchers blasted large spouts of water off the beam. The machine guns stitched rows of splashes across the bright blue water.

A few minutes after the gun testing, there was a thud and a groan at the bridge door. Meredith turned. Ensign Gerlach was stooped over in the doorway, helping the messenger to his feet.

"What happened?" Meredith asked.

"Sorry, sir," Gerlach said as he straightened up. "I was in a hurry, and I didn't see the messenger coming out the door."

Meredith looked closely at Gerlach. "What position did you play in football?"

"Fullback."

"Didn't you look to see if there was a hole in front of you when you carried the ball?"

"Not often, because I hardly ever carried the ball. I blocked mostly, and there was always some one in front of me, usually a linebacker. It was my job to run over people."

Meredith put his hand up to his face, trying not to laugh. "I see. Well, think of yourself as a halfback and try to avoid people. We might run out of messengers."

Gerlach helped the messenger to rearrange his clothing. "Sorry," he said. "I'll look next time."

The messenger grinned tentatively and cringed against the bulkhead. "So will I, sir."

Gerlach turned to Meredith. "Captain, the depth charge battery is ready for a live drop. I thought you and Lieutenant Sorenson would like to observe it from the after deckhouse."

"We certainly would. Lead the way, and remember what I told you."

Back on the after deckhouse, Meredith leaned on the barrel of the 4-inch gun and talked with Sorenson. Gerlach, holding a clipboard and stop watch, charged between the K-guns and the depth charge racks, bowling over men who weren't quick enough to get out of his way.

Meredith turned to Sorenson. "Maybe it's too early for Gerlach to learn what I told him to do about watching out for people, but keep after him before he hurts someone."

Gerlach looked up at the Captain. "Ready, sir."

Meredith nodded. "Go ahead."

The word had been passed about the test drop, and many of the crew were allowed to leave their general quarters stations and line the rail of the amidships deckhouse to observe.

"Commence drop," shouted Gerlach.

The first charge rolled off the starboard rack on the fantail. Seconds later one rolled off the port rack, and at the same time the two after K-guns fired. The arbors pushed the charges up high in the air, landing about 50 yards from the side of the ship. Then another charge rolled off aft, and the middle two K-guns fired. This was followed by another charge rolling off aft and the two forward K-guns. Finally a fifth charge rolled off one of the after racks.

There was an expectant silence for a few seconds. Then the first charge exploded, and in sequence the other charges went off. Great white and black bulges of water pushed geysers of foam 50 feet high. Eventually the bubbly foam covered an area a hundred yards wide and over two hundred yards long. As each charge went off, the deck vibrated and shook under their feet.

Sorenson laughed exultantly. "Damned good! I know some U-boats in the Atlantic I'd like to see under those."

Gerlach looked up for approval.

Meredith leaned over the rail. "Fine job, Mr. Gerlach."

Gerlach turned and weaved toward his men who backed away and flattened themselves against bulkheads or stepped behind equipment.

Sorenson said, "We mustn't forget that we're only carrying 98 depth charges. That makes about nine full patterns. When we run out, we'll have to drop cases of Vienna sausage."

Meredith laughed. "I like those sausages. Let's make that cases of canned salmon."

•   •   •

The next day, Durham leaned against the polished steel rail at the main control area of the forward engine room. He took off his cap and wiped the perspiration from his face with a rag. Most of the air coming down the ventilator cooled the area where the throttleman stood his watch, and Durham didn't want to interfere with it.

They were building up speed for a four-hour full-power trial, which would allow the ship to make about 30 knots if everything worked right. With four boilers, the *O'Leary* had done 34, but no ship had yet gone to sea with one boiler removed, so 30 knots was only the yard's estimate. It would be about an hour before they were ready for full power. This period would be used to check the performance of the recently overhauled machinery and to look for steam leaks before opening the throttles wide.

The watch messenger tapped Durham on the shoulder and pointed to the bottom of the access ladder. A pair of khaki-clad legs, followed by a khaki shirt and Meredith's unmistakable mustache, came down the ladder.

Durham walked over to the bottom of the ladder and saluted as Meredith turned around. "Welcome to your old home."

Meredith's mustache lifted, and he grinned broadly and returned the salute. "It's good to be back. I spent many a day down here. How do you think you'll do?"

Durham hesitated. "Well, it's kind of like a three-teated cow. We'll do our best as far as maximum speed is concerned, but we'd be better balanced if we had four boilers. We'll have to steam with the firerooms cross-connected."

A messenger brought a mug of steaming black coffee over to Meredith, and he beamed as he tried to sip. "Nothing like black gang coffee."

Within an hour they were at full power. High pressure steam sang as it entered the straining turbines, and the vibration of the propeller shafts roiled the water in the bilges. At the end of the four hours, Meredith went over to the ladder, sweating but smiling. Durham followed him.

Meredith said, "We have a ship that's fast enough to go in harm's way."

"I just hope we don't encounter too much from the air," Durham said.

"Speed and maneuverability brought us through several air attacks in the Philippines," Meredith said. "I feel better knowing we can do 30 knots. Our speed kept the Japs from sinking us. Well done with your full power trial."

Durham watched Meredith's legs disappear up the trunk and took a deep swallow from his coffee mug, hoping 30 knots would be enough.

•   •   •

Point Loma Light loomed above the low-lying fog bank ahead that filled the entrance to San Diego Bay. Even after a night with the operations and maintenance manuals and a day going over the radar installations, Meredith was reluctant to try navigating by radar in the fog. But as they neared the entrance, the fog lifted.

"All right," he announced. "We'll navigate by radar anyway. We need the practice. Officer of the Deck, station the special sea and anchor details."

Entering the harbor was easy, and they anchored off the Sonar School, which was also the home of the Underway Training Command.

As soon as the accommodation ladder was lowered, a large motor launch filled with officers and senior petty officers, each carrying a clipboard, came alongside. An older lieutenant came up the ladder first, and Sorenson met him as he stepped on the quarterdeck.

"Lieutenant Hicks, in charge of Underway Training Unit One," he said.

"Glad to see you aboard," Sorenson said.

"Thanks. After two weeks you'll wish we'd never been here. But this will be a picnic compared with the North Atlantic. I just spent the winter there."

"I know. I've spent a winter there, too."

"Then you know how it is. Old four-pipers roll their guts out. You freeze your ass off, and the Krauts have a field day."

"Will you have some coffee while your officers and men come aboard?"

"Thanks, but we're anxious to get started. I'd appreciate it if you'd come with me while I call on the Captain and lay out your schedule. Today we'll inspect your men and ship at anchor. At dawn tomorrow we'll get underway."

• • •

For Sorenson, the next two weeks were a blur. Every piece of equipment was opened, inspected, and tested. Every officer and man was instructed and tested. Every possible drill, exercise, and firing was done. Nights were no exception. Their day ended at midnight and started at 0500.

It was tough but not as bad as the North Atlantic, Sorenson thought.

• • •

Chuck Steiner climbed wearily to the fire control platform. On the last day they were scheduled for a long-range firing of the 4-inch battery. At first light, a wallowing tug towing a long screen-like target on a very long tow line came over the horizon. When all was ready and they were at general quarters, they steamed away at high speed, turned, and began an approach to the target on a parallel and opposite course. The training command officer chose a course so that the O'Leary would pass the target about 5,000 yards abeam, but personnel in the gunnery department were not allowed to look at the target until the training command officer shouted, "Surface target starboard! Fire at will!"

Steiner turned and looked at the target through his binoculars, now about 6,000 yards away. He estimated the range at 5,500 yards and yelled, "Surface target starboard. All guns train out, match pointers, and load. Range five oh double oh. Target speed zero five. Target angle two five zero!"

The fire controlman operating the small computer attached to the director spun the dials as the director trained out.

Steiner shouted, "Commence firing, up ladder!"

The guns below fired in unison. The computer operator immediately increased the range by 500 yards, and the guns boomed again. A second time the computer operator added 500 yards, and a third salvo went out.

Steiner watched the red-dyed splashes rise. He could see that the first salvo was short and the second a little over, but both were in line with the target. He ignored the third salvo, still in the air, and shouted, "Down two. No change." The correction was made, and the fourth salvo was fired. As he expected, the third salvo landed well over, but the next was right on, raising red spouts of water around and just beyond the raft. Steiner shouted, "No change! No change! Rapid fire!"

The remaining salvos continued to fall close to the target. Then Steiner called out, "Cease firing!" He let out a breath and took off his telephone. He was sure they had made a good score.

Then he was aware that the training command officer was tugging at his sleeve. The officer pointed at the range finder operator leaning on his 3-foot wide instrument located at the front of the fire control platform. "But you never used your range finder! That's a violation of doctrine!"

Steiner laughed. "Go take a look through it."

The training command officer walked over to the range finder, bent over, and looked through the eyepieces. "Damn, I can't see a thing. It's vibrating too much."

"Join the club," Steiner said. "It'd be great if we were firing at 10 knots, but at our battle speed of 27 knots, it's useless."

The officer shook his head. "I don't know how you did it, but you estimated the range within 200 yards."

Steiner laughed. "Lots of practice, and a good teacher. Our former gunnery officer taught me a lot off of Java."

•   •   •

In the forward engine room, the underway training command group was just completing the last of a series of inspections and engineering casualty drills.

Durham was cooling off under the ventilator with the ship's chief machinist, a twenty-year veteran who had spent more than ten years on the *O'Leary* in the Asiatic Fleet.

"Well, Chief, how do you think we did?"

The chief took a long drag from his coffee mug. "Well, Mister Durham, I think we passed. The chief from the training command found a label on a pump valve he didn't like, but I think we reached an agreement."

"How so?"

"He claimed the label was written in Spanish."

"Was it?"

"Naw. It was in Tagalog. A Filipino yard worker installed it. We know what it means."

"What did it say?"

"Ang Balat."

"What does that mean?"

"Fuel oil pump."

Durham grinned. "How did you get to him?"

"He liked the brass plate and wanted to put it on his desk. He'll bring a replacement out tomorrow."

"Good. Anything else?"

"Well, there was a couple of other plates he missed. They were really Chinese, or at least they were installed in Chefoo."

"But in English?"

"Yes. They're on a large valve wheel. One says 'open' with an arrow."

"And the other?"

"It's supposed to say 'shut.' "

Durham grinned expectantly. "And it says?"

" 'Shit.' I made sure his glasses were steamed up when he was near it."

Durham shook his head and smiled. "I'd like to have that wheel for *my* desk."

The chief kept a straight face. "You'll have to find me a replacement."

•   •   •

The day after completing refresher training, the *O'Leary* lay at anchor loading ammunition. Sorenson, seated in his stateroom, heard a heavy knock on his door frame. "Come in."

Gerlach pushed back the door curtain and stepped inside, thudding against the door frame.

Sorenson said, "Remember what the Captain said about watching where you're going. You almost carried away my door frame. Think like a halfback. What's up?"

"You won't believe this. An hour ago we got dispatch orders to transfer Chief Mortland to the Eleventh Naval District to await further orders."

"Jesus," Sorenson said, "We just finished refresher training with him. We can't afford to leave without a chief boatswain's mate."

"We won't. A Chief Bellows from the Fleet Reserve just reported aboard."

Sorenson laughed. "A great name for a chief boatswain's mate. What do you think of him?"

"He's about sixty, gray haired, and a little shaky. He had to use both hands to hold his coffee cup steady."

Sorenson shook his head. "Well, do the best you can. I've got to get ashore. I'll see you when we get underway tomorrow."

•   •   •

The *O'Leary* sat at anchor off the San Diego Sonar School ready to leave for Panama. Meredith had watched discreetly from the bridge as the last officers came aboard. Sorenson was somber, but sober. Durham had obviously been drinking, but was under control. The sly smile on his reddened face was a barometer of his success. Doctor Fineman, close behind him, looked sober but tired, and obviously glad to have the long night over. Meredith hoped he had been at least mildly successful in restraining Durham.

Meredith had his breakfast sent up to the bridge on a tray so he could watch preparations for getting underway. By now he was confident that Steele could handle the bridge, but he just wanted to watch. He noticed the new chief boatswain's mate shuffle across the forecastle with the beginning creakiness of old age. He was slightly bent forward, and his knees didn't straighten out as he walked. The strands of hair visible below his cap were gray, but he was physically trim with no evidence of a belly.

"Damn," Meredith muttered, "Some bastard ashore stole Chief Mortland. The seagoing guys always take it in the neck."

At 0730 the special sea detail was stationed. Steele

darted about the bridge. Meredith watched him with increasing satisfaction. Then Durham appeared on the bridge, clean and sober, but a little shaky. Bronte handed him a coffee mug, and Durham drank deeply. When his hands began to tremble, he put down the mug and thrust his hands in his pockets.

Meredith said, "I didn't expect you up here."

Durham laughed, obviously trying not to jar his head. "Why not? I didn't even have time enough to warm up. I'll save the rest for Panama City. I just wanted to report that the engineering department is ready for getting underway."

Sorenson came up to the bridge, passing Durham on the way down. He walked over to Meredith and said, "Good morning, Captain."

"Good morning. How was San Diego?"

"Good. I have an aunt living there."

"Thanks for not saying anything to Durham."

Sorenson grinned. "He's a real pistol. He has a hell of a good time, but he always seems to be ready when it counts. I'm working on getting him to stick to the chain of command."

"Any success?"

"Not much."

Meredith laughed. "My fault as much as his. Keep trying."

At 0800, after colors, Steele asked permission to get underway, and Meredith nodded.

Steele turned to the talker. "Forecastle, heave right up. Main control, stand by to answer all bells."

The forecastle crew began to hoist the anchor, and the incoming links grated on the steel deck. Chief Bellows peered over the rail. Then he turned toward the bridge and bellowed in a gravelly voice, "Ha-forty ga-fiff hafadems hona ha-dick!"

Meredith's eyebrows shot up, and he sat forward in his chair. "What did he say?"

Sorenson laughed. "Forty-five fathoms on deck, I think."

In a minute, Chief Bellows turned again. "Ha-tirty hafaddems hona ha-dick!"

"I got that," Meredith said. "Thirty fathoms on deck."

"It's simple," Steele said. "Cancel all the h's and guess the rest."

Sorenson said, "I think we'll have to get a dentist to work on his dentures."

By the time Chief Bellows reported "H-da henkers hona ha-dick," Meredith had almost forgotten Chief Mortland. Chief Bellows was too good a show to miss.

"A real Asiatic sailor," he announced.

But is he as good a chief boatswain's mate as Chief Mortland, Meredith wondered. Even if he is, a misunderstood command could cause trouble.

Meredith turned to Sorenson, "Tex, let's get him to a dentist as soon as possible."

Chapter Six

Three days later, Sorenson watched the green coast of Panama rise over the horizon early in the morning. Panama City's profile bulged above the flat coast. Sorenson walked across the bridge to Meredith's chair. "I hear this is a wild place."

Meredith nodded. "In some sections every other building is a cathouse. It would take a year to try them all. The alternate buildings are either bars or souvenir shops."

Sorenson laughed. "Durham's kind of place."

Steele, who had the watch, joined them. "This place has a reason to look run down. It's been destroyed at least six times."

"Who the hell would bother?" Sorenson asked.

"The Carib Indians did it twice. Then the Spanish, and finally the English. It would have happened more often, but several Spanish and English armies disappeared in the jungle on the way across the isthmus."

"I'd rather go through the canal," Sorenson said.

Steele left them and stepped out on the wing.

Meredith said, "Tex, Doc tells me Bull was lucky when he went ashore in San Diego. I hope he'll be more careful here."

"Don't bet on it."

Chumley came up to the bridge with a dispatch.

"Good news?" asked Meredith.

"Good and bad. We're to anchor off the Pacific entrance to the canal and be ready to begin transit of the canal at 0800 tomorrow."

Sorenson whistled. "That doesn't give us much time for liberty for the crew."

Meredith pulled at his mustache. "They must need us badly in the Atlantic. In San Diego, they told me that the German subs were having a field day. We'll just have to divide the crew in half and send the first party over from 1000 to 2100. Then the second half from 2100 to 0700. You can take the whole time, and Bull, too. I promised it to you."

"Are you sure you don't want to go ashore for a while, Captain? I don't need Panama City."

"No, I was here when I was an ensign. That was enough. I need to spend a lot of time studying. I'm not going to let those junior officers know more than I do."

By 0900 they were anchored in the middle of a group of merchant ships that were joined by others as the day wore on.

When the *O'Leary*'s first liberty boat was alongside, Sorenson leaned over the bulwark and watched it being loaded with the men and officers ready to go ashore. When it was almost full, Durham clattered down the ladder. Sorenson grinned. He could almost smell Durham's usual cloud of aftershave. When Durham sat down, the officers near him coughed and laughed.

Sorenson went below to change into his liberty clothes. He was not very enthusiastic about going ashore, but he needed the exercise of a long walk. A beer would be nice, too, but he resolved to avoid anything stronger. The dreams of struggling in cold water were going away, and he thought he could do without a stronger drink.

•   •   •

The next morning Meredith took his place at the head of the wardroom table and ordered his usual breakfast of fried eggs and hominy grits. The only officers present were Sorenson, Steele, Gerlach, and Doctor Fineman. Meredith picked up his coffee cup and looked at Fineman. "Doc, where is everybody? On the sick list?"

The doctor lowered his fork. "Just about. We have the

expected number of hangovers, but most of the crew is also suffering from gastroenteritis."

"What happened?"

"I warned them all not to drink the water or allow anyone to put ice in their drinks, but most of them didn't listen. Next time they'll believe us."

"That won't help us today. What can we do right now?"

Sorenson said, "Our chief machinist's mate, several leading engineering petty officers, and three firemen were aboard all night fixing a feed pump. We'll be able to steam through the canal without any other watch standers. I plan to go down below for getting under-way."

Meredith laughed. "You, an engineer?"

Sorenson said, "Why not? I took the same engineering courses you did at the Naval Academy. This is a simple plant compared to the one we had on the *Berry*, and I qualified in my spare time as engineering officer on her."

Meredith said, "Call if you need me. I know every nut and bolt in her."

Steele said, "Gerlach and I had the shore patrol and duty yesterday. I took the early duty and then went ashore with the patrol at 2100. Gerlach can handle the after deck house, the chief boatswain can handle the forecastle, and Alvarado came back early. He'll be able to steer all the way through. That's all the men we really need. The canal pilot is aboard, and he says they'll provide line handlers."

Meredith perked up. "Well, let's go."

• • •

When Meredith arrived on the bridge, the topside looked deserted. Chief Bellows stood by with three young deck hands, two of whom were retching over the side. The anchor was hoisted without incident, and the deck hands leaned against the number one gun, leaving the rigging and handling of lines to the canal employees. Gerlach stood on the after deckhouse, with one sagging seaman, watching the two tugs coming up astern.

With Alvarado at the wheel, they passed through two sets of locks without trouble and arrived at Gatun Lake in two hours. The sun was beginning to heat the decks, and the young seamen on the forecastle had slid down to the horizontal. Meredith looked down on the forecastle, watching them carefully for signs of physical trouble.

Meredith began to relax, and sent for a cup of coffee. He looked for some one to talk to. "Steele, you said you were ashore on shore patrol last night. Did you find any trouble?"

Steele paused and looked at Alvarado. "No, sir. Just about average, I guess. Nobody on report."

Meredith thought that Alvarado seemed to sigh with relief.

Steele walked out on the bridge wing, as if he were trying to avoid further discussion.

Meredith's curiosity was aroused. When Bronte emerged from the charthouse, Meredith beckoned him over to his chair. "You were on shore patrol yesterday. Tell me all."

Meredith could see Alvarado's jaw muscle bulge and noticed that he looked over his shoulder at Bronte, but Bronte wasn't looking at him.

Bronte took a deep breath. "Well, sir, we were out on patrol in a pick-up truck when the radio said there was a disturbance at La Libertad Bar, and we were told to investigate. We parked in front and went in." Bronte paused.

Meredith noted that Alvarado heaved a resigned sigh, and he began to watch Alvarado closer. "Go on," Meredith said.

Bronte continued. "We went in, me right behind Mr. Steele. At the back of the room were about six of our guys standing over Kendrick, the gunner's mate. Kendrick was out colder than a whore's heart."

Meredith cleared his throat. "Then?"

"There were about a dozen Spics standing over at one side in a group."

"Spics? You should have called them Panamanians."

Meredith looked at Alvarado out of the corner of his eye, and noted that Alvarado rolled his eyes.

Bronte finally looked at Alvarado.

Bronte said, "Well, Alvarado here is a Spic, and he doesn't care if we call him that."

Meredith said, "It would be more accurate if you referred to him as a Mexican or Spanish-American. But go ahead. This is just getting good."

"Mister Steele walked over to the group of Spics ... ah ... Panamanians, and said, 'Gentlemen, what's going on?' "

"They didn't speak much English, so Alvarado translated."

"Alvarado was there?"

Meredith noted that Alvarado was concentrating on the compass.

"Uh, yes, sir, but he got back early."

"By request, I suppose."

"No, sir. He was fine. We gave the whole group a ride back."

"Then?"

"It turned out that a big Panamanian had decked Kendrick because Kendrick had called him a dirty Spic. Mister Steele said that was not right and that Kendrick would apologize. The big Panamanian said he couldn't because he was unconscious.

"Mister Steele walked over to a table, picked up a pitcher of ice water, and poured it over Kendrick. Kendrick came up fighting, but the rest of the group was quiet. Mister Steele told him he should apologize, but Kendrick was pretty foggy, and he couldn't understand. The Panamanians got a little pissed and moved forward. The big one sneered and said something."

"You could hear what he said?"

"Oh, yes, but I don't speak Spanish. Alvarado told Mister Steele the man had said that he was too little to control his men. Mister Steele laughed. I guess that set the big guy off. He moved in front of Mister Steele and started a hell of a haymaker. I moved behind Mister Steele to catch him when he fell. Mister Steele moved a little to one side and the haymaker swished by. Then the damnedest thing happened. I couldn't see it exactly because I was behind him, but Mister Steele, he moved forward a step and his shoulders moved, one after the other. The big guy gasped twice, and his hands flew up in the air. The next thing I knew he was on his back, and he was really out, worse than Kendrick."

"Then what happened?"

"The group of Panamanians stood there with their mouths open. Mister Steele walked over to them and said he would apologize for Kendrick and would they please tell that to the man on the floor when he came to. Alvarado translated for him. Then we all left the cafe and came back in the pickup truck."

There was a silence, and Meredith looked at Alvarado, who concentrated still more on the compass in front of him.

Meredith said, "Thanks. I think we'll just forget about this."

Alvarado's sigh of relief was audible to Meredith.

Steele came in the pilothouse door. "Is something wrong?" he asked.

"Not a thing. As a matter of fact, everything is all right. You might satisfy my curiosity, though. Why didn't you win the intercollegiate boxing championship in your first year, too?"

Steele was hesitant. "The first year I went out for the fencing team. I didn't like it very well, so I shifted over to boxing my second year. I liked that a lot better because I could see my opponent's eyes. The contact was a lot more personal."

"Yes, I can see that."

"Captain, what did you do in your spare time at the Naval Academy?"

Meredith looked at the overhead. "Well, ah, I mostly was on the radiator squad."

"I don't understand."

Meredith grinned. "That means I didn't take part in any organized athletics. Just sat in my room on the radiator and looked out the window."

        •   •   •

The trip through Gatun Lake went smoothly, and the green water slid by as Meredith watched it from the wing. Just before the *O'Leary* reached the Gatun Locks, Doctor Fineman stepped onto the bridge wing.

Meredith looked back over his shoulder at him and asked, "How are all of your patients doing?"

"Much better. If you'll look down on the forecastle you'll see a good many of them up and about. I used up all of my paragoric. I'd like to go ashore in Colon and replenish."

Sorenson came up on the bridge and handed Meredith a dispatch. "I picked this up from radio."

Meredith read it and noted they'd be leaving Colon in three hours. After fueling, the *O'Leary*, a Brazilian destroyer, and two patrol craft were to escort a sixteen-ship convoy to Trinidad. "Doc, I have to go to a meeting with the convoy commodore and escort commander, so you'll have that time to get what you need. How did your time with Durham go?"

Before Fineman could answer, Sorenson said, "I started off with them and had a short beer at a bar. Then Durham wanted me to go with him to a cathouse. When we got in, I took one look at the girls and said I was going for a walk. That's the last I saw of him."

Fineman said, "He left the cathouse just after you did. I was able to keep up with him until midnight, but then he shifted into high gear, and I lost him for a couple of hours."

"Do you think he used the equipment you gave him?"

"I don't know," Fineman said. "By the time I found him again he wasn't talking very much. We'll know in a few days. I hope the worst he gets is the clap. I can cure that."

Just as Fineman was finishing, Durham joined them on the wing. "How come the ship is rolling so much?" he said.

Meredith smiled. "Rolling? We're in Gatun Lake, and it's as smooth as glass. It must be you. Did you get the same bug the rest of the crew got?"

"What bug?"

"Most of the crew got a bad case of the trots. Doc thinks it was from the drinking water."

"Who drinks water? They ought to know better."

Chapter Seven

Meredith went to the harbormaster's office for the convoy conference. When he got back he was glum.

Sorenson said, "What's the matter?"

"Sixteen merchantmen under a convoy commodore who barely speaks English and thinks a zigzag is something you scratch."

"How about the escort?"

"Worse. The escort is commanded by a commander in the Brazilian Navy in command of one of their destroyers. He is at sea for the second time in his twenty-year career. I hope the ship is better than he is, or we're in real trouble."

"Any other escorts?" Sorenson asked.

"Two patrol craft converted from yachts under the command of a couple of kids who look like sea scout rejects."

"No wonder the Germans are having such a field day in the Caribbean."

"Not only there, but all over the Atlantic," Meredith said.

"We'll have to try to compensate."

Meredith shook his head. "I hope we can, but we're too new. I smell big trouble."

Early that evening the convoy sortied from Colon. The sixteen merchantmen straggled into a ragged formation as Meredith fumed and swore. "Damn! I don't think these ships ever saw a formation before, and I know the convoy commander hasn't."

Sorenson, watching the escorts take station, said, "The escorts aren't very good either. They keep leaving gaps, and the escort commander isn't doing anything about it. His ship is the worst of all."

The TBS crackled, and a cultured voice said, "Small boys, get on station."

"Speaks good English," Sorenson said.

"He should," Meredith said disgustedly. "He spent the last fifteen years as a naval attaché in the Brazilian embassy in Washington."

The first two nights the convoy commodore had ordered a zigzag, but near collisions stopped that, and the convoy plodded on in the dark on a straight course.

"Big, slow targets," Meredith muttered, as he looked back at the leading line through his binoculars.

By the third day, the convoy and its escorts had improved a little.

Sorenson walked up to Meredith. "Tomorrow we'll be close enough to Trinidad to find U-boats, or rather close enough for them to find us. The intelligence summary says they're raising hell all around Trinidad."

• • •

The next morning when they were at general quarters, a U-boat, apparently slipping by one of the patrol craft, torpedoed a merchantman. Sorenson watched through his binoculars for a minute and then lowered them. He noted that the crew of gun one was watching in silent fascination. For a moment he thought about ordering them to stand by their gun, but then he realized there was nothing for them to shoot at, and they might as well see what war at sea was all about.

Alvarado, standing next to him, said, "Damn! Those poor bastards never knew what hit them."

Sorenson said, "I'm afraid there are going to be a lot more explosions like that."

"Here we go," Meredith said as the escort commander ordered the *O'Leary* to pick up survivors.

"That doesn't make sense," Sorenson said. "The escort commander should have used patrol craft to pick up survivors and kept us in the screen."

"Nothing makes sense. Officer of the deck, let's go."

They found the merchantman burning and listing badly. Sorenson looked through his binoculars. "Some of the crew are already in the water. I don't like to do it, but I recommend we go right up close aboard and pick them up. The submarine is probably long gone."

"I don't like it either, but the sooner we get the job done the sooner we'll be back in the screen."

Meredith took the conn. He turned in a wide sweep and ordered, "All stop."

The O'Leary glided to a near stop about 50 yards abeam and up-wind, and Meredith backed the engines for a few seconds to kill their way.

Sorenson went out on the bridge wing and directed the crew of gun one to cut loose the cargo net kept rigged to the life lines for rescue. Men began to climb up, and soon all those in the water were on the forecastle. A few crewmen were still manning fire hoses on the deck of the merchantman only 50 yards away.

The explosion was blinding, even in daylight. It blew Sorenson across the wing against the pilothouse bulkhead. When Sorenson staggered back to his feet, he saw some of the men of gun one draped over the gun. Others were lying on deck against the lifelines tangled with the merchant seamen just picked up.

Sorenson leaned in the bridge door. The steel structure had protected those inside the pilothouse from the worst of the explosion, and the thick glass ports had cracked but were intact. Meredith crawled in the opposite door and stood up, shaking his head. Men inside the pilothouse were getting up and resuming their stations.

Sorenson looked over at the remains of the stricken merchant ship and then up at the towering column of smoke, water, and debris still rising above her battered hull. "Jesus!" he shouted. "Take cover! Pass the word to all stations!"

Then he realized the telephone would take too long, and he cupped his hands and shouted first to the forecastle and then to the amidships deckhouse. "Take cover! Take cover!" The gun crews crowded under the guns, and Sorenson could hear the crew of the fire control director above scrambling down the ladder to the protection of the bridge.

Sorenson looked up again and stepped inside the pilothouse, just as the first of the debris fell on the topsides. Looking aft, he could see a piece of lifeboat as big as a barrel crush the port 20-millimeter machine gun.

Sorenson pulled his head back as a rain of salt water, shards of steel, boxes of cargo, and rounds of live ammunition landed on the forecastle. A shoe, with the foot still in it, thumped down on the port wing, and a mattress, lazily turning end over end, settled on the port anchor chain. Clothing and bits of bodies littered the rigging. The cascading sea water washed some of the gruesome litter overboard, but much of it caught in the lifelines and scuppers.

The Captain yelled to the talker. "All stations, report casualties and readiness!"

Yeoman First Class Carmody, the telephone talker at general quarters, pulled a pencil from under his life jacket and began making notes on a scrap of torn navigational chart.

Sorenson turned to Meredith. "Captain, this merchantman is about to go under, and I don't see any survivors in the water. We ought to get the hell out of here before we catch a torpedo."

Meredith said, "I agree. All ahead full. Right full rudder."

After the *O'Leary* had steadied on a course for the convoy, now disappearing over the horizon, Sorenson looked over Carmody's shoulder at his shorthand notes. "How many casualties, Carmody?"

"Four of our men and two merchant sailors," Carmody said. "Doctor Fineman is in the wardroom putting a splint on a broken arm, and the pharmacist's mate is sewing up several cuts. All stations report manned and ready with all equipment in commission except for 20-millimeter mount two which is flatter than a collision mat."

"I saw it happen," Sorenson said. "I also see a lot of dents in our deck plates and a lot of missing paint."

Meredith nodded his head. "We were lucky. But what I want to know is how that damned submarine sneaked up on us." He pulled down the handle on the transmitter of the squawk box. "Steele, come out on the bridge."

In a few seconds, Ensign Steele, the sonar officer, came through the bridge door. "Yes, Captain?"

"Steele, the torpedo that finished off that merchant ship must have passed close to us. Did you ever have contact with the submarine that fired it?"

"No sir. I don't think the explosion was caused by a torpedo. We didn't hear one coming, and we would have. I think the merchantman just blew up."

Sorenson said, "That makes sense. She was burning heavily, and a lot of ammunition landed on our decks. She must have been carrying a lot of it, and the fire finally reached it."

Steele said, "I'd like to search for the submarine, if there was one, but I recommend that we catch up with the convoy. They need us badly. There are fifteen more ships up there with only three escorts."

Sorenson looked at a new chart that Ensign Jablonski, the navigator, had pinned to the bridge chart desk. "We've got the rest of today and a full night before we get to Trinidad. This latest dispatch says there have been as many as eight U-boats operating north of Trinidad and they have already sunk twenty-eight ships this month. I think we're going to find a lot of trouble."

The TBS squawked. "Valiant, this is Planter. Another ship in the port column has been torpedoed. Are you closing fast enough to assist him?"

Meredith picked up the TBS transmitter. "Planter, this is Valiant. We'll be there in fifteen minutes."

Meredith turned to Steele. "This time we'll make a wider sonar search sweep around the merchant ship before we stop to pick up survivors."

"Aye, aye, sir," Steele said as he headed out the door for sonar.

Sorenson shook his head. "We're in a lot of trouble. The Germans are making us look like amateurs."

"We are amateurs," Meredith said. "Our convoy commodores are just peacetime merchant captains. Look at our escort. Real amateurs. And even we don't add much. Despite Steele's promise, he's still just a green ensign. This is the first enemy submarine he's ever encountered. He's trying to do a difficult job with one experienced sonarman and two new ones. We do have surface search radar and the latest sonar equipment and even the new K-guns, but we haven't had a chance to use them yet against skilled and experienced U-boat captains."

The escort commander directed one of the PCs to take the *O'Leary*'s place in rescuing survivors, and Sorenson heaved a sigh of relief.

Meredith sat down in his bridge chair and turned to Ensign Chumley, who had the deck. "Chumley, take the conn and rejoin the convoy at flank speed."

As they pulled into the lead station in the screen, the lookoute reported, "Two aircraft with running lights bearing zero two zero relative."

In the growing light Sorenson could see through his binoculars the bulky outlines of two Catalina PBY flying boats. He turned to Ensign Jablonski. "How far to Port of Spain?"

"Fifty miles, sir."

Sorenson nodded to Meredith, "I guess this game's about over. Frankly, we got skunked, and I don't like it."

       •   •   •

Four hours later the convoy began entering Port of Spain, the main port of Trinidad. When the last merchantman was inside the net entrance, the escorts began to enter. A small boat came alongside each escort, and an American naval officer boarded each one. When the boat approached the *O'Leary*, Sorenson went down to the well deck to meet the boarding officer.

The *O'Leary* slowed, and the boat came alongside. A lieutenant in khakis grabbed the rungs of the rope ladder and climbed up to the top. He swung a leg over the bulwark, faced aft, saluted, and said to Sorenson, "Request permission to come aboard. I'm Cherney, your liaison officer for your stay, which will be a short one."

Sorenson bristled. "What do you mean, short? We've been at general quarters for most of 60 hours and our men need some rest."

Cherney handed Sorenson a dispatch. "Your orders

are to go to the fuel pier and to leave with a convoy bound for Norfolk tomorrow."

"Jesus! The Captain won't like this. Let's go up to the bridge and see him."

Meredith slumped visibly when he heard the news. "Not only are we tired, but this old bucket needs several days for repairs. Also we need a new machine gun. Take a look at that one back there."

Cherney turned and looked aft. "I don't think you'll need a machine gun until you hit the North Atlantic. The naval station could put one on here in a day or so, but the big cheeses want you up north as soon as possible. I think they need your speed for troop convoys to Great Britain. You'll get fixed up in Norfolk. You look like you've been through a heavy storm."

"Yeah," Sorenson said. "Heavy is right. Pieces of steel, chunks of life boat. Crates of cargo. Not to mention pieces of people."

"Sorry," Cherney said. "I didn't know."

Sorenson said, "We lost six ships."

Cherney shook his head. "Not surprising. We've lost over twenty off Trinidad this month. There are some awfully good U-boat skippers around here."

Chapter Eight

Meredith went over to the harbormaster's office for the convoy conference. The next to enter was the Captain of the largest ship, a Norwegian tanker. Meredith rose and greeted him. "Are you the commodore of the convoy?" he asked.

"Ya. I'm Captain Danson of de tanker Flicka. Dey tell me I'm de commodore, whatever dat means."

"It means you're in charge of the merchant ships. You set the course and speed of the formation. I hope you can keep them on station, closed up, and darkened at night. Do you have enough signalmen to run the show?"

"Enough? I got vun. He'll do it. If I have to, I know de code and how to semaphore a little."

Meredith shook his head, but went on. "I'm the commander of your escort."

"How many ships you got?"

"One besides us."

"Ha! You no better off dan I am."

The rest of the captains arrived soon, and the harbormaster called the conference to order.

The harbormaster counted heads and then began after introducing himself. "I'm here to lay out your sailing orders. In your packet of information you'll find a short intelligence summary, the latest submarine contacts, and the most recent sinkings of our ships. The convoy will sail as soon as you're ready this evening. I know you won't like assembling in the dark, but remember any submarine out there won't be able to see you until you're well clear of land."

The convoy commodore interrupted. "Only four ships. Ve form a box. You guys get in formation and keep closed up. Uddervise you get sunk."

The harbormaster continued, "We're routing the convoy between Jamaica and Haiti to the east of the Bahamas, then directly to Norfolk. We're sending you east of air coverage from Florida because several German and a few Italian submarines are known to be in the channel between Florida and the Bahamas."

"How you know?" asked the convoy commodore.

"They sank three ships in the last week, all tankers."

"Dat's good enough for me."

The harbormaster asked Meredith if he had anything to say.

Meredith cleared his throat. "The commodore and I have already talked about how important it is not to straggle. You must be careful not to show any lights. There will be only one escort besides the *O'Leary*. Both of us will be at the front of the formation. If you drop back, you'll be on your own."

The other three captains looked at each other, but no one spoke.

The harbormaster looked around the room. "Very well, if there are no questions, the conference is over. Good luck."

The convoy commodore came over to speak to Meredith. "I see you in Norfolk."

"I hope so," Meredith said.

•　　　　　•　　　　　•

On the first morning at sea the warm, blue waters of the Caribbean slid by. A breeze pushed small waves from the east. Flying fish erupted from wave fronts and then flipped back into their element.

Next to Meredith, Sorenson leaned on the bridge bulwark watching. "Pretty day," he said, "but it's the same salt water you left in the Pacific."

Meredith stroked his mustache he had just trimmed. One side felt a little scraggly, and he knew he would have to trim it again. He missed his wife, who usually did it when he was home. "This water joins the gulf stream and swings up past Ireland and Iceland."

Sorenson nodded. "Maybe so, but there's still plenty of cold water up there. You last about ten minutes."

"How long were you in the water?"

Sorenson paused for a few seconds. "I really don't know. It seemed like years, but I suppose it was only about ten minutes."

"What were you wearing?"

"Just khakis, a foul weather jacket, and a life jacket. It wasn't enough, but I didn't expect to have to swim."

"That reminds me. When we get to Norfolk, have our new supply officer order another fifty percent of our allowance of cold weather clothing."

Sorenson frowned. "Do you think that's possible? The Navy Supply Depot won't honor our requisition if we're up to allowance."

"Then survey half of it. Claim dry rot, or something. If we have to pick up survivors up north, and we will, we'll need clothing for them."

"You sound certain we're going north."

"Of course. That's what we're in the Atlantic for. Escorting convoys. And most are going to Great Britain and Russia."

"How about the Mediterranean?"

"Some. Maybe we'll get lucky and get a convoy there, but the majority will be north through cold waters. That reminds me. Also get a double order of medicinal brandy."

Durham, standing nearby, brightened. "Now you're talking. Pints or quarts?"

Meredith laughed. "Neither. Get the individual bottles. They're easier to store and the dosage is exact."

That first day Meredith was apprehensive, expecting a repeat of the disaster on the voyage to Trinidad, but the commodore kept his charges well closed up, and two aircraft from Trinidad patrolled along the track.

The period of calm gave him a chance to think about the *O'Leary* and her readiness for the difficulties ahead, and he called Sorenson up to the bridge. They went out onto the wing where they could talk privately.

Meredith said, "I'm concerned about the *O'Leary*."

"Why? I thought we were making progress."

"Maybe, but it's too slow. I think we got good equipment in the yard, but not much of an overhaul. I wonder if the engineering plant will keep going in the months ahead."

"I agree with you about the equipment. If we can make it work right we can kill submarines. You know more about the engineering department than I do."

Meredith went over to the bridge door and told the messenger to ask the duty mess attendant to send up two cups of coffee, both black. When he returned to the wing, he said, "If we assume the equipment is okay, and the engineering plant will work, how about our officers and men?"

Sorenson paused for a moment. "Looking at them individually, I think they're all potentially capable of doing their assigned jobs. You know more about Steiner than I do, and I know he came through in the early days of the war. Therefore, I think the gunnery department will be all right. Steele certainly has promise, but we have to realize that he's inexperienced. The radars and communications seem to be working all right. The last is Bull. Again, you know more about his knowledge of engineering than I do, and I know you can fill in if there's some technical help needed."

Meredith and Sorenson took their coffee cups from the mess attendant and began to drink the bitter black brew.

Meredith said, "Not as good as the engine room coffee. I guess I'd agree with you about the officers. The enlisted men are another problem. We have a mixture of experienced hands and new ones. I know and trust the old ones; we'll have to depend on them when we get in tight fixes until we can test the new ones."

Meredith put his empty coffee cup on deck behind the pelorus. "The part of all this that concerns me most is what I call team training. I know we had an exhaustive test during refresher training. But in peace time that same training takes six weeks. We missed a lot, particularly damage control and antiaircraft firings. Then we haven't even fueled at sea. I've never conned this ship or any other destroyer during a fueling. Have you?"

"No. But I saw the *Berry* do it both when I was on watch in the gun director and on the after deckhouse at my fueling station."

Meredith shook his head. "Maybe you and I are the weak links. Are you in good mental shape yet?"

Sorenson frowned. "Yes and no. I still have dreams about swimming in cold water. As you know, I used to try to drown them out with booze or hard work. Lately I get up and stand in a hot shower for a few minutes, but we can't spare all that fresh water."

Meredith grinned. "As an ex-chief engineer, I agree."

Sorenson went on. "I try to tell myself to forget about flying and concentrate on a new career, but it's hard. Every time I see an aircraft fly by, I get that old feeling."

Meredith nodded. "I think it will pass with time. I also think you are doing a good job as executive officer, and you seem to be getting along all right with Bull."

"I'll get along with him. He just has to accept me. There have been some occasions where he has gone directly to you instead of working through me."

Meredith shifted uneasily and grinned. "I know, and I'll work on it."

* * *

Toward the end of the fourth day, Meredith could smell Jamaica and Haiti ahead. The odors of sugar cane, tropical flowers, and rotting jungle vegetation wafted past him.

He was dozing in his chair, dreaming of a tropical island and a native girl sitting next to him on the beach, when someone shook his arm. Meredith sat up. "Yes, Maloma?"

Chumley chuckled. "Afraid I'm not Maloma. I'm Chumley. I have a priority message for you."

Meredith blinked his eyes and started reading the dispatch. Halfway through he looked up at Gerlach, who had the deck. "Gerlach, plot this position on the chart and lay out a track to it."

Gerlach took the message and started to work. Meredith got out of his chair and looked over his shoulder. "That's close enough. Gerlach, ring up flank speed, and take that heading. Chumley, draft a message to the patrol craft and to the convoy commodore. Tell them we've been detached for a rescue mission, and the commanding officer of the patrol craft is to take over as escort commander."

Meredith turned to `the messenger. "Ask Mister Sorenson and Mister Jablonski to come up to the bridge."

In a few minutes both came clattering up the ladder. "What's up?" Sorenson asked.

Meredith turned away from the chart and said, "We've been designated to rescue survivors from a ship sunk off the coast of southern Haiti. Jablonski, check the plot, and give me an exact course at 25 knots and your estimated time of arrival. I make it about two hours. We should get there before dark."

Jablonski worked for a few minutes and gave Meredith a slightly different course. "Two hours it is."

Meredith said, "Tex, rig ship for rescuing survivors, and pass the word as to what we are going to do. There are lots of sharks around here, so have some riflemen ready." Then he grinned. "Get Kendrick to man a rifle. I hear he has some frustrations to work out."

Shortly before the O'Leary reached the area, Meredith ordered the ship to general quarters. Some of the gun crews were excused to man the boat and the cargo nets, which were hanging over the side.

Meredith approached the area cautiously, zigzagging at 17 knots, the maximum speed at which the sonar would operate satisfactorily.

Then a lookout called, "Raft one point on the starboard bow. Five miles."

Meredith raised his binoculars and located the raft. He turned to the talker. "Tell the gunnery officer to keep a sharp lookout for periscopes. The sub may still be around."

•   •   •

Sorenson watched the raft as the O'Leary approached it and studied the occupants through his binoculars. In a few minutes, Meredith took the conn and maneuvered the O'Leary alongside the raft. O'Leary men climbed down the cargo net and assisted the survivors up the side.

Sorenson went down to the main deck to supervise

operations there. The first man up wore a battered officer's cap with the remnants of gold on its visor. Sorenson asked, "Are you the Captain?"

The officer spoke in a language unfamiliar to Sorenson, who knew only English and Spanish. He turned to Chief Bellows. "Can you understand him?"

Bellows said, "Ho-yes. He ha-spik in Polish. He says he ha-the ha-Captain hov the ha-ship ha-*Maria*."

Sorenson said, "I get it. Ask him if all his crew were saved."

Bellows spoke in Polish for a few minutes to the Captain, who seemed to understand him. Sorenson thought maybe the softer Polish was easier on the chief's dental plates than English.

Bellows said, "He ha-says ha-yes."

"How come you speak Polish?" Sorenson asked.

"Ha-name used to be ha-Bjelowski."

Sorenson found another survivor who spoke English and found out that the submarine that had torpedoed the *Maria* had surfaced soon after. It had come very close alongside the raft, and the Captain had leaned over the side of the bridge and told the survivors that the nearest land was close by and the daily patrol plane they had grown accustomed to seeing was due soon. The survivor said the U-boat crew was young, smiling, and friendly, but that the submarine submerged soon and left.

• • •

After the last man was aboard, Meredith moved the ship away from the raft and ordered the gunnery officer to sink it with machine-gun fire.

Steele came over to the side of the bridge to watch the sinking. "Captain," he said, "The submarine may not be far away. I recommend we conduct a 17-knot expanding square search until dark."

Meredith said, "Tell Chumley to lay it out on the chart, and we'll start with an easterly leg. We'll stay at general quarters until it gets dark."

On the third leg a sharp echo interrupted the monotonous succession of pings. The contact was clearly recognizable on the bridge speaker. Meredith was on his feet even before Steele's voice boomed, "Sonar contact!

Probable submarine! Bearing two four five! Range two oh double oh!"

Meredith swung the ship to the bearing and waited.

Steele's reports came steadily. "Definite submarine! Recommend full depth charge pattern set on medium depth! Range closing rapidly! Up doppler! Submarine speed five knots! Recommend five degree lead!"

Meredith kept the head of the ship five degrees to the left of the bearings, and as they neared the submarine, Steele said, "Shifting to short scale! Stand by!"

Meredith paced the bridge nervously. He had made a few practice attacks on friendly submarines, but this was only the second he had made on an enemy submarine. It was the real thing. Soon he would unleash thousands of pounds of high explosives on a steel hull containing fifty human beings. But the bad feeling faded as he thought about the hundreds of ships and their crews already sunk by German submarines. By the time Steele recommended, "Stand by," he was ready to go again.

Steele called, "Drop!"

Meredith, watching his stop watch for the correct amount of time, turned to the talker and ordered, "Drop depth charges!"

Lookouts and signalmen turned aft. The K-guns fired with loud pops, and the rest of the pattern was fired or dropped. Small swirls marked where depth charges hit the water. There was a momentary silence as they waited. Then the first charges exploded with a rumbling roar, and the others followed. The sea erupted, and then it looked like it had been snowed on. The bubbles began to subside.

Meredith opened the range for another attack, and sonar reported the submarine was still there.

Twice more they attacked, but no debris came to the surface. Then sonar contact was lost, and they circled for a half-hour with no success. Meredith spotted an area of patchy oil and came alongside it. Chief Bellows dropped a swab over the side, and when he hoisted it he shouted, "Ha-diesel ha-oil!"

The evidence was not conclusive, and no more contacts were made. At dark Meredith reluctantly ordered a course for Kingston, where they had been ordered to unload survivors.

As they steamed along, Meredith, Sorenson, and Steele bent over the plot in the new combat information center and examined the pencilled track chart. One track showed the submarine and the other the *O'Leary*.

"Do you think this was really a submarine?" Meredith asked.

Steele said, "I think there's a fifty percent probability. Of course it could have been a school of fish, but no dead ones came to the surface after our depth charge attacks. The track is continuous and shows a speed of about four knots. The submarine, if that is what it was, made a course change here. I can't explain why we lost him. He could have gone deep below the thermal layer."

Meredith pulled at his mustache. "There are lots of wrecks around here. Perhaps that's where the diesel oil came from."

"And hundreds of small fishing boats," Chumley said. "They could have pumped it out of their bilges."

Meredith nodded. "I hate to give up, but the convoy needs our protection. There are four important ships in it."

Steele stretched his arms over his head. "I think you're right, Captain."

Meredith rubbed his neck. "We all need a rest before we arrive in Kingston."

*   *   *

Early the next morning, they rounded Port Royal and began the short transit into Kingston Harbor. Durham was leaning on the starboard bridge wing watching Fort Charles pass by.

Steele came over and joined him. "1692," he said.

Durham looked at him curiously. "What happened then?"

"The encyclopedia in the wardroom says there was a terrible earthquake, and most of Fort Royal was submerged. What you see over there is about a third of the original point of land. I guess it wasn't too bad, though. Almost all of the area that went down was bars and whorehouses."

Durham laughed. "What do you mean, not too bad? That's my kind of place over there." He took off his cap and held it over his heart. "May they rest in peace, and I hope they all died with their boots off and their glasses filled."

After unloading the survivors, the *O'Leary* left the harbor and set course for the strait between Haiti and Jamaica.

Durham looked at the chart over Jablonski's shoulder. "When do we get back to the convoy?"

"At 25 knots, we can catch them day after tomorrow." On the afternoon of the second day, the lookouts reported a column of light smoke ahead.

Meredith shook his head. "That smoke is a beacon for every submarine within 20 miles."

In an hour the surface search radar reported four surface contacts ahead.

Chumley, who had the deck, said, "Maybe one's been sunk."

Meredith, proud of his new-found knowledge, corrected him. "The patrol craft is still below the radar horizon. We'll pick him up in about 15 minutes."

He was right. Soon the radar operator reported the patrol craft patrolling ahead of the convoy.

In an hour, they steamed up the starboard side of the convoy and took station ahead. As they passed by the tanker, the signalman on watch, looking through the large telescope, shouted, "They're sending a semaphore message. Stand by to write!" Then he laughed. "The old guy sending it is a little slow and creaky."

Meredith said, "It may be the commodore himself. He said he had only one man who could communicate, and he might have to help out. Maybe he's trying to remember the semaphore positions he learned twenty years ago when he was a third mate."

After a few false starts, the signalman reported, "He says glad to see you back."

Meredith thought about telling him about the smoke column but thought better about it. He said to the signalman, "Send a message directly to the ship making smoke and tell him we could see his smoke for 20 miles and so could a submarine."

•   •   •

A day later they passed the net at the entrance to Chesapeake Bay, and Meredith speeded up for the long 90-minute transit to the Norfolk Naval Station. "I'm glad we brought that old salt and his convoy in safely, and I hope to see him again," he said to Sorenson. "Let's send him a nice message."

They rounded the ends of the piers at the Norfolk Naval Station and Meredith turned to Sorenson. "Tex, take her in." Then he smiled. "If you have any trouble, ask Ensign Steele for advice."

Sorenson made a delicate landing against a tide pushing across the pier. When they were secured, Meredith said, "This is the last of the easy stuff. When we go to sea again, it will be a lot tougher. Tex, go over to the Navy Supply Depot tomorrow and try to get the additional cold weather clothing we talked about. The stuff we got in California is fine for rain, but it won't do much to keep out the cold in the North Atlantic. I know you'll do better than our new supply officer could. He's pretty green."

"I know what you mean. I'll be there early."

Chapter Nine

The next morning Sorenson strode into the office of the commanding officer of the Naval Supply Depot. He stopped at the receptionist's desk. "Lieutenant Sorenson, executive officer of the *O'Leary*, to see the commanding officer."

The receptionist kept her head over the typewriter. "Please have a seat."

Sorenson sat down and picked up a dog-eared copy of the *Saturday Evening Post*. He leafed through it, but something prompted him to look up at the receptionist. Her head was tilted, and short black hair hung forward and obscured the side of her face but not her graceful neck. He tried a few more pages, but then he remembered the voice. It had been low, pleasant, and if not sexy, at least interesting. He looked up again. He caught her eyes turning away from him. A gentle curve of cheek and finely angled jaw outlined her profile. He noticed the neat way her features fitted together. His gaze wandered lower. Only the top of her was visible above the desk. Her strong, tanned hands flew over the keyboard. Supple wrists protruded from the lace cuffs of her white blouse. The top of her blouse was closed with another piece of lace, but in between Sorenson liked what he saw. The blouse obviously was backed by a slip over a loose brassiere which permitted her moderate but shapely breasts to tremble slightly with the efforts of her vigorous typing. Sorenson pursed his lips and whistled silently. Very nice. She looked up again, and he could see that her eyes were blue and topped with generous eyebrows.

The buzzer rang, and she picked up the telephone. "You can go in now," she said.

Sorenson's business took very little time. The commanding officer had a son serving on a destroyer, and his sympathies were obvious. He gave Sorenson everything he asked for.

When Sorenson came out, he stopped in front of the receptionist's desk and waited for the typing to cease. Finally, she stopped and looked up at him. "Yes?"

He wasn't encouraged by her neutral expression. A wooden nameplate sat on her desk. Sorenson read it. Ferren May Holderman, it said.

She saw him reading it. "My married name is Holderman."

He verified the bad news by noting that a small gold band circled her ring finger. He hadn't been able to see it across the room.

She went on, "My first name is Ferren, and my maiden name was May. I'm a widow."

Sorenson felt better. "Ah, I'm a stranger in town. Could you possibly show me Virginia Beach tomorrow afternoon?"

She was silent a few seconds. They seemed like an hour to Sorenson. "Well, I have plans for tomorrow night, but my afternoon is free. Tomorrow is Saturday, and anything for the war effort. I'd be glad to. I don't suppose you have a car yet. Where can I pick you up?"

"At noon in front of the Naval Base Officer's Club. I'll bring some refreshments."

Her low-pitched throaty laugh teased him. "Don't bother. I'll bring a basket and a cooler full of Cokes."

Sorenson smiled. "I'll see you tomorrow, then."

As he walked out, she said, "And you can bring the wine and beer."

The next morning Sorenson sat at breakfast idly stirring a cup of coffee. Meredith looked at him. Sorenson seemed to be inspecting a spot on the opposite bulkhead, but Meredith followed the direction of his gaze

and could see nothing of interest on the bulkhead.
"What's the matter, Tex, don't you feel good?"

Sorenson's eyes focused. "No, I'm all right, or at least
I think so. I know you said that I should stay aboard in
Norfolk and take care of our repairs and supplies, and
I am happy to, but I'd like to go ashore this afternoon
for a little while."

Meredith said teasingly, "A date?"

Sorenson colored. "Well, yes, sort of. I asked a supply
depot secretary to show me Virginia Beach. I promise to
be back by sundown, and we'll only have light refreshments."

"Beer included?"

"Well, a little, but the wine was her idea."

"Who is this paragon?"

"A girl named Ferren May Holderman."

•   •   •

She drove up to the portico of the officer's club in a red
Ford convertible coupe. In the bright sun her black hair
glinted, and the highlights in it were so bright they were
almost silver. Sorenson hurried down the steps and got
in. In the back were an umbrella, a blanket, a picnic basket, and a cooler. Sorenson leaned over the seat and put
a paper sack of wine and beer bottles in the cooler.
"Drive on," he said.

"In a hurry?"

"Don't want to miss a minute of this sunshine."

She laughed. "All Saturdays are wonderful."

She was wearing a flowered dress that buttoned up
the front, and the lower two buttons were open. She
drove rapidly along Little Creek Boulevard toward the
beach. The breeze blowing in the open car toyed with
her skirt and revealed a pair of shapely knees and lower
thighs that matched the rest of her.

She noticed Sorenson's appraisal and laughed. "Don't
get excited," she said. "I have my bathing suit on under
my dress."

"Can I change out there?"

"Sure. In the dunes."

"That sounds like a pretty private area if I can do
that."

"It is. We'll drive south of the city of Virginia Beach."

At the spot she picked, no one else was in sight to enjoy the sweep of the dunes or the waves driving in on the tan sand except a few skittering sandpipers, soaring sea gulls, and an occasional passing pelican. Sorenson worked the shaft of an umbrella into the sand as Ferren spread the blanket. Sorenson suggested a walk up the beach. As they walked, they had to skirt patches of tarry oil and debris.

Sorenson said, "Looks like some of our ships didn't make it."

Ferren stared at the swirling foam and clasped her arms across her chest.

Sorenson asked, "What's the matter? Did I say something wrong?"

She was silent, but then she looked out at the horizon. Sorenson followed the direction of her gaze. Two destroyers were leading a small convoy north toward the entrance to Chesapeake Bay. Suddenly Ferren kicked the foam of a wave toward the ships. Then Sorenson could see the tears in her eyes.

"My husband went down on one of those damned destroyers."

Sorenson took her in his arms. He could smell a faint aroma of gardenia in her hair. They stood in the swirling water for several minutes before Ferren was able to talk. Then Sorenson took her hand, and they walked slowly back toward the distant umbrella.

"Please tell me about it," Sorenson said.

She wiped the tears away and smiled faintly. "I don't even know your real first name."

"It's Alden. My mother calls me that. But all my friends call me Tex."

She shook her head. "I think I'll keep on calling you Tex."

Sorenson smiled. "If you call me Alden, my friends won't even know whom you are talking about."

She glanced up at him. "My, my, you even speak correct English."

"That's another thing nobody will believe about a Texan. I like classical music, for example. But enough of me. I want to know about your husband. I know it may be painful, but maybe it will keep me from saying the wrong thing."

"We were married about a year ago. Very happily, and I liked the Navy. So did Jerry. But then the situation in the Atlantic got steadily worse, and his ship was out more and more. Then the Japanese dragged us into war. One day a chaplain knocked on my apartment door and asked to come in. I knew from his expression that the news was bad. Jerry had gone down with the *Truxton*."

"An old four-stacker like the *O'Leary*. I'm sorry. Maybe you shouldn't say any more about it now. I hope there will be plenty of other times to talk."

She sighed. "I like talking to you. Please tell me about yourself."

"I grew up on a cattle ranch in Texas. Now my brother operates it, and we share the profits when there are any. I like the Navy, and I may never go back to the ranch, but it will always be there. I went to the Naval Academy and then right out to a carrier as a deck officer. I always wanted to fly, and I asked for and got flight training, but I failed flight training just before the end of the advanced phase. Maybe that failure will send me back to Texas after the war."

"What happened to your Texas accent? You sound almost like everybody else."

He laughed. "At the Naval Academy they teach you to fit into one mold. It isn't a bad one, and when they took away my accent, I just never got all of it back. I can only tell I've changed when I go back home on leave."

"What about your home? How big is your ranch?"

"About as big as the cities of Norfolk and Virginia Beach combined."

She whistled, just like a boy would whistle, he thought.

She asked, "Are you one of those rich Texans?"

"I don't know. We don't pay much attention to money. When we want something, we sell a few head of cattle and buy it. At the end of the year we use all the profits we make to buy more land and cattle."

They swam for a while. The water was cold, but it was invigorating, and Ferren soon regained her spirits. A beer or two helped, and the afternoon passed with a mixture of conversation and silence while they stretched out on the blanket under the sun.

As the sun began to slide toward the horizon, Sorenson said, "I hate to end this day, but I have to get back to the ship."

They gathered up their belongings and went back to the Ford. She patted it. "I suppose you have something grander back in Texas."

Sorenson said, "No. Only pick-up trucks."

"Several?"

"Well, maybe a half dozen. We use horses most of the time."

She laughed. "I noticed that you are a little bow-legged."

"Yes, but you aren't."

She drove him back to the Naval Base slowly, and when they pulled up to the *O'Leary*, he said, "May I see you soon?"

She smiled. "I'm free Tuesday evening."

"Seven o'clock for dinner and dancing?"

"I'll be ready."

Sorenson could smell gardenia as she drove off.

• • •

The next morning Sorenson sat at the wardroom table nursing a cup of coffee. Meredith came in and sat down. "Tex, this is getting to be a habit."

"What is?"

"You. Staring at the bulkhead. You didn't even say good morning."

"Sorry, Captain, I think it's a great morning."

Durham came in and said, "Good morning."

Meredith said, "Good morning, Bull, your usual big breakfast?"

"The same. I need it."

"I hear you got back late last night."

"Who told you so?"

"Doctor Fineman."

Durham laughed. "He's getting to be a regular nurse-maid."

"Yes. I sicked him on you in Panama, but he lost you."

"Sorry about that, but I got a little bored. I didn't

want to involve him, so I gave him the slip and went to the best whorehouse in town."

Meredith moaned. "I was afraid of that. You probably caught everything in town."

Durham was pensive. "I don't think so. I never touched the ladies."

Meredith put down his coffee cup with a clatter. "What?"

"After I gave Fineman the slip, I went to a second whorehouse and sat down to have a couple of beers. Then I looked around at the girls, and I felt sorry for them. They were a ragtag lot, even if they were the best in town. I began to wonder what I was doing with my life. I ended up by paying the Madam for two hours of her time and just sitting and talking to her. I improved my Spanish and actually had an interesting evening. She was a nice lady in a tough racket. After last night, I'm glad I didn't do anything more."

Down the table Fineman heard the last of the conversation and groaned. "I wasted three hours."

Meredith tried his coffee cup again. "At first I was going to diagnose your case as incipient middle age, but now I think you may be in love."

"I'll buy that," Fineman said.

Durham said, "No, but I might be later."

Meredith laughed. "Bull, you're always in love after you hit a new port. It's always someone like the babes you used to find in Chefoo or Tsingtao. I'll bet the latest one is named Babette, or Vanya, or Sonya, and that she is blonde, six feet, and a thirty-eight D cup."

Durham bristled. "Dammit! That's all over. I'm tired of looking at a girl's chest when I dance with her, no matter how big it is. The only thing you got right is her name. It's Sonya."

"How about the rest?"

"Well, if you must know, she's about five feet three, and has dark red hair. She's a white Russian who left Shanghai in 1937."

"By request?"

Durham put his fork down firmly. "No. Her husband, an American businessman named Atkinson, was accidentally killed by the Japanese. She's legally an American citizen who came to Norfolk because her husband's relatives live here."

"What does she do for a living?"

"She runs a tea house."

Meredith guffawed and Sorenson tried to hide a laugh. Durham noticed snickers among the junior officers, and he reddened slightly. "I don't know why you guys are laughing. She runs a very respectable business, and she lives in an apartment above it."

Meredith said, "With a few other girls?"

"Dammit, no, she's no whore. She lives alone. Her business doesn't make much money, but she doesn't need much. After her husband was killed, she liquidated all of their holdings and bought jewels, mostly diamonds. She's got enough to last for a long time."

"Diamonds or boobs?"

Durham threw his fork down. "Oh, shit, you guys don't know romance when you see it."

"How did she get the diamonds out?"

"She smuggled them out in her brassiere. She showed me the chamois bags she used. She had to shift to a D-cup for the trip out."

Durham pushed back his chair. "To hell with you guys, I'm leaving."

Meredith and Sorenson watched him go. Sorenson said, "You were a little rough on him."

Meredith sobered. "Maybe so, but I don't think Bull has changed that much. We'll see. By the way, I'm glad to see you have some interest beside hard work. When are you going to see this girl again?"

"Tomorrow, if it's all right with you. I promise not to be out late. I've got all the repairs and loading of stores in hand. The replacement depth charges will arrive by barge tomorrow."

"It'll have to be tomorrow. We're sailing early the following day with a convoy for Iceland."

•   •   •

Sorenson went to his room to catch up on his paperwork. A stack of letters filled his desk. When he was half-way through them there was a loud knock at his door.

"Come in."

The drape was pulled back and Carmody, a yeoman first class, entered. Carmody had joined the ship in San Francisco. "Good morning, sir. I've got some more great paperwork for you."

Sorenson groaned. Carmody looked over his shoulder at the outgoing letter Sorenson was reading. "Good, Mister Sorenson. I see you've crossed out a word in ink instead of sending it back for re-typing. My last exec wouldn't do that."

"Carmody, I went by your office yesterday, and the floor looked like it had been snowed on. Can't you keep it a little neater?"

"Well, when I made a mistake, I always save the carbon paper, wad up the rest, and aim it for the waste basket. The only trouble is, there ain't much room in that little cage, what with the leading storekeeper, two typewriters, two file cabinets, and me. We can only fit in one wastebasket, and when it's full, the floor gets the rest."

"Can't you use paper bags?"

"We do, but at sea we soon fill up to the overhead. After that, it's the spud locker when we've eaten down the spuds, but the storekeeper claims that's his territory. Then I have to use my bunk. I wish we could at least throw the unclassified stuff over the side. Some damned thing about security. The Germans might pick up a copy of an invoice and find out what we pay for toilet paper."

Sorenson rolled his eyes and picked up a letter from the pile in front of him. "What's behind this letter?"

"Shaky Bellows asked me to write it. Seems the deck force is short of rated men."

"So's the whole damned Navy. We're turning out ships like rabbits, and they have to be manned. Why do you call Chief Bellows 'Shaky?'"

"Everybody does. I think it's because his hands shake so much when he drinks coffee."

"I can understand that, but I thought they'd call him 'Loud' Bellows, or something like that."

"He's loud all right, but he's even shakier than he is loud. Speaking of voices, Mister Sorenson, I noticed from your service record that you're from Texas. Are you in cattle or awl?"

"The Naval Academy taught me to call it oil."

"I notice you've lost a lot of your Texas accent."

"Yeah, awl or oil, we don't have any. We drilled but only got dry holes. We just raise cattle."

"Maybe after the war my daddy and me can give her another try. I'm a roughneck, and we can find awl anywhere."

Sorenson sighed. "While we're waiting, do a little drilling through the paper on your office floor. Maybe you can find linoleum."

• • •

Ferren picked up Sorenson at the ship and drove down the pier. "Where would you like to go?" Sorenson asked.

Ferren laughed. "You're not going to believe this, but the Air Station Officers' Club is the best place in town. Trust me."

She was right. The lights were low, the three piece orchestra of women played sedately and well, and Sorenson savored his rare steak.

"These are almost as good as the ones we used to raise in Texas," Sorenson said.

"They came from Kansas. I make sure the club gets the best, and in turn, when I come in, they make sure I get the best."

"With the rationing, meat must be pretty tough to get."

"It is. I can't get anything from my neighborhood meat market, but the military gets taken care of. The price of meat has doubled in two months."

Sorenson laughed. "I guess that's why our married officers bring their families to the ship so often."

"You've got it, Tex, let's dance."

When she came into his arms it was unlike anything that had happened to him before. She floated, always responsive to his slightest whim, and the faint gardenia scent brought back memories of his high school prom. It was restrained, but provocative. After the second dance he was so aroused he had to sit down.

"Would you like some dessert?" he asked.

"No, I'd like to dance again."

"Ah, if you don't mind I need to rest for a few minutes. We need dessert and maybe some coffee."

She looked puzzled, but she had no trouble with a large helping of sherbet.

"How do you keep that wonderful figure with all that chow?"

She blushed slightly. "Never had any trouble. I exercise a lot."

Soon they danced again, and Sorenson managed to control his feelings by talking. After coffee, he asked if they could leave. She said yes, and they walked slowly out to her car. "Would you like to see my apartment?" she asked.

"Very much."

The compact apartment had subdued framed prints that complemented the living room rug. It was strictly functional, but still comfortable and feminine.

"I moved here after I lost my husband. Our place was too big, and the memories were too strong."

Sorenson nodded. "I like this."

"Please sit down, and I'll get some brandy."

Sorenson said, "Coffee for me."

She came back with two coffees. "This doesn't fit the image I've gotten about you from my friends. They say you are distant and troubled and sometimes drink too much."

"Friends?"

"Oh, yes, there's a wives' network in the Navy. I don't like taking other peoples' opinions and I don't like gossip. I'll make up my own mind about you. So far I like you, but there's something about you that seems to be in conflict. I hope you'll work it out someday."

"Thanks," Sorenson said. "A fair trial and a reasoned verdict is all I ask."

They talked for two hours, and Sorenson hoped he would recall most of the conversation in the coming days and nights at sea. He thought it would ease the bad dreams. Finally, next to her on the small couch, he put his arms around her. She didn't resist. Then he kissed her gently. She gasped and pushed him away. "I'm sorry, Tex, but I can't yet."

"I'm sorry, too. It's obviously too soon for you."

She colored. "I hope you won't think there is anything wrong with me. After all, I was a happy wife."

"I don't, and you're right, it is too soon, but I hope you'll change your mind some day soon."

She frowned. "It won't be soon. I know you leave tomorrow and won't be back for quite a while. You see, that's part of the trouble. I won't let myself care about someone who's going back out ... there, in all that damned icy water."

"How do you know all this?"

"Oh, don't be silly. I'm not just a receptionist. I'm also the Supply Depot Commander's private secretary. I have to know all there is to know about ship movements so I can help schedule supply deliveries for you. For instance, your young supply officer has ordered a delivery of fresh food for you on arrival back in Norfolk."

"But he doesn't know when we're coming back."

"He doesn't need to. I take care of that when I find out when you are due to arrive. Incidentally, he's a nice young fellow. He asked me for a date."

Sorenson bristled. "What did you tell him?"

She smiled. "I told him I had a date with an older man."

She drove him back to the *O'Leary*. He kissed her very tenderly and got out of the car. He thought he could see a tear in her eye before she drove off. He turned and walked slowly up the brow.

"Good evening, Mister Sorenson. You're back early."

"Good evening, Bronte." Sorenson saluted and walked below. It would be a long voyage.

Chapter Ten

Doctor Fineman leaned on the starboard bridge rail, watching Meredith get the ship underway. It was early morning, and a light fog swirled over the piers. Meredith backed the ship across a strongly ebbing tide and a 20-knot wind, which was rapidly dispersing the fog. Fineman marveled at the precision with which Meredith dodged passing merchantmen and several ferries. Sort of like a surgeon, he thought, bypassing the intestines to find an offending appendix. Nick a bowel and you endanger a patient's life. If Meredith nicked a ferry, he might endanger the ship and would probably lose his command.

Sorenson, one of Morales' doughnuts in one hand and a cup of coffee in the other, joined Fineman. "He's getting better," he said. "You wouldn't know he hasn't handled a ship much."

Fineman pursed his lips. "How much have you handled one?"

"Once or twice with the *Berry*. I'm not very good yet. I tend to think I'm flying an airplane, and this ship doesn't respond that fast. I didn't mean to be critical. It's just that neither of us is very experienced yet, and I worry sometimes."

Fineman nodded. "I understand. You could say the same thing for a lot of the officers and petty officers we have. It's a result of the rapid war-time expansion. We all have to learn fast."

"Yes. We had to transfer two more experienced petty officers to new construction last week."

Sorenson went into the pilothouse, leaving Fineman to his thoughts.

The *O'Leary* rounded the last Norfok Naval Base pier, and the shoreline of Ocean View slipped by. Fineman's reverie was interrupted by the arrival of newly promoted Lieutenant Junior Grade Chumley.

"Good morning, David," Chumley said.

"Good morning, Jerry, you look great this morning. Is married life agreeing with you?"

"Oh, yes. My wife had a nice apartment ready. She had a hell of a time getting across country by automobile. Someone tried to steal her tires in the middle of the night, and she had to threaten to shoot him from her motel room. But I think she liked the adventure. She said she enjoyed dickering with the gas station attendants and seeing how much mileage she could get out of a tank of gas. She even changed the spark plugs to try to get more mileage."

Fineman said, "That's good. There's no telling what she can do if you give her a challenge."

Chumley colored slightly. "I know she likes one. When I showed up she was very ... passionate."

Fineman chuckled. "That ought to tell you something. In your case, keep your wife busy or in suspense and be more unpredictable. I think you'll find your married life will be better."

Chumley sighed. "I can't take much of it at this speed." Then he brightened. "Maybe going to sea has its points."

Fineman sighed. It sounded like Chumley and his wife were mismatched sexually. Fineman usually had complaints the other way.

Chumley left to take over the watch, and Fineman idly watched Sorenson on the main deck. Sorenson was inspecting the securing of the ship for sea and heavy weather. When he finished he came to the bridge and joined Fineman again. They both watched Chief Bellows on the forecastle.

"Pull da bight tight," Bellows shouted.

Fineman's eyebrows shot up. "Listen to that! Even I could understand him."

Sorenson said, "I got him an emergency appointment with the false chopper guys, and they spent the night working on his new set. The new plates seem to have eliminated the extra 'H's. What's left is Polish accent."

Fineman said, "Tell me about your new girl friend."

"There's not much to tell. I've only known her for a few days. She lost her husband at sea several months ago. I know she cared about him, and she feels the loss very deeply. I'm not sure I can take that. I don't know whether she will ever forget him."

"You wouldn't want her if she could completely forget him, and you wouldn't want her to forget you if she lost you. Her feelings are a sign of good character. Don't try to turn them off. If she falls in love with you, time will change the relationship, and she will learn to love you. You will have to be patient. Your position in her affections may increase with time, and I think you'll find that you can accept her former husband's role."

Sorenson sighed. "Thanks, Doc."

Fineman said, "You'll have a lot of time to think about it. I hear we won't be back for at least a month."

•   •   •

Inside the pilothouse, Meredith paced the small area, and thought about their departure from the Norfolk Naval Base. He knew he had done well, and he cherished the admiring glances from the young officers and petty officers on the bridge as he had maneuvered the ship. But he knew the days ahead would be taxing, and he would have to call on all his energies. His wife had nourished him, both emotionally and at her high-calorie table. He knew he worried too much at sea and ate too little. Every week at sea seemed to cost a pound, and he did not have too many pounds to spare nor any excess energy.

He thought back over his too few days in port with his family, and he was grateful that Sorenson had taken over the burden of preparing the ship for sea in order to give him a little more time with his family. His wife and children were the center of his universe, and he missed them the minute they faded from view on the pier.

But now he had other responsibilities, and he watched the Coast Guard cutter ahead as they approached the net vessel at the entrance to the Chesapeake Bay.

The Captain of the cutter, a few years senior to Meredith, would be the escort commander, and they would pick up three more escorts off Halifax. Meredith tried to remember the faces of the eight merchant captains he had met at the conference the day before, but they merged into a conglomeration of pipes, mustaches, beards, and foreign accents. He knew he would do better remembering them when the ships assembled outside the net and he could associate the captains with their ships. When they arrived off Halifax, twelve more merchant ships would join.

The cutter slowed and stopped, and the *O'Leary* kept station behind. The net tender slowly pulled back the large steel net strung from buoys, and the vessels speeded up. They were to patrol off the entrance for an hour before the merchantmen came out.

The pinging sonar found nothing but occasional schools of fish. At 0900 the first merchantman poked its bluff bow out into the Atlantic. The others soon followed and struggled ahead, occasionally belching puffs of black smoke, but obviously trying to control their boilers. They eased into a formation of four columns of two ships each.

The escorts ranged ahead, patrolling their stations on each bow of the convoy.

Meredith pulled down the transmitter handle on the squawk box. "Sonar, this is shallow water with a lot of wrecks on the bottom. Keep that in mind."

Steele poked his head inside the bridge door. "Aye, aye, sir. We've got them plotted on the chart. You'll be glad to know that we've established communications with the two aircraft that are to escort us until dark. They've searched ahead and report all clear. They'll have reliefs here at dawn and as long as we're in range."

Meredith said, "I don't think we'll have any trouble the first few days. We'll have air patrols from here and then from Halifax. The intelligence briefer said yesterday that most of the German submarines have withdrawn from the coastal areas, and the Germans are beginning to use new tactics. Did you get any different information?"

"A little. They are going to form groups of submarines called wolf packs," Steel said. "The Antisubmarine Center over at the Fleet Command said they will work in groups of five to ten and make radio-coordinated attacks, mostly at night."

"The Germans seem to like the word wolf."

"Yes. To them it means vicious, offensive, and terrorizing."

"I don't think wolves are all that bad."

Steele shook his head. "You can bet the German U-boats will be worse. They like the word so well the first wolf pack will be nicknamed the sea wolves. They will have about twenty-four packs eventually, each with a name. We may run into the first one on this trip."

"A sort of double wolf?"

Steele ignored him. "That's not all. You remember the intelligence officer told us in San Francisco the Germans were designing a new class of U-boat based on the Type IX. They called it the Seawolf Class."

"Yes, I remember that."

"Now they're starting to build it. You will also remember it will be bigger than we are."

"And full of torpedoes?"

"No, not yet. The first three will be supply submarines and minelayers. The fourth and subsequent ones will be wolf pack flagships and attack boats. They will also have a much bigger deck armament than the Type IX."

Meredith slumped in his chair. "Well, that will give us a few more months before we have to face the attack version. I'll be dreaming about wolves from now on."

Steele said, "We all will."

"They didn't tell us much at the convoy conference," Meredith said. "They said we can expect a three-submarine group about the end of the third day beyond Halifax. Ask the executive officer to hold a meeting of all officers in the wardroom after lunch so you can brief them on the convoy conference and the latest intelligence. I don't want to leave the bridge, so I won't be there."

•   •   •

For three days the convoy sailed unhindered, practicing emergency turns by whistle signals and simulating evasion. At dawn the air patrols thundered overhead and then swept out ahead over the horizon, returning in an hour from another direction and then starting out on a new sector. There were no contacts by aircraft or by sonar.

At the end of the third day the second section of the convoy joined from Halifax, and the extra escorts reported for duty. By nightfall the second section had settled in their positions and the screen had grown to five escorts in a bent line screen ahead. Meredith watched the joining process and hoped that they would have at least two more days to settle down before they ran out from under air cover.

But that night, as Meredith was dozing in his chair, one of the *O'Leary's* lookouts shouted, "Surfacing submarine on the starboard bow! Two miles!"

Meredith said, "It can't be! The intelligence guys promised us a few more days of quiet." He ran out to the wing, and he could see the submarine easily because of the foam from the water passing in and out of her super-structure vents. He wondered why it was surfacing so fast and so close, and he decided it might want to be seen. If so, it could be a decoy.

The radar picked it up immediately and reported it to the bridge. Gerlach, who had the deck, gave the orders, "Right full rudder! All ahead flank! Sound general quarters!"

Meredith said, "Whoa! Belay the course and speed changes! We may be dealing with more than one sub. This one may be a decoy. If we leave a gap in the screen, another may come through it. It's all right to head for the sub, but slow down. The escort commander has to evaluate the situation and issue orders."

Meredith picked up the TBS handset and transmitted a contact report to the escort commander. The acknowledgement was calm and clear. "Maintain position," the escort commander ordered.

Watching the range close slowly to the contact was agonizing. The submarine had turned away, and the foam from her vents was no longer visible. The director could not see the reduced profile well enough in the dark to fire the guns, and the range was not yet close enough for sonar contact.

Then the escort commander's flagship reported sonar contact on another submarine. Meredith said to Chumley, who had relieved Gerlach at general quarters, "See, if we'd left station that second bastard might have gotten through the gap we left and there would have been hell to pay."

Soon the director reported on target, and Meredith ordered, "Commence firing!" Almost immediately the guns that could bear fired and recoiled smoothly.

The first salvo missed, and by the time the second arrived, the submarine was beginning to submerge.

Meredith sighed with mixed relief and disappointment, but the period of quiet was short.

There was a tremendous explosion toward the rear of the convoy. The intense light outlined the plodding lines of merchantmen. There was no doubt that a third submarine had attacked aft.

The TBS crackled, ordering the *O'Leary* astern of the convoy to assist and look for the submarine.

Chumley shouted, "Right full rudder! All ahead full!"

This time Meredith left the officer of the deck alone. The *O'Leary* was the second escort in the right side of the screen, and when she reversed course, they were headed almost directly for the right hand column. Meredith was worried about passing the column of merchantmen that was now ahead of the *O'Leary*'s track. If he passed too close, he ran the risk of having the *O'Leary* cut in two if one of the merchantmen suddenly sheared out of column. The *O'Leary* would be passing the ships in the column at a relative speed of over 30 knots, and there would not be enough time to avoid a massive hulk.

Sorenson came up to the bridge. He had been back on the after deckhouse at the new battle station recommended by the Destroyer Type Commander as a means of separating the captain and executive officer so that both would not be lost by a hit on the bridge area.

"Captain, I'm sorry, but I can't stay back there when we're doing this. The *Berry* went down in a situation much like this, and I think you need all the help you can get."

Meredith said, "I understand. I need you up here anyway."

Sorenson said, "If you sheer out too far, you'll take too long to reach the area. If you come in too close and one of those big bastards loses his orientation, he'll run right over us."

Meredith said, "We'll compromise." He pushed down the transmitter handle to the squawk box, "CIC, give me a course to pass the column by one thousand yards."

Almost immediately Jablonski's voice came back. "Recommend two two zero."

Meredith took the conn. "Come to course two one five. All ahead flank. That'll give us a little more room."

He turned to Sorenson's barely visible form. "Is that better?"

"Yeah. It is."

Meredith said, "Chumley, keep track of the formation, particularly the outboard column, on the surface search PPI. Let me know when we're abreast of each ship. Tex, stand in the doorway and I'll stand just outside and we'll keep track of the ships with our binoculars."

Chumley moved to the PPI and leaned over it. "The lead ship is forty degrees on the starboard bow at one five double oh."

Meredith said, "I see him. Now shift to the next one."

The second one Sorenson saw first and reported it to Meredith.

As Meredith watched the second merchantman draw abeam, he thought how much the commanding officers of small ships depended on the skills of junior officers like Chumley and Jablonski.

Then Chumley said, "The third ship is forty degrees on the starboard bow. He's a little behind station, but on a steady course."

Meredith could not see him, but again Sorenson reported the low-lying tanker hull.

In a minute Meredith said, "There he is. I have him."

There was nothing ahead now but a burning ship and a submarine. He could see the ship plainly, but where was the submarine? He thought for a minute what a paradox this was. He feared the merchantmen they had passed more than he feared the submarine. The unpredictability of the merchantmen made them dangerous, but by now he felt that he could fight the submarine on his terms.

His thoughts were interrupted when Sorenson said, "We should slow to seventeen knots and commence a sonar search. I'm going back to the after deckhouse now."

"Thanks for the help," Meredith said.

In a few minutes Steele's voice boomed over the bridge speaker. "Sonar contact! Probable submarine! Bearing two one eight! Down doppler!"

Meredith changed course to head for the contact and reported it to the escort commander. Back came the answer, "Attack. Rescue survivors later."

The range wound down to 1,000 yards. Steele reported, "Submarine is headed directly away! Bearing two one two! High down doppler! Speed five! Recommend zero lead angle!"

Meredith said, "Steer two one two. Depth charges, standby. Shallow pattern."

"Shifting to short scale! Range two double oh! Bearing two one three!"

"Steer two one three," Meredith echoed.

As they passed over the sub, Steele said, "I think he changed course at the last minute. Recommend drop anyway."

Meredith ordered, "Drop depth charges!"

After the last charge had gone off, Steele said over the squawk box, "Captain, recommend change course to zero one zero to regain contact. I'm coming out to the bridge."

In a few seconds Steele appeared at Meredith's elbow. "Captain, I think he changed course at the last minute to throw us off and expelled a cloud of air bubbles.

We've seen these clouds before, but this one is very big."

Meredith could hear the pings of the sonar going out, but there was only a mushy return. "Very well, tell Jablonski to set up a search of the area. If there's no contact soon, we'll make a wider search."

The search was fruitless, and Meredith didn't want to leave the torpedoed ship too long, or the escort short-handed too long. He reported to the escort commander, "Contact lost. Recommend I render assistance."

"Affirmative," the escort commander said. "Get back as soon as you can. We've lost another ship."

As the *O'Leary* approached the wallowing merchantman, Meredith could see men running about the deck. The ship was not listing, but it was deep in the water, and there were large fires on her topside.

Meredith judged she was sinking and made an approach to pick up swimmers. The seas were too rough to permit bringing the *O'Leary* alongside, and Meredith remembered the merchantman that had exploded off Trinidad. The merchantman was making no move to lower boats, so Meredith let the *O'Leary* drift into a hundred yards so that they could get to the swimmers.

Meredith said to the talker, "Tell Mister Steiner to have the crew of gun one man the cargo nets on the forecastle."

The *O'Leary* nosed in closer, but Meredith didn't want to come in any more. On the forecastle, the gun captain tied several heaving lines together and secured them to the backs of the life jackets of two volunteers. They climbed down the cargo net and swam to some of the merchantman's crew who were obviously poor swimmers. As soon as two faltering swimmers were grabbed by the *O'Leary* men, the gun captain had the heaving lines hauled in and the men were soon on deck.

Meredith hoped he would get clear soon, but suddenly a tremendous flash from the merchantman seared Meredith's eyes, and the concussion drove him from the bridge door across the pilothouse and into the opposite bulkhead. The world went black.

·   ·   ·

Steele bolted from the charthouse and into the pilothouse and looked around. All those on the bridge appeared to be unconscious. The Captain was lying against the bulkhead. There were bloody patches on his face, but no arterial bleeding. Alvarado, who had been steering, was lying near the captain, his forearm badly cut. Steele could see spurting blood. Chumley and the other members of the watch were in a tangled mass under the Captain's chair. It was so quiet he could hear the flames crackling on the remains of the merchantman.

"Bronte!" he shouted. "Come out and take the wheel! Take care of Alvarado! He's bleeding badly!"

Steele ran out on the port wing. The empty forecastle indicated the crew of gun one had been blown over the side. He ran back to the ladder leading down to the well deck and shouted, "Anybody down there? We need help up here!"

Chief Bellows was coming topside from his station with the forward repair party. "Yah?"

"Take all the men you can find and get up to the forecastle. Standby to pick up the crew of gun one. They must all be in the water, and they may be unconscious."

Back on the bridge wing, Steele searched the nearby water. By the light of the fire from the merchantman, he spotted a cluster of men floating in life jackets. Some of them were face down. He began to maneuver the ship to bring the bow closer, shouting orders in to Bronte. Soon Bellows could reach some of the men with a small grappling hook. He threw the small device gently so that its prongs would not injure the men. The hook caught in their life jackets, and soon two men climbed down the cargo net to bring men up.

As the first man was being brought on deck, Sorenson appeared on the bridge, dragging his leg. "Are you all right?" he asked Steele.

Steele turned to him. "Bronte and I are all right. All the personnel up here are either groggy or unconscious, and Alvarado is bleeding badly."

Bronte interrupted. "He's okay. I made a tourniquet out of my belt and a pair of dividers."

"The rest of the personnel in the charthouse are pretty badly shaken up and can't function very well. I was lucky. See what you can do for the Captain and the others."

Sorenson said, "I stopped on the way up and told the doctor to come up here. He's right behind me."

Steele said, "With your permission, I'll keep the deck and conn."

"Of course. Well done! I'm taking over command until the doctor has a good look at the Captain."

Steele watched the stretcher bearers remove the Captain, Alvarado, and the other members of the watch. Then he turned and watched the men on the forecastle. For several minutes Bellows and his men labored to bring up more men.

Finally Chief Bellows yelled up, "We got 'em all. Some is pretty bad. De doctor is working on 'em."

Steele said to Dionte, "I'll take the wheel. The PPI is out. Go inside and give me a course to the convoy." He reached over and set the annunciators on full. There was nothing he or the *O'Leary* could do for the burning hulk. No one aboard could have survived the blast. As they gathered speed, new men came up to the bridge to take over the ship control positions, and soon Steele felt he had the situation under control. He turned to Sorenson, "Sir, you are obviously in pain, and I see some blood on your shirt. Why don't you go below. I'll call you if I need help."

Sorenson sighed. "A good idea. Please keep me informed and let me know when you approach the convoy."

• • •

In the wardroom Sorenson could see Fineman working on a man on the table. His pharmacist's mate was leaning over a man on the deck, sewing up a large cut. Blood and bandages littered the deck. Meredith sat in a chair watching, his head lolling against the bulkhead behind him. Two bodies lay at the other end of the wardroom, beyond help. Chumley, a small bandage on his forehead, was covering them up.

Fineman turned to Meredith. "You're next."

Meredith grimaced. "I hate that table. I'm okay below the waist. Fix me right here."

Fineman leaned over his chair and began to examine

him. Meredith groaned as Fineman's hands passed over his skull and then down his upper body. Finally Fineman straightened. "You're lucky you're conscious now. You were out for almost an hour. You had a serious concussion. When we found you, your helmet was off. I think it came off when you were blown across the pilothouse, and the back of your head hit the opposite bulkhead. There's a helluva bruise back there and a large cut. Without an x-ray machine, I have to be very conservative, and you'll have to stay horizontal for a while. Beside your head injury, you have an assortment of bumps and bruises and some facial cuts from the flying glass. You'll get over all those in a week, but the concussion may take longer. I'm going to sew up your cuts, give you some pain-killer, and put you in your bunk."

Fineman turned to Sorenson, who had been circulating around the room, looking at the wounded and talking to them. "And now for you. I see you're limping and there's blood on your shirt."

Sorenson suppressed a groan. "I'm okay, Doc, just a little cut that needs a Band-Aid and a sprained knee. I've got to get back up on the bridge."

Fineman grinned. "Not before you've had a couple of medicinal brandies."

"How about me?" Meredith asked.

"Not for you. Aspirin is all you get until we see how you react."

Sorenson said, "Not for me either. I've got to keep a clear head, but there are a lot of others who could use some."

Meredith said, "We've got a lot aboard."

Fineman shook his head. "If this keeps up we won't bring back much."

.   .   .

Back on the bridge, Sorenson eased into the Captain's chair and pulled his leg up. He knew he was violating tradition; no one sat in the Captain's chair except the Captain. He had to do the job, though, and he knew he couldn't stand long. The pain was increasing, but he didn't want to take morphine or brandy. It would be a long night.

They were still at general quarters, and gradually the full bridge watch was reconstituted as Chief Bellows sent men up from the gun crews to take over. Bronte turned the wheel over to a helmsman and then went back into CIC.

Sorenson said to Chumley, who had taken over the deck, "I'll take the deck and conn. I can't get around very well. Take a trip around the ship and see if there is any damage or other injuries we don't know about."

Chumley was back in twenty minutes, closely followed by Durham.

Sorenson turned to him. "Any troubles, Bull?"

"I'm afraid so. The explosion gave us a helluva underwater shock. Must have been ammunition stowed below in that merchantman. It loosened a lot of boiler brick in the forward boilers. It will have to be repaired, probably in a navy yard. Our boilers didn't get a full brick replacement at our last overhaul."

Sorenson said, "How will it affect our speed?"

"We're making twenty knots now, and it isn't getting any worse, but I wouldn't want to push that. I'll watch it carefully. If any bricks fall out, I'll have to secure that boiler to prevent the casing from burning through. If I have to shut down both forward boilers, we'll be down to a single boiler and fifteen knots."

"All right. Make up a casualty report. We'll transmit it visually to the escort commander tomorrow morning and by radio from Iceland to Norfolk."

Chumley said, "I've got some items to add to that report. We've got a lot of holes in the forecastle sides and deck and in the forward bulkhead of the bridge structure. Chief Bellows has the shipfitters patching the holes temporarily, but they'll have to be welded in a yard. Also I think gun one may be badly damaged. It won't train. Otherwise, we're all right. We have two dead, and the remainder of gun one's crew won't fight for a while. You know about the personnel casualties. They're the same as when you left the wardroom. Chuck Steiner is making up a replacement crew for gun one."

Sorenson laughed in spite of his pain. "I'll bet there weren't many volunteers."

"Oh, yes, there were. Morales wants to be the gun

pointer. He says he manned gun two in the Phillipines. Mister Durham says he was a corker."

"Tell him he has the job."

"And Kendrick says he wants to be gun captain."

"Did Chuck twist his arm?"

"Not much. Steele says he owed him one."

• • •

Dawn was breaking when they caught the convoy, now reduced by six ships. The other torpedoed ships had sunk, and the survivors were aboard escorts. When the *O'Leary* settled in formation, Sorenson went below to the main deck cabin to visit Meredith, leaving Gerlach with the deck. His descent was slow and painful, and he thought about asking Fineman for morphine, but by the time he had negotiated the last step of the ladder, he had decided against it. Now that he was temporarily in command, he wanted to set a good example.

Meredith had three blankets draped over his thin form, but he was alert and cheerful. Several holes in the forward bulkhead of his cabin were crudely stuffed with wooden pegs wrapped in rags. The effect was odd, but only a little cold air came in around the bulging patches.

Sorenson shivered. "Jesus, Captain, don't you want to move below? I'll move out of your lower cabin."

"Hell, no! I like it up here. Beside, I have to get used to the cold. This is only a sample. Wait until December. By the way, when do we get to Iceland?"

"The day after tomorrow we're scheduled to turn this convoy over to three British corvettes that will take what's left to Great Britain. Then we go into Reykjavik to fuel. We should be all right from now on. Our air cover starts today."

The buzzer from the bridge went off, and Sorenson picked up the phone. "Sorenson," he said. After a few seconds he said, "Thanks. That's good news."

"What is?"

"Radar just picked up our air patrol. They'll be on station in a few minutes."

• • •

Back on the bridge, Sorenson tried to relax, expecting a peaceful day. He sent for coffee. Before he could finish it, a torpedo was reported on the other side of the convoy passing the convoy commodore's flagship. There was consternation on the TBS as the convoy commodore tried to communicate with the escort commander, and whistle signals sounded stridently as he tried to maneuver the convoy. There were several near collisions, even in daylight. The torpedo that missed the convoy commodore's flagship hit a ship in the next column. Both patrol aircraft were called in and dropped depth charges.

Jablonski listened to the aircraft frequency and kept the bridge informed. "One thought he had dropped on a periscope, but the other pilot said it wasn't moving through the water and it was a swab handle."

After dropping all their depth charges, the aircraft gave up and resumed patrol. Jablonski reported, "They're a little pissed off. They think the U-boats are supposed to be afraid of aircraft, and this guy practically thumbed his nose at them."

Sorenson said, "I guess the poor bastards on that torpedoed ship are pissed off, too."

•   •   •

Two mornings later, radar reported three surface contacts, and soon three British corvettes rose over the horizon. After a brief relief over the radio, the American escorts departed for Iceland.

At dawn the next day, about three o'clock in that latitude, most of the crew was on deck to watch their entry into the harbor of Reykjavik. Behind the harbor, rugged hills, geysers, and steam vents dotted the bare, undulating ground.

Alvarado, back on the bridge with his arm in a sling, said, "It looks like Yellowstone Park in the winter."

Carmody, standing beside him, laughed. "It sure ain't Texas, but I'm sorry we're not getting ashore. I'd like to see it close up."

Bronte walked out of CIC and looked over at Alvarado. Alvarado turned away with out saying anything.

Carmody said, "Why did you do that? I know you're mad at him, but I hear he might have saved your life by putting a tourniquet on you the other night."

"Maybe, but I can't like him as long as he keeps running the *O'Leary* down. It's my home, and these young guys have got to keep their mouths shut. After all, they didn't see what she did in the Philippines."

Carmody shivered. "I'm sorry about that. I came up here this morning to watch Mister Sorenson bring the ship in."

"Why?"

"He invited me, and it might be a good show."

"Naw. He understands the *O'Leary*, and it will be routine."

It was.

Chapter Eleven

While they were alongside the tanker, Alvarado stayed on the bridge and talked with the sailors lounging on the tanker's main deck across from the *O'Leary*'s bridge wing. Bronte came out to join him with two mugs of coffee, but Alvarado walked away. "No thanks, the signal bridge coffee is good enough for me."

"What's the beef?" asked Bronte.

Alvarado looked back, "I don't like guys that don't like my ship."

Bronte shook his head, turned away, and began to talk to the sailors on the tanker.

One sailor said, "You guys are missing a lot. These blonde babes here really like us."

Bronte said, "Maybe they just like your cigarettes."

"No, they just know we'll be here for a while."

"We're coming back," Bronte said.

Alvarado, listening to the conversation, knew his heart wasn't in it. He moved to the side away from the tanker and looked over toward the shore. He thought the countryside looked harsh and inhospitable, and he wanted to get back to a hot Norfolk summer, but most of all, he wanted Bronte to stop putting the *O'Leary* down. Bronte, when he came aboard, had been his best friend, and he missed the periods of quiet conversation in the charthouse.

Alvarado was glad when Sorenson said they were

ready to get underway and directed Chumley to take the ship out.

Chumley backed the ship away from the tanker smartly, and steadied up on a course toward the harbor entrance.

Alvarado nudged another signalman. "Good job. The kid is learning."

As they steamed out astern of the other escorts, Alvarado watched the rugged mountains behind Reykjavik disappear in a gathering mist. He felt relieved to be back at sea even if it meant going back to the cold of the Atlantic and the ever-present U-boats. The sea and the O'Leary had become his home, and he hated the Germans who were trying to take it away from him. Alvarado went over to the signal bridge coffee pot and drew a mug of hot, black coffee. It took the chill from the strong breeze, and he went to the port wing to watch for signals from the escort commander.

Later that morning Alvarado searched the horizon with his telescope, trying to beat Bronte who was manning the surface search radar by spotting the masts of the convoy they were to meet before the radar detected them. Just before the surface search reported them, Alvarado sighted the tops of several masts, and he felt proud that he had not lost his touch.

Soon signals went up on the yardarm of the escort commander assigning stations, and they were off to relieve the British escorts. Alvarado watched the merchant ships come over the horizon. Two vessels straggled, belching black smoke as they labored to take station. Alvarado frowned, thinking how easy it would be for other men like himself on the U-boats to see the smoke.

In half an hour the escorts were on station, and the convoy steamed off on the long voyage west, the two stragglers still marking their location with black smoke.

•   •   •

The second day they cruised under the umbrella of anti-submarine patrol aircraft from Iceland. After breakfast, Sorenson looked over at the 30 ships they would escort to Halifax, and he hoped they would do better at protecting them than they had the ships on the east-bound trip. He felt the situation was safe enough so he could leave the bridge, and he went below to Meredith's cabin. He knocked and entered. Meredith was propped up in his bunk with a towel draped over his chest. Doctor Fineman sat on the edge of the bunk.

Sorenson laughed. "What's this? Getting a shave and a haircut?"

Fineman picked up a small pair of scissors and a set of tweezers from a tray balanced on Meredith's chest. "No, I'm taking the stitches out of these facial cuts." He swabbed several areas on Meredith's growing beard and began to remove the stitches.

"Can I stay here?"

"Sure, sit down."

Sorenson said, "Captain, I sent a dispatch to Norfolk outlining our personnel casualties, material casualties, and supply needs. Since that time, we've discovered that our air search antenna is badly damaged and will need replacement. On the other hand, we've freed gun one so it can train, but it will need a new shield."

"Sounds like we'll need a few weeks in the yard. Ouch!"

Fineman said, "That shouldn't have hurt."

"I think you pulled a whisker along with that stitch by mistake."

"Maybe so. I tried to leave as much of your mustache as possible intact. Some of these whiskers are growing close to the scene of the action."

Sorenson sent on, "The new crew for gun one is green, but they've been working overtime on the loading machine. They can load, but I'm not sure if they can hit anything."

"Don't worry about that. Morales is good. Maybe a little rusty. We have to hope the old hands from China and the new men we picked up in the States will begin to work together better. Now they've played together and, more importantly, fought together. I'm just sorry to lose some of our Asiatic Fleet veterans. They went through a lot of battles with us out there. How about the injuries, Doc?"

"Many bruises and cuts, but nothing serious."

Meredith said, "Back in Java, when we were hit by

the Japanese, I hated to lose my engineers. Losing people is one of the worst things about a naval career."

Sorenson said, "They were both good men."

Meredith sighed deeply. "What can I do to help?"

"I have some rough letters here, together with the men's service records. It would take a load off of me if you could write letters to their next of kin. We couldn't take their bodies back to the States. I had them transferred to the tanker. They have enough refrigerated space to do the job. We'll have a memorial service this afternoon."

Meredith said, "I'll be there, and if Fineman will let me, I'll be up tomorrow to take over."

Fineman finished the last of the stitches and examined the healing cuts. "No, not for a couple of days. I'm still concerned about your concussion and your dizziness. If there were an emergency I'd say take a chance, but there isn't. Maybe you can go up for a bit of fresh air, and you can go to the memorial services, but you don't go back to duty until I'm sure there are no lasting effects from your concussion."

Sorenson said, "As long as you've got all of your equipment, will you take a look at this little cut I have here under the Band-Aid?"

Fineman's eyebrows rose. "What cut?"

Sorenson stood up and opened his shirt. "This."

"Where did you get that?" Fineman said. "I didn't know about it."

"Your pharmacist's mate put a Band-Aid on the other night. I didn't want to bother you."

Fineman pulled the bandage off. "Looks healthy. Just leave it uncovered."

Meredith asked, "How did you hurt your knee?"

"You remember you had me stationed on the after deckhouse when we got that directive suggesting that the captain and the executive officer be separated at general quarters?"

"It worked."

"It did, but I could have been of better use if I'd been in CIC. Young Steele was there, and he came out on the bridge and did a wonderful job. I think we ought to consider awards for him and Chief Bellows."

"Okay on both counts, you can come up to the CIC from now on at general quarters. To hell with the directive."

Fineman said, "You didn't say what caused your knee injury."

"I was standing in front of the compass binnacle looking aft to make sure there weren't any subs in sight behind us. The gun crew had gone below to man the K-guns, and they were protected from most of the blast. I was blown against the binnacle. It kept me from being blown overboard, but something on it caught me just above the knee. There is a bruise just above the knee and the joint is sprained a little, but I think it will get better without treatment. Something projecting from the binnacle cut me a little. I didn't want to use morphine or brandy, so I didn't bother you. Your pharmacist's mate took care of it."

Fineman finished, and Sorenson buttoned his shirt. As he walked out the door, he paused, turned back, looked at Meredith, and grinned. "If you're going to come up to my bridge, you'll have to shave that black fuzz off of your face, except for your mustache of course."

• • •

That afternoon, all those not on watch gathered in the well deck below the bridge for the memorial service. When all was ready, Meredith was helped out and put in a chair. The well deck was the best protected area on the ship, although the muted roar of the fireroom blowers aft made it hard to hear.

Remembering the high noise level, Sorenson had arranged for Ensign Steele to read appropriate parts of the burial service, taken from the Navy hymnal. Steele's vibrant voice could be heard easily, but when Sorenson stepped forward to deliver a short eulogy, he had to remind himself to turn his voice up to full volume. The service ended with the Lord's Prayer, and then Doctor Fineman led them in a verse of the Navy Hymn.

Sorenson watched the somber men leave the area and hoped that the press of duties and the thoughts of returning to Norfolk would lift their spirits.

• • •

The next day Sorenson's knee was better, but he still sat in the Captain's chair. The convoy left their Iceland-based air cover. Sorenson heard two quartermasters discussing what had happened on the trip east in the same area. "Maybe those damned seawolves will be waiting for us again," said one.

The other shook his head. "Out in Montana we used to shoot wolves, but we can't see these bastards."

Just as he was dozing off, a rumbling explosion came from astern. A straggling ship had been torpedoed. The TBS came to life, ordering the *O'Leary* back. After a twenty-minute search around the dying merchantman, Steele's voice came over the squawk box. "Sonar contact! Positive submarine! Up doppler, making about four knots!"

The range closed, and Sorenson took the conn from Jablonski. He headed directly for the contact at 17 knots. Then Steele's voice boomed, "Down doppler, but decreasing! Bearing drifting right! Recommend ten degrees lead and deep pattern! He's had time to go deep!"

Sorenson turned to the talker, "Depth charges, stand by! Full deep pattern!" He gave the helmsman a course to lead the submarine by 10 degrees. The range continued to decrease and the "pings" came faster when the sonar operator shortened the scale.

"Lost contact due to short range! Recommend drop on time!"

Sorenson ordered the depth charges dropped after his stopwatch indicated enough time had gone by to compensate for the *O'Leary*'s movement after losing contact and for the depth charges to sink. He noticed that none of the bridge watch bothered to look aft. Neither did Sorenson. Instead he concentrated on regaining position for the next attack, and when the after deckhouse talker reported no debris, he began another run.

"Firm contact," reported Steele. "Recommend head for it."

Then Sorenson was aware that Meredith was standing in the bridge door. "Jesus Christ!" Sorenson said. "You shouldn't be up here."

Meredith said in a small voice, "The Doc said I could get some fresh air. I'll just sit in my chair and be quiet."

"Fine, Captain, but please don't forget, I'm running the show."

"Don't get huffy, Tex, I'm still too weak to do anything but watch. Good luck."

Sorenson was already concentrating on the next attack. Like the first one, it seemed like a good one, but there were no visible results. The third seemed better. The contact was firm all the way in, and the submarine had slowed.

"I think he's damaged," Steele said. "He's not maneuvering, and he's only making one knot. Recommend no lead and a full medium depth pattern. He may be coming up."

The range grew shorter, and the bearing was still steady.

"Lost contact due to short range," came from Steele.

This time Sorenson felt confident, and he sent Chumley aft on the bridge to observe the results. After a few minutes, Chumley shouted, "Large oil slick and a lot of debris!"

Steele reported, "Contact dead in the water. May be sinking. Think we can hear him breaking up."

Then the submarine apparently sank below the thermal layer, and there was no further contact.

Steele came on the bridge. "Sir, I'm fairly certain we sunk it, but the claim won't stand up unless we get enough debris."

"We're on our way," Sorenson said.

Chief Bellows hoisted aboard parts of several life jackets and a bucket full of papers. As they grappled for more odds and ends, Gerlach tried to translate the papers. Finally he shook his head. "Too much oil and blood. Some of these are personal letters, and this is a manual of some kind. We'll have to send this stuff ashore to the experts in Norfolk."

Steele said, "The big cheeses ashore will have to assess all of this. Besides this physical evidence, they'll have certain intelligence information I can't talk about. I'd give this one about a fifty percent chance of being declared sunk."

Sorenson shrugged. "We can't wait any longer. It's about to get dark. We'll claim it, and see what happens.

Hopefully there's one less seawolf out here. Right now we have to take care of that torpedoed ship."

The hull was only a few miles away, and Sorenson headed toward it. Ugly black smoke billowed from her after cargo holds, blotting out occasional tongues of flame, and she was listing badly. As they closed in the growing darkness, Sorenson noticed that the officers and men on the bridge seemed apprehensive. He knew the situation was much like the tragedy of a week ago. The fires flared up, and Sorenson noticed that Alvarado, at the helm seemed, flinched involuntarily. Sorenson remembered the suddenness and the searing heat of the blast. "Steady," he said, "I don't think it will happen again."

Alvarado's breath whistled through his teeth.

They closed to 100 yards, and the crew of the merchant didn't seem to be able to lower a boat. They jumped in the water and swam over to the O'Leary.

When the survivors were all aboard, Sorenson backed the O'Leary away. He decided that they should sink the hulk with torpedoes. Gunfire would take too long. He turned to the telephone talker. "Tell the chief torpedoman to come to the bridge."

Chief Skelly clattered up the bridge ladder, his thin arms flapping as he slid his hands up the side rails. All 130 pounds of him slid to a stop in front of Sorenson. "Yes, sir?"

Sorenson said, "Slow down. We're going to torpedo this ship." He called over the first class torpedoman who was manning the torpedo director on the bridge wing. "I want the depth mechanisms on our torpedoes set at four feet. How long will it take?"

Skelly grinned. "They're set now. Captain Meredith wanted it that way. Herman, here, told me how bad the depth control was on the torpedoes they fired off Java."

"All right, let's do it. I'll move a thousand yards off, and you'll be able to shoot directly on her beam."

The torpedo impulse charge flashed briefly, and the torpedo chuffed out of the tube and belly-flopped in the waiting waves. The slight phosphorescence of the rising gas bubbles of combustion enabled the watchers on the bridge to follow the course of the torpedo toward the wallowing ship.

Most of the watchers leaned on the rail, watching without interest. Sorenson knew they were physically and mentally tired, and they knew the hulk wouldn't shoot back. Sorenson sensed their mood, and turned to the talker. "Tell Mister Steiner to have the lookouts keep a sharp watch away from the merchantman."

Satisfied that the lookouts, sonar, and radar were busily searching, Sorenson turned back to watch the course of the torpedo.

Jablonski was watching the hand on his stop watch. "Now!" he shouted.

Nothing happened.

Sorenson cursed. "Stand by to fire another torpedo." Another torpedo followed the first. The explosion was blinding, destroying the night vision of all those who had not learned to close their eyes on Jablonski's "Now!"

Sorenson opened his eyes and could see. There was no doubt the hulk was going to sink.

"All ahead full," he ordered.

    •   •   •

Sorenson leaned against the bridge behind Meredith for a few minutes rest, but then he remembered the boilers and called down to main control to see if the depth charges had done any damage.

"No," Durham said, "but there are a lot of men down here who can use a shot of medicinal brandy. That last torpedo blast shook us up."

"Sorry, we've got a tough night ahead," Sorenson said. He turned to the messenger. "Find Doctor Fineman and tell him to issue medicinal brandy to the men we saved."

"I'm glad we got the extra brandy and the cold weather clothing," Meredith said quietly.

Sorenson suddenly remembered Meredith was on the bridge. "Tell Doctor Fineman to save a brandy issue for Lieutenant Commander Meredith."

Meredith laughed. "What about you?"

Sorenson smiled in the dark. "Even the acting commanding officer only gets served after the crew is taken care of."

· · ·

Before midnight they had lost two more merchantmen. Sorenson kept the ship at general quarters, and he could see the weariness growing in the eyes of the bridge watch. The man on the annunciator dozed off several times and had to be poked by the helmsman. At dawn they were sent to investigate a periscope sighting by a merchantman. Sorenson headed for the area, but a circular search was fruitless, and Sorenson brought them back to a course to rejoin. On the way back he set condition III. The added risk was worth taking to give the crew some rest. His own eyes were heavy, and his leg was beginning to hurt again. He eased into the Captain's chair, and welcomed the blessed relief. In seconds he was asleep.

Fifteen minutes later he was jolted awake by an explosion. Two miles ahead a merchantman in the rear line of the convoy was spewing steam and smoke. "General quarters!" Sorenson shouted.

The general quarters bridge crew soon came back to their stations, dull-eyed and stumbling. The talker cursed as he fumbled trying to adjust the telephone harness. Sorenson shook his head and slapped his cheeks, trying to hold off the fatigue. They had now been without sleep for over forty-eight hours, and none was in sight. Sorenson was grateful for the weather, which was cold enough to help them keep awake, but not cold enough to hinder their functioning.

The merchantman went down quickly, and all that was left when the O'Leary arrived was a few lifejacketed men and a spreading blanket of oil and debris. A steel barrel was the biggest piece, and Sorenson could see parts of clothing and insulation coming to the surface as they closed to pick up the men. By now they were so skilled at the job that the process of hauling up the oil-soaked men took less than five minutes. Sorenson had made a wide sweep of the area before approaching without sonar contact, and after picking up the survivors, he made another. Still there was no contact, and after a second circle he headed back. This time overhauling the convoy took an hour, and another attempt to rest by setting condition III was more successful.

As they took station on the port side of the screen, an escort at the front of the screen reported a contact. Sorenson held off going to general quarters as long as he could. Five minutes later sonar reported a sonar contact, and they were off again at general quarters to develop the contact.

After one depth charge attack, they lost it. Steele came out to the bridge. "Sorry, sir, I think the sonar operators are losing their sharpness."

Sorenson yawned and stretched. "I don't blame them. So am I. Tell them to do their best."

Late that day two more merchantmen went down. Their survivors were picked up by escorts on the other side of the screen, but the flurry of activity drained Sorenson. Sorenson stumbled over to the chart and looked at their track. If all went well they would come within air patrol range of Halifax in twenty-four hours. He wondered if they would have any merchantmen left in the convoy by that time. Then he remembered the U-boats that had attacked them on the way east within air patrol range and he groaned. Maybe even the air patrol wouldn't help.

Back in the chair he slumped and leaned his head against the chair back. He was so tired that he could not sleep, but the time passed faster when he was comfortable. He thought about Ferren, and he could see why she was hesitant about their relationship. After all, his chances of surviving were not good. Now he was so tired he hoped he wouldn't survive. He dozed off, still thinking of Ferren.

The TBS woke him, and he came to rapidly as he heard the *O'Leary*'s call. In a minute they were off after another sighting. One depth charge attack failed to produce results, and Steele was doubtful about the contact anyway. Sorenson held off on another attack, and a run through the area showed a few dead fish.

"The merchantmen must have seen the swirls from the school of fish near the surface," Steele said.

Sorenson agreed, and they went back to condition III.

Sorenson noticed the sagging faces of the oncoming watch and wondered if he looked the same. He rubbed his unshaven face vigorously, but it didn't seem to help the dead feeling.

In an hour the first air patrol roared overhead, and Sorenson grinned. Maybe they would make it now, he thought.

For another day they approached the area of Halifax without losing any more ships. At dawn the next day three Canadian corvettes came over the horizon and took over the remnants of the convoy.

•   •   •

A few hours sleep rested Sorenson enough so that he began to think about problems other than surviving, and he remembered that he hadn't looked after the survivors they had picked up. He sent for Fineman, who took him down to a section of the forward crews' compartment where four injured survivors had been placed in bunks.

Fineman said, "Their stomachs were full of oily water, and they had bad cuts. One has a broken leg."

Sorenson bent over the first man, a grizzled older man who grinned through a week-old beard. Sorenson said, "How are you?"

"Great! Best chow I've had in years."

Sorenson laughed. "Is this your first trip?"

"Hell, no. My tenth. And my third swim."

"Are you going to sea again?"

"Sure, skipper. What else is there?"

Fineman nudged Sorenson and pointed to the next bunk. "A different kind of case," he said.

Sorenson looked carefully at the young merchant seaman lying rigidly under two blankets. His face was pale and gaunt under a scraggly blond beard. Sorenson said, "Can you hear me, son?"

There was no answer, and the man didn't move.

Sorenson asked, "Can he talk?"

"Maybe in a few days. He has a few injuries, but nothing serious."

Sorenson was pensive as he climbed the ladders back to the bridge. From now on he would pay more attention to the merchantmen. It was tough enough fighting the Germans with an armed ship and a full crew, but going to sea in a helpless, lightly-armed merchantman took a special kind of courage.

•   •   •

On the first day of August, the surface search radar reported the Chesapeake Bay net vessel on the scope, and soon they were safely inside the net.

Sorenson had no trouble mooring the ship in the Portsmouth Naval Shipyard, just south of Norfolk. After the ship was secured, he went to Meredith's cabin. Meredith wasn't there, but Sorenson found him standing on the forecastle, shaved, alert, and looking 5 pounds heavier.

"Good morning, sir," Sorenson said, "Doctor Fineman says you're fit for duty. I'm ready to return command to you. Are you ready for it?"

"Am I ever. I had to chew my lip to keep from coming up to the bridge while you were making that landing."

"What was wrong with it?"

"Nothing. Your landing was fine, and I thought you ran the ship superbly while I was down. The problem was that I was beginning to think I wasn't needed around here any more."

Sorenson laughed. "That's not true. I've run my butt into the deck trying to get along without you. Now that you're back in the saddle, I have some urgent business ashore. I won't leave the ship until I'm sure that Durham, Steiner, and Gerlach have the yard work well in hand."

Meredith said, "I appreciate that. I do want to see my family. As soon as I'm squared away, I want you to take a week's leave."

"Maybe. That depends on what I find ashore."

Chapter Twelve

The day after they arrived at the Portsmouth Naval Shipyard, Sorenson sat in his room going over the ship's mail. Above him the riveting hammers chattered, punctuated occasionally by the hiss of welders' torches. Shouts from workmen and the rumblings of giant cranes added to the din as Sorenson tried to concentrate, hoping to catch up on the ship's official business, so that he could go ashore the next day.

Half way down the pile of official letters, all opened and carefully sorted by Carmody, was a personal letter, still sealed. The return said, "Ed Sorenson, Sorenville, Texas." Sorenson picked it up and said, "Good old brother Ed. I miss him."

He opened the letter, and a check fell on his desk. Sorenson picked it up and read the numbers on the check. He whistled.

"Jesus," he said softly, "fifty thousand dollars."

Carmody knocked on the door and came in. "What was that, sir? Somebody suing you for fifty thousand dollars? Jealous husband?"

Sorenson grinned. "No, better news than that." He handed Carmody the mail he had finished. "Get on with this, and step on it. As soon as we're caught up, both of us can go ashore."

"Off I go."

Sorenson picked up his brother's letter. As he read it, his eyebrows went up steadily. When he finished, he stood up and banged his fist on the desk. "Wow!" he said. "I'm rich!"

He read the letter again. His brother said that he was selling cattle to the government as fast as he could deliver them, and prices had tripled in the last six months. Sales for the six-month period had already passed the two million dollar mark.

"I'm a millionaire," Sorenson muttered. "A lousy lieutenant millionaire. And he says the government will buy all the cattle they can drive to market."

He went up on deck, and, oblivious of the snaking hoses and wires, walked up and down the forecastle until his feelings returned to normal. He had to tell somebody, but should he tell Ferren? He decided he would have to play it by ear, and he went below to finish his paperwork.

* * *

The next day, after he was sure that the yard work was in good hands, he dressed carefully in a good uniform and went ashore. At the gate, he hailed a taxi and told the driver, "The nearest Buick dealer."

The cabby whistled, "Won't do you much good, bud, they don't have many cars."

They didn't, and Sorenson had to settle for a green four-door demonstrator. An extra five hundred dollars convinced the reluctant salesman. Sorenson drove off to the nearest bank to open an account with his check. Paying for the automobile had nearly exhausted his modest Texas checking account, but his brother had said there would be other checks soon. Sorenson shook his head and wondered what he was going to do with all that money. Buy War bonds? Spend some? Give some away? Damned right, he thought, all of that good stuff and more.

His next purchase was two dozen red roses. He called Ferren's office from the florists. A strange voice answered, and he asked for Ferren. The voice hesitated, "Is this Lieutenant Sorenson?"

"Yes."

The voice perked up. "Mrs. Holderman has taken a few days leave. I'm holding down her job. She left a message for you to call her apartment."

Afraid that she might tell him she did not want to see him again, Sorenson drove to her apartment, parked his car, and walked, carrying the roses, as fast as his ailing knee would allow. Before he could knock, the door opened, and Ferren was there. She was smiling, but there were tears in her eyes.

"Tex, I'm so glad to see you. Are you sure you're all right?"

He opened his arms, and she filled them, scattering the roses. He had never felt so complete.

"Why did you ask if I was all right?"

From somewhere deep in his coat front, she said, "I read the *O'Leary's* casualty report. I know you lost two men, your Captain and several others were wounded, and that your ship was damaged."

He followed her into the living room. They sat on the couch and talked for hours. He put his arm around her, and she didn't resist.

She said, "I liked your Captain's wife and children."

"How did you happen to meet them?"

"I knew he was wounded, so I went by to see her. I thought it was better for her to see me than having a chaplain show up."

He ran his fingers through her soft black hair.

Then she said, "Oh, Tex, it's no use. I wanted to tell you not to come to see me any more because I couldn't face the thought that I might fall in love with you. I've thought for days, and I can only come up with one answer. Life is too short to waste a single day. If you really want to keep seeing me, I'm willing."

He said, "I don't want to rush you. I know how you must feel, and I'm ready to wait as long as necessary."

She sighed. "You have strong arms. Please just hold me for a while. Then I'd like to get to know you better."

"You'll have a chance. I'm on a week's leave, and we'll be in the yard for two more weeks."

"Where will you be staying?"

"The BOQ, I guess."

"How about trying the FMQ?"

"Where is that?"

"Right here. It's otherwise known as the Ferren May Quarters. But you'll have to use the couch."

He patted the cushions with his hand. "After the bunk I've been used to this will be great. But won't the neighbors talk?"

"The ones I know won't. The others I don't care about."

"If you're sure, I have my gear in my car."

"Your car?"

"Yes, I just bought a green Buick."

"Where is it?"

"Out front."

"You can rent a garage here when you're at sea. Many people don't have cars these days because of gasoline rationing, and there's a shortage of automobiles for sale."

"I found that out. I had a hard time getting this one. Apparently the automobile factories are busy making tanks and jeeps."

"A Buick is expensive. Where did you get the money for it?"

"My brother sold some cattle. A lot of cattle."

In the dim light he could see her frown. She said, "Are you now a rich Texan?"

"Well, I haven't put horns on my pickup trucks, but I am well off."

She said, "I'll think about how I'm going to put up with a rich Texan. I don't really give a damn about a lot of money. My husband left me well off."

"That's okay, but you'd be surprised what we can do with it."

The next day they awakened early, and Sorenson said, "That couch was pretty good after my bunk on the ship. I've got something to do today. I'll be back at noon for another trip to the beach."

She said, "I've got some shopping to do anyway. You eat a lot."

He laughed. "I'm not worrying about food. I'll be working on a surprise for you."

•   •   •

Durham got out of a taxi in front of the Oriental Tea House, paid the driver, and turned to look at it. He thought the front looked nice. The ground floor had a central door flanked by two large windows. On one was a gold and black 'Oriental' and on the other the words 'Tea House' in the same color scheme. On one side was a door which led up to the upper two floors.

Durham was carrying a compact bouquet of yellow tea roses, and as he went in the front door, he put them behind his back. He stepped inside the door and removed his cap. A hostess was in the back of a large room filled with tables and chairs, and he looked around the room as she came toward him. The decoration was Oriental, but tastefully subdued.

The hostess, a pretty Chinese girl, said, "Good evening. I'm Ling. Would you like a table?"

Durham catalogued her for possible future reference. "No thanks. I'm looking for Mrs. Atkinson."

"Ah, you mean Madam Sonya." She pointed a forefinger tipped with a long red fingernail upwards. "She's upstairs." Then she smiled. "You must be Lieutenant Durham."

Durham grinned. "None other. How do I get up there?"

"There is a back inside stairway, but I think you'll want to use the outside stairs." Durham could see her trying to suppress a grin. "More privacy."

Durham thanked her and went to the outside stairway. He bounded up the stairs, two at a time, but he knew Ling must have been faster on the intercom because Sonya opened the door as he reached the top.

"Bull!" She shouted, and she laughed as Durham took her in his arms. He could feel the swell of her pointed breasts pressing into his chest. She was full-figured, but not overly plump, and very attractive. Her face was full also, but not fat. Her large brown eyes, slightly slanted so that they had an Oriental appearance, dominated her face. Her skin was fair, and her hair a dark red, neatly falling about her face in short waves.

Durham pulled back and handed her the roses.

Her eyes sparkled. "Just what I like. Yellow and petit."

Durham said, "I've come to like small things, too. A guy on my ship opened my eyes."

Sonya took him by the hand and led him into the living room. "Sit down, or better yet make yourself a drink. There's your favorite brand of Scotch on the bar. I'm going into the kitchen to put some cheese snacks in the oven."

Durham looked around the room. The furniture was plain, modern, and probably expensive. There were no Oriental pieces in sight.

She came in with a tray of cheese pastries. Durham said, "Why is downstairs so Oriental and upstairs so American?"

She laughed. "I guess I had my fill of Oriental furniture in China. What you saw downstairs is authentic Old Kingdom and beautiful. I had most of it sent out from Gumps in San Francisco. As for myself, I'm trying to become an American."

Durham looked at her hair. "You've got the hair for it. I never heard of a red-haired Russian."

"Don't be silly. There are some. Peter the Great imported Scots engineers to help modernize Russia. My family name was Dougald."

They sat together on the large sofa, finishing the snacks and later several sandwiches. One bottle of Scotch disappeared and another was opened. They talked about the Orient and even found some mutual acquaintances from Tsingtao and Chefoo. Durham had never spent this much time in conversation with a woman before, and he liked it. By now, his shirt, tie, and shoes were off, and Sonya had found some old slippers for him. She had shed her shoes and pulled her legs up on the couch under her.

About midnight they were talked out, and Durham said, "I'll race you for the bed."

"You're on!" she said. She won because Durham stopped to take off his trousers. She was everything Durham had ever wanted, and their lovemaking was long and passionate.

Finally Sonya pulled back and laughed. "You've got to be a little less . . . ah . . . vigorous. You'll shake the expensive chandeliers off the ceiling down below."

• • •

Sorenson drove to a small airfield south of Norfolk. He pulled up to a small hangar and got out.

A man in dungarees and a leather jacket was sitting in a chair in front of the hangar door. "Howdy," he said.

Sorenson leaned against the hangar wall. "Hi, I'm looking for an airplane to fly and someone to check me out for a private pilot's license."

The man pushed back his hat. He was fifty-ish, with gray hair and two days worth of graying stubble on his leathery face. He closed one eye and looked up at Sorenson through the other blue one.

"I'm Charlie Curtis. I got a plane I'd rent. Gas is the problem."

"Don't you have any?"

"Just some I've been saving for something special."

"Is five hundred bucks for fifty gallons special enough?"

"Yup. That's special all right."

Sorenson said, "Let's look at your plane."

Curtis hoisted himself off the chair, and they walked into the dim hangar. When his eyes became adjusted to the dimness, Sorenson whistled. The two-place biplane was old, but its radial engine gleamed.

Curtis said, "I know it's an old crate, but this beauty will do anything you ask of it. It's designed for aerobatics, and it's gentle if you want to learn to fly."

Sorenson laughed. "I know how to fly. I just need to qualify for my license."

Curtis's eyebrows shot up. "Well, if you've got the money, I've got the time. Grab the other side, and we'll roll her out. Then we'll see if you can fly."

Sorenson could fly. When they came down, Curtis taxied up to the hangar door and cut the engine. Curtis climbed down before Sorenson could extract his sore knee from the cockpit.

Curtis watched Sorenson come down the steps. "Well, sonny, you sure can fly. Where did you learn?"

"Pensacola. I got through basic training just fine. I was a week away from graduating from advanced training and heading for the fleet when I bilged out."

"I was wondering why you didn't have any wings on your khaki uniform shirt. What the hell happened?"

"It wasn't the flying. I could do anything they asked. I got caught one day in a bad situation. I flat hatted."

"That wasn't very smart."

"No. I found that out in a hurry."

"Well, live and learn. Let's get on with the paper work for your license. You've got a written exam to take and some forms to fill out. Also some cross-wind landings and a cross country flight to make. Then some spin recoveries to do. You shouldn't have any trouble. I've got a coverall I can lend you to keep your uniform clean."

Sorenson got his license the next day and rented the plane for the next two days.

•   •   •

That night he told Ferren to get ready for a surprise the next day.

She said, "I've got a surprise for you, too. Today a delivery man came to my door. He brought a large box. The return address said 'Soren Ranch, Sorenville, Texas.' Where is that?"

"Oh, it's just a small town my grandfather started."

"I opened it, and it was full of filet mignon steaks. So many that I had to take most to the supply depot freezer for storage. And what was that thingy on the top?"

"What thingy?"

"A big circle with an arrow across it."

"Oh, that's our brand. It's supposed to represent straight shooting."

She thought a minute and then said, "I didn't know Texans were straight shooters."

"They can shoot a gun straight, all right. They certainly shot at a lot of Indians and Mexicans and did them out of their land, just like my great grandfather did."

"Did he start your ranch?"

"Yes. I'm not proud of what he did to get his land, but I guess it was about average for Texas history. Sometimes I've felt guilty at what we have now, but my brother tries to make up for it by taking care of our ranch hands and their families. They eat as well as I do, and they think they eat a little better."

"Don't they like filet mignons?"

Sorenson laughed. "As a matter of fact, they don't.

When we butcher, they ask for the tougher parts. It makes better chili."

Ferren grimaced. "I hate chili."

"So do I. But I had to eat it twice a day until I was ten."

"What happened then?"

"I found out that there were other parts of a steer, including filet mignon."

"Ah, Tex, thank your brother for me, but all this high living may be too much for me. And you ... I see you are learning to live with a lot of money without being obvious about spending it."

"What do you mean?"

"You bought a Buick when you could have had a Cadillac."

"I couldn't do that. The skipper only has a Chevrolet."

      •   •   •

The next day they drove out to the airfield. He parked, and she looked around. "Big building, but what is it? It looks like an old movie set."

"A hangar. You get to come inside and help roll out the airplane."

Curtis met them at the hangar door, and Sorenson introduced him to Ferren. He could tell that Curtis was attracted to Ferren. He looked at her carefully, even longer than Sorenson felt necessary, and then went off to find a set of flight gear to fit her.

"Tex," she said, as she was putting it on, "I've never flown before, not even commercially. I hope I won't embarrass you."

"You won't. We'll start out easily. You'll have a paper bag if you get sick."

During the first hour they flew up and down Virginia Beach, and Sorenson pointed out their particular stretch of beach.

Then they made gentle turns. She said over the voice tube, "I think I like it. You don't have to be so easy on me."

The last hour he showed her what the plane could do, and she endured every maneuver without complaining.

When they landed, she was reluctant to get out, and

when he helped her down, she put her arms around him and said in his ear, "My God, that was almost as good as sex."

For the rest of Sorenson's leave, they flew in the mornings and lay on the beach in the afternoons.

On the last day, Curtis said, "I hate to tell you this, but you've used up all my gas."

Sorenson laughed. "Let me pay my bill. You need a vacation, too." Then he added a hundred dollar bill to the check.

Curtis put the bill and check in his wallet. "Thank you. I liked watching you fly. The Navy is wrong if it doesn't want you. Why do you want to fly so much if you can't fly for the Navy?"

"I think after the war is over aircraft will be used for a lot of new purposes. For instance, I grew up riding horses, then pick-up trucks, and someday I hope to run cattle with light aircraft."

Curtis scratched his head. "If your operation is big enough that might work. Maybe you could use me."

"The operation is big and getting bigger," Sorenson said. "I've got your address."

* * *

The next two weeks, Ferren had to go back to work. Sorenson became involved in the *O'Leary's* repairs and getting ready for sea. Still, the evenings were theirs, with long hours of talking and exchanging of confidences, and they became closer and closer.

One night he asked, "Have you changed your mind about marriage?"

"I want to marry you, all right, but not until the war is over. But I might change my mind. What are you going to do when the war is over?"

"I don't know. I hated the Navy after I was kicked out of flight training. I wanted to fly ever since I was a kid, and I was so close."

"What happened?"

Sorenson told her.

"And you still want to fly?"

"Yes. I've come to like destroyers, particularly since I've had a chance to command one, even though it was only for a couple of weeks. There's nothing like commanding a ship, except flying an airplane. In the airplane you get a lot of wind in your face, or at least you do in the open cockpit type we were flying in. In the ship, there's a lot of salt water in the wind. But in either case, you tell the beast what to do."

"Do you think you might stay in the Navy?"

"Maybe. I'd like to command a ship at sea, but I don't think I'd like shore jobs."

"You could always go back to the ranch."

"I've been thinking about that. When I was a kid I busted my butt and burned my skin on the back of a horse. I didn't think I'd ever get all the dust out of my ears. Then I got the bright idea of using pick-up trucks. They can't traverse very rough areas, but the shade was great, even though they bounced like hell. Now I'm thinking of adding light aircraft." He grinned. "And I've even got old Curtis to volunteer to join me as a pilot. We could get you to the city, too, for quick shopping and some entertainment."

Ferren laughed. "Maybe I'll put a brand on you some day after the war." She paused. "If I do, I'll be glad to share you with either the Navy or your ranch or both. You'll either be the richest lieutenant in the Navy or the first flying ranch hand."

       •   •   •

Carmody arranged for Alvarado and Kendrick to go ashore with him. He knew this was a strange combination, but he felt that there was animosity between Alvarado and Kendrick and he wanted to talk about it in a relaxed atmosphere ashore. They saluted the petty officer of the watch, showed him their liberty cards, turned, and saluted the colors aft. Then they walked down the brow and up the pier, laughing and talking.

Before they could reach the base of the pier, Bronte yelled from behind them. "Hey, guys, wait up. Can I come with you?"

Alvarado muttered something, but before he could say anything out loud, Carmody said, "Sure."

Even a couple of Budweisers in the nearest Portsmouth bar failed to thaw Alvarado. Carmody watched him. He felt that Alvarado's mood was almost as dark as his black hair. Carmody noted that his features were regular, and he knew the women thought he was handsome. Carmody noted his slightly prominent and flat nose and felt that there had been a South American Indian somewhere in his ancestry. He look like the Mexicans back in Texas, thought Carmody, but a little taller and handsomer.

Carmody thought Bronte was exactly the opposite, with fair coloring in his face and hair. He had heard Doctor Fineman say that Bronte was a mixture of the ancient tribes of Britain and maybe a visiting Viking. He knew he was smart and ambitious, and had heard that only the lack of a college education kept him from a commission.

Bronte broke the chill. "All right, Alvarado, out with it."

Alvarado took another swig of his beer, but said nothing.

Kendrick looked at him. "Come on, Spic, what's on your mind?"

Alvarado straightened up and looked back at Kendrick. "Okay. Bronte told the Captain all about that night in the bar down in Panama."

Carmody said, "Well, what he said musta been good. I heard the Exec and Steiner talking about you, Kendrick. They said you were a damned good petty officer, particularly when you were sober, and a helluva good gunner's mate. Sorenson said the Captain liked you, too. He said you were the kind of guy he would like on his side in any fight, except when you were fighting Spics."

Alvarado said, "I figured Bronte had screwed both of us up."

"No," Bronte said. "You didn't do anything wrong and I said so, and I couldn't hurt you with them. The Captain and Mister Durham think you guys who were with them in China walk on water. As for you, they and the exec think you are as good or better than Kendrick."

Kendrick frowned. "Not better."

Bronte sighed. "As good as."

"Okay," Kendrick said, "but there ain't no Spic better then me." He was getting excited and his New York accent showed.

Alvarado picked up his beer bottle and dribbled some beer in Kendrick's lap. "Look, amigo, You can call me Spic if you want to, but do it in a friendly way."

Kendrick grunted and tried to sweep the beer off his trousers. "Okay, okay, but you've ruined my best whites. What'll people think when I stand up?"

"They'll just think you pissed in your pants like you did when that big Spic floored you in Panama."

Carmody perked up. "That must have been a helluva night. Tell us about it."

Kendrick glared at Bronte. "Enough of this crap. I won't hold it against you for telling the Captain, but nobody else needs to know."

Bronte lifted his beer bottle and took a long swig. "Hell, everybody on the ship knows about it except Carmody. They don't talk about you, Kendrick. All they want to know about is how Steele managed to deck that big guy without even mussing up his own uniform. I tell them he did have a little trouble."

The men at the table leaned forward expectantly.

Alvarado said, "Out with it, or I give you the beer-in-the-lap treatment."

Bronte grinned. "Well, I noticed that one of his knuckles was bleeding. He ain't perfect."

As they started to get up to leave, Alvarado said, "There's one thing more. Bronte keeps running the *O'Leary* down. He's got to quit it."

Bronte sighed. "Admit it, Jaime, the old girl is a bucket of tired bolts."

Alvarado glared at Bronte. "You young bastards think you know everything because you read books. The *O'Leary* came through when the chips were down, and she's my home. Keep your opinion to yourself."

Carmody shook his head as he watched Alvarado stalk out of the bar. "Lost another round."

    •   •   •

On a day at the beach, Durham and Sonya were lying on a blanket on the sand, idly watching a swimmer body surf a mile or so away.

Sonya said, "Do you think he'll get any closer?"

"No, the waves aren't any good here. That's one reason I suggested we come here. There aren't any body surfers. Sorenson told me about this beach. He's been here before. Even if the surfer comes closer, we don't have to put on our suits. I'll wrap you up in the blanket and cover myself with sand."

"No you won't. My sun-burned bottom is sore enough as it is. This blanket is wooly, and you're too rough."

"I could be gentler."

She sighed, "Never. I'll bring a cotton blanket next time."

She reached back and patted her buttocks gingerly. "I think I'll take a dip and cool off."

Durham watched her go, admiring the jiggle of her full buttocks. He knew her pointed breasts were doing the same thing in front, keeping time with the slow movement of her beautiful legs.

He rose and followed her, hoping that he could control his erection until he reached the cooling water. But then he walked faster, stopped worrying, and let it happen. By the time he reached the warm shallows, even the splashing water couldn't dampen his passion. He ran and caught Sonya by the ankle just as she dove in. He hoped that making love in the water would be as good as it had been on the blanket.

•   •   •

Across the table from Doctor Fineman at breakfast, Gerlach engulfed a double omelette. Next to Gerlach, Ensign Renard, the new supply officer, nervously toyed with a bowl of cereal. The shiny new Supply Corps insignia gleamed in the light of the overhead light fixtures.

Fineman had long since finished an order of dry toast and black coffee, and now he was playing Mozart's 38th Symphony in his head, nodding slightly with the delightful second movement.

Renard cleared his throat nervously and began to talk. Fineman reluctantly shut off the music in his head and dragged himself back to reality. "You were saying?" he asked.

Renard said, "I was saying that I have ordered sets of L. L. Bean ski suits for all topside watch standers, although I don't know why we need them. The regular Navy issue should do."

Fineman looked carefully at Renard's eager young face, blue eyes, and light brown hair. "You weren't at sea with us last trip. The weather was fine here, but off Iceland it was cold, and it was still summer."

Gerlach said, "Standing watch up there without any glass in the ports off Iceland was bad, almost like being on an open bridge in the British Navy."

"What do you mean?" Renard asked.

"Some of the Brits I met at the club told me they stand their watch on an open bridge above a tiny pilot-house. They said they freeze their balls off in almost any weather. And we may go farther north than Iceland in winter."

Renard swallowed. "I guess the Exec was right to get the extra L. L. Bean ski suits."

Fineman kept a straight face, "I notice that the Executive Officer brought two sets aboard and gave one to the Captain."

"Holy Moses!" Renard said. "That would have set him back over two hundred dollars at a sporting goods store."

Then he blushed slightly. "Sorry, Doctor, I didn't mean to take the name of Moses in vain."

Fineman shook his head. "Doesn't bother me. I'm not Jewish."

Fineman asked for another cup of coffee and looked carefully at Renard as he stirred the black brew provided by Morales. He guessed that Renard was still uncomfortable in the formal wardroom atmosphere after his university days and the hurry-up regime of supply officer school. Fineman tried to put Renard at ease, and he asked, "How did you manage the L. L. Bean thing?"

Renard perked up. "I met a very nice girl in the Supply Depot Commander's office a couple of days ago. She gave me anything I asked for."

"Nothing personal, I hope."

"No, but I wish she would. She's a beaut. I've asked her several times for a date."

"Any luck?"

"No, she always says she has a date with an older man."

"Do you know who he is?"

"No."

Fineman looked up the table, his eyes fixed on Sorenson, who was talking to Meredith. Fineman raised his eyebrows slowly.

Renard followed the line of his gaze. He paled. "Jesus Christ, No!"

Gerlach smirked. "Now you've offended another religion. Next time try Wodan or Buddha."

Chumley was listening now and laughed. "You might also try Shiva."

Renard put down his spoon and said in a low voice, "Do you think he knows?"

Fineman restrained a smile. "I'm sure he does."

Renard slumped. "Oh, God!"

Gerlach said, "That's better. Stick to generalities. That way you offend us all equally."

Renard reddened. "Stop kidding. What am I going to do? He might have me sent to Murmansk."

Fineman shook his head. "We all might be going there. But no, he won't send you anywhere. He likes you."

Gerlach laughed. "Maybe he thinks of you as the son they'll have some day." Gerlach leaned over and looked at Sorenson. "See, you both have the same coloring. By the way, did you order a big enough size L. L. Bean suit for me?"

Fineman noted that Renard seemed to be glad to have the subject changed, and Renard brightened. "Sure. An extra large."

Fineman looked at Gerlach's bulging shoulders. "That won't do. He'll need a Wodan size."

Renard went back to his cereal, obviously happy the subject had been exhausted. Fineman hunched over his coffee and returned to the symphony in his head. The soaring notes filled his head, but he was unhappy. He had missed most of the second movement.

* * *

The last few days in the yard were frenzied for Sorenson. He was able to see Ferren at night, and he was up early to return to the ship. Ferren had encouraged him to continue to use her couch, even though he was no longer on leave.

The last minute welding was finished, and a late-arriving shield for gun one was installed. Steele and Chumley were able to supervise improvements in the new CIC. The newness of the concept of the CIC meant that they had to scrounge a few illegal pieces of equipment because they were not available in regular stock. A new brass label saying Combat Information Center appeared on the door. Supplies and spares were loaded, and four cases of medicinal brandy, courtesy of Ferren, were locked away.

That evening, Sorenson went ashore for the last time. The evening was somber. Ferren choked back tears as long as she could, but in the partial darkness of the living room, she dissolved and cried in his arms for over an hour.

When all else failed, he turned on the lamp beside the couch and took a small black box out of a pocket.

Ferren sighed, wiped her eyes, and asked, "What's that?"

Sorenson opened the box. The lamp light reflected off a large diamond.

"Wow!" she said. "A real headlight!"

He slipped it on her ring finger before she could protest. "If you won't marry me now, at least we can be engaged."

"All right," she said, turning the ring for the diamond to catch the light. "But I'm only going to wear it in private with you."

"Are you ashamed of me?"

She gripped him tightly. "Oh, no, I'm proud of you, but if anything happened to you I don't think I could go through all that sympathy thing again."

"I understand, and maybe you're right. I want you to know that I've made certain arrangements to take care of you. I'll leave the title of my car with you. Also, you're the beneficiary of an insurance policy for two hundred thousand dollars."

"But Tex, I told you I don't care about money. I just care about you."

She began to cry again and stopped only after Sorenson kissed her gently.

She drove him to the Navy yard in her red Ford. He kissed her longingly and got out.

"Don't look back," she said.

But he did, and watched the red Ford disappear around the corner of a warehouse.

Chapter Thirteen

Meredith sat at the family breakfast table, watching his three children eat breakfast. Johnny looked a lot like Meredith, tall and angular under a shock of black hair. Beth, two years younger, was just starting school. She resembled her mother, who was bustling about the small kitchen. A second son, born while Meredith was in the Philippines, sat in a highchair.

Linda had tried every known recipe for potatoes, but nothing seemed to stick to Meredith, although sharing them had put several pounds on Linda. Meredith liked her a little plump and enticed her into joining him in the potatoes and gravy and biscuits she produced every night. He watched her long blonde hair swaying about her shoulders. The last three weeks had been the longest time they had been together in the last two years other than the yard period in San Francisco.

Before the *O'Leary* had returned to the States, Meredith's family had been evacuated from the Philippines a year before the start of the war there.

Meredith looked at his older son. "Johnny, how are you doing in school?"

Johnny frowned. "All right, I guess, they do things differently in every school I go to."

Linda put a plate of fried eggs, sausage, and hominy grits in front of her husband. "He's been in four schools in four years."

Meredith shook his head. "That's about par for a

Navy kid. I hope we'll be here for at least three years so that Beth will have a good start."

Linda sat down and began to eat her sparse breakfast of dry toast. "I liked Tex's girl friend."

"Ferren? I haven't met her yet, but she's been good for him. He seems much happier."

"She came by and spent most of an evening with me before you got in from your last trip. From the casualty report you sent in, she knew you'd been injured and could tell me that your wounds weren't serious. She said she had studied to be a primary grade school teacher, but doesn't have a Virginia license yet. She offered to tutor our kids."

Johnny grinned. "She's nice."

Beth put down her fork. "Daddy, when will you be back?"

He looked at her fondly. "About a month, I think."

He left an hour later, sad to go, wondering if he was ready to face the Atlantic.

·   ·   ·

After Linda dropped him off, Meredith walked along the pier, looking up at the *O'Leary*'s freshly painted upper works. The dark gray wartime color scheme was in stark contrast to the light gray of her pre-war years. The new shield on gun one glowed dimly with its purposely dulled paint. The new air search radar antenna on the foremast rotated slowly. The glass ports replaced in the bridge structure glistened, and he could barely make out where the holes in the bridge structure and side had been patched. She looked ready to go.

Sorenson met him at the brow and saluted after Meredith had come aboard. "Ready for sea, Captain, except for loading ammunition. We'll be ready to get underway at 1400."

Meredith's eyes swept the quarterdeck. "She looks good, Tex. Let's go up to the bridge and talk. I've had breakfast."

At the top of the bridge ladder, Meredith turned to the door in the back of the old charthouse. The first thing that caught his eye was the new brass sign on the door. "Combat Information Center," he said, "I see you,

Chumley, and Steele have been at work. We're not legally supposed to have one of these yet."

"Let's don't worry about what we call it. Take a look inside."

Sorenson pushed the door open. Bronte looked up and yelled, "Attention on deck."

Meredith waved a hand. "Carry on. Bronte, tell me about the new gear."

"The DRT has been improved and a dimmer has been added. The air plot is new." He pointed to a large, vertically-mounted, transparent plotting board where the pipe rail bunk had been removed. "That small desk between the DRT and the sonar console we made ourselves, and the yard installed the new radio terminals.

"Now Mister Sorenson or the CIC watch officer can run the whole show right from there. He can see all of the plots without moving. He can tell you what he sees and make recommendations over the two-way squawk box. The bridge squawk box is mounted right by your chair. That way you can talk directly to whoever is in charge. You can also use the voice tube if something goes haywire with the electronic stuff."

Sorenson said, "Some day a captain may fight his ship from CIC."

"Maybe so," Meredith said, "but most captains would want to see what's going on."

"Yes, but they can't see much outside at night or in fog," Sorenson said.

"You're right, but it will take time. By the way, who will stand watch in here? We have some new officers and we should use some of the leading chiefs."

Sorenson took out a piece of paper. "I think I have it figured out. This shows the chief engineer and the navigator off watch, unless we need them, and Steiner, Steele, and Chumley standing officer of the deck watch. They will have as assistant officer of the watch, Chief Torpedoman Skelly, Chief Gunner's Mate Aronson, and Chief Boatswain's Mate Bellows. Here in the operations center will be Ensign Gerlach, Ensign MacIntosh, the new torpedo officer, when he gets here, and Bronte, who has just made first class radarman. Until MacIntosh arrives, Jablonski will stand CIC watches. Doctor Fineman and Renard will do the decoding."

"I know the new officers, but I don't know Chief Aronson. Tell me a little about him."

"I don't know how long we'll keep him. He's a re-called reserve. He was in college and could have stayed until graduation and then been commissioned, but chose to be recalled as an enlisted man as soon as war was declared. As a first class gunner's mate, he was as-signed to a new destroyer and made chief quickly. Then it was sunk, and he was sent to us. I don't think he has adjusted to the *O'Leary* yet. He thinks it's a waste of his knowledge of the 5-inch gun system, and I'm sure it is. The Navy does strange things sometimes. But I'm glad we have him. He'll be needed soon in new construc-tion. By the way, he looks like he is twenty-three years old. Youngest chief I've ever seen. He does shave, though. He's a strange contrast to Chief Bellows."

"Chief Bellows talks well now. You did a great job getting him some dental help."

Sorenson smiled. "I had to. Sometimes even I couldn't understand him."

• • •

Chumley took the ship out, with Meredith pacing the bridge trying to look unconcerned. Chumley did well, and they were soon anchored at the ammunition an-chorage off the Norfolk Naval Base. Sorenson and Steiner supervised the ammunition loading, and Meredith left in the gig for the departure conference to be held at the Norfolk Naval Base.

He was back in two hours, and strode up the accom-modation ladder and onto the quarterdeck. "Tex, call a conference of all officers as soon as possible. Let Steiner keep on with the loading."

In five minutes the officers were either sitting at the wardroom table or in the lounge chairs. Meredith called for a cup of coffee as they settled down. He stroked his mustache, now fully recovered from the small gaps in-flicted by Doctor Fineman's repairs.

He looked around the wardroom and began, "We leave Norfolk at 1400 or as soon as we finish loading ammunition. We join another destroyer, the *Bulmer*, off the entrance. We'll make a transit at twenty knots to Halifax and pick up a high-speed troop transport convoy off the port. It will only have three ships, and we will escort it at seventeen knots to Iceland."

The bachelor officers grinned at each other. Meredith knew they were remembering the rumors about the girls of Iceland.

Meredith paused. "We'll be there two nights, so I think you bachelors can test the local climate and, ah, the hot baths."

There was a spreading murmur of appreciation down toward the end of the table where most of the bachelors sat.

Meredith went on, "Then comes the bad part. With the *Bulmer* we will go out to meet a group known as 'Operation Easy-Unit' composed of the heavy cruiser *Tuscaloosa* and the destroyers *Rodman* and *Emmons*."

"What's that unit going to do?" Sorenson asked.

"Take some equipment to Russia. Our part is a little vague. It seems that a convoy of thirty-eight ships bound for Murmansk has just been decimated by German submarines and land-based aircraft operating out of Norway. Also, some German surface ships sortied from their continental ports and apparently scared the out-manned escorts into scattering the convoy. Only five ships made it to Russian ports."

"Five out of thirty-eight!" Sorenson said.

Meredith nodded. "The British declared they weren't going to send any more convoys to Murmansk. The Russians protested so much that the Americans agreed to send some high priority electronics equipment and personnel by cruiser and destroyer. These ships are loading now in Great Britain, and we will meet them in the Barents Sea and act as a distant anti-submarine screen, looking for submarines ahead of them."

Sorenson asked, "Do we go into Murmansk?"

"Yes, if we survive, and then back to Norfolk via Iceland."

From the end of the table Renard asked, "Will we need to issue the new cold weather equipment I just got?"

Meredith looked puzzled and turned to Sorenson.

Sorenson cleared his throat. "I had Renard order enough special cold weather equipment to outfit the bridge watchstanders. It's like the set I got for you."

Jablonski said, "I've got the piloting instructions here. They say that the mean average temperature for Iceland at this time of year is fifty degrees. That's not bad."

Steele chimed in. "Maybe, but the nightly lows are near freezing even in summer, and in the Barents sea the water temperature is near freezing, and the air temperature can get below freezing even in the summer."

"Right," Jablonski said, "and the fogs are awful. Also the winds and heavy seas."

Sorenson said, "That might be good for us. If we can't see surfaced subs, they can't see us either. And we've got surface search radar. They don't have it on their subs yet."

Meredith pulled at his mustache. "Hold the cold weather outfits until we need them. The standard Navy outfits will do."

Steiner poked his head in the door. "Captain, we're finished loading ammo, and the engineers report they're ready for sea."

Sorenson turned to Gerlach. "Gerlach, you and Chief Bellows check to see that everything, both topside and below, is secured for sea. We may hit some heavy weather."

Jablonski nodded. "Likely to. There's a large low pressure area moving up the central Atlantic."

Sorenson said, "Gerlach, do a good job. I'll be right behind you."

"Let's go," Meredith said. "Station the special sea detail."

• • •

The trip out the channel gave no hint of the weather farther out in the Atlantic. The sky was a deep blue, Blue October weather, the locals from Norfolk would call it, even though October was two months away. Meredith sat back in his chair and breathed in deep lungfuls of crisp salt air. In an hour they passed out the net and were joined by the destroyer *Bulmer*, another old four-stacker that had escaped the Java disaster.

Sorenson leaned on the bridge bulwark next to

Meredith, watching the *Bulmer*. "Must be like old times for you," he said.

Meredith said, "Maybe so, but I don't like this side of the world. I don't trust the Atlantic. It can be cold, unpredictable, and rough as hell. These old four-stackers will roll their rails under. Also, all of our transits will be made with the prevailing swells on our beam. I hope you've got your bunk rigged for heavy weather."

"I've done the best I can. I have an extra blanket and my life preserver under the inboard side of my mattress. That makes a sort of U-shaped hammock, but I wish we had the old-fashioned hammocks themselves. Sometimes I think the progress we think we've made in the last fifty years is really backwards."

Meredith said, "The last time I visited the Antisubmarine Force Headquarters, they were pessimistic as hell. They said sinkings of merchant ships were way up, and more and more German U-boats were showing up on our convoy routes."

"Can't we do more?"

"I think we're doing all we can with what we have. Apparently our shipyards are working twenty-four hours a day turning out merchant ships and escorts. I don't see how we can change much on our end. Our convoys have to stay on routes that can be covered by land-based air patrols. The U-boats know how far out the aircraft can cover and they stay beyond that range."

"Any chance of increasing the range?" Sorenson asked.

"Steele says our airdales are working on extending the range of our present aircraft and adapting other longer range aircraft to ASW work. There are some improvements in the works in ASW equipment for us. We may have them installed by our next trip."

"That won't help us this time."

"No, but we have speed," Meredith said. "At least the U-boats can't end run us."

"I tale it the mood at headquarters must have been bad."

"Very bad. Right now they think we're losing the war in the Atlantic."

"What about the big U-boat, the Seawolf?" Sorenson asked.

"The mine-laying and provisioning versions are at sea. The attack version is almost finished. We'll have a few more months before we have to face it."

"Face it, hell! I want to go look for it," Sorenson said.

Meredith laughed. "We'll see it soon enough."

. . .

Meredith was senior to the commanding officer of the *Bulmer*, so he placed the two destroyers in front with two thousand yards between ships and began zigzagging. From CIC the sharp, recurring pings of the sonar could be heard. Meredith put the ship in condition III with one third of its batteries manned.

Sorenson came to the bridge after inspecting the ship and stopped beside Meredith, who was staring out to sea toward their destination. "What are you looking at, Captain?"

"Those steadily building wave troughs. We're beyond the continental shelf, and the water is deeper so that the waves will continue to get higher and with larger distances between their crests. We're rolling fifteen degrees now, and I don't like the wind. The barometer is continuing to drop. It may get nasty before long. But I guess the North Atlantic is better than the Russian front. Three thousand miles over there, millions of men on both sides are fighting and dying in mud and stinking filth. At least it's clean out here in the open sea."

"Yeah, beats the Russian front."

"I'm sure several million German and Russian soldiers would agree."

Sorenson looked down at the wake surging by the side and throwing spray over the after decks. "That water hides a lot of grief, too. We've lost almost two thousand ships in the last year in the Atlantic."

"No wonder there's despair over at Antisubmarine Headquarters. The plan the Germans call 'Parkenschlag' is failing, but they'll think of something else."

"What the hell's that German word mean?" Sorenson asked.

"It means, 'the roll of the drums.' They've tried to overwhelm us with sheer numbers theoretically marching to their drums, but we've fought them to a standstill with more escorts and more land-based antisubmarine patrol planes. They've made a difference, even though not enough yet to turn the tide. We'll be seeing aircraft all the way up to Halifax, where we pick up our convoy, and then they'll stay with us for another day before we pass out of their range. Then we'll meet the latest German idea again, the 'wolf pack' of several submarines grouped together under a single commander."

"Wolf pack? I didn't like the sound of that on our last trip."

Meredith nodded. "The briefers were beginning to use the term then, but I don't think the Germans were well organized that early. The groups of submarines we ran into then were not good as teams." Meredith took a last deep breath of salt air. "Let's go below for chow."

He had difficulty keeping his balance during the trip down as the O'Leary's roll increased. When they entered the wardroom, Morales grinned. "Save on mess bill tonight. Not many officers eat."

Meredith looked around. Renard was hanging on to a stanchion, waiting to sit down. Doctor Fineman was ready. He hadn't missed a meal yet. Chumley and Gerlach were hanging on to the other stanchion, and the lashed down chairs moved slightly with the increasing roll. The mess attendants had wet the table cloth to keep the plates from sliding.

"Dinner is served," Morales said.

All those present managed to get into their chairs without too much trouble, except Gerlach. He tried to hop over one of the chair arms, but got a foot tangled in a securing line. He bounced off Chumley and sprawled across the table. Chumley yelped and dropped the silverware the mess attendants had handed him.

"Damn!" Chumley gasped. "You broke my rib or something."

Fineman looked at him carefully. "I think you'll be all right, but you'll need a new fork. That one's bent double."

The mess attendants served by bringing in one dish at a time and handing it to each officer. Water glasses and salt and pepper shakers were dispensed with.

When the main course arrived, already served on plates, Renard looked at it for a few minutes, and then asked to be excused. He could be heard running along the passageway forward to the head.

Sorenson looked over his shoulder. "Well, at least he got past your room, Doc."

Fineman nodded. "Nice kid. He'll make it. I predict he'll be eating normally in two days."

.   .   .

The next day the seas grew larger, and meals in the wardroom were reduced to sandwiches and coffee in heavy mugs, but most of the officers and crew were back to eating again.

The O'Leary and Bulmer arrived off Halifax on schedule in spite of the weather and joined the high-speed convoy. Meredith could see hundreds of life-jacketed troops walking about the promenade decks of the converted passenger liners.

The local escorts that had brought the convoy out of Halifax reported to Meredith for duty. A Navy captain, aboard the largest transport as convoy commodore, set a course for Iceland and ordered the convoy to begin zigzagging. Meredith noted the Alvarado was in good spirits, presiding over the signal bridge watch that was signalling to the other escorts. Two days later they passed out of the range of air cover but almost immediately entered a heavy fog bank. The convoy commodore stopped zigzagging just before the gray blanket enveloped them.

The next two days passed quickly as the seas moderated, but the nights grew steadily colder. Meredith worried about the transports full of troops astern but could do little for them except keep track of them on the surface search radar. Occasionally two contacts came close to merging, and Meredith could hear whistle signals as the ships got close enough to see each other, and there were no radio reports of collision.

Two days before the convoy was due in Iceland, the fog lifted, and Meredith searched anxiously astern. The transports had straggled badly, but now they began to close up. In an hour the formation had steadied and the convoy resumed zigzagging.

The CIC reported radio contact with an antisubmarine patrol plane and soon reported it as a radar contact. Subsequently, a lookout reported the welcome sight as a Catalina dipped to a low altitude and passed close by the *O'Leary*.

Meredith was relaxing in his bridge chair when the radio messenger brought him the message board. He looked up after reading it and said to Jablonski, who was working at the chart desk, "You shore-goers won't like this. We aren't going in to Reykjavik Harbor. We've been told to fuel in Seydisfjordur. Look that up."

Jablonski thumbed through the Piloting Guide. "Small port on the northeast coast. Population three thousand."

Meredith said, "I promised you liberty in Iceland and I'll keep my word, but this sounds like a small farming or fishing town."

       •   •   •

Meredith conned the *O'Leary* alongside a tanker in the small but well-protected harbor. After fueling, they shifted to an anchorage.

Chief Bellows came up to the bridge with Ensign Gerlach. Bellows was holding the kind of sounding lead used to test the character of the bottom. A large hole in its bottom was filled with wax. Bellows held it up and said, "Captain, don't like da bottom. Mostly rock. Tink you have to keep steam up all night."

Meredith nodded. "The chart says poor holding ground." Meredith turned to Sorenson. "Keep the special sea detail on the bridge manned. Also a skeleton crew on the forecastle, and tell main control we'll want the engines on two minutes notice."

"What about liberty?" Sorenson asked.

"I didn't think you'd be going ashore," Meredith said.

"Just looking out for the crew. I'm not going ashore."

"Okay, Tex, start liberty for half the crew, taking into account the need for special sea detail reliefs, and end liberty at 2400. If what I hear about these Icelandic girls is true, the crew won't last beyond 2400 anyway. Anybody still game is welcome to get a standby tomorrow and try again."

       •   •   •

The next morning at breakfast in the wardroom, Meredith looked down the table. Almost all the officers were present. "What happened ashore?" he asked. "Was all that rough weather too much for you?"

Renard cleared his throat. "Nothing much happened, Captain. I think your rumor was wrong. Most of the girls were away. And those still here were mostly engaged. They weren't even all blonde. There were many dark-haired ones."

"What's wrong with that?" Meredith asked.

"I guess nothing, but we'd all heard that Scandinavians were blonde and sexy."

"Nothing wrong with being brunette and sexy."

Fineman said, "And they all aren't Scandinavians. Some of the early settlers came from Scotland and Ireland."

Nobody else spoke up. Renard studied the overhead carefully.

Meredith said, "Well, this little place may be a farming and fishing community and the people have to get up early. I'll try to get us into Reykjavik next time. It's a lot bigger."

•   •   •

The next morning Sorenson watched the *Tuscaloosa* group come into the harbor and fuel, and soon the escorts got underway and formed a screen off the entrance. That morning, the British destroyer *Onslaught* joined the group, and Meredith was ordered to take the two four-stackers 50 miles ahead of the *Tuscaloosa* group and conduct an antisubmarine sweep, keeping their relative position during the high speed transit. Again a heavy fog surrounded them, shrouding them from submarines and apparently grounding the Luftwaffe. The German Air Force usually ran patrols from the airfields they had taken in Norway.

Except for the increasing cold, Sorenson thought the run was easier than he had expected, but he realized that the fog had kept the German Luftwaffe away. The *O'Leary* and *Bulmer* stood in to Murmansk early in the morning. The *Tuscaloosa* group sent a message stating they were going in to Vaenga Bay to discharge their cargo of urgently needed war supplies and RAF personnel. Then the *Tuscaloosa* would load American Navy men and merchant marine men from vessels that had been sunk in the last disastrous convoy.

Off Murmansk, Sorenson watched from the bridge as a Russian pilot boarded the *O'Leary*. The pilot managed to bring the *O'Leary* to a berth without damaging the ship, although Meredith appeared to be on the verge of taking the conn back several times. He muttered to Sorenson, "This pilot doesn't understand how much engine power he's controlling and how little rudder control we have with a single rudder."

Once the pilot asked for "back full," and Sorenson gritted his teeth as the shuddering stern almost met the picr on the other side of the slip before the pilot could correct the situation.

After they had moored to a pier, Sorenson met a delegation of Russian officials on the quarterdeck and escorted them down to the wardroom for coffee. The smiling Russians displayed several stainless-steel teeth that glinted in the wardroom lights.

Meredith welcomed them in the wardroom. The Russian interpreter's fractured English was incomprehensible. Meredith sent for Bellows, and the chief tried his Polish and a few words of Russian. One of the Russians spoke Polish, and after some initial confusion while the Russian was getting used to Bellow's dental plate, they got along fine.

Bellows said, "Dey say dey tank you for bringin' lot of parts dey need. Dey wanta show der appreciation. So dey invite de crew to a dance. Dey not got enough women, so some of de men haveta dance wid each udder."

Meredith covered a laugh by adding his hand to his mustache. "Tell them, thank you. We'll have a group ready in an hour."

The Russians left, pocketing the packs of cigarettes Renard had produced.

Meredith asked Chief Bellows to sit down and sent for Sorenson, who had gone up on deck seeing to the security watch posting. He told Sorenson what the Russians had said. Sorenson broke up in raucous laughter but soon came back to normal when he realized they had to solve the problem. "Wow," he said, "Chief, what do you recommend?"

Bellows cleared his throat. "I tink you gotta do it. I understand dis a new area of de port, and da man I spoke wit said after the Russkys built de new piers up here dey built de whorehouses. Better our guys dance dan screw."

Meredith put his hand back up to his mustache and said, "Thanks, Chief. Very wise."

•   •   •

Sorenson thought the conduct of the men at the dance would be so important that he went on shore patrol himself. He took with him the biggest and toughest man he could think of, Gunner's Mate First Class Kendrick.

The dance started slowly with about twenty Russian women present, half women workers still in long wool dresses and boots and another half obviously off-duty prostitutes. An accordion and a violin provided loud music with a strong beat. One of the Russian visitors of the afternoon brought out several bottles of vodka which soon broke the ice.

Sorenson stood at one side of the dance floor behind Alvarado and Bronte, who were looking over the milling and laughing women. Sorenson heard Alvarado say, "Look at those two women across the room. Their slanted eyes make them look Chinese."

Bronte said, "Could be descendants of the Mongols. They swept over a lot of Russia."

"How do you know?"

"I read."

"What the hell, so do I."

Bronte turned, looked at Alvarado and raised his eyebrows, but said nothing.

Alvarado said, "Well, I read some, but I've never heard of Mongols before."

"They came from the east."

Sorenson could see Alvarado's neck redden. Alvarado shook his head and said, "I don't care who their ancestors were or where they came from! You talk too much." He walked away, and Sorenson stepped up beside Bronte. "I didn't mean to be listening," he said, "but I don't like to see you and Alvarado quarreling. You two are leading petty officers and key men in our crew."

Bronte laughed. "Alvarado's the one with the problem. I like him."

"You could have fooled me, and the younger enlisted men don't understand it either. Try to keep your differences hidden. Why don't you go dance with a Russian lady."

Bronte laughed and walked over to a young prostitute to ask her to dance.

Sorenson shook his head and began watching the dancers. All the women were on the dance floor with members of the *O'Leary* crew, and a few Russian men were dancing together.

Alvarado came back to Sorenson. "Sir, what was Bronte telling you?"

"Nothing. I was telling him, like I'm going to tell you, that I hope you two will stop arguing."

Alvarado frowned. "But he's such a young smartass."

"Yes, he's young and also smart. But the ship needs those qualities just as it needs your maturity and experience. It's our duty to figure out how to get the best out of Bronte and others like him."

Alvarado said, "I'll try. Mister Sorenson, why aren't you out there dancing?"

"I'm on shore patrol. I can't."

"But Kendrick is wearing a shore patrol brassard, and he's out there."

"I know. I sent him out there to get the dance going and to help keep order on the floor."

Alvarado said, "Kendrick is another guy I have trouble with. I spent several years on the Asiatic Station with him trying to keep him out of trouble ashore. Now I've given up."

Sorenson wiggled his toes and folded his arms trying to relieve the fatigue that was creeping through his body. A week at sea without much sleep was catching up. He watched Kendrick, who was in the clasp of a young, buxom girl almost as big as he was. She wore a long wool skirt, just a little shorter than the others about the floor, a pair of big boots, and a red kerchief tied about her hair. The red ends fluttered behind her as the couple twirled, a warning to all behind her. Beads of perspiration grew on Kendrick's forehead. The excess trickled down his cheeks, detoured by the deep wrinkles of his large smile. He seemed oblivious of the other dancers who bounced off his partner's ample rear.

Sorenson watched Carmody almost go down and laughed. "Quite a show," he said to Alvarado.

Alvarado shook his head. "Yeah, just like a small town rodeo. Smells the same, too."

Sorenson felt the weariness creeping higher, and sat down on a bench at the side of the room. While his vigilance was relaxed, some of the crew managed to sneak out of the room and, as Chief Bellows would say, screw.

•   •   •

The next morning, after Jablonski had assured him that he had plotted their course in the channel and the minefields so that he could navigate them out, Meredith conned the O'Leary away from the pier a few minutes early so as to avoid having to take aboard the Russian pilot. As they pulled away, the Russian pilot ran up the pier, waving his fur hat and shouting in Russian and broken English.

Chief Bellows, on the forecastle, listened carefully and shouted up to the bridge, "I can't understand him very good, but I tink he say come back or dey don't invite us to da dance next time."

Meredith laughed, "Tell him we're sorry. We liked the dance very much, but we have to get back to Iceland for an urgent date."

Chief Bellows shouted for a minute in Polish and stopped. "He don't understand me," he said.

The Russian pilot was now too far away to hear Bellows, and he disappeared from sight, pacing up and down and shrugging his shoulders.

Meredith watched him. "The poor guy will probably end up in Siberia," he said.

Chapter Fourteen

Meredith took the two American destroyers almost due north for two hours and then turned to the west. He knew that the *Tuscaloosa* group astern would draw most of the German Luftwaffe efforts, and that the newer ships had the antiaircraft armament to cope with it.

The two old four-stackers weren't designed to fend off air attacks. Their best defense was high speed and radical maneuvering to avoid bombs. Each had six 20-millimeter machine guns, and only Meredith's begging had prevented the Mare Island Navy Yard from taking off the ancient 3-inch gun from the fantail. The gun was officially classed as an antiaircraft gun, but was used mostly for firing starshells. It had no method of control other than a direct open sight. When used against aircraft, all of the fuzes were set at two thousand yards, giving a fixed barrage that attackers would have to fly through.

Meredith lifted his binoculars and looked at the *Bulmer*'s stern. Her 3-inch gun had been removed. "Damn!" he said, and he sent for Steiner.

Steiner soon joined Meredith on the bridge. Meredith looked at him over his shoulder, as he watched the *Bulmer* take station on the beam of the *O'Leary*. "Chuck, we've got to figure out what we're going to do if the Luftwaffe comes after us. I think this far north we'll only see Heinkel 115s with torpedoes. There isn't usually enough ceiling up here for high-level horizontal bombing. That means they'll all be at a medium level while searching and will make only low-level attacks."

"Captain, they've been fired at lately by American destroyers with 5-inch antiaircraft guns, and maybe they'll think our guns are the same kind."

"Good thinking. If we fire our 4-inch guns at them, they'll have to think it over. If the 3-inch gun fires, they'll see the bursts from it and think all our guns are firing bursting antiaircraft projectiles."

Steiner chuckled. "Might help, and it will give our gun crews something to do. If the Krauts come in close, I think our twenties will do well."

"All right, go instruct your gun crews."

By the time they were ready to head southwest, fog had begun to form, and a rainy drizzle cut the visibility. By the next morning, the fog became patchy, and the thermometer dropped to 34 degrees. Meredith authorized the issue of the L. L. Bean clothing, and the bridge watch soon appeared in dark blue nylon parkas and trousers. Some even had fur around the hoods. Meredith laughed as Alvarado strutted back and forth on the signal bridge, calling for a set of ski poles.

Two hours before noon, CIC reported four scattered air contacts that seemed to be in a search pattern. Meredith called the crew to general quarters, and the strident clang of the general alarm hurried the men to their stations.

The patches of fog lightened, and the air search contacts came closer and closer. One closed to 5 miles and burst out of the overcast. A lookout shouted, "Aircraft! zero four five relative. Position angle ten. Range five miles."

At Meredith's order, the *Bulmer*, a mile north, started to open the range to give both ships an opportunity to maneuver freely. Meredith lifted his binoculars, but before he could identify the aircraft, the talker reported that it was a Heinkel with a torpedo. Steiner requested permission to open fire. Meredith turned the ship to port so that most of the guns could bear, and then the 4-inchers roared. They were elevated enough to bear on the Heinkel, and soon the smoke obscured the guns so that the pilot would have had trouble identifying them.

The 3-incher astern began to pop away, and its projectiles burst well in front of the aircraft. The Heinkel turned away and flew back into the overcast. The gun crews cheered.

The air search radar followed the aircraft as it circled. "He's calling in his pals," Meredith said.

The other two aircraft closed and emerged from the overcast for a simultaneous attack from different bearings. Meredith increased speed to 25 knots and headed to keep the nearest attacker on the beam.

The guns banged away again but did no damage. The nearest Heinkel bored steadily on their beam and at a thousand yards dropped its torpedo.

"Right full rudder!" Meredith shouted.

Alvarado spun the wheel so fast its spokes blurred. The ship heeled, and the signalmen on the bridge rushed to the side to watch the torpedo wake.

"Get back!" shouted Sorenson, who had come out from CIC to watch the attack. "If it hits near you, the blast will take your heads off!"

But it missed ahead at least a hundred yards, and Meredith was already busy looking for the next Heinkel. It dropped its deadly fish even closer, and Meredith backed the inboard engine to increase the speed of his turn. Again the torpedo missed, this time about 20 yards ahead. By coming closer, the Heinkel gave the 20-millimeter guns a better chance. They poured a steady stream of projectiles into its side. Meredith could see the pilot fighting the controls. The big aircraft slowly rolled and caught a wing in the water. The bomber cartwheeled and lifted a spray of white water.

A shout went up aft where most of the 20-millimeter guns were located. The bridge talker grinned. "Twenties aft report they shot down an aircraft!"

Sorenson said, "Good job!"

Meredith nodded his head and looked for the third aircraft. It was nowhere in sight, and radar reported it had headed south.

"Send one to us next time," the *Bulmer* signaled.

There were other air contacts during the day, but the

fog increased. They skipped from bank to bank without being discovered.

• •

The third day they were released by the *Tuscaloosa* group, and Jablonski recommended that they turn south just beyond Jan Mayen Island in the Greenland Sea. Two days later they rounded Iceland and sighted Reykjavik.

By noon they had fueled and moved to an anchorage. Meredith and Sorenson looked carefully at the chart and noted that the holding ground in their assigned anchorage was good. Chief Bellows put a sounding lead over the side. When it came up, he examined the bottom material brought up by the wax in the end of the lead and shouted up to the bridge, "Mud . . . goot stuff!"

Meredith laughed. "That's good enough for me, Tex. Start liberty."

Fineman was leaning on the bridge bulwark studying the shoreline. Meredith joined him. "What do you see, Doc?"

"A lot of volcanoes, geysers, and steam vents, but not many people."

"It's cold. They may be inside."

"Not necessarily. It isn't cold for them."

Sorenson came over and heard the last remark. "It's cold for me, and I think it is for the crew out in the open. I think we may be back up around here again this winter, and I'd like to make sure that our men don't freeze their balls off."

Fineman said, "Not much chance of that. Their fingers and toes might suffer, and they don't perform well when they're cold."

Sorenson said, "Captain, I'd like permission to draw a real cold weather outfit for each man topside at general quarters."

Meredith stroked his mustache. "That sounds good, but I don't know whether we can get that many outfits or whether our limited budget can pay for it."

"If I can swing it, can I do it?"

"Sure."

• • •

The next morning Bronte invited Alvarado and Carmody into the CIC as a peace gesture to Alvarado after the lecture by Sorenson at the dance. Bronte had rigged a coffee pot for the sonarmen and radarmen. Bronte, as senior radarman, rated the padded seat at the surface radar, and Alvarado got the similar seat at the air search radar, but Carmody, as a visitor, had to make do with an upturned wastebasket. Bronte used his finger to stir his coffee.

Carmody shuddered. "You wouldn't do that with Texas coffee. It'd burn your finger off."

Bronte said, "Speaking of burns, I sure wish I'd had some of this hot stuff ashore. I damned near froze my pecker off."

Alvarado smirked. "You should have kept it in your pants."

"I did. No chance to use it except to take a leak, and then I had to use a snow bank. Icelanders don't seem to believe in public heads."

Bronte said, "Did you have any luck, Alvarado?"

"Sure."

"How come? Ain't any Spics over there."

"That shows how ignorant you are. There are some traces of them. Spanish and Portuguese came across the seas to Iceland in the old days. Many early settlers came from Ireland and Scotland. Many of the people of Iceland have dark hair." He raised his eyebrows and looked at Bronte. "I read about that in a book I borrowed from the wardroom."

Bronte ignored the opening. "Guess I didn't get to see many of them with their hats off."

Alvarado said, "They don't have dark complexions. I guess they got bleached out over hundreds of years by lack of sunshine. I found a nice dark-haired girl who liked me very much, but she couldn't understand when I tried to tell her where I came from. I'd like to see her again."

Carmody had been quiet, listening but not saying anything. Bronte said, "Why so quiet, Carmody?"

"No reason."

"Come on! Did you meet a girl?"

"Well, kind of."

"Did you have any luck?" Bronte asked.

"Yes and no."

"What does that mean?"

"Yes, I was ready, and no I didn't. I thought of the girl I met in Norfolk, and I lost my urge."

"I'll bet that made you popular," Alvarado said.

Carmody sighed. "She was a knockout. I hope I won't regret it."

Bronte laughed. "I think you will. The girls in Norfolk are pretty tough for sailors to get close to."

Carmody raised his eyebrows. "How would you know? You hardly ever go ashore."

"I don't any more, but I did when I first got there."

Alvarado said, "I remember. What made you stop?"

Bronte said, "I met a very nice girl and we had several dates. Then she took me home to meet her folks. They treated me like I was a leper."

Carmody sighed. "I know what you mean. Most civilians don't like sailors. I hope my girl's parents will change their minds."

"Did you have some trouble?" Bronte asked.

"Yes. My girl friend and I got along fine, but she wouldn't take me home to meet her folks. She said nobody in Norfolk likes sailors."

Alvarado nodded. "I can understand that. There are a lot of them in Norfolk and many of them raise a lot of hell."

Bronte said, "Losers like us have to pay for their coffee. That'll be a nickel."

• • •

The next morning Fineman stepped into the wardroom early and found Chumley and Gerlach each laying in large amounts of Morales' waffles. Breakfast in the wardroom was loud and cheerful. The early end of shore leave had given even the carousers time to sober up, and Fineman noticed the cool climate stimulated their appetites.

Steiner, Chumley, and Gerlach were describing their experiences in a public steam bath. Chumley said, "This wasn't at all like Fineman said public steam baths were like in Japan."

Fineman tried to hide behind a cup of coffee, but nobody was paying any attention to him anyway, and he put it down and listened.

Chumley went on. "He said everybody was naked there. Here, they all had bathing suits on, and old-fashioned ones at that. Gerlach wore trunks, and the women spent all their time coming over and looking at his muscles. I didn't know what they were saying, but they did a lot of giggling and pointing at his trunks."

"Probably wanted to know if he was big all over," Steiner said.

"Aw, cut it out," Gerlach said, but he was obviously pleased.

Steiner said, "And even the men came over. They were bold enough to try to feel his muscles."

Fineman started to say something, but thought better about it and filled his mouth with a piece of waffle.

Gerlach asked Renard, "Charlie, what did you do ashore? We never saw you."

"I had a little supply business to do, trying to get some fresh fish for the crew. I met a very nice girl in the fish market who invited me home for dinner. She spoke pretty good English, and the beer was good."

Gerlach smirked. "What did you do after dinner?"

"We used the family hot bath."

"Did she have a funny bathing suit?"

"It seems the Icelanders only wear them in public baths now that the Americans have come to Iceland. The reason the suits look so old-fashioned is that they haven't been used for a good many years."

"Well, how did she look in her bathing suit?" Gerlach asked.

"Ah, well, she didn't wear one."

Fineman suppressed a laugh and went on listening.

Gerlach asked, "What did you use for a bathing suit?"

"Nothing. I didn't want to offend my hostess."

Gerlach leered. "If you didn't have any clothes on, where did you keep your rubbers?"

"Didn't need any. There were some right next to the soap dish. American, too. Lend-Lease, I guess."

Gerlach stopped eating and laughed. "Pretty good."

Renard blushed slightly. "I don't know how they were. I didn't try them."

Gerlach put down his fork. "No, that wasn't a question. Just a statement about these waffles. They're pretty good."

Renard let out his breath and smiled. "Pretty good! They're great!"

Fineman agreed, although he had only had one. Listening to the conversation had slowed him down. He called Morales over. "Another waffle, please."

Morales shook his head. "Sorry, sir, Mister Gerlach ate the last one."

Fineman made a mental note in his case book that all that young officers thought about was food and sex, in that order. Then he realized that he had eaten only one waffle and had had no sex recently, and he resolved to bring himself back up to par in both areas.

•   •   •

The trip back was so rough that no submarine could have found them if it had been there. The remnants of a hurricane swept through the area and dropped blinding rain which beat down the breaking spray from the mountainous swells. The barometer dropped an inch and the temperature plunged 20 degrees in an hour. The two ships they escorted were fast troop ships, and the need to make as much speed as possible to keep up with them made the two old four-stackers pound badly. Much of the topside gear was damaged, and one K-gun was twisted so badly that it would need replacement.

When the weather began to abate, Fineman climbed up to the bridge to get the mixture of stale smells out of his lungs. At the top of the ladder he saw Meredith glumly looking at the long high rollers still coming from the south.

Fineman watched the roll of the ship and chose a moment at the top of a roll to let go of the edge of the flag bag at the top of the ladder. He skittered across the deck and grabbed the rail next to Meredith. When he was sure he was safe, he said, "You look bushed. Will you take some time off when we get to Norfolk?"

"I guess so."

"I hope you'll be more enthusiastic than that. How you take your time off is as important as if you take it."

Meredith shook his head slowly. "I know I'll feel better when we get in. It's just this damned ocean. I hate it. The Pacific was much better. Also I have a feeling that the Germans are gaining ground against our convoy system. We can't afford to lose ships at the rate they're going down."

"I agree. If we don't stop these German subs we could lose this war."

• • •

By the time they dropped the fast troop ships off at Halifax, Steele was more than ready for a return to Norfolk. He stopped by CIC the next day to make sure the sonar was operating at peak efficiency.

"No Krauts today," reported Terrill, his leading sonarman. "None likely around here."

The TBS suddenly crackled with a reported sonar contact by the *Bulmer*.

"Damn!" Terrill said. "I don't believe it!"

Steele went out on the bridge and joined Meredith, who put the *O'Leary* in a circle following the *Bulmer* around the contact.

The *Bulmer* reported, "Course one eight zero. Speed three. Intend to attack."

Steele asked the Captain to close in a little, and then the *O'Leary* picked up the contact, too. Steele listened intently for a few minutes and then went into CIC and conferred with Terrill. Then he straightened up and went out on the bridge.

"Captain, I think that's a school of fish. It's moving erratically at slow speed and it varies in size."

Meredith conferred with the Captain of the *Bulmer* over the TBS, suggesting the contact was fish, but the other Captain was adamant.

Meredith reluctantly transmitted, "Make an attack."

The *Bulmer* headed for the contact and dropped a full pattern. The explosions boiled up and then subsided. The *O'Leary* headed for the contact and passed through the area of the depth charge explosions but didn't make an attack. Meredith and Steele looked over the side as they passed through the foam. There were a dozen large fish floating in the bubbles.

The TBS squawked. "Any debris?" the *Bulmer* asked.

Steele grinned. "Shall I tell him?"

"No," Meredith said, "I'll get it."

Meredith picked up the TBS transmitter. "No debris. Contact evaluated non-submarine. Resume formation and course."

Steele said, "That was kind."

Meredith grinned. "I won't be as kind when I see him in port."

Steele said, "We could have picked up a few of those fish."

Meredith raised his eyebrows. "What for? Norfolk has great seafood."

* * *

Two days later Sorenson leaned on the bridge rail as they entered the Chesapeake Bay. The trip up the channel was routine. It was hard to believe that the raging Atlantic had given way to Norfolk's Blue October days. The air was crystal clear and the sky a clean and brilliant blue, as it had been when they departed. Sorenson's spirits lifted.

Sorenson watched the shore line slip by as the ship approached the Naval Base piers. He suggested that Meredith entrust the landing to Gerlach, who put a small dent in the bow. Sorenson regretted his recommendation for a moment, but decided to stick by his premise that young officers would make mistakes. Gerlach maneuvered a ship like he walked down the deck, bulling over any obstacle. Sorenson hoped that he had learned that a pier could not be run over. Meredith made no comment and did not appear to be disturbed.

Meredith left the ship, bound for home, almost as soon as the lines were doubled up. Sorenson went to the brow to see him off and then started immediate liberty for the eager crew. Then he went below to the wardroom and sent for Renard.

When Renard entered the wardroom, Sorenson thought he looked apprehensive, so he grinned at him and motioned him to a chair.

Renard eased into it. "Yes, sir?"

Sorenson drummed on the table. "Renard, I want you to do everything you can to get a set of L. L. Bean cold weather clothing for every man of the crew who will be topside at general quarters."

Renard bit his lip. "But, Mister Sorenson, that's about fifty sets. Over five thousand dollars. And I don't think the supply depot has that many. I was lucky to get eight. They said that all the rest were being shipped out to the west coast for the Aleutian campaign."

"The Aleutians? What the hell do they want them for?"

"That's what they said, and besides the ship doesn't have any money left in its allotment for this quarter. We used all the rest of it up on medicinal brandy."

Sorenson reached in his pocket and pulled out a set of car keys. Then he took out his check book, wrote a check, and handed the check and keys to Renard.

Renard looked at the check. "Holy Shiva!" he said.

"What was that?"

"Er, nothing, just something Chumley taught me."

"Well, next time you cuss just like I cuss. Take my car and cash this check. Start with the sporting goods stores in Norfolk. If you can't find the suits in Norfolk, start north and try Washington, D.C., and then head for the Pennsylvania ski resorts."

Sorenson reached in his pocket, took out his wallet, and extracted several twenty dollar bills. "Take these, too. And tell Carmody to make out a set of temporary duty orders for you so that you'll be covered."

"Where will I find your car?"

"It's at a garage at Mrs. Holderman's apartment." Sorenson suppressed a smile. "You do know who she is?"

"Er, yes, sir. I'll call her."

Sorenson got up. "Give her my love and ask her to pick me up at the ship at 1800."

Renard rose slowly, looking at the check and pile of money on the table. "Jesus, Mister Sorenson, you must have won a lot of jackpots at the club. This check is for five thousand dollars."

Sorenson said over his shoulder, "Don't worry about it. Just use it, and remember this is just between you and me."

Chapter Fifteen

After he looked at the important mail and sent Carmody on his way, Sorenson showered, shaved carefully, used a minute drop of aftershave, and put on his blues. At 1800 he impatiently paced the quarterdeck. In a few minutes the familiar red Ford raced down the pier scattering the liberty party. They whistled, and Ferren waved back.

Sorenson dashed down the brow and climbed into the right hand seat.

He leaned over and kissed Ferren. "I've missed you."

"I missed you, too. I'm glad to see you back in one piece."

      •   •   •

Two miles away, on the outside stairway of the Oriental Cafe, Bull Durham bounded up the stairs, this time three at a time, hoping to get to the front door before Sonya could open it. He failed, and Sonya met him with open arms. "I was watching for you out the front window."

Durham kissed her passionately. After a few seconds she pushed him away and said, "I think you need a drink."

Durham grinned. "If you insist, but that's not what I really want."

As she pulled him inside the door, she said, "A girl named Ferren called and told me you were all right. Who is she?"

"The Exec's girlfriend. She said I was only all right! I'm superb, and I'll prove it, but first a drink or two. All the time down there in that damned hot engine room has shrivelled me up."

Sonya laughed. "Maybe that will make things easier for me."

About midnight Sonya got up from the couch and made a dozen small sandwiches. Durham began to wonder if she could cook, but decided he didn't care. They could always go down to the tea room for meals.

In the morning she had an enormous breakfast sent up, and after eating all of it, Durham tipped over the coffee pot chasing Sonya across the bed for what he called one last frolic for the night.

•   •   •

Four days later Renard knocked on Sorenson's door.

Sorenson looked up and smiled. "Well, I thought maybe you'd gone over the hill. Come in."

Renard looked exhausted. "Sir, you sent me over the hill."

"How did you make out?"

"Mission accomplished. I've got a truck coming this afternoon with fifty L. L. Bean suits of cold weather clothing. I had to take some odd colors and a few women's suits, but they're big enough for the smaller men."

Renard pulled the keys to Sorenson's car and a few bills out of his pocket. "There's not much money left here. I hope you can afford it. I need a little sleep now. I've been driving night and day around the New York and Pennsylvania ski resorts. That took a lot of black market gasoline."

•   •   •

In early October, Meredith was ordered to a conference to be held by the Commander Task Force 34 in the Hotel Nansemond in Ocean View. Meredith asked around the yard as to what Task Force 34 was, but nobody knew. He drove to Ocean View, which was located along the shore of the channel leading out of the Chesapeake Bay. He parked his car near the hotel and passed through a screen of armed Marine sentries.

Two hours later he returned to the *O'Leary* and immediately called a conference of all officers in the wardroom. After they had gathered, he sat at the head of the table for almost a minute, stroking his mustache. Then he looked down the table.

He began. "Fineman, please tell the mess attendants to leave the pantry and close all the doors."

When Fineman returned, he went on, "Pardon me for delaying, but I hardly know where to start. I've just spent two hours listening to a crazy scheme. To give you the ending first, we will depart about the 24th of October and help escort a group of transports to the Casablanca area of North Africa. Troops will land there and attempt to take over the northwest coast of Africa from the French."

"Will we be landing from the Mediterranean?" asked Gerlach.

"No, all the targets are on the Atlantic coast of North Africa. It will take me hours to tell you why this will be extremely difficult, but I'll try to give you as much as I can today, and I'll give you the rest as soon as we get the written plans and orders aboard.

"Frankly, I'm astounded, apprehensive, and maybe a little afraid. Only stupid but brave Americans would attempt such a difficult task with untrained forces."

Sorenson broke in, "You mean we'll have a dangerous job?"

"Oh, no, our job will be doing what we do best, screening against submarines. It's just what the rest of the force will be doing that bothers me. The force will attempt an amphibious landing on a dangerous coast known for its high waves. The Army troops have had no training in amphibious warfare. The landing craft have never been used in that kind of assault. The escort carriers haven't proved that they can operate the types of aircraft they're to be equipped with. Add to that we don't know what the French will do, or what defenses they have. It may be a hell of a fiasco."

Fineman said, "This sounds as risky as the Gallipoli landings and the land campaigns after them in World War I."

Sorenson groaned. "I agree. Captain, can you give us a few details?"

"Sure, but some more coffee first, and as soon as the

mess attendants are out of the wardroom, we'll continue. I must ask you all to remember that secrecy is paramount. We must not talk about this to anyone."

Morales and his stewards rapidly re-filled the coffee cups and left. Meredith stirred an extra spoonful of sugar into his coffee and waited for the mess attendants to close the doors before speaking again.

"First, as to secrecy, even though we aren't to talk ourselves, the political types are arguing among themselves as to how much to tell the French. The French are a proud people, and that goes particularly for the French naval officers. None of the intelligence types nor staff politicos has any idea as to what the French will do. They don't know whether to warn selected French officers about the invasion. Advance notice might facilitate a surrender or it might give them time to prepare for an all out fight."

Gerlach said, "My father says the French people don't even trust each other."

Meredith nodded and went on. "Anything can happen. The French might surrender quickly or fight for a while to protect their pride and placate the Nazis who are occupying France."

Steiner asked, "What kind of French naval opposition will we face?"

"In the Casablanca area, there's the partially completed French battleship, *Jean Bart*. She has a forward turret of 15-inch guns that will work, but her unfinished engineering plant won't allow her to get underway. There are also a destroyer leader, five destroyers, eight submarines, and several minesweepers and light patrol craft. There may be more, and other French forces may move up from Dakar."

"What do the French have in Dakar?" Steele asked.

"The best estimate is a battleship, several cruisers, and a dozen destroyers. Intelligence will fill in this data later. We hope to keep the forces there by heading toward Dakar until the last few days before the landing and then turning our forces northeast toward Casablanca."

Steele said, "Will the German and Italian subs hit us off North Africa?"

"We're trying to delay them. After departure, our task forces will scatter and head northeast so that any submarines sighting them will think they're headed for Great Britain."

"That'll only buy us a few days," Sorenson said. "All those ships will be a hell of a target for subs. They'll show up before it's over."

Meredith nodded. "You can bet on that. We've got a lot of other problems. To start with, D-Day will be 7 November. The transports the landing force will use are still being converted from merchant ships. Their crews will be green as hell, and they won't all get a chance to train much or rehearse.

"The landing craft will be a mixed bag. Some will be Higgins boats with no ramps. Some will be a new design with a bow ramp, and a few will be a new steel landing craft capable of carrying medium tanks. Shortage of these heavy landing craft will require a large ship to land most of our heavy tanks at a pier in Safi. These tanks will be needed for the drive up the coast from Safi to take Casablanca from the rear.

"The plan for getting this ship to the only pier capable of unloading her is a real Rube Goldberg. Two fourstackers, the Cole, and Bernadou, will be converted and manned to enable them to force their way into Safi Harbor. The Army troops embarked will land and capture the pier."

"Do we go with this group?" asked Jablonski.

"Yes, but we may be shifted to any other area as needed. There will be three landing areas with a support group for each one. The northern force will land near Port Lyautey, the central force near Casablanca, and the southern force at Safi. We will start with the southern force, but we may be shifted.

"We will have a strong covering force, which will be available to render fire support ashore when it is not fighting the French Navy. There will be a covering group composed of the new battleship *Massachusetts*, two heavy cruisers, and fifteen destroyers.

"The northern force will have a surface group supporting it composed of the old battleship *Texas*, a light cruiser, and an air group composed of two escort carriers. All will be screened by destroyers.

"The center force will have a surface support group of three cruisers, two carriers, and escorting destroyers.

"The southern force will be protected by a surface group of the old battleship *New York*, a light cruiser, and escorting destroyers."

Steiner said, "Sounds like the center is the place to be. Most of the naval action will be there. That's where the *Jean Bart* is, right?"

Meredith turned to him. "Yes. That French battleship can do a lot of damage, and that's where all the French submarines are. Down south we'll meet a lot less opposition."

"Only if the forces at Dakar stay put," Sorenson said.

"What the hell," said Fineman. "As for me, I'd like to stay in Norfolk."

Meredith said, "We will for several weeks. We may escort some of the landing craft up the bay to Solomon's Island for exercises, and maybe some of the transports out to Virginia Beach, but mostly we'll stay in port, study the plans, attend conferences, and get ready. We should be thankful that we're not getting the treatment the *Cole* and *Bernadou* will be getting."

Sorenson raised his eyebrows. "What's that?"

"For the assault on Safi, they are to be considered expendable. All topside hamper and weight is being removed. All masts are to go and only stubs of stacks will be left."

Meredith sighed. "Well, that's enough for today. We'll meet at least once each week as we know more."

•　　　　•　　　　•

Meredith left the ship preoccupied with the upcoming invasion. As he drove home, he failed to stop at a stop sign and narrowly missed a collision. Fortunately, no policeman was on hand to ticket him.

At dinner he was preoccupied, and Linda had to urge him to finish his mashed potatoes. When the children were asleep, she brought him a scotch and soda and pushed aside the newspaper he had been staring at for several minutes.

She looked at him searchingly. "What's the matter?"

He smiled at her fondly. "Sorry I've been so distracted tonight. It involves the war, and I can't tell you what it is."

She sighed. "We've always been able to share our problems. Why not this one?"

He reached forward and stroked her hair. "This isn't our problem. It's the country's, and it's top secret. You'll know all about it in a few months."

"You're going out on a big operation."

"Of course. The war will be full of big events from now on. But don't ask me any more. Let's go to bed."

When they were in each other's arms, Linda tried again, but he silenced her with a long kiss, and that led to a period of tender lovemaking. Then they made love another time, more passionately, and Meredith fell into a deep sleep.

The next morning, he was up before the children, and they ate a quiet breakfast together. After Linda served him, she sat down with a cup of coffee. There was a hint of knowledge in her smile. She said, "I know all about it."

Meredith looked up in alarm. "Know what?"

"Africa . . . landings at Casablanca."

"My God, How did you find out?"

"You talked in your sleep. You sounded troubled."

He sighed. "You're right, but for God's sake don't tell anyone what you know."

She put down her coffee and said with a sly innocence. "Your secret is safe as long as you don't sleep with any other women, particularly those who can stay awake."

Chapter Sixteen

A week later, the *O'Leary* was ordered to accompany a transport to a beach on Solomon's Island inside the Chesapeake Bay where it would try out its new landing craft. The *O'Leary* escorted the transport up the bay, where it anchored and prepared to exercise its boats as if in combat. Another destroyer anchored off the beach to act as a control ship. The *O'Leary* was ordered to lie to near the transport and to assist boats as necessary.

Through his binoculars, Meredith watched the boats being hoisted out and the loading of boats alongside the transport. Now and then he groaned. Finally he put the binoculars down and laughed.

"What's so funny?" Sorenson asked.

"Looks like a Chinese fire drill over there. I don't know how they can be ready to unload under combat conditions by the end of the month." Meredith sat down in his chair and sent for a cup of coffee.

Sorenson lifted his binoculars and watched the transport. When he put them down he shook his head. "You're right. There are a lot of men topside waving their arms and blowing whistles. They've almost dropped a couple of boats, and some of the boats in the water won't start. Also the winch operators lowering the equipment into the boats are obviously unskilled."

But in a half-hour, all the boats were in the water, gathered in an assembly area, and heading for the distant control ship.

"A minor miracle," Meredith commented.

One boat turned and headed for the *O'Leary*. For a moment it looked like it would run into the side, but the boat passed close aboard. Meredith watched with an open mouth. The coxswain was leaning over the compass in front of him and seemed unaware of the *O'Leary*. Meredith jumped out of his chair and called to the officer of the deck, "Come around to the right and follow him."

The *O'Leary* swung about and paralleled the errant landing craft, slowly pulling up abeam of it. When it was about 50 yards away, Meredith picked up a megaphone. Before he could use it, Chief Bellows on the forecastle shouted through cupped hands, "What yer doing, Coxswain?"

The coxswain looked up in surprise and then tried to answer, but his diesel engine drowned out his voice.

Bellows waved for him to come alongside. The *O'Leary* slowed, and deck hands rigged a sea ladder over the side. Meredith ordered Jablonski and Durham to go aboard and inspect the boat. When the boat arrived alongside, the two officers climbed down.

After a few minutes, they climbed aboard and Meredith could hear Jablonski telling the coxswain to carry out his orders. The boat left and reversed course toward the other boats. Meredith turned the *O'Leary* back toward the transport.

When Jablonski and Durham arrived on the bridge, Meredith asked, "What happened?"

Jablonski said, "You won't believe it. Those kids were about twenty, and they say the rest of the boat crews are just out of boot camp. The coxswain said he had never been in any boat except a canoe. That made him more experienced than anyone else."

Durham laughed. "The engineer had taken a motor shop course in high school. That qualified him. Unfortunately he studied gasoline engines, and the boat engine is a diesel."

"Where was the coxswain going?" Meredith asked. "In an hour he'd have gone aground on the Eastern Shore."

Jablonski said, "He was ordered to join the rest of the

boat group and go to the control ship. Unfortunately the ship told him to simulate night conditions, and he was given a course to steer. He didn't know how to use a compass, and he steered by the lubber's line on the back of the compass instead of the line on the front. That's why he was on a reverse course."

Meredith rolled his eyes. "Multiply that kid by a hundred and you'll see why we may be heading for disaster."

Durham said, "And you said they told you at Task Force Headquarters that many of the boats they will use haven't even got any engines in them yet."

The trip back was somber.

· · ·

The next morning the messenger knocked on Sorenson's door frame. "Sir, Ensign MacIntosh is reporting for duty."

Sorenson turned and said, "Come in."

A tall ensign, about Sorenson's height and build, stepped in. Sorenson smiled and said, "I'm Lieutenant Sorenson, the executive officer. Welcome aboard."

"Thank you, sir, I'm Ensign Finlay MacIntosh."

"Please sit down."

As MacIntosh settled himself, Sorenson noted a pencil-thin mustache over a firm mouth and under angular cheeks. Reddish-brown hair fell over his forehead, and Sorenson made a mental note to remind him to get a shorter haircut. Sorenson sent for coffee. "We're glad to see you aboard. Chief Skelly has been doing a good job, but we need you. Tell me about your background."

"As you can hear from my accent, I'm of Scottish descent. I came to the United States in 1930 with my family and became a citizen. I enrolled in California at Berkeley and joined the NROTC. After graduation, the Navy sent me to a bunch of schools, ending with torpedo school, and here I am."

"You've lost a lot of your accent."

"Aye. I try hard, but when I'm under stress, it comes back."

"Like now?"

MacIntosh laughed. "I guess so."

"Let's go to see the Captain. He's been expecting you."

In the captain's cabin after introductions, Meredith grinned and extended his hand. "I see we have another mustache in the wardroom." He passed his hand over his own. "But you'll have to build yours up a little. Please sit down."

MacIntosh sat down and pulled his sleeves down, but they were still two inches short of his angular wrists.

Sorenson noted that MacIntosh was obviously still nervous, and he tried to put him at his ease. He said, "MacIntosh came to this country in 1930 from Scotland."

Meredith said, "I thought I detected a Scottish burr. We'll have to put him in charge of the breakfast oatmeal."

MacIntosh smiled and Sorenson thought he was relaxing. "Why did your family come to this country?"

MacIntosh cleared his throat. "My uncle operates a big sheep farm in Colorado. He never married, and he wants to pass the farm to me someday."

Sorenson said, "The war will prevent that for several years."

MacIntosh said, "About the oatmeal, I hate it."

Sorenson said, "You won't have to eat it. Just make sure Morales keeps the lumps out."

• • •

A week later, Meredith came back from his second conference on Operation Torch and called a meeting of all officers. Again he was upset. He started off without even waiting for coffee. "I couldn't believe what I heard today. Every time something came up that was unusual, a staff officer would jump up and telephone someone in Washington. The Task Force Commander's staff and the Landing Force Commander's staff aren't even in the same town. I don't know what kind of a plan we'll get, but it's due next week. I do know that we're still in the southern force but we're to be ready to shift to the central force if the destroyers there are required to go close inshore and provide fire support."

"How about us?" asked Steiner. "We can do close-in fire support."

Meredith laughed. "Yes, but they didn't know it. I had to tell them to include that capability in their plan in case we are needed."

Sorenson said, "Are we sure we have the capability, Chuck? We don't have all the equipment the *Berry* had."

"Sure," Steiner said. "With navigational fixes we can locate our position on an Army chart on the DRT. The chart shows the terrain ashore, and spotters can radio us the coordinates of the target. We locate them on our chart and measure the direction and distance from our position on the DRT to the target. The distance is the range to set on the fire control computer on the director, and the direction is the direction to train the director. Maybe our computer isn't as fancy as the computers on the newer destroyers, but it works. We just set zero speed and any course on the target dials, and we're ready to fire. If the target is a tank, we treat it just like a ship and set in the course and speed of the tank that's given to us by the spotter ashore."

Sorenson scratched his head. "I knew the *Berry* had that capability when I was gunnery officer, but we were never in an amphibious operation. Maybe I need to have you give me a course in CIC capabilities."

Chumley said, "Good idea. You're the man who has to know since you're in charge in the CIC at general quarters. We can start tomorrow."

•   •   •

One evening Sorenson worked after dinner, trying to dispose of a stack of paper work Carmody had left on his desk in the room that had been Meredith's cabin. He noticed the sound of music, classical music, with soaring passages. The sound seemed to come from the passageway across the wardroom. He pushed back his door curtain and walked across the wardroom and up the passageway, following his ears. There was no doubt; the music was coming from Doctor Fineman's room. He knocked, but the music was so loud that there was no answer to his knock. Sorenson pushed the curtain aside and stepped inside.

Fineman was stretched out on his bunk, eyes closed, one hand behind his head, and the other waving in the air conducting the absent orchestra. A black record whirled at 78 rpm on a portable phonograph on the floor.

Sorenson sat down in Fineman's chair, put his feet up on the desk, and closed his eyes. The music soothed his churning mind, and he felt a sense of peace.

When the record stopped, Fineman opened his eyes and started to get up to change the record.

"Good God!" he said. "What are you doing here?"

Sorenson opened his eyes. "Listening to your wonderful records. Mozart, isn't it?"

"Yes, how did you guess?"

"I didn't guess. I like classical music, but I don't know all of Mozart's works. I'm more a Wagner-type man, and for semi-classical stuff, I like Ferde Grofe's 'Grand Canyon Suite.' "

"You amaze me."

"Why? A lot of people like classical music. Ferren likes jazz better, but I'm introducing her to the classical variety."

Fineman said, "I'm glad I met Ferren. She really is something, just like you said."

"We'll arrange a get-together when we get back next time. Ferren has a lot of girlfriends. Maybe she can fix you up."

"I'd like that." Fineman leaned over the box of records. "What would you like to hear next?"

"Nothing now, but I'd like to borrow some of these to try on Ferren. All she has is jazz and popular stuff."

"Are you sure you two are compatible?"

"Oh, yes."

"Maybe so, but there's still some unresolved problem in you."

"That's what she told me."

"Very perceptive. I'd like to help."

Sorenson sighed and thought of how he still wanted to fly. "There's nothing anyone can do except me, and I'm working on it."

• • •

The last week before sailing was frantic for Meredith. He spent hours with the thick operation order. He looked at the meteorological data and directed Sorenson to store their new cold weather clothing below. The temperature should be mild, but storms could produce up to 15 foot swells on the landing beaches.

He talked to Durham, who remembered the light plywood bottom on the runway landing craft he had boarded off Solomon's Island. When Meredith told him about the possibility of heavy swells, Durham said, "A lot of those landing craft might be banged up so badly they won't be able to get off the beach."

Meredith noted that they would fuel at sea at least twice enroute to Africa and many times thereafter. There would be Navy tankers with each force, but destroyers were directed to be ready to fuel also from the escort carriers and transports. Meredith had never been on the bridge during fueling at sea before, so he spent time reviewing the procedures with Gerlach and Chief Bellows, and he asked Sorenson to remember what he could about his days on the *Berry*.

Sorenson said, "We fueled several times, but my station was aft. I didn't see much."

Meredith went to other destroyers to ask their more experienced captains what to expect when conning his ship alongside. He got general help, but those who had fueled before had conned the more modern destroyers and knew little about the characteristics of a four-stacker. He could not find anyone who had even seen a four-stacker fuel the modern way without using the old cumbersome towline.

•   •   •

There was a last minute flurry of loading fresh provisions and spare parts, and then all was ready. Both Meredith and Sorenson went ashore for one last night.

Sorenson drove his green Buick out to Ferren's apartment so that he could leave it there while he was gone. She opened the door before he could use his key. She was somber, but there were no tears. She drank more than usual that night before dinner, and Sorenson fixed himself a stiff Bourbon and branchwater, Texas style.

She nodded at his glass. "You haven't been drinking anything but beer. You're worried."

"Yeah. I guess you could say so."

"I know you haven't told me anything about where

you are going next, but I see all the papers in the office, and I know it's big and in Africa."

"I couldn't take a chance on telling you. If you let something slip in the office, your boss would know where you got it. You're right about what you know."

"Do you think you'll be in more danger than usual?"

Sorenson thought of the massive 15-inch shells the *Jean Bart* might unleash. "Hard to predict. We'll be one of many targets, and an insignificant one. There's always the chance we'll take something meant for someone else."

"That would be awful."

"That's not what keeps me awake, though. I wonder if the ship will be able to do its job . . . if I've prepared the ship and crew properly."

"We'll be with some big boys. Battleships, carriers, cruisers, a lot of modern destroyers. None of our officers, even the Captain, has ever seen a carrier conducting actual war operations, and the only big ships he's ever seen have been Japanese, except for a few of our cruisers."

"You'll be doing things you've never done before?"

"Yes, like fueling at sea and shore bombardment. Everybody else is about as green as we are. And then there's the problem of fending off aircraft attacks. The Captain has already proved that he can maneuver the old girl expertly in the open sea, but we may not have that freedom in a large formation or in restricted waters."

"Sounds like Jack will be able to handle it."

"But I'm worried about his lack of physical stamina. He got weaker and weaker the last time we were at sea. I've been told I would be ordered to command one of our older destroyers as soon as Meredith declares me qualified. But I don't think I should leave the *O'Leary* now. The crew will need me if Meredith doesn't hold up."

"Now I know why you look so worried."

"I keep thinking of all the time in my years in the Navy when I should have been studying or asking questions. The only thing I ever cared about was flying, and they wouldn't let me do that."

She went over and sat down beside him. He took her in his arms.

She said, "I'm beginning to understand why you are so unhappy. It's not just not getting a command. It's this flying thing. You've got to let it go and get on with your life."

"Thanks," he said, "I feel okay now. You are my life."

The next morning, just after dawn, she drove him down to the ship. "You aren't crying this time," he said.

"I won't until the ship is gone."

    •   •   •

The night before their departure, Meredith unburdened himself to Linda. "I don't know if I can hack it," he began. "I've never fueled at sea or operated with carriers. I don't know much about amphibious operations and the transports we are going to escort know less. The failure, if there is one, could be, as Fineman says, worse than the one at Gallipoli in World War I."

"You're making too much of this. All you have to do is the best you can. You've got a good group of officers and a fine crew, and your ship can do a lot of things, even if it is old and tired and many of your men are green."

He said, "Another thing that bothers me is Bull. You know we used to be like brothers back in the Asiatic Fleet. He never gave a damn about what happened to the ship. I know I'm not like that, but watching him operate released a lot of tensions in me, even if I was only a spectator. I know he hasn't kept me up to date professionally, but he's trying very hard now. Every ship captain needs a first-rate engineering officer. Frankly, Bull isn't one now. I just hope he can get up to speed and come through if we have a crisis."

"How is Sorenson as an executive officer? You said he did well when you were wounded."

"He did, but that was only for a short time. He hasn't had much time in destroyers. I just hope he learns quickly and holds up for the longer run. But then I'll have to recommend him for command, and I'll lose him."

He sighed and took her tightly in his arms. "We could use a dozen like you aboard. The chow would be better, and your can-do attitude would help a lot of us. There is one thing I know I can do, and that is dodge aircraft. Even so, air attack really worries me. I don't know if I'll have any maneuvering room. It's our best defense."

"You'll just have to do the best you can. Give me a kiss. I'll make you some pancakes tomorrow."

Chapter Seventeen

Meredith paced the bridge the next morning as the early morning mist began to lift. Their departure had been delayed a day, although some of the transports had left the day before. Meredith was anxious to get underway. The extra time had given him an opportunity to study manuals and wiring diagrams, but they were no substitute for physical activity.

Meredith checked around the nests of ships still remaining and planned how he would back out into the channel amidst the ships that would be leaving about the same time. The senior destroyer commander had issued a sortie plan, designed to keep order amongst the destroyers leaving, but it called for careful timing. Meredith knew that if any destroyer was late in backing out, the error would compound itself, and later ships would pile up in the channel.

When the appointed time arrived, the ships of the first nest began to leave, their whistles blasting and tooting to signal they were leaving their slips and their engines were backing. When the second nest began its turn, one destroyer had trouble getting its lines in and backed out behind schedule.

Meredith took a deep breath when the *O'Leary*'s turn came. Watching the destroyers astern maneuvering in the channel, he purposely backed with only one-third power, and the tide set the *O'Leary* toward the pier to starboard. He corrected with full rudder and a little more speed, but the momentum put him in the channel too soon.

A tangle of gray ships choked the channel, all trying to twist and find their proper order. Meredith could see that the *O'Leary* was going to be out of order, and he decided to proceed down the channel anyway. He glanced astern and noted the destroyer that should have been ahead of him rounding up astern. Her signal light began to blink.

The signalman read off the message as each word arrived. " 'Thanks,' " he read, " 'I'll take my proper position when we round the Naval Base.' "

Sorenson nodded. "Well done, Captain. If you'd waited, there would have been a hell of a mess."

Meredith bit his lip. "I'm afraid this is just the first of many foul-ups."

The destroyers rapidly cleared the piers, but the larger transports ponderously backed and wheeled as they tried to avoid each other in the channel. The destroyers proceeded down the long channel toward the Chesapeake Bay entrance and through the opening in the net. Meredith looked back down the channel, where a column of gray ships stretched as far as the eye could see. It was a splendid sight, one he thought would give the Vichy French trouble if they could see it.

Outside the net, the destroyers steamed for patrol positions assigned by the sortie plan, so that they could clear the approaches to the bay area of submarines. Overhead floated two silver blimps, recent additions to the Atlantic Fleet, plodding about like obese waitresses. Farther out, antisubmarine patrol aircraft orbited on the horizon.

An hour later, the transports and tankers shuffled past the net vessel and wheeled into their assigned places in the rectangular cruising formation. They were better at it than the merchantmen had been in the convoys the *O'Leary* had previously escorted. All of their commanding officers were Navy and Coast Guard officers. The destroyers began to take their stations in an antisubmarine screen ahead and on the flanks of the main group. The task force pointed northeasterly, a course designed to make it appear they were headed for Great Britain.

When the formation settled down, Meredith gave the conn to Steele, who had the first watch, and joined Sorenson, who was watching the ships from the bridge wing. Meredith said, "Quite a sight. I hope the rest of the trip goes as well." He glanced at the blue-green water sliding by the side.

Sorenson nodded at the water. "Still on the continental shelf," he said. "This calm won't last long. The Atlantic is treacherous and always lulls you the first day out."

"I didn't have an opportunity to talk to you about the conference yesterday. There were over a hundred officers from all services, but no Marines."

"I think they're mostly in the Pacific."

"Yes, and General Patton, who will command the landing force, said he didn't need any. He also said that all the Navy had to do was land him within fifty miles of the proper beaches. Somehow I got the impression that he meant himself and not his troops. I'll bet he thinks he can walk on water."

Sorenson said, "From what we saw at Solomon's Island, they'll be lucky to end up *only* fifty miles away from their beaches."

•   •   •

The next morning, after a breakfast of fried eggs and grits, Meredith leaned on the bridge wing railing. A formation of flying fish burst from the blue water of the Gulf Stream. The shimmering gray shapes of two porpoises glided alongside the bow as if they were harnessed to the ship.

Fineman joined Meredith and Sorenson. "Porpoises are supposed to bring good luck," Fineman said.

Meredith nodded. "We'll need it. I can't get over General Patton's remarks the other day. I like his spirit, but it doesn't help some poor bastard put ashore with only a rifle against a strong enemy force."

A large patch of Sargasso weed floated by. Meredith pointed to it. "That weed started out east of the Caribbean. In a few months it will float ashore in Ireland."

"Are we still in the Gulf Stream?" Fineman asked.

"Yes. Part of it passes by Ireland. That's one reason the south of Ireland is so temperate."

"When will we pass out of it?"

"Tomorrow. We head north and rendezvous with the Center Force, which left the day before we did."

"Will the weather get worse?"

"Not necessarily," Meredith said. "The weather in this part of the Atlantic is generally good at this time of the year, but I never trust it. I just hope we can fuel the first time in good weather."

•   •   •

Meredith went up to the bridge early on the 26th. Their force was scheduled to rendezvous with the center force and the covering force that morning. About 0900 the radar operator on watch reported many contacts to the north, and soon dozens of masts appeared over the horizon. By noon the newcomers had jockeyed into their positions in the new cruising formation, and the two screens had merged.

Early that afternoon, the radar operator reported a large body of ships to the south. Meredith was puzzled because the covering force was expected to join from the north, having come from Casco Bay in Maine, but soon the comforting top hamper of battleships could be seen.

The covering force, headed by the new battleship *Massachusetts*, took station ahead, with the *Brooklyn* between the covering force and the main body of thirty-five transports and auxiliaries. The old battleships *Texas* and *New York* guarded the flanks. All the units were screened by numerous destroyers.

Meredith surveyed the giant armada, so large that some of the ships on the flanks and ahead were well over the horizon.

"There are so many big targets out here, maybe we'll be safe," said Chumley, who had the deck.

Meredith shook his head. "Not necessarily. A lot of ships get sunk when torpedoes miss their targets and hit some innocent bystander."

"Oh, well, there are a lot of folks to pick us up."

Meredith didn't have the heart to tell Chumley that there weren't many survivors when a destroyer took a torpedo because the small ships went down so fast.

The seas had turned a more greenish hue when they left the Gulf Stream. Meredith looked over the side and studied the swells. They were very long and coming from the south. He knew they'd started in the South Atlantic, and had a long time to build up. He hoped they wouldn't get any worse because they'd have to fuel in a few days.

The formation steamed on a westerly course until the 28th, when the air group joined the armada. The O'Leary's position with the convoy screen was too far astern for Meredith to see the carriers, but soon their aircraft began regular antisubmarine patrols, and Meredith could see the morning sun glinting off their windshields just after they took off.

Sorenson, standing next to Meredith, watched them for a long time. Then he lowered his binoculars. "I wish I could be up there flying."

"Tex, you'd have only one aircraft. Or maybe two as a lieutenant. Down here you're responsible for over a hundred men and a lot of fire power. In a year you'll be in command of this ship, or another one like it. You can do a lot more with a ship than you can with a few aircraft."

"Maybe so, but I'd still like to be up there."

"Most of the officers manning these ships are reserve officers, and a majority of the men are under twenty. Your Naval Academy training and your experience are badly needed."

Steele had the deck, and he came over to Meredith and Sorenson. "How do you like our new art work on the bridge wing?"

Sorenson leaned over the side and looked down at the O'Leary's painted trophies. "I didn't know we had gotten credit for the German submarine."

"I told the Captain, but I guess in the press of getting underway I forgot to tell you. I went over to the headquarters of the Commander in Chief of the Atlantic Fleet the day before we sailed. They told me that we were being given credit for the submarine we attacked."

"Why?" asked Sorenson. "We never found much debris."

"They said they had independent sources that confirmed our sinking."

"That's interesting," Meredith said.

"They wouldn't tell me much more, but I think they listen to German submarine radio frequencies, and I think they've broken their codes. When a wolf pack sub fails to check in with its commander every day, they begin to ask about that submarine. The officer I was talking to let slip that the wolf pack commander had reported back to base that he had lost the submarine we attacked."

"So you painted the submarine on the bridge wing," Sorenson said.

"Yes, sir. The Captain gave me permission, and you were ashore."

Meredith coughed apologetically. "Sorry, Tex, I told Steele I'd tell you, and I forgot."

"No problem, I'm very happy about it. We've got more important problems to worry about, like working in the green hands we just got aboard."

•   •   •

The good weather continued, the long swells abated some, and on October 30 the ships began fueling. Meredith was too nervous to eat breakfast, and anxiously waited for their assignment. He was greatly relieved when they were assigned to a tanker instead of a transport. The tanker's straight sides and underwater structure permitted the water to pass down her side relatively undisturbed, not like the turbulent water along the sides of a cruiser, battleship, or transport. The tanker would not have the over-hanging flight deck of the escort carriers.

An hour before noon, the *O'Leary* was ordered to standby station astern of a tanker. After an hour, the ship ahead completed fueling and wheeled ahead. Meredith gripped the bulwark in front of him and ordered, "All engines ahead standard."

The *O'Leary* accelerated and began to draw near the tanker's port quarter. On the tanker's decks, the crew rearranged the tangle of lines and hoses just taken in from the previous destroyer so that they could be passed quickly. When the *O'Leary*'s bow was abeam of the tanker's stern, Meredith slowed to 8 knots, the signaled fueling speed. Almost miraculously to Meredith, who was trying to conceal his nervousness, the *O'Leary* slowed and slid into place about 120 feet abeam of the tanker. This was too far out, and Meredith could see the tanker Captain waiting patiently on his bridge before ordering the lines to be passed.

Meredith wanted to close quickly to 50 feet, but the process was new to him. The *O'Leary* had rarely fueled underway in the Asiatic Fleet, and Meredith had always been in the engine room. This was the first time he had seen a fueling from the bridge. He cleared his throat, which had tightened, and ordered, "Steer zero nine zero." This course was two degrees to the right of the tanker's course.

The gap began to close, and in a minute the *O'Leary* had slid in to 70 feet. The tanker Captain turned to his talker and gave a series of orders. On deck, the tanker's crew whirled monkey fists, small weights in hemp balls attached to heaving lines. The lines snaked over to the *O'Leary*. On the forecastle, waiting men gathered the lines in and rapidly hauled the slack in, pulling the larger lines carrying the forward fuel hose. Aft, Steiner's men hauled in a similar sequence of lines attached to the after hose. Just forward of the bridge, a small line known as the distance line, festooned at regular intervals with colored tufts, was passed over and held taut giving an accurate gauge of distance between ships. While the lines were being rigged, Meredith ordered the helmsman to parallel the tanker's course.

Meredith concentrated for a few minutes trying to estimate the combination of speed and course that would keep them in proper position. Finally he had them riding steadily at the proper position. When he had it figured it out, he looked around to see how Sorenson was doing with the fueling arrangements. All seemed to be well as the huge hoses began to pulse with oil.

•   •   •

On the signal bridge, Alvarado, who had been allowed to turn the helm over to another quartermaster after they were settled down, looked up and recognized an old friend on the tanker's bridge. He held up his arms and began to semaphore to him, using his hands instead of semaphore flags. After a short exchange of messages, the friend on the tanker signaled, "Where did you find all those Japs and Krauts painted on the side of your bridge?"

Alvarado sent back, "They found us."

His friend signaled, "You have more trophies than any ship we've fueled yet."

• • •

The captain of the tanker looked down at Meredith and waved. He lifted a megaphone and said, "Good job, skipper. I'm sending over a couple of good movies."

Meredith waved back, and he suddenly realized that his empty stomach was demanding food.

He turned to the messenger and said, "Ask Morales to send up my lunch."

When they finished and the lines were hauled in, Meredith ordered, "All engines ahead flank."

Sorenson looked at him. "Jesus, isn't that a little too much?"

But Meredith was too exhilarated to care, and the O'Leary boiled away from the tanker's side at 25 knots. When spray kicked up over the forecastle, Chief Bellows looked about to protest. When he saw Meredith's beaming face, he apparently thought better and jammed his chief's hat down firmly on his head so it wouldn't blow off.

• • •

For Meredith the next two days were peaceful. He felt he had put one of his major fears behind him, and the weather continued to get better. The skies cleared, and the wind moderated. There was still a long swell, and Meredith eyed it with caution. Still, today was today, and he leaned back in his bridge chair and almost relaxed before he remembered what they were heading for. Next week would be faced when they came to it.

They continued to make a good 14 knots zigzagging by day, and the ships of the formation got better and better at keeping closed up. Miraculously, there were no breakdowns and no submarine contacts. On the November 3, they changed course to pass north of Madeira and the Canary Islands. Their goal of appearing to head for

Dakar to hold the French forces there had been accomplished.

The next day they fueled again, and this time Meredith was so confident that he let Sorenson conn the ship while they were alongside. "Tex, next time you do the whole thing," he said.

Sorenson didn't look up from the distance line, his knuckles white as he gripped the railing of the bridge wing. "Please don't distract me now," he said.

After a few minutes, his knuckles eased, and he grinned and said, "Not quite as easy as keeping station in an aircraft."

Now the force was ready, and it had made a four thousand mile transit without incident. Meredith knew that in just three days, thousands of men would find out whether their efforts would bring a terrible disaster or a great victory.

Chapter Eighteen

Later that day the weather worsened. Alvarado, as one of the senior petty officers living in the forward compartment, tried to help the newer and younger men. He showed them how to use bunk straps to keep from being rolled out of their bunks, but most of them were too sick to care. Some were too sick to get in the upper or even middle bunks, and Alvarado wedged their inert bodies in the corners of the compartments with life jackets. The crew's living compartments became a shambles, as clothing, equipment, and parts of occasional meals all mixed together and among the men lying on the decks.

Only sandwiches could be served, both in the crew's compartments and the wardroom. The continuous movement of the ship and the lack of fresh air below tired everyone. Only the old hands like Alvarado avoided seasickness. There was little time left to each man for personnel affairs after standing eight hours of watch and doing a minimum amount of maintenance on assigned equipment.

When Alvarado felt he had done all he could in the compartment, he packed several sandwiches in his pockets and went up to the signal bridge. He stayed there for the most of two days, wedged between a flag bag and the side of the bridge structure, staring out over the tops of the rollers.

The morning of the second day, Bronte came out of CIC, gingerly balancing a mug of hot coffee. He skittered across the signal bridge to Alvarado, holding on to the rail of the flag bag. He tapped Alvarado on the shoulder, "Coffee?"

Alvarado reached back and took it, but still stared straight ahead.

Bronte followed the direction of his eyes. "You're looking in the wrong direction. Home is aft."

Alvarado shook his head and patted the bridge rail. "You still don't understand. This is my home."

· · ·

Meredith studied the weather reports and predictions. A rising west wind and heavy swells, on top of the long, low swells from the south, rolled the ships heavily in a corkscrew fashion. Even some of the large ships reported damage as the invasion force tried to sustain its speed of advance. The smaller *O'Leary* rode over some of the larger swells, but she rolled 30 degrees, with some rolls to 40 degrees.

Meredith knew he was losing weight, but his stomach felt queasy when he thought of food, and he didn't eat much. Sometimes he remembered the wonderful dinners Linda had cooked for him. He tried to think of something else, and went into the CIC to study the thick operation order.

He wedged himself into a corner between the DRT and the air status board and opened the Operation Order, trying not to damage the tracing paper taped to the top of the DRT. Through the tracing paper he could see the outline of the Safi Harbor area. He pulled the tape loose from one side of the tracing paper and rolled it back so he could get a better look at the Army map underneath. The map was crossed by vertical and horizontal reference grids and had many squiggly blue terrain lines showing altitude above sea level. It was totally unlike any nautical chart Meredith had ever used, and he spent several minutes studying it.

He noted the Army unit symbols placed here and there denoting enemy and friendly units and the symbols showing French artillery. From the friendly symbols, broad arrows swept back into the countryside, showing the expected path and direction of advance. The landing beaches were marked with colors. They were narrow but seemed to be usable, although Meredith had no experience in amphibious warfare.

He opened the Operation Order to the section covering the southern force because the *O'Leary* would be part of it. In Safi Harbor, two pierside areas were marked off where the converted destroyers *Cole* and *Bernadou* would land their troops and where the specially configured ship would land the heavy tanks of the force. Meredith shook his head, thankful that they had not been converted for their sister ships' jobs.

He put the tracing paper back down on the DRT and went back to the Operation Order, noting the neat index tabs Chumley had inserted. He turned to the northern force section. The objective there was Port Lyautey, situated about six miles up the winding Sebou River. The landing beaches were located north and south of the river entrance, and the plan of maneuver was to land and envelop the city in a pincers movement. The landing did not seem to present many problems, but Meredith carefully read the section that required a four-stacker, the *Dallas*, to penetrate the Sebou River and try to reach the city itself.

Meredith noted the depth of water in the channel and the numerous mud bars. The *Dallas* would literally have to crawl like a catfish over some of the bars, her propellers in the mud. Meredith shuddered, and grabbed the corner of the DRT as a particularly nasty roll dislodged him. He hoped they would avoid the northern landing area altogether, and he turned his attention to the most important area, the responsibility of the central force. He guessed that the *O'Leary* would end up with this force because of the submarines near it.

The forces assigned to the central area were the strongest, and the possible enemy forces were substantial. If the French Navy fought, rather than surrendered, all the power of the covering forces would be needed just to counter them.

Meredith turned to the small map of the landing area. Casablanca did not concern him. The suspected minefields off the harbor entrance and the large French naval force in the harbor dictated that the initial landings would be made at Fedala, about 15 miles north of Casablanca.

He shook his head and turned to the southern group section of the plan again. The *O'Leary*'s group would provide antisubmarine protection for the transports off Safi Harbor. They would have a good view of the action in the inner harbor.

The rolling began to make Meredith queasy, and he put the Operation Order in the drawer under the DRT, stepped out to the signal bridge, and moved forward to the port bridge wing. The fresh air revived him, and he walked into the pilothouse and sat down in his chair.

He noticed that Chief Gunner's Mate Aronson was the assistant officer of the watch. Aronson was carefully plotting the positions of the guide and the ships adjacent to the *O'Leary* by making grease pencil marks on the face of the PPI. The last daylight was beginning to fade, and the reflected phosphorescence on the face of the radar scope outlined Aronson's young face. Meredith decided that there was both youth and maturity there, and he hoped they could hang on to Aronson for a while. He had recommended him for a commission, but that would probably mean he would be ordered to another ship.

If Aronson left, Kendrick would be senior gunner's mate. Kendrick had been on the *O'Leary* for eight years, almost all of his enlisted service. There was no doubt that he knew every nut, bolt, and wire in the gunnery department, but he had limited intelligence. Aronson, on the other hand, could reach beyond the nuts and bolts and innovate, improvise, and help the gunnery department. If he left, Steiner would have to take up the slack.

Aronson tapped the face of the PPI. He did it again. Then he looked at Meredith. "Sir, something's wrong with the surface search radar."

Over the squawk box Bronte said, "Bridge, the surface search radar is out."

Meredith resisted the temptation to ask what was wrong with it. He knew that Bronte would have to find out, using a variety of test instruments and electronic gear. He drummed his fingers on the chair arm trying to be patient. He knew the *O'Leary* would be useless if the radar was not fixed by the night of the landing. Without radar, the Task Force Commander would give them some unimportant station out on the periphery.

After a few minutes, Aronson tapped the PPI again. "Sir, it's back." Bronte's voice confirmed the report.

Meredith asked over the squawk box, "What was wrong?"

Bronte said, "I had to replace two burned-out tubes and a resistor. The tubes are the only spares of that kind we have. If the new ones don't hold up, we're in trouble."

Meredith said, "Thanks. Keep me informed."

He sat back and ground his teeth. There didn't seem to be any easy way to command a ship, particularly a small one.

Meredith yawned wearily, remembering that he had not slept for two days. As the darkness settled, he thought about his crew. He knew that ninety-eight percent of the officers on the ships in the force were either reserves or ex-enlisted men. On the *O'Leary*, many of the old hands who had served with him in China had been promoted and sent to newly commissioned ships. The gaps had been filled with young sailors just out of recruit training, and many of them were draftees. The newest arrivals had not been tested in combat, and he wondered if the ship as a whole would do well. Then his head slumped forward on his chest and the world turned black.

·   ·   ·

Meredith was aware that someone was shaking his arm. He sat forward slowly and blinked his eyes. Chumley was standing in front of him. "Sorry, Captain, but I thought you should see this message."

Meredith looked around. "Where's Steele? He had the deck."

Chumley laughed. "He was relieved by Gerlach, I relieved him. You've been sleeping for most of the night. We thought you needed it, and you looked comfortable."

Meredith stood up and stretched. "I don't think I'll ever straighten out. I hurt all over. But I feel better and I'm hungry."

"It's just after midnight. I'll have the messenger get you a sandwich from the wardroom. But first read that message."

Meredith sat down again and read the message using a red flashlight. It was a weather report from Washington. "Jesus!" he said, "This predicts 15-foot waves on the beach on D-Day and terrible sea conditions in the transport areas. It says landing conditions will not be favorable."

Meredith remembered the chart he had recently studied. The beaches weren't very wide, and a few boats piled up could cause serious delay or even stop the whole operation.

Chumley said, "Now Admiral Hewitt is faced with a difficult decision. He has to postpone D-Day or reschedule the landing for other areas inside Gibraltar."

Meredith said, "I don't envy him. Neither alternative is good. In either case the Germans and the French will know we're coming, and we may suffer heavy losses to ships and troops."

Doctor Fineman came up the bridge ladder, clutching a dispatch form in his hand. "You'll want to see this right away. I just decoded it."

Chumley looked so curious, Meredith told him what was in it, "Admiral Hewitt says D-Day will still be the 8th. His aerologist predicts moderating weather and four-foot waves on the 8th. The landing will go on as scheduled."

"A gutty call," Chumley said.

Meredith was almost speechless. "It's gutty, all right. If he's right, nobody will remember. If he's wrong, he'll be on his farm in a month. But that's what responsibility is all about. If you don't like it, the Navy's not for you."

Chumley sighed. "Maybe the Navy's not for me." Then he brightened. "But my wife would love this stuff. She'd make a good naval officer."

Sorenson came up to the bridge, and Meredith showed him the messages. Sorenson said, "The weather is moderating already. I think you should go below for a shower and a mustache trim. That thing looks awful, even in this dim light. You should also get a little sleep. I'll call you if you're needed."

Meredith laughed. "All right, if you put it that way. Can you stay up here on the bridge while I'm gone?"

"Sure. Take your time."

Meredith started below, and then turned to Chumley, "It's not that I don't trust you when I'm gone. If anything happens, Admiral Hewitt himself would need help, and I guess you know what I think of him after today."

Chumley grinned. "That's good enough for me."

•   •   •

Meredith turned in fully dressed. His restless and fitful sleep was interrupted by dreams of 15-inch shells whistling overhead and bombs dropping close aboard. One of the bombs blossomed into a white light. Meredith jerked upright and found a flashlight shining in his face. The dream faded, and he knew he was coming back to reality.

"Yes?" he said.

Someone snapped on the reading light over his bunk. When he could adjust his eyes to the sudden glare, Meredith saw Chumley's anxious face bending over him, with Bronte close behind.

Chumley cleared his throat. "Sir, we've got trouble. The surface search radar is out again. Bronte has been working on it for an hour."

"Yes, sir, I've found the trouble, but we don't have the parts I need."

"My God, why not?"

"We've got our allowance and a lot more that I bummed in the yard. The replacement parts we are allowed are supposed to be for the parts that burn out the most often. I used some spares yesterday, but this is a different part. We don't have any. At radar school they told us this dingus never went out."

"Dingus?"

"Yes, sir. That's what we called it at radar school. Here's the official name and number." He handed Meredith a slip of paper.

Meredith read it. "I see why you call it a dingus. This official name doesn't mean a thing."

He turned to Chumley. "Jesus, we've got to get the surface search radar back in commission. We're just about to go in close to shore at night and mill around with a dozen ships. We'll get run over in the first hour. What'll we do?"

Chumley took a deep breath. "We've got to tell the Task Force Commander so he can allow for our problem in his plans. In the same message we'll include the description of the part we need."

"Good idea. The Task Force Commander will send a message to the other ships of the force to see if there's a spare available."

Bronte said, "One of the bigger ships should have one."

Chumley said, "Captain, I thought you'd think that way. Here's a rough dispatch."

Meredith said, "Well done. Leave it to me, and I'll get it out."

After Chumley and Bronte had departed, Meredith added his shoes to the clothes he had worn to bed and went up to the bridge. Just as he arrived, the officer of the deck sounded the general alarm for morning general quarters.

Meredith sat down in his chair and studied the rough dispatch. He changed a word and signed his name to it. Meredith handed it to Alvarado who had just come to the bridge. "Send this yourself. Make sure you get the part numbers right. No mistakes. Take your time so the guy on the other end receives it properly."

Alvarado scanned the message quickly and added the call signs of the addresses. "Aye, aye, sir. I see what you mean."

He ran over to the signal light nearest to the Task Force Commander's flagship and began to send. The light shutter clicked rapidly as he twisted the handle, sending out flashes of light. In a few minutes he called over his shoulder to Meredith, "Captain, they've receipted for it."

The next two hours were agony for Meredith. Then Alvarado shouted, "The flagship is calling us."

Meredith jumped out of his chair and stood by Alvarado, listening to him as he called out the words. First came the call signs. Meredith tapped on the rail, waiting for the text to begin.

Then Alvarado said, "Break. *Massachusetts* has required part. Close her and pick up soonest. Good luck. Break."

"That's it!" Meredith said. "Where's the *Massachusetts*?"

Alvarado grinned. "You can't miss it. It's that horizontal skyscraper on the port beam."

Meredith said, "Officer of the Deck, all ahead flank. Call away the forecastle transfer detail and head for the *Massachusetts*."

Gerlach had the deck, and Meredith took the conn. Meredith said, "CIC, give me a course to the *Massachusetts* at 25 knots."

In a few seconds, Bronte's voice came back, "Recommend zero three zero. The next course change in the zigzag plan is in ten minutes. Twenty degrees to starboard."

"My God!" Meredith said. "I forgot we were zigzagging. I hope the Task Force Commander will stop while we're alongside."

Sorenson said, "He won't. Too big a chance to take. Besides, you won't have any trouble staying in position during the turns. It'll just be like flying an airplane in formation."

"Not for me," Meredith said. "I don't like the idea."

In fifteen minutes they had closed the *Massachusetts*.

"Jesus," said Kendrick, who had taken over as helmsman so Alvarado could be free to signal. "That thing looks like a big apartment house in the Bronx on a Saturday night. There're guns hanging out of every apartment window."

As they came up astern, Meredith's confidence increased, and he eased in to 80 feet after slowing abeam.

The next zigzag turn was to be to the side away from the *O'Leary*. Jablonski shouted, "Mark."

Meredith started to turn with standard rudder, but knew immediately that he had made a mistake. The battleship, with its double rudder, would turn much faster than the *O'Leary*. "Belay that order!" he shouted in the pilothouse door. "Steady as you go!"

He looked up at the towering superstructure and felt like it might fall on him. He looked aft at the huge wake. When he could see a slight swirl in the burbling torrent of white water and the stern begin to swing toward him, he gave the order, "Right full rudder." He kept on watching the battleship's stern, and by making small changes, was able to keep parallel to its huge side.

After an agonizingly long time, Sorenson called from the gyro repeater in the pelorus on the wing, said, "On course, Captain."

Chief Bellows, on the forecastle, pulled in the light transfer line, and soon a small canvas bag came over on the line. Bronte pounced on it and ran back off the forecastle.

When the lines were clear, Meredith pulled ahead. When the O'Leary was well clear, he turned the conn back to Gerlach with orders to return to station.

Then he started aft to look over the side of the bridge to see how Bronte was doing. As he reached the top of the ladder leading below, there was a yell from the lower radar room.

"What was that?" Meredith asked.

Alvarado was standing nearby. He laughed, "That smart-assed Bronte must have stuck his finger in a live socket."

Feet clattered up the bridge ladder and Bronte ran into Meredith standing at the top of the ladder. He looked up at Meredith, and a huge smile spread over his anxious face. "Sir, it works!"

Meredith's smile was almost as big. "Well done!"

"If he's so smart, it never would have broke in the first place," Alvarado muttered.

•   •   •

They continued on a northeasterly course, and at daybreak on the 7th, the southern force departed for Safi, leaving the other forces to continue to their destinations. The weather continued to moderate, and Meredith was more impressed than ever with the ability of Admiral Hewitt's aerologist and the courage of Admiral Hewitt. The six transports of the southern amphibious group formed a column, and it was screened by a dozen destroyer types on either side. Ahead was the battleship *New York*, screened by the fast minesweepers *Howard* and *Hamilton*. A cruiser, an escort carrier, a tanker, and other ships steamed astern. Further in the rear was the ship carrying the heavy tanks.

Two hours before midnight, they headed into the wind and slowed so that the transport *Lyon* could transfer the combat troops to the *Cole* and *Bernadou*. The *O'Leary* was assigned as a lifeguard, 500 yards astern of the ships conducting the transfer. Chief Bellows and the crew of gun one stood by on the forecastle with life rings and a grappling hook in case it was necessary to fish a soldier from the water. The ships making the transfer used hooded lights, but otherwise the night was black. Meredith paced the bridge for an hour until the transfers were completed without injury.

They were scheduled to arrive in the transport unloading area at midnight, and Jablonski carefully plotted their position as they progressed. Meredith was puzzled because they were ahead of schedule, but the problem was solved when it became apparent that the group commander, Admiral Davidson, wanted to make his approach to the area with combatant ships between the transports and the beach. Two ninety-degree turns brought them into the area exactly on time. The stage was now set, and Meredith hoped the moonless night would prevent the audience ashore from seeing the players at sea in the drama about to start.

Chapter Nineteen

Two hours before dawn, Sorenson looked on as Jablonski moved his navigational equipment from the bridge to the DRT in the CIC. As navigator, he would need to plot the ship's position on the DRT if the *O'Leary* were required to render gunfire support, and he would have to navigate by radar before dawn. Because the control console for the surface search radar was in CIC, he would have direct access to it.

At Bronte's invitation, Sorenson drew a cup of coffee from the pot maintained in CIC and inspected the plot. He was uncomfortable with the Army map on the DRT, but he felt more comfortable as Bronte, who was manning the surface search radar, read off the range and bearing of points ashore. Sorenson leaned on the DRT as Jablonski quickly plotted the points, marked the fix with the time, and started up the DRT. Thereafter the point of light would progress across the chart, and the bug could be adjusted as new fixes revealed the effects of current and wind.

Sorenson put down his coffee cup and moved behind Bronte's chair. Bronte showed him the grease pencil plots he was maintaining on selected ships. Sorenson could see the transports in a line off shore. Many smaller pips showed the boats milling around the transports. At first, the movements seemed to be random, but then he recognized that they were moving in small circles on both beams. Some of the boats were scheduled to embark troops from other transports. Sorenson remembered the young coxswain who had wandered in the Chesapeake and wondered how many like him would get lost tonight.

Then he shifted his attention to the dots that could only be the *Cole* and *Bernadou* moving slowly toward the end of the breakwater of Safi Harbor. The lead ship, the *Bernadou*, seemed to be following her assigned path, closely followed by a small covey of landing craft, but the *Cole* was obviously lost. Sorenson watched her approach the base of the breakwater, almost a half mile too far to the south. She was headed right at it, and Sorenson dashed out on the bridge. "Captain, somebody should tell the *Cole* she's headed into trouble!"

Meredith trotted into the CIC and peered at the radar console. "The *Cole*'s in trouble all right, but I don't think we should break radio silence to help her. All hell might break loose. We're supposed to keep radio silence until the French start to fire."

The *Cole* continued to approach the breakwater, but at the last minute reversed course and headed out to sea.

The *Bernadou* rounded the breakwater and appeared to be heading for her assigned landing area near the inside base of the breakwater.

The CIC talker jerked upright. "The *Bernadou*'s under fire from the beach."

Meredith ran for the bridge. Machine gun nests around the harbor and many small artillery pieces raked the *Bernadou*. Star shells followed, and the harbor was washed with a pale green light.

The *Bernadou* opened fire, and the heavy fire from the French batteries diminished.

The American destroyer *Mervine*, assigned to render support fire, broadcast, "Batter up," which meant that the French were firing on American ships.

Admiral Davidson immediately broadcast, "Play ball," which released all American ships to fire back at the French.

Arching projectiles from the *Philadelphia* and *New York* impacted around the French guns with muted yellow flashes. The rumble of gunfire echoed across the water. The *Bernadou* could be seen as a light pip on the bridge

PPI coming alongside some rocks near her designated beach. Over the TBS she reported that her troops were ashore, moving into the area behind the jetty.

Then the *Cole* rounded the breakwater and headed for her berth a few hundred yards north of the *Bernadou*. Now it was light enough to see the shore, and Meredith raised his binoculars. The *Cole* appeared to have trouble mooring to the pier, but he could see that by 0545 she was secure, and her troops began to land. The way seemed to be clear for the *Seatrain* to enter the harbor and discharge her tanks.

Renard clattered on to the bridge waving a dispatch at the Captain. "Sir, the *O'Leary* is ordered to depart immediately at best speed and report to the central group screen commander off Fedala."

Meredith read the rest of the dispatch and turned to Chumley. "Apparently the French ships at Casablanca are about to leave the harbor and all of the covering force may be needed to cope with them. This says there are eight submarines, a light cruiser, two destroyer leaders, and six destroyers."

Meredith pressed the transmit lever on the squawk-box. "What's the course to Fedala?"

"Zero two one. But we'll have to adjust as we get nearer to Casablanca."

Meredith ordered Chumley to come to the course and to increase speed to 30 knots. Meredith remembered that they had been able to get 30 knots out of three boilers on their full speed trials, and wondered if they could do it again. He knew that they had a hundred miles to go, and that they had started north at about 0545. That would put them off Casablanca about 0900. Meredith called Sorenson and ordered the crew fed again. It had been hours since the pre-dawn breakfast, and who knew when they might have time to eat again.

Sorenson said, "I'll get right on it. Should we consider zigzagging for safety?"

"I don't think there's any point in zigzagging at this speed. The sonar can't operate at this speed, and there shouldn't be any reason for a submarine to be here."

"I agree," Sorenson said.

Meredith leaned back in his chair. "I'm going to catch

a few winks here, and I suggest you do the same below. We may not have this much time off for days."

Before he dozed off, Meredith called for the engineering officer. Durham came up to the bridge, obviously grateful to have an excuse to get some fresh air.

Meredith asked, "How's the plant doing?"

"Fine. The fire brick we repaired in Norfok is holding up so far, and we're just a hair under thirty knots. I think we could do thirty-one with a clean bottom and a lighter load."

"Thanks, Bull," Meredith said. "You can go back below."

Durham took a deep breath, "I wish I could enjoy more of this fresh air, but I don't know if this old gal can hold up at full power."

Meredith watched him go. He didn't envy Durham his responsibility, but he thought Durham was doing better.

About 0700 the CIC reported that, on the air control circuit, which had a longer range than the TBS, they could hear reports from spotting aircraft that French submarines were leaving Casablanca Harbor and that French surface forces were under way.

Shortly afterwards, the *Massachusetts'* spotting plane reported that the *Jean Bart* was firing at the *Massachusetts*. The *Massachusetts* began firing at the shore batteries and at the *Jean Bart*. Their spotting plane reported several hits and that the *Jean Bart* had stopped firing.

About 0745, aircraft from the carriers reported sighting three French submarines still in port, but they also reported that eight others had escaped and submerged.

Meredith shook his head. "There's the trouble we will be expected to take care of."

At 0900 the lookouts spotted the top hamper of the battleship *Massachusetts* maneuvering off Casablanca. As the *O'Leary* got closer, Meredith could see masses of flames welling up from her hull at thirty-second intervals as flights of 16-inch projectiles hurtled toward the shore batteries that soon rose over the horizon. Meredith raised his binoculars. He said, "Those projectiles are making a hell of a mess, but the explosions are smaller than I expected."

Sorenson said, "I'll bet they're armor-piercing projectiles. The Task Force Commander probably expected the large French force from Dakar to appear, and the *Massachusetts* was ready for them."

"Probably right," said Meredith, "but I don't like all those shore battery rounds falling around the larger ships. Jablonski, give me a course to take us well outside of the battle area."

The *O'Leary* changed course to the left 10 degrees and began to pass to seaward of the firing ships.

Sorenson said, "I can see French ships going north toward the Fedala landing area, and they're starting to fire on the transports."

Steiner, who had a better view from the fire control platform, reported that the American ships were pounding the French destroyers and had sunk several.

By 1000, the *O'Leary* was north of Casablanca, and Meredith had a clear view of the running battle between the French ships and the American forces. Then over the TBS there were several reports of torpedo sightings, and the *Massachusetts* and *Tuscaloosa* reported maneuvering to dodge spreads of torpedoes.

Meredith looked at the light cruiser *Brooklyn*. He watched her rapid-fire 6-inch guns training around, and when they opened up, their continuous blast wreathed the ship in flame and smoke.

Sorenson, now in CIC, reported over the squawk box, "A spotting plane has just sighted a group of French ships coming north from Dakar."

Within minutes the TBS sputtered. The Task Force Commander ordered the *Massachusetts* to intercept, and she steamed south at high speed with her escorts.

Meredith, watching them disappear over the horizon, said, "I hope she can handle them all. If she can't, we're in trouble."

Meredith waited anxiously for half an hour. Then Sorenson reported to the bridge, "The contact report is false, and the *Massachusetts* is on the way back."

Meredith felt relieved, and eased into his chair.

Soon the *O'Leary* cleared the battle area and approached the transport area. Meredith reported for duty to the screen commander and received a screening assignment. Jablonski rapidly plotted the limits of the station, and in minutes the *O'Leary* reached station, slowed to 17 knots, and began sonar search.

By 1100, the *Massachusetts* was back on station.

"She's firing on a French destroyer," Steiner reported.

Meredith swung his binoculars to watch the action and spotted the destroyer just as it sank in the middle of an enormous column of water raised by a salvo of 16-inch projectiles.

Then there seemed to be a lull in the firing around Casablanca Harbor to the south, so Sorenson directed Renard to feed the crew sandwiches and coffee at battle stations.

But their lunch was disturbed by reports that another group of French ships had left the harbor at Casablanca and was headed north for the transport area. The *Brooklyn*, the *Wichita*, and three destroyers headed for the French, but they were too far away to engage them immediately.

Meredith moved the *O'Leary* to the southern edge of their station. When Steiner reported that the nearest French ship, a destroyer minelayer, was in range, Meredith ordered, "Commence firing!"

Steiner fired a salvo using a radar range from CIC rather than a spotting ladder, and the second salvo was close aboard the nearest French ship. Before the third salvo landed, strings of bombs dropped by carrier aircraft exploded near the target, and then shells from the rapidly closing cruisers landed. The thicket of the *O'Leary*'s projectile explosions, *Ranger* aircraft bombs, and cruiser projectile explosions enveloped the French vessel.

From the fire control platform, Steiner shouted, "Those damned clowns are sinking our target!"

Then the geysers subsided, and the French ship emerged. It had turned away and zigzagged at full speed for Casablanca, spouting black smoke.

Meredith laughed and shouted up to Steiner. "You didn't want that one anyway. She was too small."

Meredith ordered the officer of the deck to return to their station.

Jablonski called out to Meredith from the CIC, "Captain, we're getting very close to the beach. Recommend we move back nearer the midpoint of our station."

Before Meredith could reply, he heard the whistle of a shell. "What the hell is that?" he yelled.

A spout of white water rose 10 yards on the port side.

Steiner yelled, "I can see the bastard! There! An artillery piece on the beach! In that cloud of smoke and dust! Counter-battery fire! Target, field gun! Bearing zero six eight! Approximate range six oh double oh! Rangefinder, give me a range on it!"

"Commence firing when ready!" Meredith ordered.

Meredith held his breath, waiting for another round from the beach. He raised his binoculars and spotted the gun. Then he realized he ought to make the enemy fire-control problem more difficult, and he shouted, "Right full rudder! All ahead flank!"

He was too late. The whistling came again, and Meredith held his breath. An explosion on the well deck rocked the ship.

The telephone talker said, "Captain, the gunnery officer is about to open fire."

Within seconds, a salvo of 4-inch projectiles was on its way, the blast shaking Meredith.

Meredith estimated the gun to be a French 75-millimeter, probably a World War I artillery piece. The O'Leary's first salvo landed close, scattering dust over the gun. The gunners tried to drag their weapon back toward a hiding place where it had been awaiting an unwary ship that ventured too close to the beach.

More salvos boomed out. Shells from the third salvo flipped the gun on its side. Several of the gunners sprawled around the shattered weapon. Two survivors crawled into the bushes.

"Cease firing," Meredith ordered.

A last salvo went out before Steiner could restrain his eager gunners.

•　　　•　　　•

The talker in CIC turned to Sorenson. "Captain wants you to go below and check for damage."

Sorenson opened the door to CIC and heard Chief Bellow's voice from the well deck. He ran from the bridge to find Bellows bent over two reddened forms. Bits of flesh and bone were strewn about the deck.

Sorenson bent over the two men on deck. "Is it bad?" Sorenson asked. "The doctor is on the way."

Bellows stood up and pointed to the men. "Dey ain't bad, but our dinner is. Dey was gettin' sides a beef outa da refrigerator when de first round hit. De rest is tomato juice cocktail dey was coolin' in da fridg. Dey was plannin' a big feed for us tonight."

Sorenson wiped the red gore off the faces of the men on deck. They were the two ship's cooks.

Fineman poked his head out of the hatch leading up from the wardroom where he had been at his battle station. "Do you need me?"

Sorenson said, "Don't worry, I've rendered first aid, and they should be able to get up in a minute."

"Jesus!" said Fineman, looking at Sorenson and the flesh on the deck.

Sorenson said, "No, divine intervention wasn't required. I just wiped the tomato juice out of their eyes. I think they've got a few small cuts on their faces that will require some stitches."

"I'd better look at them then," Fineman said.

While Fineman examined the men carefully, Sorenson looked at the refrigerator, a large cubical structure on the port side of the well deck. It was a shambles. Sides of beef hung out of it at strange angles, and butter was smeared all over the deck around it. On top of it all was a slimy coating of red tomato juice.

Sorenson and Fineman helped the two cooks to their feet, untangling them from the pieces of beef hanging from their clothes.

Renard came up from below from his general quarters station at the coding machine. "Jesus!" he said.

Sorenson said patiently, "We've been through that Jesus thing already. The French did the damage, and I raised your cooks from the dead."

Renard looked around the well deck and shook his head. "Looks like I'll have to change the menu for tonight to hamburger and tomato sauce."

Sorenson laughed. "You're getting the hang of destroyer life."

•   •   •

After the flurry of action, the first part of the landing was over, and the *O'Leary* settled in a routine patrol of an assigned area that lasted two days. Meredith requested a fueling assignment and they went alongside the oiler *Winooski*. Meredith was anxious all the time they were alongside, requiring the lookouts to keep a careful watch for submarine periscopes. After fueling, Meredith quickly backed the *O'Leary* away from the tanker.

Sorenson was standing on the bridge near the torpedo director watching the tanker. He heard footsteps behind him, and Chumley stepped up beside him and said, "We really needed that oil."

"Yes, we were pretty low," Sorenson said.

"But I still didn't like being alongside. It's about time for U-boats to show up." As he started to turn to go back to the pilothouse, a giant column of water shot up the *Winooski*'s side and an explosion battered Sorenson's ears. Sorenson started to say something to Chumley, but suddenly realized he wasn't there. He looked down. "Jesus!" he shouted. "Send for the doctor!" He knelt beside Chumley and could see a jagged piece of metal protruding just above Chumley's left eye from a bed of brain matter and blood. Sorenson held Chumley's head until Fineman arrived.

Fineman bent over, felt his neck, and stood up. "Gone," he said.

Sorenson managed to reach the rail before he vomited.

•   •   •

After he had supervised the preparation of Chumley's body for burial, Fineman came back to the bridge and spoke to Meredith and Sorenson. They were leaning on the bridge rail, talking quietly. Fineman interrupted them. "I guess you'll want to have a burial at sea as soon as possible."

Meredith said, "We were talking about the possibility of transferring his body to a transport which would have the necessary facilities for taking him back to Norfolk."

Fineman shook his head. "That won't be necessary."

"Why not? His wife is there."

"She's not there."

Sorenson said, "Where is she?"

"I don't know. I knew the Chumleys were having trouble, and I went over to their apartment to see them two days before we left Norfolk. She wasn't there. Neither was their car nor her clothes. She just disappeared. Gerry was sitting in the dark and just staring into space."

"Didn't he know where she went?"

"She didn't even leave a note. I got a drink in him and brought him back to the ship. He felt better when he got to the ship and asked that I not say anything. While we were driving back he said he was an orphan and if anything happened to him he wanted to be buried at sea."

Meredith sighed, "I wasn't looking forward to notifying Miss Margaret."

•   •

For two days, as the *O'Leary* plodded back and forth on her station, Meredith looked over reports of submarine sightings. He turned to Sorenson, who was watching him plot the contacts, "There's trouble here. A lot of submarines are headed this way. We're going to lose some ships."

"Goddam submarines," Sorenson muttered.

Chapter Twenty

The next day, the transports continued their unloading operations. Meredith hoped they were sparked by the knowledge that they might be torpedoed. Three were. The transports were torpedoed about 1800, apparently by the same submarine, and the locations of the targets indicated that the submarine had probably come in at the end of the screen, close to the shore. All three ships were obviously doomed, and the many landing craft in the area were taking off their crews.

Steele came out on the bridge. "Captain, this latest intelligence bulletin says the nearest wolf pack to our area was disbanded and sent toward our area three days ago. I think we're seeing the first arrivals."

"Christ! Just what we need. Those wolf pack bastards!"

Two sonar contacts were reported by escorts on the other side of the screen, and Meredith said, "There are two more of them."

Meredith watched helplessly, repeatedly asking for permission to leave station and head for the location of the submarine attacks, but his requests were denied. He pounded the bridge rail in frustration, watching the transports list and sink.

"Jesus!" he said to Sorenson. "Are we going to let these bastards do that and then let them go? These God-damned seawolves will chew our asses off! If a destroyer doesn't try to find them and attack, they'll just move around inside the screen and torpedo other ships."

Sorenson's jaw tightened. "The least we can do is get the transports underway before the other two penetrate the screen."

The signal to get underway fluttered from the flagship's yardarm and the remainder of the transports quickly got under way and stood out to sea, screened by destroyers.

The *O'Leary* was left behind to patrol off the harbor entrance, Meredith wondering if she had been forgotten. Meredith paced the bridge restlessly, hoping to locate a submarine.

For two days Sorenson watched Meredith's frustration grow. "We're not going to find anything. These Krauts are too smart to get near us unless there is a merchantman they can attack."

Meredith sighed. "I know you're right, but I'd like to get a crack at something after the screw-ups of the last few days."

"We'll have plenty of chances later."

On the 15th, the *O'Leary* received a dispatch ordering it to become part of the escort for the remaining transports returning to Norfolk.

When Meredith announced the contents of the dispatch to those on watch on the bridge, there was a loud cheer, and the word soon spread below.

Meredith listened to a conversation between Alvarado and Bronte on the bridge wing.

"It ain't that I don't like to fight," Alvarado said, "but this has been ridiculous. I hate to fight old minelayers and World War I artillery pieces. Even the subs ain't any fun. They sneak along the beaches, attack our ships, and then run like hell, and we ain't even allowed to look for the bastards."

"Yeah," said Bronte. "but it's the only war we've got."

"Maybe getting back to the North Atlantic will be better. Those Germans put up a good fight, and I'm getting pissed off at them. You can have the French. But before we get back in the front lines of the German sub business, we fight the battle of Norfolk."

Bronte's eyes widened. "Yeah!" he said.

Meredith grinned and turned to the door leading into the bridge. "I hope you'll both get your wish," he said.

•   •   •

On the afternoon of November 15, the transports and one tanker left Casablanca harbor and formed a square formation. The *O'Leary* and four destroyers formed an antisubmarine screen around them. A division commander on one of the destroyers took command of the screen. Meredith kept a wary eye on the other ships in the screen and listened to the sonar. That afternoon he felt safe enough to go below to the well deck for Chumley's funeral service and burial.

Sorenson had assembled the officers and men off watch on the well deck. Chumley's flag-draped body, sewn tightly in canvas by Chief Bellows, lay on a mess table placed so that one end was adjacent to the bulwark.

Meredith read a short service, and MacIntosh read a poem by Robert Burns that Chumley had liked. Fineman led the group in a verse of the Navy hymn. After the hymn, Meredith read a short prayer of committal and nodded to the four junior officers standing by the sides of the table. They lifted the inboard end of the table and tilted Chumley's body over the side.

Meredith wiped his eyes and directed Sorenson to dismiss the crew. Meredith had liked Chumley and thought he had been doing well. Freed of his wife's influence, he thought he would have made a fine naval officer.

The crew dispersed in a somber mood. It was two days before Meredith saw a smile in the wardroom.

•   •   •

The convoy headed southwest for two days to avoid the most probable paths that the German subs might take from their Central and North Atlantic stations. There were only a few contacts, all false. But the unpredictable Atlantic weather blew enormous swells up one day. Then the wind changed directions abruptly and formed cross swells which caught the *O'Leary* on one wave peak and rolled her over 45 degrees without any warning. When Meredith asked for damage reports, he heard from Morales that he had lost half of the wardroom crockery on that one roll.

One morning the Task Group received a dispatch from General Patton. Meredith sat in his bridge chair, wedged in against the increasing rolls, reading the dispatch. Now and then he laughed.

Sorenson hung on to the chair, trying to read the message over Meredith's shoulder.

Meredith laughed again. "Listen to this, Tex. General Patton says 'It is my firm conviction that the great success attending the hazardous operations carried out at sea and on land by the western task force could only have been possible through the intervention of Divine Providence manifested in many ways. Therefore, I shall be pleased if in so far as circumstances and conditions permit, our grateful thanks be expressed today in appropriate religious services.' "

The helmsman snorted. Meredith looked at him but didn't say anything.

Sorenson said, "Well, I guess we're off the hook. Today is Monday. We were a day late in getting this dispatch."

Meredith shook his head. "A day late. Just like the rest of the operation. I think a lot of credit for success is due to Admiral Hewitt's courageous decision to land on the scheduled date."

"And a lot to those kids in the landing craft," Sorenson said. "If you really want to, Doctor Fineman could say a silent prayer."

Meredith laughed. "No, I don't think that's necessary, but we should all be thankful that we got out alive after that operation."

"Maybe we're too hard on the Army," Sorenson said. "After all, they did take on a tough job without any squawking, and they did the job with a minimum of casualties."

Meredith smoothed his mustache. "Yes, but the Navy ended up with more casualties than the Army. I added up the daily casualty reports."

•   •   •

The weather worsened, and the waves grew to green, white-topped monsters. The high winds blew the wave

tops over the bridge and into Meredith's eyes when he
ventured outside the pilothouse.

When Steele took over the watch the next day, he was
smiling.

Meredith asked from the bridge chair, "What are you
so happy about?"

"The weather," Steele said.

"It's awful. Why should that make you happy?"

"It's awful for subs, too. If they're on the surface, they
can't see us. By tomorrow we'll be out of the area where
they've been operating."

"How's it below?"

"Terrible. We're back on sandwiches, and not many of
them. The men are exhausted, and that makes them lia-
ble to seasickness."

Meredith brightened. "But that solves another problem. Without our refrigerator, we would have been on
beans and rice anyway."

　　　　　•　　　　　•　　　　　•

For the first week of the passage, Meredith had been
anxious about fuel, consulting with Durham over fuel
expenditures and the necessity for ballasting because of
the bad weather. They calculated that they could just
make Norfolk without fueling. Durham went below to
put into effect all possible fuel economies.

Unfortunately, if the heavy weather continued and
fueling were impossible, they would have to ballast
empty fuel tanks with seawater to insure stability in the
heavy swells. The seawater used could never be completely pumped out at sea and might get in the fuel
lines later.

Meredith would have to decide about ballasting, and
either way, it would bring problems. Just after a last
consultation with Durham, when Meredith had resigned
himself to ballasting and a rough weather fueling, the
weather moderated. They passed out of the storm, and
the seas dropped to the usual long swells coming out of
the south.

The screen commander quickly arranged a fueling
schedule, and just after lunch, the first normal meal in
days, the O'Leary started alongside the same tanker they
had fueled from on the transit east. Meredith, in a burst

of optimism, gave the conn to Sorenson and watched. Sorenson had no trouble coming alongside, and soon the lines and fuel hoses were over and fueling began. Sorenson took off his cap and stuffed it behind the pelorus to prevent it from blowing overboard in the gusts. Meredith noticed how his short blond hair stayed close to his scalp even in the wind. Maybe like an old Roman charioteer, he thought. He took off his own cap and felt his longer hair flapping in the breeze. He shook his head and put his cap back on. Some heads were designed to look well without coverings. Others, like his, did better covered.

Meredith looked over at the tanker Captain and waved at him. The tanker Captain pointed to his ears and took the inter-ship telephone from his talker. Meredith did the same and adjusted the head piece.

The tanker Captain said, "Welcome. Can we do anything for you?"

"You sure can. We took a hit on our refrigerator, and we don't have any fresh meat or other fresh provisions. Can you help us?"

The tanker Captain looked back toward the *O'Leary*'s refrigerator. "Good God, who did it?"

"A French shell."

"Did you fire back?"

"Oh, yes. We haven't had time yet to add an artillery piece to our collection on the bridge wing."

The tanker Captain pointed at the *O'Leary*'s bridge wing. "That's the damnedest collection I've ever seen. Looks like you destroyed at least one of everything in both oceans. You've got more there than all the rest of the ships we've fueled. By the way, your conning officer did a good job of coming alongside."

Meredith turned to Sorenson and relayed the compliment. Sorenson grinned and waved to the tanker Captain.

Meredith thanked the tanker Captain and returned the telephones to the talker. He walked aft on the bridge and looked down at the well deck. Renard was already directing the receipt of several sides of beef. Meredith figured they would have to eat roast beef for two straight days to keep it from spoiling. Oh well, he thought, such are the fortunes of war.

•   •   •

The last day, crossing the Gulf Stream was almost restful. Sorenson went up to the bridge and talked to Meredith. "Steiner says the crew would like to have a ship's party soon after we get in. He's willing to arrange it."

Meredith sighed. "I hope he knows what he's getting into. I remember our last party on the China Station."

"Steiner says he was on leave."

"Oh, yes, I remember. Maybe it's best that I don't tell him about that party. He might lose his nerve."

They passed the Norfolk net after the transports and tanker and moored at the Norfolk Naval Base piers. Meredith went ashore after the lines were secured, but as usual Sorenson had to wait until liberty was started and the ship settled down to a routine before he went ashore. Then he called Ferren.

Ferren whizzed down the pier with her usual aplomb and skidded to a stop in front of the brow. The petty officer of the watch waved appreciatively and gestured up to the bridge wing where Sorenson was watching. "He'll be right there, Ma'am."

Sorenson clattered down the ladder from the bridge and ran down the brow. He got in the other side of the red Ford and swept her into his arms, gear shift and all.

•   •   •

When Sorenson and Ferren arrived at her apartment, Ferren quickly fixed a dinner she had already partially prepared. After dinner, Sorenson said, "I almost forgot. I've got to send some filet mignons over to the Captain. We haven't had much fresh meat in the last two weeks, and I think he'd appreciate them."

Ferren murmured, "You don't have to bother. I've already taken care of it."

"How did you know?"

"Your logistics request. You didn't ask for much fresh meat. What happened?"

"Our refrigerator got blown up."

"Leaky pipes?"

"No, a leaky defense. A French artillery piece popped

us when we weren't looking. Damned thing was so old it should have been in a museum."

*   *   *

The night of the ship's party, Sorenson took the duty and sent all the officers ashore to the party. Then he looked into the pantry and said to Morales, "Give all the mess attendants liberty for the party tonight. Just leave the keys to the pantry with me."

Morales said, "But what will you eat for dinner?"

"Don't worry. I'm having it brought in."

Ferren arrived at 1800. Sorenson went down to her car and helped her carry aboard two large paper sacks. As he started aboard he stopped and felt one of the sacks. "Is this what I think it is?"

Ferren colored slightly. "Well, I've never seen you turn down a bottle of beer."

Sorenson grinned. "Thanks for trying, but I can't bring this aboard. Go ahead, and I'll put it back in the car."

Dinner that night was simple, but wonderful in Sorenson's eyes. Ferren had brought a half-dozen crab cakes, a quart of potato salad, and two large chocolate milk shakes. He didn't even miss the beer.

After polishing it off, Sorenson opened the pantry and, with Ferren's help, brewed a pot of strong, black coffee.

They sat in the two lounge chairs at one end of the wardroom and finished two cups. Then Ferren said, "Can you lock these doors?"

"No, did you have something in mind?"

She came over to his chair and sat on his lap. "Not really. I just wanted to be alone with you."

"If the messenger knocks on the door, I have to be ready to answer him. There may be an emergency. Even this arrangement with you on my lap may not work. Can you get off of my lap in time?"

She giggled. "Not with your hand on my knee."

"Sorry, I'll save that until some other time."

She said, "Can I see your room?"

"Sure. Which one. I've lived in two."

"Let's see where you started." They got up and went to Sorenson's first room, now occupied by Doctor

Fineman, which was at the head of the passageway. They went in, and she looked around. She said, "This doesn't look like you."

"No, it's now Doc Fineman's room. I'll show you the Captain's old room where I live now."

He led her to his new room and they went in. She said, "This is more like you, but you don't have a picture of me."

He pulled down the fold-up desk. On the safe door were taped several small pictures of Ferren, taken at the beach.

She said, "That's better. You passed that test. Now what did those two notches in the bunk rail in your old room mean?"

Sorenson colored. "Ah, I'm not sure. All I know is that I didn't put them there."

"That's not good enough. Tell me more."

"Well, rumor has it that some of my predecessors, all bachelors of course, used the bunk for ah . . . personal purposes."

"I get it. You don't have to spell it out."

Sorenson said, "Let's go back to Doc Fineman's room. I'd like to show you something."

They pushed aside the drape at Fineman's door, and Sorenson bent over and opened the cardboard box full of records. "I'd like to play you some of these."

"Oh, yes, I liked the ones you brought out to the apartment."

Sorenson brought the record player and the records out to the wardroom and put on a record of Beethoven's Ninth Symphony.

Ferren listened intently for a few minutes. Then she said, "Stop. That sounds too much like the stuff I used to have to play when I was taking piano lessons."

"Can you play?"

"Sure, but only blues and that sort of stuff."

"Nothing wrong with that. Maybe a little Tchaikovsky would be a little more up your alley."

She liked it, and they worked up to a little Brahms before she said, "Let's dance."

Sorenson rummaged in the box and came up with a Stan Kenton record. "I think you'll like this. It's slow enough so that we can maneuver around in this small space." He pushed the wardroom chairs as far back as they would go, started the record, and took Ferren in his arms.

After a few minutes Ferren stopped. "Why didn't you go to the ship's party tonight?"

"I wanted to let all of the officers go. Besides, the exec puts a damper on a party."

"You mean that's an exec's duty, like fending off young ladies on your lap and turning down beer aboard ship?"

Sorenson sighed, "Yes, all of those things. But I've decided I like being an executive officer. Most of all, I like the idea of commanding a destroyer some day, and the only way to do that is to be a good exec first."

They started to dance again, but after a few minutes Ferren said, "Sorry, all this close contact maneuvering in such a small place is getting to me. I've got to go. Besides, I have to be at work early tomorrow.

"By the way, I've been looking at those notches on the wardroom table. This place must have been a real den of iniquity."

Sorenson laughed. "Those are for a different reason. Meredith and Durham put them on the table after they each had surgery on it."

*   *   *

The next morning, after the party, Sorenson met the Captain at the bow. Meredith grinned expansively. "You missed a great party last night, Tex."

"How long did you stay?"

"We got there just in time for the entertainment and left right after. I didn't want to put too much of a blanket over the party. Come down to the wardroom, and I'll tell you all about it."

The wardroom was full of officers finishing their breakfasts. There were a few blood-shot eyes, and Gerlach had a small shiner and two scratches on his cheek. Some of the officers made a tentative move to leave quietly, but Sorenson looked down at them with his eyebrows raised, and they avoided his gaze and went on with their breakfasts.

Meredith said, "Gentlemen, that was a fine party last

night. I commend all of you, and particularly you, Chuck."

The junior officers sitting at the end of the table looked at each other, but no one said a word. Steiner studied his eggs without looking up. "Thank you, sir."

Meredith went on. "I thought Chief Bellows was great."

Sorenson said, "Tell me about it."

"He sang two songs, and believe me he shook the walls. I told him I liked his Polish songs. He looked at me and said, 'Dey was in English.' I tried to save the day, and I said, 'I meant, would you sing the same songs in Polish?' He did, and I couldn't tell the difference."

The officers at the other end of the table now were relaxing and listening.

Sorenson suspected something. He said, "The mess attendants said Morales was pretty good, too."

"He was. He taught the new hands how to sing and dance the famous Filipino song 'Planting Rice.' Then after they had learned it to his satisfaction, he christened them all Asiatic Sailors."

Sorenson moaned, "Oh no! Bull told me about that one day."

Durham laughed. "Sorry you missed it. We'd have christened you, too."

"It wasn't bad," Meredith said. "He just poured a little beer over their heads. The bartender didn't have any rice wine."

Down at the end of the table there was a titter, but it was quickly stifled with a loud cough.

"Well," said Meredith, "there you have it. Next time you can go, and I'll take the duty."

He got up and went above to his cabin.

As soon as he was through the door, Steiner said to Sorenson, "Sir, we've got to talk . . . in private."

Sorenson grinned, "That doesn't surprise me. Come into my room."

After Steiner had eased gingerly into the extra chair in Sorenson's room, Sorenson looked at him and laughed. "I've been to ship's parties before. Tell me all."

Steiner shook his head. "You won't believe it." He

pulled a piece of paper from his pocket and laid it on Sorenson's desk.

Sorenson studied it. "Go ahead."

Steiner said, "The party started off all right, and it was on track until the Captain left."

"It always is. Wasn't Bull still there?"

"No, he said he had some urgent business to take care of."

"Urgent?"

"Yes, Sonya looked pretty urgent."

"Go on."

"Then the dancing got a little wild, and the beer flowed. The first thing that happened was that Gerlach asked to dance with Kendrick's date. She agreed. He picked her up and twirled her so fast her feet actually left the floor. When they finished, Kendrick's girl challenged Kendrick to do the same. They got along for a couple of twirls, and then Kendrick lost control. They crashed into a table and broke the hell out of it."

Sorenson looked down at the piece of paper. "Yes, the table leads the list. What about this other stuff?"

"Well, a little later the crew started a basketball game."

"What?"

"Yes. They used the dance floor for a court and two wastebaskets for baskets."

"And, I suppose, a beer pitcher for a ball."

"Yes, and they were getting along all right until one of the players hit a wet spot on the floor."

"Left over from the Morales christening ceremony, no doubt."

"How did you know?"

"I've been to some of these parties, but not any with a lot of ex-Asiatic Fleet sailors. You seem to have good ones."

Steiner perked up. "That's right. We had a good time. I wish you'd been there. I heard you used to be a great band leader."

"A little in high school. Did you miss me last night?"

"Oh, no. Doc Fineman was great. I thought he was a musical egg-head, but he came through fine. He even knew some songs for a sing-along, and he accompanied

Chief Bellows on the piano." Steiner brightened. "Sorry you missed that."

"I suppose I can figure out the charges for the beer pitchers, but how about the mirror?"

"I was getting to that."

"After the slip on the beer?"

"Yes, one of the players slipped while making a long pass."

"And broke the mirror?"

"Well, actually he only cracked it, but the proprietor insisted on replacing it."

"And the chairs?"

"They got caught in the chariot race."

"And you stopped that?"

"Yes, and then Ensign Steele, who had the shore patrol, dropped by and helped remove some of the more, er, active, party-goers."

"How did Gerlach get his wounds?"

"He volunteered to sit on those waiting to, er, be escorted out by the shore patrol."

"And?"

"While he was sitting on Kendrick, Kendrick's girl came over and bopped him with her handbag. Then when he grabbed it, she, ah, scratched him."

"I take it that all ended well."

"Oh sure, we all threw our glasses at the bar when we left."

Sorenson looked at the bill for damages. "That explains the hundred glasses."

Steiner wrung his hands. "That's about all, except that we used up all of our funds paying for the party. We don't have enough in the recreation fund to pay for damages."

"How much do you lack?"

"Five hundred dollars."

Sorenson laughed. "Well, leave this with me. I'll go to see the proprietor and see if he'll come down any."

Steiner looked relieved, but still doubtful. "I don't know. He was pretty mad."

Sorenson said, "How did you get the crew to leave?"

"Well, our last entertainment was a strip tease girl

that Carmody had hired. She was pretty good, but she wouldn't take off the last piece."

"Why should she? This isn't Chefoo, or any of those other ports you used to visit."

"That's what Alvarado said, and he said he knew a place down the street where they took off everything."

"And there was a stampede for the door."

"Yes, but luckily Steele got it open in time, so it wasn't added to our bill."

"How was the other place?"

"Closed for repairs, and when the crew got back to the old place, it was locked up."

"And that ended the party?"

"Yes, except for the chase after Alvarado."

"Did they catch him?"

"No, he used to be a high school track star."

·   ·   ·

Sorenson parked outside the club, looked up at its sign to make sure it was the right one, and got out of his car. The door of the club was open, and he walked in. Two men were mopping the floor and two others were moving in new furniture.

Sorenson said, "Pardon me, is the proprietor around?"

One of the men looked up. "He's in the office in the back. The last time I saw him he was holding his head."

Sorenson went to the office in the back of the building and looked in. There was a man sitting at a desk there massaging his temples.

Sorenson said "Are you the proprietor?"

The man looked up and said, "Afraid I am. What can I do for you?"

Sorenson, said, "I'm the executive officer of the *O'Leary*."

The man moaned. "I hope I never hear that name again."

Sorenson sat down and took out a check book. "I have a bill here for repairs totalling five hundred dollars. Is that correct?"

"Cheap at that price."

Sorenson wrote out a check and shoved it in front of the man. "Maybe this will make you feel better."

The man read the check and looked up, "Do you mean this?"

"Yes, just a little extra so you will welcome the *O'Leary* back next time."

"Sure, any time, but please, just a few guys at a time."

Chapter Twenty-one

The *O'Leary* was ordered to remain at the Norfolk Naval Base until January 4 for upkeep, leave, and manufacture of a new refrigerator. Sorenson took leave first so that Meredith could take leave later and spend Christmas with his family.

Although the weather was too cold for swimming, a warm spell allowed Ferren to arrange a picnic at their favorite beach, which included Renard and his girl friend from Ferren's office.

Sorenson and Ferren visited the airfield south of Norfolk, and found out that the owner had more aviation fuel.

Sorenson grinned. "Where did you get it?"

Curtis shrugged. "Can't tell you, but it's yours for a price."

Sorenson bought it all, and they flew every morning for the week of his leave. At the end of the week, Sorenson pronounced Ferren ready for soloing, provided Curtis checked her out, but she wanted a few more days instruction before trying.

One morning Sorenson took Fineman to the airfield. He gave Fineman a short course of instruction in the hangar. After they were airborne, he demonstrated the basic maneuvers and some simple aerobatics. Fineman caught on quickly and was able to duplicate them easily, but when they landed, Fineman climbed down slowly. His face was white and his legs were wobbly.

"Sorry," Sorenson said, "I thought you liked what we were doing."

"I did. I want to do it again, but I can't seem to convince my stomach. Now I know why you were unhappy about leaving Navy flying, but it's not for me."

The days passed rapidly, and then Christmas was upon them. They were invited to the Merediths' for Christmas dinner, and Sorenson saw that Ferren was getting very close to the Meredith children.

Then the holiday period ended, and they had to get ready for sea.

•   •   •

At the end of their third week in port, Meredith was having breakfast in the wardroom. About half of the officers were on leave, but those still aboard were there. Meredith said, "How about another ship's party before we leave?"

Steiner choked on his coffee, and there were several snickers from the end of the table.

Sorenson shook his head and said, "Captain, I think we'd better let that one alone for a while."

"Aw, come on, Tex. I thought the last one was a huge success."

"Captain, take my word for it. It's not time yet."

Meredith twitched his mustache and put his coffee down. "Tex, there's something about that party that you're not telling me."

Sorenson sighed. "Yes, sir, there are some things captains don't need to know."

The awkward situation was relieved by the messenger, who knocked on the door and announced, "Captain, there's a barge coming alongside with the new refrigerator."

Sorenson rose, obviously glad of the interruption. "Captain, please finish your breakfast. I'll have Durham take care of the barge."

•   •   •

On deck, the senior ship's cook, his assistant, and Durham watched the barge come alongside. On its deck was a new refrigerator, somewhat larger than the old one. Several workmen and a supervisor stood alongside it. When the barge was secured alongside, the men came aboard, and the supervisor came over and reported to Durham. "We've come to install your new refrigerator. The old one sure was a mess."

Durham said, "Glad to see you. We've missed the old box. Looks like the new one will be just right."

The supervisor went over to the senior ship's cook and said, "The guys over at the shop where we built this want you to know that we know how much you're doing to win the war. Cooks don't usually get much credit, or get into the action. Your shipfitter who came over with the work order told me you two were right in the action when the old box bought the farm."

The senior cook said, "Yeah, it was a real humdinger."

The supervisor looked at him closely and noticed the healing scars on his face. "I understand you got wounded. How did it happen?"

"A rib bone, I think."

The supervisor looked a little puzzled and turned to the junior cook. "You've had a few stitches, too. How did you get yours?"

"Don't know for sure. Musta been a flying tomato juice can."

The supervisor laughed. "Now I know you're kidding me. Say, me and the boys wanted to show our appreciation. You'll find a case of beer in the back of the box."

The senior cook looked over at Durham to see if he had heard, but Durham was looking up at the crane.

The supervisor said, "Maybe we should have made it a dozen."

The senior cook said. "Thanks, but I think we'll have to do our drinking ashore . . . like Mister Durham."

"Guess you're right. Wouldn't want to fight those Kraut subs with somebody too drunk to do their job," the supervisor said. "But don't worry. We stenciled 'medicinal brandy' on the cases."

The senior cook looked bleak. "We can't have strong booze either. What we have is locked up under the doctor's supervision."

The supervisor looked surprised, "Whada ya mean? We heard this ship has enough brandy stored below to keep a French whorehouse going for a month."

The junior cook pulled at the sleeve of the senior

cook. "Joe, don't you think we could drop by the shop and pick up the cases of beer?"

Durham strolled closer to the group. The senior cook shook off the junior cook's hand and said to the supervisor, "Thanks for everything. We've got to get lunch started."

•   •   •

The morning after New Year's Day, Renard decoded a dispatch assigning the *O'Leary* to escort a small convoy to Bermuda, leaving two days later. He showed it to the Captain, who announced it at lunch. There was a loud cheer.

Fineman said, "I prescribe a day on the beach for everyone."

Two mornings later Jablonski conned them down the channel toward the net vessel. The weather was cold, but bearable. Renard came up to the bridge and asked if he should issue the new L. L. Bean cold weather clothing.

Sorenson shook his head. "No, the temperature will be mild after the first day and pleasant in Bermuda."

The convoy consisted of three ships, with the *O'Leary* and a PC as escorts. The 700-mile trip was over almost before they had shaken down.

The only incident was a report of a submarine by the High Frequency Direction Finding System, which Meredith hoped would help them turn the tide against the U-boats. Several radio direction finding stations, including the one at Bermuda, listened twenty-four hours a day to frequencies used by German submarines reporting back to their bases. Even though the transmissions were brief, the stations could get accurate bearings on them. A central station plotted the location with great accuracy.

Meredith waved Steele over to show him the message.

Steele looked it over. "A few months ago a contact was reported off Bermuda, and an aircraft from Bermuda found the submarine within the hour with the crew sunbathing on deck."

"What happened then?" Meredith asked.

"The aircraft sank it."

"Good. I guess the members of the crew on deck were properly dressed for a swim."

Meredith looked at the contact that Jablonski had plotted. It was 500 miles to the north.

"Well, that's one we won't get, and it's too cold for a swim up there."

.   .   .

On the day before they were to arrive, Alvarado and Bronte lounged on the port flag bag, nursing mugs of coffee. They were watching Ensign MacIntosh and Chief Torpedoman Skelly working on the base of the torpedo director. The base closure plate was lying on the deck beside a tool box.

MacIntosh straightened and pulled out a tartan-colored handkerchief. He carefully wiped a speck from his eye and put his handkerchief back in his pocket.

"What the hell was that?" Alvarado asked Bronte.

"Tartan."

"What's that? And don't tell me you read it in a book."

"I did. It's a design which indicates which Scottish clan he belongs to."

"Looks like it would make a good signal flag."

"What would you use it for?"

"Fire drill, or just as a 'What-the-hell' flag. It sure had a lot of colors in it."

"Speaking of books. Would you like to read about your Mexican ancestors?"

"Sure."

Bronte looked surprised. "Okay. We go to the public library next time we're in Norfolk."

Alvarado looked at Skelly and MacIntosh again. They were deep in conversation, but he couldn't follow it. Then MacIntosh pulled out a wire with a part attached to it and held it up in front of Skelly.

Skelly said, "Easy, MacIntosh, that's no sheep gut."

MacIntosh laughed. "Okay, I'll put it back. I think you found the trouble anyway."

Bronte took the two empty coffee cups and went into CIC.

.   .   .

Later that afternoon, Durham came up to the bridge for some fresh air. Alvarado was leaning on the port flag bag looking at the adjacent ships in the formation. When Durham's head appeared above the top of the ladder, Alvarado turned and grinned. "Afternoon, Mister Durham."

Durham walked over to Alvarado. "Hi. Got any of that gun grease?"

"Sure. Back in a minute." Alvarado returned with a mug of coffee. "Black and bitter," He said.

"Just like I like it," Durham said.

They sipped in silence for a few minutes. Then Alvarado said, "Why do people call you Bull?"

"Simple enough. What does that bag of tobacco in your inside pocket say?"

Alvarado pulled out a small bag of tobacco, closed by string pulls, and looked at the side. "Durham Tobacco Company."

"Look at the trademark."

Alvarado looked up. "There's a bull on it."

"Sure. At the Naval Academy any man named Durham is automatically called Bull. Just like guys named Rhodes are called Dusty."

"Do you have any stock in the company?"

"A little. Why?"

"I was wondering if you are the one who paid for the damage after our party."

"No. You might ask the exec."

"I did. He won't say." Alvarado put the tobacco bag back in his pocket. "I envy you the time you had at the Naval Academy. I never even finished high school."

"Do you ever go back there?"

"Once. The only girl I ever dated was gone. My parents are dead. I don't have any friends left in my home town. Now the only home I have is the *O'Leary*."

"You've been with her a long time."

"Eight years."

"Don't you ever want to go to a newer ship?"

Alvarado grinned. "No. Only when I have dust-ups with Bronte or Kendrick or some of the new guys."

"What's your problem with them?"

"I don't like it when Bronte runs the *O'Leary* down. He calls it an old bucket of bolts."

Durham laughed. "It is, but a good bucket of bolts. I like her, too, as long as I can keep her kettles going."

Alvarado suppressed a smile. "So you can get ashore with the babes."

Durham handed the coffee mug back to Alvarado. Over his shoulder he said, "Maybe."

* * *

The next afternoon they rounded the northwest end of Bermuda, bound for the American naval base in Great Sound. By the time they passed Ireland Island, the merchant ships had anchored in the sound. The *O'Leary* headed for the pier at the naval base, on an island connected to the main island by a causeway. Within the hour they were moored at the naval base pier, and Meredith had gone ashore to call on the base commander.

He returned with a box of what proved to be travel brochures, and sat down at the wardroom table. All the officers had been waiting eagerly for his return.

Meredith grinned and pointed at the box. "The main industry of Bermuda used to be tourism, and you can also guess that no one is interested in traveling to Bermuda by sea now. These brochures are useless, since most of the hotels they describe are closed, but if you want to read them, you'll know what you missed."

There was a groan.

"Don't be quite so down. There are still enough of the bars and restaurants open to take care of the Bermuda Naval Air Station, the Bermuda Naval Base, and all the military transients here. The beaches are still open and are among the best in the world. Hamilton, the main city, is only five miles away by ferry, and if you want to try it, only eight miles by bicycle."

"Bicycle?" said Renard.

Meredith looked down the table. "I thought you knew. There aren't many taxis here, and the roads are very narrow. Walking and bicycling are some of the main sports here."

Gerlach said, "That wasn't the sport I was thinking of."

Durham said, "You can try a little rugby. That should slow down your hormones."

. . .

On the first day out on the way back to Norfolk, Fineman came up to the bridge.

Meredith asked, "How did the visit to Bermuda go?"

Fineman said, "For me fine, and I don't think the crew caught anything but sunburn."

"They seemed to come back exhausted every night."

Fineman laughed. "I don't think that's what they were exhausted from. The Bermuda girls are healthy and the percentage of males here is very low."

"Did you get around the island much?"

"Yes, even as far as the Bermuda Naval Air Station on the other end of the island. I met an old college chum who flys Liberators."

"Liberators? Aren't those Army Air Force aircraft?"

"Yes, normally, but the Navy uses their model for long range antisubmarine patrol as far out as a thousand miles. There will be one in front of us on the way back to Norfolk, and they range quite far north."

Meredith stroked his mustache thoughtfully. "I think air power will do a lot to help the antisubmarine battle in the Atlantic. Also, I hear that the Navy is going to form several hunter-killer groups around the type of escort carriers we saw off Africa. That way the whole Atlantic can be covered, and the wolf packs won't have any place to hide or refuel."

"Refuel?"

"Yes, they've started using some of those converted type IX U-boats we heard about that they call milk cows. Just bigger submarines stripped of all armament with extra fuel tanks and storage areas. That way the active German submarines can rendezvous with them and provision and fuel. That saves a lot of unproductive transit time, and keeps the best subs out there longer."

"Clever guys."

"Yes, they'll be tough to beat. When we meet the attack versions they call Seawolves they're making out of the big type IXs we'll be in trouble."

On the third day they sighted Virginia Beach, and by noon were back at a pier in the Norfolk Naval Station.

After they moored, Renard brought a decoded dispatch up to Meredith, who read it and frowned.

Sorenson asked, "Bad news?"

"Good and bad. We go to New York on the 20th. That's good. And we leave on the 25th with a convoy for Londonderry."

Sorenson thought a moment. "That might not be so bad. I've always wanted to see Great Britain. Ireland will be a start."

Meredith shook his head. "You forget the price of the trip. Two weeks in the North Atlantic in the dead of winter."

Chapter Twenty-two

At lunch their first day in port, Meredith said, "Tex, Linda wants to visit New York when we go up there. Have you gotten any feeling from Ferren yet whether she wants to go?"

"Feeling? She's already put in for leave. Do you think Linda would like to ride with Ferren in my car?"

"Sure. Train tickets are hard to get, and I wasn't looking forward to turning her loose with our old car. Also gasoline rationing would be a problem."

"Ferren figures that she'd have hers, mine, and your ration coupons for January, and she has about twenty pounds of sugar saved up. She thinks the sugar and her meat ration coupons can be traded for at least twenty gallons of gas. Then there's always the black market."

"How about inviting Mercedes MacIntosh to join them?" Meredith asked. "The MacIntoshs haven't been married very long. She needs a little Navy wife counseling. That would be another set of ration coupons."

"That would be fine. I'd thought of asking Chuck Steiner's wife, but she's pregnant and wouldn't want to travel. Bull says Sonya can't leave her tea house now."

• • •

On the 20th Ferren left, driving the green Buick north carrying Linda Meredith and Mercedes MacIntosh. Mercedes was starry-eyed, obviously glad to be on the road, even if she was alone in the back seat with some of the luggage that wouldn't fit in the trunk.

Linda said, "How are you and Finlay getting along?"

"Fine. I like Navy life. Now I'm about to see New York, and I loved traveling across the country when we came here from California. What an adventure that was! I'd like to tell you about it."

Ferren said, "Just as soon as we get out of town. Right now I have to be careful with Tex's car. Maybe you've got some good advice for us, and I know we've got some for you. This will be a long trip up to New York."

"Oh, I know how to get extra gas and everything."

Ferren said, "We may need the extra gas. Let's hold the everything until we get out on the highway."

•   •   •

A hundred miles at sea the O'Leary steamed under a cloudless sky marred only by passing antisubmarine planes. They tried out the repaired boiler brick in a 30-knot power trial. Meredith said, "Making thirty knots on a calm sea on a beautiful day is one of the few rewards for going to sea in a destroyer."

Sorenson, standing next to him, was pensive. "I know you're right, but in an aircraft you can always go up a little higher and find weather like this. On a ship, we're stuck with what's on the surface, and this is a rare winter day in the Atlantic."

On the morning of January 22, the O'Leary eased past the entrance net to New York Harbor and headed for the Brooklyn Navy Yard. Meredith watched the deck force, standing at quarters on the forecastle, gawking at the Manhattan skyline. After mooring, a liberty party scurried over the bow, obviously bound for the big city.

Sorenson dropped by Meredith's cabin where Meredith was shaving before putting on his blues. "Captain, we'll find our ladies at the Waldorf Astoria."

Meredith dropped his razor with a clatter. "What! We can't afford that."

"Don't worry. I know a rich Texan who likes the Navy, and he's going to pick up the tab for the rooms and all of our meals there."

Meredith picked up his razor, inspected its blade for nicks, and finished shaving.

"You Texans are strange people. On second thought, you're great people."

Meredith, Sorenson, and MacIntosh hailed a taxi, and when they arrived at the Waldorf, they found their wives in choice suites. Linda was ecstatic. "Jack, have you heard about this? Tex's friend arranged it. And we have show tickets waiting for both nights."

Ferren interrupted, "Well, that's not quite right. The second night is for a symphony."

Meredith said, "Who cares? With the money we're saving, we can afford to pay the sitter we left with the kids."

•   •   •

The first night they had dinner at the Twenty One Club, and Meredith felt relieved when Sorenson picked up the check afterward.

"For your friend, Tex?" Meredith asked.

"Yes, I'll get it to him."

At the theater, a new musical, they found seats reserved at the box office and settled in them.

Linda looked around at the entering crowd and suddenly tugged Meredith's arm.

"Look over there a couple of rows in front of us. Isn't that group of men from the *O'Leary*?"

Meredith followed the direction of her eyes. Ten enlisted men in uniform were sitting across the theater.

Alvarado looked up and waved at them. "Thanks, Mister Sorenson."

Meredith's eyebrows rose and he leaned over to Sorenson, "Your friend again, Tex?"

"Ah, I guess so. He really gets around."

•   •   •

Sorenson had arranged a suite with adjoining rooms for himself and Ferren, but there was a door between them. After entering his room, he went into Ferren's room through the inner door.

He took her in his arms and they were quiet for a while. Ferren said, "That was nice of you, Tex, to arrange all this. The wives will never forget this trip."

Sorenson laughed. "Neither would the husbands if they knew the size of the bill."

They fell asleep on Ferren's bed, fully dressed, in each other's arms. They slept that way until Sorenson heard a peculiar noise through the open window. It sounded like all the *O'Leary*'s machinery had suddenly run out of oil. He got up and went over to the window. It was garbage trucks loading refuse from the hotels. A huge floral wreath protruded from one garbage can. He closed the window and returned to the bed.

Ferren stirred. "What was that?"

"Just garbage trucks picking up garbage and dead flowers."

Ferren was quiet for a few minutes. Then Sorenson could feel her trembling, and when he felt them, her eyes were wet.

"What's the matter?" he asked.

"Oh, Tex, please don't ever mention death. I don't want to lose you."

He patted her back. "Don't even think about it. Old Maria said I'd live to eighty."

"Who's Maria?"

"An old Indian woman on our ranch."

"You said all the Indians had been chased out of Texas."

"I did, but Maria is married to one of our ranch hands, and she's like an aunt to me."

"How did she make her prediction?"

"She put my hand in the smoke of a mesquite fire and then read the lines in my palm."

"I suppose that's as good a way as any. Your hands are pretty lively."

"Go to sleep." Sorenson said, and they slept until hunger awakened them at noon.

•　　　•　　　•

After a large lunch in Peacock Alley in the Waldorf Astoria, Ferren asked Sorenson to walk with her down Fifth Avenue. The store windows were partially filled with meager stocks depleted by the shortages of war, but Cartier's was as glittering as ever. Ferren resisted, but Sorenson insisted that they go in. He tried to buy her a large diamond pendant, but she turned it down.

"I'll never be able to wear that, Tex. How about something less extravagant?"

"You could keep it hidden under your dress. I'd know it was there. I insist."

Ferren wore it under her blouse that night as they

filed in to the auditorium for the symphony. Mercedes MacIntosh had told Ferren that she wasn't sure she would like that kind of music, but at the last minute the MacIntoshs joined them. After they were seated, Linda searched the surrounding seats.

"What are you looking for?" Ferren asked.

"I wanted to see where our men are sitting."

Ferren said, "I don't think you'll see them here. They have a table at the Chez Martinez."

"That rich Texan again?" Linda said.

"That's right," Ferren said.

Ferren changed the subject. "Have you done any shopping?"

Linda rustled her program, "Yes, but I didn't buy anything. The prices were too high for a naval officer's wife. Did you buy anything?"

Ferren fished the pendant out of her blouse and showed it to Linda. "Just this."

Linda looked at it, and her eyes widened. "That's the most beautiful piece of jewelry I've ever seen."

"Do you really like it?"

"Oh, yes. It's gorgeous."

Ferren saw the wistful look in Linda's eyes, and she turned and saw Sorenson watching them. He inclined his head toward Linda. Ferren took the pendant off and gave it to Linda. Linda put it on and twisted it so the diamond glinted in the overhead lights. Then she started to take it off. Ferren put her hand on Linda's wrist. "Keep it. It will always remind you of this trip."

Linda's eyes widened. "I can't do that. It must be worth at least a thousand dollars."

Ferren laughed. "It's just glass. I can get another one, can't I, Tex?"

Sorenson nodded and said, "Sure. There's plenty more where that came from."

The curtain began to go up, and Ferren became more and more interested in the music as the symphony went on. At intermission she said, "Tex, you've made a convert. I want to hear more of this kind of music."

"You will," he said.

Mercedes MacIntosh did not seem to be impressed by the music, but Ferren could see her eyes glow as she watched the well-dressed New York women walking around the lobby. Even by wartime standards, some of the gowns were impressive.

Ferren watched her and said to Sorenson, "I think Finlay is going to have a little trouble taking her home to a sheep ranch."

"Just what sheepherders deserve," Sorenson said.

•   •   •

The convoy was slow in loading and they stayed a third day. That morning Sorenson and Ferren were at Cartier's when it opened. Sorenson bought her an even bigger pendant. That night Sorenson watched Ferren put it around her neck. "No gem ever had a nicer setting," he said.

The next morning the three men said good bye over a magnificent breakfast in the Waldorf Astoria dining room and helped load the green Buick.

By ten o'clock they were back aboard, and Meredith was off to a convoy conference. Sorenson leaned on the bridge railing and stared at Manhattan. New York was about to become a memory.

Chapter Twenty-three

Sorenson paced the bridge. The *O'Leary* was ready to get underway, but Meredith hadn't returned from the convoy conference. Sorenson had inspected the ship to make sure that all was secured for the heavy weather they expected in the North Atlantic. He stopped pacing and leaned on the bridge rail, idly watching the civilian longshoremen working on the pier. Alvarado stood next to Sorenson with a short telescope, looking up the pier to catch the first glimpse of Meredith. Doctor Fineman came up to the bridge and joined them.

Sorenson asked, "Doc, did you enjoy New York?"

"Yes, I met a medical school classmate at the naval hospital."

"I'd have thought you could have found something more interesting."

"Oh, I did, but after I did my business."

"What kind of business?"

"I needed to pick up some drugs that weren't available in Norfolk, particularly a small supply of something called Penicillin. A British scientist discovered it in a mold. It may be a breakthrough in the treatment of certain infections. It's new and hard to get."

"Why is it so good?"

"We don't exactly know yet. It's been tried on a number of infections and has been almost miraculous. On the other hand, some kinds of infections it doesn't touch at all."

"Is it expensive?" Sorenson asked, thinking of the ship's limited funds.

"Yes, but I got some free from my classmate, who is conducting tests with it."

Alvarado, still watching the head of the pier, said, "There's a Navy pickup truck coming down the pier. But I don't think the Captain is in it."

Fineman said, "I think that's my Penicillin. It will have to go in the refrigerator. See you later."

A sailor got out of the truck and brought a small insulated package aboard. Fineman went down to meet him.

Alvarado lowered his telescope. "Mister Sorenson, we had a hell of a good time in New York. We'd like to write to your friend who made all the arrangements for us."

Sorenson laughed. "He'll like that. Just give the letter to me, and I'll see that he gets it."

"Do you suppose your friend enjoys making money as much as we like spending it?"

"I'm sure he does."

"Mister Sorenson, that answer was just a little too quick. Is there something about this deal I don't know?"

Sorenson grinned. "Maybe, but don't worry about it. It's all legal."

Alvarado shook his head. "Something's fishy."

Sorenson heard him and chuckled.

An engine muttered, and a Navy sedan turned the corner. Alvarado looked up the pier and said, "That's the skipper. I can recognize his mustache."

Sorenson went down to to the quarterdeck to meet him.

•   •   •

When the officers had assembled in the wardroom, Meredith began. "I've just come back from a convoy conference, and we're still scheduled to leave in about an hour and join the screen of convoy SC-118, bound for Londonderry. Londonderry is the second largest city in Northern Ireland, the section that still belongs to Great Britain. The rest of Ireland is independent and neutral in the war."

"I don't see how anybody could be neutral where Hitler is concerned," Fineman said. "Does anyone know how the war is going?"

Steele answered, "At Antisubmarine Warfare Headquarters they were pessimistic. They won't really say it, but I believe they think we're losing the war at sea."

Sorenson said, "The situation seems to get worse each month. I heard we lost at least a hundred merchant ships last month."

Steele shook his head. "More than that. They told me the United States lost 800,000 tons in November alone. That's well over a hundred ships. The British lost about as many. The Germans did all this damage with only about fifty U-boats on station in the North Atlantic and a few more in the Caribbean."

"How much tonnage are we building?" Sorenson asked.

"November was the first month in which we built as much as was sunk," Steele answered. "We sunk thirty-three German U-boats and Italian submarines, more than they built that month."

Meredith said, "I read in an intelligence bulletin that we have an average of six convoys at sea in the North Atlantic at any one time. The average convoy has thirty-four merchant ships and seven escorts."

Sorenson said, "We'd better hope the tide turns in our favor."

Steele said, "If it doesn't, we could lose the war."

Meredith shook his head and sent for another cup of coffee. "I need this," he said. "There wasn't any heat in that damned car."

"What will our route be?" Sorenson asked.

Meredith rubbed his hands together and said to Jablonski, "Spread out that chart of the North Atlantic that I asked you to bring down."

The officers rose and leaned over the chart. Meredith's pencil traced their route from New York to Londonderry. It paralleled the coast of Canada about a hundred miles off shore until it reached Newfoundland. Then it headed for a point about 50 miles north of Ireland and finally dipped south to head in to Londonderry. Meredith drew rough arcs of about 600 miles in radius and centered on Newfoundland, Iceland, and Londonderry.

"This is our expected track and the arcs represent the extent of aircraft coverage using present aircraft. Air operations are limited to daylight and good visibility. The German submarines will try to attack us at night or in fog, or in the areas not covered by our air patrols. As you can see, the track keeps us as far inshore as possible and bulges slightly north of our destination to avoid westward bound convoys."

"Because the British drive on the left?" Jablonski asked.

"As good a reason as any," Meredith said. "Anyway, that's the playing field. Now let's sit down again and go over the players."

Meredith consulted some mimeographed papers he had brought back in his briefcase. "MacIntosh, now that you've taken over communications in addition to being torpedo officer, the radio call signs, the communication plan, and the other junk you need are all in here. You'll have time to set it up as we go out the channel."

He pushed some of the papers down to MacIntosh, and riffled through the rest. "We start out from here with thirty merchantmen and three escorts."

Durham interrupted. "Only three!"

Meredith looked up. "There hasn't been any trouble from submarines this close in for almost a year. Too much air patrol. Before we get off the Canadian coast on January 31, another section of the convoy will join us, bringing the number of merchantmen up to sixty-four."

"And escorts?" asked Steele.

Meredith grinned. "Now I'm coming to the good news. The second section of the convoy will be accompanied by seven British and Canadian corvettes, all experienced and built just for ASW."

Gerlach frowned. "Maybe they're built for it, and they're maneuverable and well equipped, but they have limitations. A corvette can only make seventeen knots, no faster than a surfaced U-boat."

Steele said, "They do have a new weapon, called the

hedgehog. It projects twenty-four small projectiles ahead in a wide oval pattern. They won't go off unless they hit. An explosion means a hit. Unexploded hedgehogs don't disturb the water. Of course, a ship can combine hedgehogs and depth charges, projecting the hedgehog ahead, before the submarine can maneuver, and then passing over the submarine and dropping depth charges."

"The hedgehog projectiles can't be very big," Gerlach said. "I'm for the big stuff, even if we can't throw it very far."

Renard laughed. "Just like Kendrick and his girl at the ship's party."

Meredith saw Steiner raise an eyebrow, and Renard began to study his notes carefully.

Meredith looked around with a puzzled frown but didn't question him.

Sorenson said, "Captain, please go on. We don't have much time before getting underway."

"Right," Meredith said. "We pick up another escort, a Coast Guard Cutter, off Newfoundland, and if we need them, two or three escorts off Iceland. There will also be a specially equipped rescue vessel with us. The *Toward* will do the nasty job of picking up survivors."

"She have any other jobs?" Steele asked.

"Yes, she has the capability of taking radio bearings and plotting them."

Fineman said, "You told me what you called a HUFF-DUFF was before, but I thought it was on land. What's it doing out here?"

Meredith said, "It is just a single station on the *Toward*. With only one bearing, triangulation isn't possible, so all we get is a bearing."

Jablonski said, "Don't forget that a single bearing can only give us direction. The transmitting submarine might be hundreds of miles away."

"Yes, but it will be a very accurate and prompt initial bearing," Steele said. "The strength of the signal should give some indication of range."

Sorenson said, "I just hope the escort commander doesn't run our balls off searching down single bearings."

Meredith laughed. "He won't. We've already talked."

Steele said, "Did the merchant captains have anything to say? They must be getting discouraged."

"Some of them looked really down. The odds against them are pretty bad. One of the merchant captains said, 'Why are you trying to control forty ships by whistle signals? Why don't you use radio?' "

"What did the harbormaster say?"

"He told them we can't use medium frequency radio because it has too much range, and the U-boats would hear it. He also said, 'TBS radios have limited range because they are very high frequency, but if we tried to put TBS radios on all merchantmen we would have great difficulty making them all work. Even warships have trouble with them. Whistle signals, even if we don't like them, will be more reliable than TBS.' "

Sorenson laughed. "I see his point. Ours is fairly good, but it takes a lot of Bronte's time."

Meredith said, "We would seem to have a respectable escort force, but the wolf packs will be tough to handle. The Seawolf Group will be one of the wolf packs waiting for us. If there isn't anything else, let's set the special sea detail and get out of here."

•   •   •

On the bridge, Meredith told Sorenson to get the ship underway and settled in his chair. Two other escorts backed from their berths. Along the Brooklyn waterfront, tugs nudged three merchantmen into the stream.

Meredith looked back toward Manhattan, trying to pick out the Waldorf Astoria, but the maze of tall buildings obscured it. It was a visit he would never forget, and he hoped the others felt the same way.

Meredith decided Sorenson was doing well, and turned to inspect the other escorts. The commanding officer of the large Coast Guard Cutter, a senior commander, was the escort commander, and his ship forged ahead down the channel. HMS *Beverley*, a British fourstacker that had been visiting New York, brought up the rear.

When they cleared the harbor entrance net and the channel, Meredith directed that condition III be set.

Sorenson turned the conn over to Gerlach, came over to Meredith's chair and asked, "Cup of coffee, Captain?"

"Sure," Meredith said. "Let me buy this one. You bought everything for the last three days."

"Well, not exactly. I passed all the bills on."

"Hmmm. Sure you did. Someday I'm going to find out the truth."

Sorenson laughed, but before he could reply the coffee arrived, and he took a deep swallow.

MacIntosh came out of the CIC. "I've got the convoy formation plotted. Could you both come into the CIC and have a look?"

Meredith carried his cup into CIC. They leaned over a sheet of maneuvering board plot, a circular arrangement of concentric rings representing distance from the center.

MacIntosh said, "I've put the guide, who is the convoy commodore, at the center, and the rings represent one thousand yards. The convoy formation is square, with the merchant ships in eight eight-ship columns. Only thirty stations will be filled until the second section joins. The merchant ships are six hundred yards apart, and the columns are one thousand yards apart."

Meredith whistled. "A helluva big formation."

MacIntosh pointed to two of the ships leading columns. "This is the convoy commodore's flagship, and this one has the vice commodore. The three-ship bent line screen will change when the other seven join. Then we'll have a circular screen about six thousand yards out from the center of the convoy formation."

"Will they leave some of the rear stations empty?" Sorenson asked.

"Yes," Meredith said. "The escort commander told me he may put one escort astern as a trailer hoping to prevent the Germans from approaching from the rear. He also has a position about five miles ahead if he feels the Germans will run ahead on the surface and then wait for us either submerged or surfaced."

Sorenson shook his head. "I think we'll be all right as long as we have air cover to keep the subs down, but when we don't, the nights will be long and cold like they were on the *Berry*."

"Speaking of cold," Meredith said, "I could use another cup of coffee."

"So could I," Sorenson said, "but we haven't seen cold yet. After we get closer to Newfoundland, we'll freeze. Or at least the ship will. We'll need to have sledges, chipping hammers, and scrapers broken out to chop the ice that collects on the topsides from the spray."

"You're the expert," Meredith said.

"Captain," Sorenson said, "I'd like to break out and issue the special cold weather clothing."

"Whenever you think we need it."

•   •   •

The trip was uneventful until the convoy was joined by the second section, which filled the sixty-four stations in the convoy formation and the ten stations in the screen. Another escort, the Coast Guard cutter *Bibb*, joined the escort force and was assigned to the station astern.

That night, the temperature dropped to the low 20s, and Sorenson ordered Renard to issue the L. L. Bean clothing.

The next morning Meredith came up to the bridge for dawn general quarters with his blue L. L. Bean suit on. "Nice and warm," he said. He settled back in his chair and listened to the talker's reports. Soon all reports were in, and Meredith raised his binoculars, searching the lightening horizon ahead for conning towers or periscopes. Satisfied that there was nothing unusual ahead, he lowered his glasses and looked down at the forecastle at the crew of gun one.

"Good God!" he said.

"What's the matter?" Sorenson asked.

Meredith pointed down at the forecastle. "Look at that!" He got up out of his chair and looked aft at the amidships deckhouse. "And that!"

Sorenson looked down and then aft, and began laughing. The crew wore parkas in a variety of colors, ranging from dark blue to yellow and pink. Some of the parkas were fur-trimmed, and the boots were of all colors and designs.

Meredith frowned. "For Christ's sake, it's not funny. If

we get close enough for anyone else to see us, we'll get laughed out of the formation."

Sorenson stopped laughing, but he was still smiling. "I don't think so. They'll want to know where we got them."

Just then Renard arrived on the bridge.

Meredith scowled. "Are you responsible for this?"

"Yes, sir. Aren't they great?"

Meredith groaned and held his head. "Do you know what you've done?"

"Yes, sir, I've carried out the executive officer's orders."

Meredith asked, "Where did you get the pink and yellow suits?"

"Ski resorts," Renard said. "As you can see, they're on the smaller men. They didn't like them at first, but when they saw how warm they'd be, they forgot about the problems."

"What problems?"

"They're for women. Can you see the zippers on the sides?"

Sorenson said, "And no zippers on the front?"

"Exactly. A little problem in logistics because it will be rough to take a leak. But you told me to get them at any cost. It was those or nothing."

Meredith began to smile. "I guess we'll just have to use them. If they're as warm as mine, the men on the topside will appreciate them."

Sorenson said, "If you like, we can take them off when we fuel."

"Hell, no. Let 'em laugh. This war needs a little levity. By the time we get to Londonderry, they'll be looking for us."

•   •   •

For the first two days after the rendezvous, no submarines were sighted. Before dawn on February 4, lookouts reported a sudden bright cloud of illumination above the convoy. Frantic voices chattered on the TBS. After an hour of communication, the convoy commodore reported that one of the foreign ships had accidentally set off a mortar-like device known as a "snow flake." This projector shot up a firework display, which merchant ships could use to provide illumination when they used their guns against surfaced submarines.

For several hours Meredith paced the bridge, afraid that the accident had alerted U-boats. Apparently it had, because HMS *Beverley*, on station 5 miles ahead, reported a surfaced submarine ahead of her. The convoy changed course to avoid the contact. *Beverley* reported that she was having difficulty taking it under fire because the heavy seas obscured her view of the target. The corvette HMS *Vimy* was sent to assist her and soon gained a sonar contact. Both ships made hedgehog attacks and the *Beverley* dropped depth charges.

MacIntosh had his ear close to the TBS. Many garbled transmissions could be heard faintly as the two ships dropped behind the formation. Suddenly MacIntosh straightened. "They got her! The sub has surfaced, and both ships are shooting at it!"

He bent over again, and in a few minutes straightened. "The sub has sunk, and the escorts are picking up survivors."

All went well for the rest of that day, probably because they were just on the fringe of air coverage, but that evening a radar contact ahead forced the convoy commander to make an emergency turn to starboard. The weather apparently prevented the column leader of the third from the left column from hearing the whistle signal, and the three left hand columns continued on. In the total darkness the convoy split.

Meredith stood over the PPI and muttered. The convoy commodore was alerted, but the formation was divided by a 15-mile gap. Some ships that did hear the signal straggled in the middle. The *O'Leary* was detailed to round up the stragglers. Meredith headed for the nearest radar contact.

The only means of communication that could not be seen by the enemy was by a blunder buss-shaped signal gun designed to project flashing light in a narrow beam. It had to be kept aimed at the receiving ship, a difficult task on a rolling deck. Meredith watched Alvarado signal the first ship they approached. Alvarado cursed in the dark, fighting each roll.

Finally Alvarado's assistant, looking at the ship through binoculars, said, "I think he's got it."

Meredith asked CIC where the next straggler was, and they were off again. Several sonar contacts were reported over the TBS, and depth charges rumbled over the water, but no results were reported.

Just before dawn, the last straggler was herded into place in the rebuilt formation, and the *O'Leary* went back to her station.

Meredith stretched to relieve his weariness and said to Sorenson, who had just come out of the CIC, "Tex, I don't feel so good. I'm going below to take a hot shower. Maybe that will warm me up a little." Sorenson stayed on the bridge and sent for a breakfast tray and Doctor Fineman.

Fineman arrived as Sorenson finished his toast. "What's up, Tex?"

Sorenson sipped his coffee. "I don't think the Captain feels very good. Would you look at him? Don't tell him I sent you."

Fineman nodded. "Maybe he has the cold that's going around. I've got several cases."

Fineman was back in a few minutes. "He says he began to have cold symptoms in New York, and they've been getting steadily worse. I don't like the sound of his lungs. I'll watch him closely because this could become pneumonia."

• • •

No further contacts were reported during the forenoon, and Sorenson was surprised when Meredith came back up on the bridge about noon. Sorenson looked at him closely, and noticed that Meredith was pale and shivering.

Sorenson walked over to him. "Captain, you ought to turn in. Everything's calm. We'll be getting three escorts tomorrow morning from Iceland plus an air patrol."

Meredith looked at him. "To mix a metaphor, the calmest period is just before the roof falls in. I'm going to stay here."

As the TBS crackled, Sorenson wondered if Meredith were right. A straggler from the preceding night, still 5 miles astern, reported being torpedoed, and the *O'Leary* was ordered astern to investigate. The rescue vessel also steamed back to pick up survivors.

About 2,000 yards from the floating hulk, Steele reported a contact, and Sorenson watched Meredith start an attack. He noted that Meredith's voice was weak, and his attention span seemed to be limited as they made a depth charge drop.

Steele came out on the bridge as they circled a tentative contact. "Captain, I don't think this contact is worth spending any depth charges on. It's too faint—probably just a knuckle of bubbles left over from the submarine's wake."

Sorenson said, "Let's try a brief search."

After a close in search, they were unable to regain contact, and circled as the salvage ship picked up survivors. The hulk soon sank, and the *O'Leary* escorted the *Toward* back to her station.

Soon the *Beverley* and *Vimy* came back from an unsuccessful attack on a contact south of the convoy, and the screen was once more intact. Sorenson watched Meredith struggle into his chair. For a moment he thought of sending for Doctor Fineman, but thought better of it.

·   ·   ·

Sorenson stayed on the bridge that night, but all was quiet. As scheduled that morning, the Coast Guard cutter *Ingham* and the American four-stackers *Babbitt* and *Schenk* arrived from Iceland. The additional escorts gave the screen commander enough ships to fill the extra stations ahead of the convoy and the trailing station astern. Sorenson plotted them on the surface plot and went out on the bridge to chat with Meredith, but Meredith had gone below.

Sorenson sent for Doctor Fineman. When he came up to the bridge, Sorenson said, "Doc, I don't like the way the Captain talks and looks. He even went below without telling me."

Fineman said, "I've just seen him, and he's got a classic case of pneumonia. I've put him on the sick list, and you're now in command."

"Can you try some of that new wonder drug you got in New York?"

Fineman said, "I already have. There are several types of pneumonia, and we'll just have to hope this is one of the varieties Penicillin will work on. The best way to administer it is by a shot in the fanny. The Captain was unhappy when I told him what I was going to do. He doesn't like shots, and he yelped when the needle went in."

Sorenson laughed. "Aren't you exaggerating some?"

"Well, a little. The needle is pretty big, and the stuff stings."

"How long will it take to work?"

"I don't really know. If he survives, you can bet that he will be too weak to come up here until we're in Londonderry."

"If he survives?"

"Yes, pneumonia is serious business."

"Thanks, Doc, I'm not looking forward to running this show alone, but it's what I've wanted, so I'll do the best I can."

Fineman said, "Ah . . . I'm sure you'll do very well."

"Absolutely sure?"

"Ah . . ." Fineman looked at the deck.

"You're not a very good liar, Doc."

"Frankly I'd feel better if you'd spent more time studying and less time watching aircraft fly by."

"So would I."

•   •   •

By mid-morning, air cover from Iceland was overhead, but their protection ended at nightfall. The wind had picked up in the afternoon, and the *O'Leary* pounded through 10-foot swells. After sunset, radio intercepts ahead became frequent. The escort directly ahead of the convoy was sent out to investigate one of them. *O'Leary* was ordered ahead to take her place in the screen.

Almost immediately, *Toward* reported a radio direction finder bearing just off the starboard bow, and the *O'Leary* was designated to investigate. Sorenson ordered the crew to general quarters and increased speed to 20 knots. They cork-screwed across the growing seas. Five miles out, the O'Leary slowed to maximum sonar speed and began to search. Sonar detected nothing, but ten minutes later radar reported a small contact ahead.

Sorenson turned to the talker, "Tell gun control to train all guns that can bear forward. Alert all lookouts. Radar has a small contact dead ahead."

Alongside Sorenson on the bridge wing, Alvarado swung his telescope through a small arc ahead, one eye tight against the eyepiece, and the other closed. Suddenly the telescope froze, and Alvarado tensed "Submarine conning tower dead ahead! Submerging!"

Gun control reported the director couldn't find it among the dark swells. Steiner's curses rained down from the fire control platform. Alvarado banged his fist on the bulwark railing after the U-boat submerged. "Damned Krauts!"

Five minutes later, sonar reported, "Sonar contact, possible submarine. Range one oh double oh."

Sorenson turned to port to keep from closing the range too fast and to allow the sonarmen to develop the contact. Then sonar reported, "Contact stronger. Definite submarine. Up doppler."

Sorenson headed for the contact. "Standby for depth charge attack. Shallow pattern," he told the talker.

The range wound down, and the sonar pulsed faster as the operator shortened the scale. Then Steele said, "Submarine turning away. Speed five knots."

Sorenson changed the lead angle slightly.

Steele reported, "Lost contact due to short range. Recommend drop on time."

Sorenson could not see the stopwatch in the darkness, but counted the seconds under his breath. When he figured they had reached the proper drop point, he ordered, "Drop depth charges."

Sorenson opened the range and turned to starboard to clear the sonar projector from the ship's baffles astern which prevented the ship's propeller noises from drowning out the sonar return. Sorenson ordered sonar to begin a standard search from the baffles forward.

The O'Leary took a heavy roll as Steele reported, "Regained contact. Five hundred yards. Up doppler. Recommend open range."

Sorenson opened the range again and turned to make another attack. He knew that the submarine had probably gone deep. If this pattern did not get him, the U-boat might get below a thermal layer. "Use deep pattern," he said to the talker.

The attack went off as planned, but Steele was unable to regain contact. He lurched out to the bridge, fighting the heavy swells. "Mister Sorenson, I think we've lost him, and he's way down deep. Terrill concurs. I recommend that we regain station."

Sorenson looked at the surface search PPI and located the convoy, which had made an emergency turn to port. He said to MacIntosh, "Take the conn and rejoin. Try twenty knots for a few minutes. If you need any help ask Jablonski."

MacIntosh took the conn and gave the orders for course and speed. The *O'Leary* rounded up on a course toward the convoy and almost immediately began to pound badly as her bow rose over the long rollers. Solid water broke over the forecastle, rattling the anchors in their housings. The forecastle had been deserted by the crew of gun one before they made the turn. Spray smacked against the bridge ports, and spume sprayed back over the open bridge wings.

"Slow to fifteen knots," Sorenson ordered.

The pounding eased, and Sorenson leaned against the Captain's chair to ease the weariness in his feet. MacIntosh made small course changes to bring the *O'Leary* back to station ahead of the convoy. Sorenson noted that he was learning fast and should qualify to be left alone soon.

Just as the *O'Leary* eased into position, a lookout reported a large explosion astern of the convoy. Sorenson and MacIntosh went out on the port wing to look at it. Just as Sorenson raised his binoculars, a blinding flash filled the sky.

"Jesus!" said Sorenson. "That was brighter than any lightning I've ever seen."

"Must've been an ammo ship," MacIntosh said.

Then the rumbling concussion of the explosion reached them, strong enough to squeeze the air out of Sorenson's chest.

"There won't be any survivors from that," Sorenson said.

"May be better than freezing to death."

"Radar contact between us and the convoy!" a voice reported over the squawk box. "Bearing two nine zero. Range three oh double oh."

Sorenson's stomach dropped, and he ran for the PPI.

"The U-boat went right through the hole in the screen left by the corvette that was sent out to investigate," he said to MacIntosh.

The TBS came alive, and the escort commander designated the *O'Leary* to close the contact and attack.

"Let's go!" Sorenson said. "I have the conn. Left full rudder. Turns for seventeen knots. Talker, tell the gun nery officer to have the crew of gun one man their gun but stay behind the shield."

The door below banged open, and feet thudded as the crew of gun one ran forward. Sorenson watched the bow carefully as they turned. Although there was some solid water coming over the anchors, it was not dangerous. They were plunging back toward the convoy at a closing speed of 30 knots. Sixty steel bows were pointed their way, and Sorenson remembered the look of the huge steel bow that had crushed the *Berry*. He swallowed and turned his attention to the radar contact. On the PPI he watched it pass between two columns of the convoy. As it passed the second ship, a dull red flash lit the *O'Leary*'s bridge. Sorenson looked up from the PPI and spotted a U-boat conning tower in the glow of the burning ship.

"Damn!" Sorenson said. "We're too late. Gun control, commence firing when ready, but watch out for merchantmen behind the target."

Sorenson could hear Steiner giving his orders to the gun battery, and in a few seconds the salvo buzzer rang just before guns one and two fired. The projectile from gun two passed close to the bridge wing, and Sorenson moved to the other wing, his ears ringing from the gun blast. He raised his binoculars again. As the second salvo went out, he shouted, "The bastard is submerging! Cease firing!"

The *O'Leary* turned quickly, heeling deeply to port, and passed between two of the column leaders. She passed close to the burning merchantman. Ships astern of the glowing ship were shearing out to pass the blazing ship, and Sorenson had to thread carefully between the oncoming bows. Then the flames began to die out and darkness closed in. Sorenson tried to fix the positions of the nearby merchantmen in his mind.

Sonar reported, "Sonar contact bearing two six one. Possible submarine."

Sorenson headed for it, but before he could steady on course, sonar reported, "Contact is a wake knuckle from a merchantman. Resuming search."

Sorenson ordered a return to a course that would take the ship through the convoy, but finding a clear course was difficult. Merchant ships of both columns were out of position.

Sorenson walked inside and looked at the PPI. "Damn!" he said. "The PPI looks like an anthill."

Sonar came to life. "Sonar contact bearing two four zero. Definite submarine." Steele's voice added, "This is a good one."

Sorenson headed for it and concentrated not only on the attack, but on avoiding the ships plodding past them. But he kept remembering how much damage the U-boats had already done to the convoy. He knew something had to be done to turn the awful tide, and he wanted to kill every U-boat possible. He focused his attention on the attack on the submarine.

Just as they were about to drop depth charges, Alvarado yelled, "Look out! A ship is headed right for us!"

In the fraction of a second before he looked up, Sorenson realized the hate he had for the U-boats had focused too much on the target. He looked up and saw the ship reported by Alvarado. The huge hull loomed high above the bridge, like some mindless black monster, and it seemed inevitable that it would crush them.

Sorenson gasped and shouted, "Left full rudder! All back emergency!"

The quartermaster at the helm, who had relieved Alvarado, spun the wheel, and the lee helmsman mashed the annunciator handles aft. In seconds the *O'Leary* began to shudder as the engineers in main control spun the ahead throttles closed and opened the astern throttles to the maximum. Sorenson gripped the PPI, waiting for the crash. The loom of the dark hull bearing down on them still seemed to make the collision inevitable, but the huge side slipped by within yards, the massive single propeller thrashing as the ends of its blades came out of the water whenever the ship pitched over a high roller.

Sorenson watched it go, transfixed by the near disaster. He shook himself. "All engines ahead standard. Rudder amidships."

He turned to Alvarado and said in a subdued voice, "Well done."

It was five minutes before Sorenson could breathe normally. While he listened to his heart beat slowing, he silently vowed never to allow his responsibility for the safety of the ship to be diverted again.

From the CIC, over the squawk box, Bronte said, "Sir, I can give you the first leg of a short search plan. It's two seven six."

Sorenson sighed and said to MacIntosh, "I'm staying out on the wing from now on. Acknowledge the recommendation and tell Bronte we're coming to his course, but it had better be clear of ships or I'm going to pour cold coffee down the voice tube all over his radar console."

MacIntosh laughed, but there was a quaver in his voice. "Aye, aye, sir."

On the second leg, they held a contact briefly, but there were many wakes present, making identification difficult. Steele said, "This is like looking for a mouse in a maze. Every time we get a good ping, he finds another corner of a wake and we lose him."

An explosion rocked the night. The CIC reported that it was the *Toward*. Sorenson cursed. The rescue ship had been invaluable, relieving the escorts of the time-consuming job of picking up and caring for survivors. Now the escorts would have to do the job. He thought about the survivors the *Toward* had picked up. Now they were being fished out of the frigid water for a second time—if they were lucky. He knew the U-boat had no way of knowing it was sinking a rescue ship, but he hated the Germans anyway. It was a tough and cruel way to fight a war, and he knew it would get worse.

The *O'Leary* was astern of the convoy, but not near any torpedoed ships. The escort commander assigned her to the trailing station.

The next morning, a muster of ships indicated that seven of them had been lost during the night, with only one submarine accounted for by the *Beverley* and the *Vimy*.

Sorenson remembered the pre-departure conversation about ship losses. The abstract statistics had become real ships full of valuable cargo needed urgently by the Allies and flesh and blood people—like the seamen they had picked up a few weeks before. Sorenson shuddered. How could they hope to win a war with losses like this?

At daylight, aircraft from Ireland reached them, and the submarines, probably aware of this hazard, did not appear. For the old four-stackers, the trouble was fuel. All of the corvettes and the Coast Guard Cutters carried enough fuel to make Londonderry, but for the four-stackers, fuel supply was marginal.

The *O'Leary* had been fitted with a large fuel tank in place of her fourth boiler, but the British four-stacker coming from New York still had the fourth boiler. If the wind continued from the east, even the *O'Leary* could not make it.

That morning, the weather moderated enough to try fueling from a tanker in the convoy. It was necessary to stop zigzagging for the two hours it would take to give the four-stackers enough fuel to make port.

Sorenson sighed deeply as the escort commander assigned the *O'Leary* to fuel last. He was relieved to know they would now try to fuel, but concerned over whether he could conn the ship alongside successfully in such weather.

The *O'Leary* took standby station astern of the tanker, and Sorenson braced himself against the bridge bulwark, watching the *Beverley* roll and pitch alongside the tanker. Once the destroyer came perilously close to the tanker's side and sheered out so radically that one of the fuel lines parted.

While the fuel line was being replaced, Fineman came up to the bridge. He watched the ship ahead for a few minutes and then shuddered. "The Captain is lucky to be out of this," he said.

"How's he feeling?" Sorenson asked.

"Not good, but I think the crisis is about here. Let's just hope the Penicillin will work. If it does, medicine has discovered a new miracle. He'd be in serious trouble without it. He doesn't even yell when I give him his shot."

"If he does pass the crisis, how long will he be on the sick list?"

"For about two weeks. He'll be very weak for that period."

The *Beverley* finished fueling and pulled away, spray flying as high as her bridge as she passed out of the lee of the tanker's hull. Down on the forecastle, Chief Bellows and his crew swung axes to bash the ice on the forecastle deck to give them traction.

Sorenson shook his head and said to Fineman, "Look at that. If the weather doesn't get warmer, we'll have that stuff coating the bridge."

"Won't that make us top heavy?"

"It sure will. If we can't fuel, we'll have to ballast with sea water, and that will increase our fuel consumption."

"Then we've just got to fuel?"

"You've got it."

"Good luck. I don't swim so well."

The tanker hoisted a signal flag indicating they were ready for the *O'Leary*. Sorenson took a deep breath and began the approach carefully, watching the swings of the tanker's head as she tried to maintain a steady course in the large seas coming from slightly on her starboard bow.

Then the *O'Leary* entered the lee formed by her large, deep hull, and the wind and seas calmed slightly. Still the waves appeared to be mountainous from the destroyer's low bridge, and the crew on the forecastle clung to the forward gun as water swept over their feet.

Waves bounced between the tanker and the hull of the *O'Leary*, throwing heavy spray high above the bridge.

Sorenson gripped the gyro repeater pelorus, which showed him the course they were steering. It was located far out on the wing of the bridge, and his position behind it gave him a good view of both the tanker and the *O'Leary*'s forecastle. Alvarado was steering, the wheel spokes flashing as he labored to keep the ship on course. The tanker was making 8 knots, and Sorenson slowed to 10 knots for a gentle approach. The *O'Leary* crept alongside the tanker and steadied about 120 feet abeam.

The crew of the tanker, on a relatively dry deck, fired line-throwing guns. Small steel projectiles arced through the spray, carrying light lines which fell across the *O'Leary* forward and aft. The *O'Leary* men scrambled carefully across the icy decks and hauled them in and then the following larger lines. Progress was slow because of cold hands and treacherous footing. Once Sorenson failed to give a course change soon enough, and the *O'Leary* veered out so far that he thought the lines would part. Alvarado was able to steady up quickly, and they moved back in to the proper distance. Then the big rubber fueling hoses were sent over and secured to the tops of the fuel trunks.

Chief Bellows shouted up to the bridge, "Ready for fueling!"

In a few minutes pumping started, and the hoses began pulsing with the pressure generated by the tanker's fuel pumps.

Concentrating hard on keeping in proper position, Sorenson was surprised when the talker reported that they had completed fueling and were about to reclaim the hoses.

When the last hose splashed into the water, Sorenson clenched his hands to stop them from shaking and let out his breath. As the last line snaked out, he changed course slightly to the left and increased speed to 10 knots. After the deckhands cleared the forecastle area, he increased speed to 12 knots. Even at this slow speed, mountainous waves smashed across the forecastle as soon as they left the lee of the tanker. He had learned his lesson from watching the ship that had fueled just before them.

Fineman came up and stood beside him, watching the waves ahead. "Good job," he said. "The Captain sends his congratulations."

Sorenson looked surprised. "Is he any better?"

"Yes. The crisis has passed. He should make it."

"He's awake?"

"Yes. We sat and talked about the old times out in the Asiatic Fleet. He never even twitched when he heard the waves banging into the bow."

"I'll be damned!"

"No, not damned. You were complimented. The old man said you would make an outstanding destroyer man if you'd forget about flying."

Sorenson said nothing, thinking it might be nice to have his own command someday.

Fineman said, "By the way, here's a prescription for you. I know you won't use it until the rest of the crew topside has theirs. You've earned it."

He handed Sorenson two small bottles of medicinal brandy. Sorenson looked at them, but did not immediately take them. Then he took them and said, "I'll give them to Alvarado. One for today's fine job, and the other for his work the other night."

Alvarado, busy turning over the helm to the regular watchstander, smiled in anticipation.

As Sorenson turned the ship slowly to head for their screening station, he made a mental note to tell Renard to find better winter gloves for the topside crew when they got back to Norfolk. Norfolk! Oh, so far away, and so nice to go home to. He could picture Ferren in her apartment, and he groaned. In spite of the weather, sexual arousal surged. Even the cold salt water dripping down the inside of his parka and trousers couldn't dampen it as he thought about Ferren lying on the beach. When would she bury her ghosts so they could get on with living . . . and loving?

• • •

The next three days were calm and peaceful as the weather, under the influence of the tail end of the Gulf Stream passing Ireland's west coast, warmed the water and melted the ice from the superstructure. Air patrols from Northern Ireland apparently discouraged German submarines, and there were no contacts.

Early on the morning of February 11, they sighted the coast of Northern Ireland.

Chapter Twenty-four

The convoy made steady progress toward Londonderry, and about noon a group of British escorts stood out and relieved them. The *O'Leary* and the other escorts steamed independently toward Londonderry.

Shortly after they were moored, an American naval officer trotted up the brow. He saluted Sorenson. "I'm Lieutenant Brodie, your liaison officer. You'll see a lot of me."

Sorenson escorted him to the wardroom and called a conference of all officers. As soon as they were seated, Sorenson called in Morales and asked Brodie if he would like coffee.

Brodie looked hungrily at the coffee pot on the side board. "Would I ever! All the Brits have is tea, and I think some of that is hedge clippings."

"Have as much coffee as you like. Would you like a pound or two to take with you?"

"That would be wonderful. I only get coffee here when American ships visit."

"How long will we be here?"

"You sail at dawn day after tomorrow. That will give you a chance to let your crew go ashore in two groups. Unfortunately, curfew in town is at 2200. The pubs close then, so any more time ashore usually ends in trouble, both for the sailors and the townsmen."

Steele asked, "Can we have some time on your ASW trainer?"

"Certainly. You can have it this afternoon and also all day tomorrow. The other American ships in your group will have to share it with you."

Steele looked disappointed.

Brodie said, "Don't look so glum. That will be all the time you'll want. Originally, it was used to train ships in elementary tactics, but we also use it now to teach coordinated attacks using two ships. Your operators can listen to the latest recordings of sonars operating against German Submarines, particularly their new trick, the Pillenwerfer."

"What's a Pillenwerfer?" Sorenson asked.

Brodie said, "A cannister of chemicals released from German submarines just after an attack. The chemicals released from the cannister form a cloud of bubbles, which simulate a submarine."

Steele said, "I think we've already encountered a few. The contact is very mushy, compared with a steel hull, and it doesn't move."

Brodie grinned. "You've got it, but it will help to refresh your operators."

Sorenson asked, "Can you fuel us at the pier?"

"Certainly. There's a fuel barge on the way now. I'm sorry that we can't give you anything in the way of fresh provisions. The situation here is very tight. You probably eat better than we do."

Sorenson leaned forward and looked down toward Renard. "Renard, see if you can spare something from your fresh stores for Lieutenant Brodie."

Renard looked up. "I think so, Mister Sorenson. I found some unauthorized ... er ... liquid provisions in the refrigerator just before we left, and I sent them ashore and replaced them with some oranges. Would they do?"

"Wonderful," Brodie said. "We haven't seen an orange in our mess for months."

•   •   •

Sorenson started liberty immediately, except for the sonarmen and radarmen; liberty for them was coordinated by Steele. The duty section fueled and repaired minor damage caused by the heavy seas.

Sorenson went to Meredith's cabin to visit him. He

knocked at Meredith's door and entered. Meredith was sitting up in his bunk, reading.

When he saw Sorenson, his mustache elevated at least ten degrees. "Am I glad to see you! It gets lonely here."

Sorenson sat down and looked at Meredith carefully. "You look a lot better."

"I feel better, but I'm damned weak. I don't get much rest in this bunk when the ship is rolling. It takes all of my energy just to keep from falling out of the damned thing."

Sorenson looked at the forward and after bulkheads of the cabin, got up, and paced the distance between them. "Let me turn the problem over to Chief Bellows. I think he can rig a hammock for you. There's plenty of room for one to swing. If he can find one ashore, our shipfitters can weld hooks to the bulkheads. Normally hooks would be put up in the overhead, but that would make the hammock too high and too hard for you to get in and out. Of course the welding will scar your bulkheads."

"I don't care about how it looks. I think it would work fine. I've often thought about using a hammock in a destroyer, but most skippers I've talked to think it's important to be able to feel the ship in case the weather changes. Enough of this. Get yourself ashore for a little recreation and a change of scene. Drink a couple of beers for me."

Sorenson was too tired to go ashore the first night. The next day, after he heard that Chief Bellows had found a hammock ashore and installed it, Sorenson decided to go ashore. As he left the ship, Chief Bellows was crossing the quarterdeck. Sorenson stopped him. "Well done, Chief. How did the Captain like the hammock?"

Bellows beamed, his leathery face one big smile. "He like it. He say he sleep in it tonight to try out."

Sorenson took Chuck Steiner ashore with him, and they headed for the officers' club at the American naval base. After a wetting-down beer, Sorenson asked, "How'd you like to try an Irish pub? I can't see coming to Ireland and staying in an American club."

"Sure," Steiner said. "Let's go."

They left the club and went to the pub nearest to the base gate, the Mossy Cat.

Steiner looked up at the swinging sign. "Do you think that's spelled right? It must be the messy cat."

"Don't think so. It rains a lot here. Probably even the cats grow moss."

They sat down at a table and ordered a beer.

"What kind, sir?" asked the middle-aged waitress.

"What kind do you have?" Steiner asked.

She rattled off a dozen names.

Steiner interrupted her. "Just bring us an Irish draft beer."

"They's all Irish drafts, sir," she said patiently.

Sorenson laughed. "Just bring us the kind you like best."

"Don't drink nothin' but tea."

Sorenson said, "Bring us two of the first brand you named."

The beer was warm, but good. They had a couple more, and decided to take a walk through the town before it got dark. The town was interesting, but depressing. The stone houses were worn, and the successive wars and invasions had obviously taken a heavy toll.

Steiner said, "Looks awfully old."

"It is. Doc Fineman says it goes back to the sixth century. They've been fighting over this place for centuries."

"No wonder it looks old," Steiner said. "It looks the way I feel every time we get tangled up with those U-boats."

●   ●   ●

In a pub a little farther from the gate than the Mossy Cat, Alvarado, Carmody, Kendrick, Bronte, and some friends sat around a circular table.

Bronte looked around at the other tables. "Alvarado, you're in clover. There are a lot of people with dark hair in here."

Carmody shook his head. "Only their hair is dark. They've got blue eyes."

One of their friends, obviously from the south, said, "Well, Bronte, you're a smart guy, tell me why this so-called beer tastes like the water my old granddaddy used to wash the mash barrels out with."

"You aren't drinking beer. I ordered ale for you."

"Well, tell them to take the damned stuff away, and order me a real beer."

"There aren't any real beers over here. No Budweisers. You'll just have to try them all until you find one you like, and they'll all be warm."

"I can buy that. Start me out."

•   •   •

At the ASW trainer, Steele had a hard time keeping his sonarmen and radarmen working. They kept asking if it was time for liberty.

Finally Steele sent half of them off on liberty and promised the remaining half an early start the next day. That seemed to get the attention of those remaining, and they crowded around the instructor. He started with a review of German submarine capabilities and equipment. Obviously the British had many intelligence sources and knew much about the improvements that were being worked on in Germany.

The instructor said, "We've been doing very well with our HUFF-DUFF, but the Huns will catch on to what we're doing and soon they should begin to use a new transmitter they're working on. It's called a squirt system. They pre-record a signal transmission and then speed up the transmission so it lasts less than a second. That way a listener will probably miss it."

Steele said, "How about recording the transmission and then slowing it down?"

"Bingo!" said the instructor, "That's what our boffins are working on, but it isn't bloody simple. This will slow down the system, and we won't have time to determine the direction as accurately."

"Now let's turn to other improvements the Jerries are making. They know what our aircraft ranges are, and they have been staying just beyond them. We, on the other hand, are extending our ranges by using drop tanks and larger internal gas tanks. The ultimate will be when you Yanks send your hunter-killer groups to sea."

Steele asked, "You mean escort carriers with aircraft modified for ASW work?"

"Bingo, again. How'd you like to join our staff?"

"No thanks, I admire your work here, but I'm happy where I am. What does your intelligence know about the Seawolf class of U-boat?"

"They know some are being built, but most will be supply submarines or minelayers. The first attack version is due to be completed soon."

Steele shook his head. "I hate to think about fighting one of those big U-boats. The smaller ones in the wolf packs were bad enough. A Seawolf will be tough."

"That's the bloody truth."

"With other ships and aircraft we'd be all right," Steele said. "If we end up alone, the Seawolf will be bigger and as heavily armed as we are."

"Quite right. Should want some of your other blokes around, if I were you."

Then the instructor got down to the main business at hand, putting each of the *O'Leary*'s sonar operators on a sonar trainer equipped to simulate the diverse sounds a sonar would pick up. Whales, Pillenwerfers, break-up sounds of sinking submarines, propeller noises, and others were presented to the operators, who were required to make rapid identification. Then operators were tested for their ability to recognize doppler changes and to see how faint a contact they could recognize.

Steele noted that Terrill did very well, even though he didn't test perfectly on the pitch-change discrimination test. He watched Terrill's lanky form hunched in the seat in front of the sonar. Steele realized how much of the ship's success depended upon him. The other operators were learning fast, but Terrill was better. Terrill didn't have the best natural talent, but he had the intelligence to use what he had. His earnest, plain face was reflected in the glass covering the range scale, as his gray eyes concentrated on the controls.

After the individual training, they were taken to the advanced trainer, for which the center was famous. Here, two or three ship's ASW attack teams were put in rooms simulating their combat information centers. In a central plotting room, a problem was run on a gigantic plotter, on which were displayed one or more submarines and up to three escorts. The movements and sounds of the submarines were transmitted to each team.

Each ship's team was able to track the submarines and to conduct liaison with the other teams. An overall commander of the surface attack unit was designated, and he could order one of the ships to attack while the others were designated to contain the submarine by circling. Then, when the submarine was supposedly reeling from one attack, the commander could order a second ship to attack immediately. The desired result was a bewildered and harried U-Boat, and eventually a kill.

The trainer session exhilarated Steele, and only the weariness of his crew persuaded him to call a halt and declare liberty.

•   •   •

Two mornings later, Lieutenant Brodie ambled into the wardroom with a sheaf of papers in his hand. Sorenson invited him for breakfast. When the mess attendant listed the menu and asked him to order, Brodie's eyes widened.

"Can I have one of each?" he asked.

Sorenson laughed. "Of course, but between bites describe our next mission."

Brodie handed him the papers. "You can read these while I eat."

Sorenson sorted them out and passed some of them down the table. Then he said, "Gentlemen, from this summary on top of the pile, I see that we're to get under way by ourselves as soon as possible and join a westbound convoy designated ON-166 a day or so west of here."

"Right," Brodie mumbled between bites.

Sorenson laughed and went on. "Then we continue to east coast ports. Ours will be Norfolk."

Lieutenant Brodie paused again from his enormous breakfast. "You'll have about forty merchantmen and an international escort. Captain Heineman, an American, will be in command of the escort, which will have one Polish destroyer, two British corvettes, four Canadian corvettes, Two Coast Guard cutters, and you. The communication call signs, frequencies to guard, and the formations are in that mass of papers just below the strawberry jam, and would someone please pass me the sugar for my coffee."

Sorenson passed the sugar. "What will the Germans have against us?"

Brodie put down his coffee cup and paused for a few seconds before answering. Then he said slowly, "A hell of a lot. They're slaughtering the British convoys, and ours aren't doing much better. We can't tell you exactly how many submarines are there, or just where they are. It'll be rough, and I wish you luck."

Steele asked, "What happened to the intelligence information we were getting?"

"If you mean the decoded intercepts, the Germans change their codes now and then, and we're in a hiatus while the British experts break the latest code."

Sorenson shook his head. "Damn! When do we leave?"

"As soon as I finish these pancakes. By the way, the weather is reported as stinking out there. That might help you a little."

Sorenson said, "In that case, we'd better get going. Please finish your breakfast. The rest of you can make preparations to get under way. Unless it's mandatory, I don't think we need a pilot."

Brodie smiled. "I'm your pilot. If you don't mind, I'll stay here for another helping until you're ready."

• • •

On the bridge, Steele supervised the last of the preparations for getting underway while giving Sorenson a running commentary on the exercises at the ASW center.

"Sounds like you did all right," Sorenson said.

Steele laughed. "The first day most of my men just wanted to leave on liberty, but they liked it so much they were at the door when it opened the second day."

"I expect you'll use all that stuff," Sorenson said. "If the intelligence summary is right, there are at least three wolf packs operating along our track. One of them is the Seawolf group, and if what Brodie said is right, there may be more intelligence doesn't know about."

"Yes, but the air coverage from here will be good out

to over a thousand miles, now that more long range aircraft are available."

"But only in daytime," Sorenson reminded him.

"The British say that surface search radar for aircraft is on the way."

"We may not last that long."

Brodie managed to get them out safely in spite of a bulging stomach and having to give orders between belches. After a small boat retrieved Brodie, the *O'Leary* set course for the assigned rendezvous. Initially Sorenson directed that they steam at 20 knots, but by nightfall the weather had worsened as predicted, and they were forced to slow to 15. Sorenson hoped it wasn't a bad omen.

Chapter Twenty-five

The next morning Sorenson and MacIntosh bent over the DRT table in CIC. Fineman peered over their shoulders. A large maneuvering board chart was taped to the glass top of the DRT.

Sorenson rubbed the thin scar on his face. "We didn't get much dope from the boys in Londonderry about the convoy, nor in these orders they gave us."

"No," MacIntosh said. "We know they'll use a square convoy formation. I've plotted one on the chart. We're supposed to have forty-two merchant ships. There'll be nine columns of five ships, with the last station in three of the columns vacant. Lieutenant Brodie told me the escort commander usually uses a circular screen on the 6,000-yard circle."

Sorenson finished a cup of coffee Bronte had fixed for him. "I think that's all we can do here. I see you've put all the information you have on the status boards."

"We're ready," MacIntosh said.

Sorenson looked at him and grinned. "I see your mustache is much thicker."

MacIntosh laughed. "I'm not trying to emulate the Captain. It's just too hard to shave closely in this weather."

Sorenson noticed that Fineman had been watching MacIntosh as he moved about the CIC. When MacIntosh left, Fineman said quietly to Sorenson, "He's developing a lot of self-confidence, and he seems to know what he's doing."

"He's learned a lot. He's qualified to take the deck by himself now. Let's go out and see if we can find our convoy."

On the open bridge wing Sorenson spotted Alvarado above on the fire control platform with his telescope. Sorenson laughed. "Doc, look at Alvarado. He doesn't believe science is here to stay. He thinks he can see the convoy before the surface search radar picks it up."

"Can he?"

"Sure. He'll see the smoke. Radar can't."

Ten minutes later, Alvarado shouted, "Smoke bearing three four zero!"

Sorenson put down his coffee cup. "See, I told you so."

Fineman said, "Mind over matter."

Sorenson frowned. "The only trouble is that the damned U-boats can see the smoke, too."

Soon the radar picked up the masts of the merchantmen and a short time later the masts of the nearer escorts.

The escort commander assigned them to the last station on the port side of the circular screen. As MacIntosh had predicted, they were on circle six, and the convoy formation was in nine columns. From CIC, Bronte reported that there were three vacant stations in the ends of three columns. Another message gave them the call signs of the other escorts and their assigned stations.

The Coast Guard cutter *Spencer*, with the escort commander, was at the head of the circle in station one. Sorenson knew from the information furnished in Londonderry that she was equipped with a high frequency radio direction finder.

On the right half of the defensive circle were the Canadian corvettes *Chilliwack*, *Rosthern*, *Trillium*, and *Dauphin*. On the left were the Coast Guard cutter *Campbell*, the British Corvette *Dianthus*, the Polish destroyer *Burza*, and then the *O'Leary*.

Sorenson plotted a course to their station, and in a

few minutes they rounded up in station, took convoy course and speed, and commenced zigzagging.

•   •   •

Later that day, Sorenson noted that the swells were increasing in height and length. The wind picked up to 35 knots and began to blow the tops off the waves. When Sorenson ventured on the open wings to take a bearing, the cold spray stung his face. Sorenson returned to the warmth of the pilothouse blowing on the bare fingers he had used to operate the pelorus.

The convoy slowed to 8 knots, and finally to 4 knots. The merchantmen wallowed, and the escorts rolled and pounded as their bows thrust into the mountainous rollers. The larger waves buried the O'Leary's forecastle up to the forward gun.

The O'Leary plunged for the bottom of each trough, and then rose sharply as the oncoming wave lifted the bow. Sorenson knew that the crew was experiencing the same sinking sensation they would have felt in a high-speed elevator beginning its drop. Sorenson went below and walked through the forward crews' compartment, threading his way between the triple-tiered bunks. Many men were seasick, and the crowded space reeked of stale clothes, old food, and vomit. Sorenson made a mental note to air bedding and scrub mattress covers and pillow covers on the first day in port.

Sorenson went to the wardroom to get something to eat, knowing that even the nimble-footed Morales couldn't negotiate the trip up to the bridge with a tray. The wardroom was deserted, and the chairs were lashed to the stanchions. A large cardboard box was lashed to the table. Sorenson waited for a steady moment, and then walked over to the table and wrapped his arm around a stanchion.

Then he laughed. In the box were the remains of two dozen sandwiches. The ones on the bottom were more or less intact, but those on top had come apart, and pieces of bread, baloney, and cheese tumbled back and forth with each roll and splatted against the sides of the box. Sorenson reached in and snared the makings of a sandwich. He held on to the stanchion with one hand and deftly assembled the parts into a sandwich with the other. Just like a cowhand rolling a cigarette on a horse, he thought.

As he ate, he thought about his future. Did he really want to subject himself to the hardships at sea on a small ship in return for the satisfaction of having a command? Life on a carrier would be much more comfortable. And what about after the war? He could have a satisfying life with Ferren on his ranch and not have to ride anything more uncomfortable than a horse. Then there was civilian aviation. After the war it would undoubtedly expand enormously and would accomplish tasks not even thought of now. That would be tempting. Staying in the Navy would be a hard choice, but he felt better about it as nourishment from the sandwich seeped through his blood stream. By the time he finished a second sandwich, his doubts had diminished. He stuffed a third sandwich in his pocket in case he couldn't come back down below again.

•   •   •

The northwesterly gale kept up through the night, and the swells increased. By dawn, two ships had straggled, but they soon caught up, harried by the escorts.

On the bridge, listening to the TBS, Sorenson was amused by the variety of accents that flavored the English language: New York, New Jersey, Boston, several southern varieties, upper-class English, cockney, Australian, and Scottish burr. The Polish destroyer fascinated Sorenson. One of the TBS radio operators had an upper-class English accent, but he seldom stood watch. The other Polish TBS radio operators acknowledged each order with a sibilant "Yesss, roger." An order to leave formation and investigate a contact brought a "Ve go, roger," a large puff of smoke, and a smashing wave across the bow as they invariably put on full speed. When this first happened, Sorenson watched them in disbelief.

"They won't last a week in these waters at that rate," he said to Alvarado.

Sorenson looked around the screen at the various escorts. In contrast to the slim destroyers, the squat corvettes were slow but more maneuverable. Unlike the *O'Leary*'s closed pilothouse, the corvettes had British-style open bridges. Sorenson shuddered as he watched their bridge crews, muffled in oilskins, huddle behind the glass windshields as spray cascaded over them.

The O'Leary was unique, unlike even her former sister ships, the British four-stackers. She had speed and dash and a low, slim silhouette, but she did poorly in heavy seas. Where the Corvettes seemed to bob over the swells, the O'Leary sliced through them, and the tops of the swells rolled back and smashed against her forward structure, threatening to sweep it off the main deck.

Doctor Fineman came up to the bridge. "Jesus, Tex, what's going on up here? I thought that last wave was going to take the Captain and his cabin and me right off the ship."

"What did the Captain do when we took that last big one?"

"Nothing. He just laughed and said for me not to worry, and that you knew what you were doing. I did notice that he had his life jacket close by, though."

"Everybody should. Where's yours?"

"Ah, I guess I left it in the Captain's cabin."

"Treat it like a second skin. It may save your life. You never know when a big one will sweep you overboard, or a torpedo will blow us in two."

Fineman shuddered. "Do you think you could save me if I fell overboard?"

"Sure, but I'd only have about five minutes to do it. That's all you'd be good for in this cold water. An L. L. Bean suit, if you had it on, might give you another two minutes. But a life jacket would hold you up even if you were unconscious, and that would be enough to give you about two more minutes."

•   •   •

The next morning the seas moderated, but the wind still gusted past 30 knots. The escort commander decided to fuel, and he started with the bigger cutters, followed by the Polish destroyer. The convoy had to head northwest into the wind and lost some forward distance, but fueling was absolutely necessary. With the rough weather the escorts had burned a lot of extra fuel bucking the seas. Most of the escorts now could not make port without at least one fueling.

Sorenson watched the *Spencer* alongside the tanker disappearing in the troughs of some of the bigger swells. Spray showered above the top of the tanker's decks as swells sluiced between the ships.

Later another escort rolled against the tanker but reported no serious damage. The tanker and the escorts kept large cane fenders rigged over their sides. If the impact was just right, these fenders would cushion the jolt and prevent major damage, but this was largely a matter of luck.

Just before the *O'Leary's* turn, Sorenson pulled a baloney sandwich out of his parka pocket and munched it. It was the tenth sandwich he had eaten in three days and the only food he had eaten. He felt a surge of energy as the food entered his bloodstream. He wondered again if he wanted to spend his life this way, facing daily danger and frustration. Then he stopped thinking, took a deep breath, and concentrated on the task ahead.

Sorenson started a slow approach that would allow him to gauge the movement of the tanker ahead. He stepped out on the wing for the final approach. Icy spray spinning over the forward bulwark worked its way into his half closed eyelids. Some of it leaked inside his parka and trickled down his chest in spite of the tightly closed neck. He thought about the poor bastards on the other escorts who weren't fortunate enough to have L. L. Bean clothing, and he realized how much they must be suffering from the cold.

As the *O'Leary* crept abeam of the tanker's broad hull, the enormous swells continued to sweep the forecastle. The forecastle crew was sheltered on the well deck, waiting for the word to go out onto the streaming deck.

Sorenson took a firm grip on the pelorus and steadied himself. More spray whipped into his eyes, and he wiped it away with the sleeve of his parka. His gloves were useless, and his fingers were numb. When he judged that they would slide into position, he slowed to fueling speed. The tanker's lee gave them some protection from the wind and spray coming from starboard, but the swells continued to come from ahead. An occasional swell caused them to change direction in spite of Alvarado's frantic efforts on the wheel. Once abreast of the tanker, Sorenson eased them in. When he judged they were in the proper position, he turned to the talker standing just inside the pilothouse door and thrust his thumb forward. The talker nodded, and Sorenson could see his lips moving, although he could not hear him in the wind. Deckhands, led by Chief Bellows, scrambled onto the forecastle.

Sorenson glanced at the tanker's bridge where the signalmen were pointing at the *O'Leary*'s forecastle and laughing. Laugh, thought Sorenson, and shiver. At least we're reasonably warm.

The men on the forecastle slipped on the wet deck, trying to heave in the dripping lines. Chief Bellows was everywhere, shouting encouragement and advice. By now the forecastle crew understood him, and "Hiv in smartly on dat line," produced a taut line.

As fast as humanly possible, deckhands hauled the large black fuel lines over and lashed them to the tops of the fueling trunks. The tanker started pumping, and the big hoses pulsed and jumped. Chief Bellows and his crew stood back and crouched behind the shield of gun one.

On the open bridge wing, the wind cut through Sorenson as he made small speed and course changes to hold position. Then a towering swell loomed ahead. Sorenson clenched his teeth and watched it with awe as it passed the tanker's bow and heaved the *O'Leary*'s bow high in the air. It hit them at a slight angle on the outboard bow. Sorenson peered into the pilothouse and saw Alvarado whirling the wheel to counter their swing, but the *O'Leary* angled toward the tanker. For a few seconds Sorenson thought they would recover, but the bow kept swinging in. Although it steadied, it was too late.

Sorenson gritted his teeth as the *O'Leary*'s side clanged against the tanker's hull. The ship shuddered, and the fenders groaned as they compressed between the ships, but the thousands of pounds of force were too much. The upper edge of the amidships deckhouse screeched as it folded against the strong hull of the tanker. The *O'Leary* bounced twice and began to swing free. On the bridge Sorenson could reach out and touch the tanker's rusty side, and for a moment he thought it would crush him and the pelorus.

The impact forced the O'Leary's bow out slowly, and the rudder began to take hold. Sorenson shouted to Alvarado to resume course before the ship yawed too far out. The O'Leary began to steady. Soon they were on their way back to the proper position, but the damage was done. Sorenson gritted his teeth and pounded his fist on the bulwark. His hand was so cold he couldn't feel it.

Bronte brought a large mug out of the CIC and squatted down next to Sorenson. "Here, Mister Sorenson, drink this and don't argue with me."

Sorenson reached down and took the mug, gripping it tightly with his numb hands. He grinned at Bronte and lifted it to his lips. It was like scalding black nectar, but nectar laced with brandy. He laughed out loud. You could never outguess the American sailors, he thought, they were marvelous. Take care of them, and they would take care of you. Then he knew that he would probably stay in the Navy. Regardless of the long bad times, the short good ones made it all worth while.

After the tanker took back its hoses, Sorenson conned the O'Leary carefully away from the tanker's side and back to station. When they were settled down, Sorenson ordered medicinal brandy for the deck force, and went back to the amidships deckhouse to see the damage. The structure had been collapsed inward about 2 feet, but the 4-inch gun mount did not appear to be damaged.

Steiner joined him. "Not bad. We can still fire, but did you see the signal yardarm?"

Sorenson looked up. The yardarm was bent down to a 45-degree angle. Sorenson said, "I didn't even notice it, and I was standing right under it. I guess the deckhouse crunch made too much noise."

Sorenson went down to Meredith. The Captain was swinging in his hammock with a book across his chest.

Meredith looked up, his face pale. "What happened?"

"A little bang-up. We took a cross-swell about forty feet high. Maybe I should have told the escort commander it was too rough to fuel."

"Why? You needed to, and you did it."

"Yes, but I banged us up."

"Hell! That's par for the course. We do dangerous things, and damage is expected. I take it the ship can still fight."

"Sure, no damage to the guns."

"Well, stop worrying. Just think about the fact that you were able to do what you had to do and no men were hurt. That's the bottom line."

•   •   •

For Sorenson the next days passed in a daze. The weather was too bad for submarine operations and also too bad to make much speed. On February 21 several high frequency direction finder bearings strong enough to be near the convoy were reported by the *Spencer*. The escort commander advised the escorts that he thought there was at least one wolf pack ahead and maybe two. His judgement appeared to be correct as new direction finder positions came in from shore stations and new bearings were reported by the *Spencer*. The Coast Guard cutters were assigned to run two of them down but found nothing. Then an aircraft sighted three submarines on the surface on their starboard quarter, and *Spencer* and *Dianthus* went to attack. They failed to find anything, but the *Spencer* made a good contact on the way back and reported a possible kill.

That evening the convoy passed out of the arc of air patrols from Ireland, and Sorenson knew they would be in trouble.

Sorenson was so tired that he had finally broken tradition for the second time and had slowly eased himself into the Captain's chair in the pilothouse. He sagged against the back and felt the blood beginning to circulate in his tired feet. The men around him were haggard and red-eyed, and they had not spent as much time on the bridge as Sorenson had put in.

Sorenson rubbed his cheeks vigorously. It was a habit he had acquired to relieve fatigue. It didn't help much, but it made the scar on his cheek tingle. He remembered the day he had gotten it. His horse had shied at something in the mesquite, and then he was flying through the air. The barbed wire had torn at his face and arm, and the pain was searing. He remembered that he shouldn't have been riding that close to the fence, but he had been in a hurry to get back to the ranch house and see his brother, Ed. Then he thought about Ed, and he was grateful that Ed was back on the ranch making it possible for him to be a millionaire. What the hell, he thought, why am I grateful? Ed ought to be grateful to me out here on this damned ocean making it possible for him to stay home. He rubbed his face again, and the scar stopped tingling.

A rumbling thud shook the pilothouse. Sorenson ran to the wing where he saw a ship sinking well away from their station. He watched with frustration as a corvette nearest to the victim was ordered to assist. He had barely eased his head against the back of the chair when a second explosion went off, nearer this time. Two U-boats, Sorenson thought. This is going to be a hell of a night.

Then he realized how routine his reactions had become. Instead of feeling compassion for the merchant seamen who had died in the explosion or would freeze in the frigid water, he had merely counted the number of explosions.

Then a stronger explosion shook the ship, and a concussion pushed air in the pilothouse door. Sorenson knew it was close by, and he pulled himself out of the chair. When his feet hit the deck, fatigue washed through him, and he almost collapsed. He caught the annunciator and pulled himself upright.

From somewhere adrenalin flowed, stimulated by the hatred he felt for the Germans and the damned U-boats. He wanted to destroy every wolf of the sea he could find, and he cursed silently as he stumbled toward the bridge wing.

By the time he reached it, Alvarado had his telescope on the blazing merchantman. "A big one," he said, "It's not going to last long."

The TBS crackled, ordering the O'Leary to look for the submarine. An adjacent corvette was ordered to rescue survivors. Sorenson shouted, "I have the conn! Right full rudder! Turns for 17 knots!"

The O'Leary swung rapidly, and Sorenson headed for

a position to port of the sinking ship. The sonar pinged
over the bridge speaker. He had almost given up when
sonar reported, "Sonar contact. Bearing three four zero.
Twelve hundred yards."

He headed for the contact, the bow pointed right at
the burning merchantman.

"Damn!" Sorenson said, and he changed course to circle the merchant ship. "The bastard is under the merchantman."

For thirty minutes the *O'Leary* circled as sonar tried
vainly to separate the submarine from the merchantman
over it. Then the corvette closed in to rescue survivors
jumping off the merchantman. Her wake further com-
plicated the sonar picture, and Sorenson pounded the
bridge bulwark trying to control his rage.

Steele came out on the wing. "Sorry, we've lost it."

By this time the convoy was well ahead, and
Sorenson knew it would need every escort. He headed
for the convoy and reported to the escort commander
who ordered the *O'Leary* to take station astern.

Sorenson turned the conn over to MacIntosh. "Make
the best speed you can. Clear the crew of gun one off
the forecastle."

Sorenson was ready to set condition III because he
knew the crew was near exhaustion, but before he could
give the order, dull flashes lit the night over the convoy.
Many seconds later the sounds of the blasts reached
them.

Sorenson was so angry and discouraged he couldn't
even swear. He sagged against the bridge bulwark.

"Just like a shooting gallery," he heard Alvarado mutter.

"The bastards!" Sorenson growled.

The TBS crackled with questions and reports; answers
flew back and forth. MacIntosh stood by the TBS
speaker and relayed information to Sorenson. Depth
charges rumbled in the distance as the *O'Leary* continued toward her station, but there were no reports of
success.

With no immediate prospects of action, Sorenson ordered condition III set. He leaned gingerly back in the
Captain's chair and tried to wedge his head between the

chair back and the forward pilothouse bulkhead so that he could stay awake for the next U-boat attack. It didn't work. Just before he dozed off, he thought that the trip had become hell on earth. Even though most of the merchantmen were empty, they were badly needed and their crews were vital. Somehow, the fight against the U-boats had to be won or the war in Europe would be lost.

Sorenson's short nap was interrupted by a report of torpedoes. He was so tired that he didn't even get out of his chair. "Where were they?" he asked.

Gerlach, who had the deck, said, "I think they were fired at the lead ship in the center column."

Sorenson knew that was the commodore's ship. "The old boy was sitting right on the bull's eye."

Gerlach said, "I don't think we will have to go."

"Thank God," Sorenson said in a flat voice. "Call me if we're assigned to attack."

At dawn general quarters, Sorenson woke up with a bad headache and a stiff neck. He was grateful that the ship had survived the night, but it had been a depressing and maddening experience. He knew there would be more to come.

Renard came up to the bridge right behind Morales, who brought Sorenson a sparse breakfast of three hard-boiled eggs, a piece of beaten-up toast, and two aspirin. Renard waited patiently until Sorenson took the tray. "Sir, here's a dispatch saying there's a seven U-boat wolf pack just ahead of us."

Sorenson groaned. "Morales, keep the aspirin coming every four hours."

During the day, Sorenson ordered the off-watch men to sleep when possible and even managed to get a few hours of rest himself. Later, when Sorenson announced the presence of the wolf pack ahead, he noticed a tension in the members of the bridge watch and heard muttered curses. He asked Alvarado, "How's the crew taking the latest news?"

Alvarado rubbed the stubble on his jaw. "Sir, I think they'll do their best, but just between you and me, they'd rather be going to a ship's party in Norfolk."

Sorenson was too tired to laugh. "Well, against my better judgement, maybe we'd better have another one."

That afternoon a bleak sun broke through for a few minutes, but the cloud cover was solid by dusk. The night was black.

Steele came out to the pilothouse. "Steele here, sir, in case you can't see me."

"I'm glad I can't," said Sorenson. "The U-boats should have trouble finding us."

Steele said, "I hope so, but with that many, they can spread out and wait for us. Then when they find us, they'll run ahead and concentrate."

Sorenson said, "I hope our radar will pick them up."

"Maybe," Steele said, "but the tops of these big seas will look like a conning tower half submerged. If they have good information on us, they can be at periscope depth and we'll never see them on radar."

In the early morning when it was still dark, the first torpedo attack just missed an escort, and the escort turned to attack. The escort commander quickly closed the gap, but while the other escorts were racing to new stations, a second U-boat apparently penetrated the gap, and a violent explosion rocked the first ship in the port wing column.

Sorenson called the crew to general quarters. Just as MacIntosh was relieving Gerlach, the escort commander reported a surfaced submarine sighted and assigned the *O'Leary* to attack.

Sorenson pulled down the transmitter switch on the squawk box. "Do you have it on radar?"

Bronte's voice came back. "There's a small pip. Might be a submarine."

Sorenson said, "Keep plotting it. We're going to investigate. Give me a course and speed."

Sorenson took the conn and ordered the ship around toward the contact.

"The contact's gone," Bronte reported. "If it was a submarine it's submerged."

Jablonski added, "I've tracked the contact and it's headed under the left column."

"Damn!" Sorenson said, remembering the close call

when they had last chased a submarine through the convoy. "This time we're going to let him go."

Two more surfaced submarines were reported ahead of the screen.

Sorenson reported the loss of their contact, and without waiting for orders from the escort commander, turned to regain station.

"Good decision," MacIntosh said. "The escort commander needs escorts up forward to take care of these latest contacts."

"What's the total number of contacts?" Sorenson asked.

"Five. There may be two more out there somewhere."

"Maybe they were too far out on the wings of the U-boat search line to get to us, but I wouldn't count on it."

The torpedoings mounted to seven with two explosions astern. Sorenson resignedly walked out to the open bridge wing and looked aft. Two towering columns of fire breached the darkness and outlined the decimated columns still plodding ahead.

MacIntosh said, "Those attacks must have been made by the sixth and seventh submarines."

Two other escorts were assigned to attack, and soon the familiar rumble of depth charges vibrated the deck.

"That's a feeling I'll never forget," Sorenson said. "Many more nights like this and the war's lost."

Chapter Twenty-six

Dawn came with agonizing slowness the next day, but the forenoon was surprisingly easy. Just before noon, the *O'Leary* and *Burza* were sent to investigate a radio direction finder fix. The *O'Leary* pounded along, with the Polish destroyer one thousand yards abeam. Nothing happened for over an hour, and Sorenson thought about recommending to the *Burza*'s captain, who was in charge of the operation, that they abandon the search. Just as he was picking up the TBS transmitter, the squawk box reported a probable submarine. Sorenson ordered general quarters and waited for another set of pings.

Then he picked up the TBS and transmitted, "Bumblebee this is Valiant, sonar contact bearing two seven three. Range one thousand. I am attacking."

"Bumblebee, yesss," came the *Burza*'s answer.

Sorenson turned the *O'Leary* to the bearing and gave the order to stand by for depth charge attack, medium depth pattern.

Steele's voice boomed over the squawk box, "Definite submarine! Range five double oh! Down doppler! Recommend use shallow pattern!"

The range wound down, and pings came faster as sonar shortened the scale. Then Steele reported, "Lost contact due to short range! Recommend drop on time!"

Sorenson watched the hand on his stopwatch tick toward the proper elapsed time. Then he ordered, "Drop depth charges."

From aft came the familiar pops of the K-guns.

Almost before the foam of their depth charges had subsided, Alvarado, who had turned the helm over to a junior quartermaster and was on the signal bridge, reported, "The *Burza* is attacking."

Sorenson speeded up to get out of her way and opened the range in preparation for making another attack. After the Polish destroyer completed her attack, she swung sharply and attacked again

Steele came running out of the CIC and looked around. "What's going on?" he asked. "The water is full of depth charges and wakes and we can't find a thing."

Sorenson laughed. "I don't think the *Burza* can either. We'll just wait until the sub clears this area. Let's start a wide circular search, and the *Burza* will chase the sub right into us."

On their second circle, Steele reported, "Sonar contact, bearing one six three! Distance eight double oh! Definite submarine!"

Sorenson picked up the TBS transmitter, but thought better about transmitting, and put it back in its holder. He said to MacIntosh, who had the deck, "We'll just keep this contact for our own."

Steele said, "Recommend head for the contact and attack."

Sorenson headed for the contact and told the depth charge battery to stand by for a deep pattern.

The attack seemed to take the *Burza* by surprise. A stream of Polish came over the TBS. Sorenson grinned and gestured to Chief Bellows, who had been called to the bridge when they had teamed with the *Burza*. "Chief, see what he wants."

Chief Bellows grabbed the TBS transmitter and answered with his own brand of Polish.

In the meantime a second attack was delivered with a full pattern of depth charges, and Steele reported rushing noises as if ballast were being pumped. "I think he's damaged and is coming up," Steele said.

Chief Bellows was still talking, and Sorenson decided to try again before the submarine could surface. This attack was hasty, with shallow settings in case the submarine was coming up.

As they were in the middle of the approach, Chief Bellows said, "He say, 'What we doin?' "

Sorenson laughed. "Tell him we're attacking."

While Chief Bellows went at it again, the depth charges began to fly and roll.

Sorenson turned to open the range and attempt to get across the circle from the *Burza*.

The TBS chattered, and Sorenson turned to Chief Bellows again. "What did he want this time?"

Chief Bellows scratched his head. "He say he think I must be from Kracow because of my accent."

A lookout shouted, "Submarine surfacing, port beam!"

Sorenson turned. A sharp bow knifed up at an angle, dripping foam and green water. It lunged forward to level, and a conning tower appeared. A slime-coated U on the conning tower stood out, but the numbers behind it were rusted over.

Above, Sorenson could hear Steiner shouting orders to his gun battery, and the guns swung toward the submarine. Then Sorenson realized that the *Burza* was directly beyond the U-boat. A shot might ricochet and hit her, and he shouted to the talker, "Tell gun control to hold fire until the bearing is clear!"

Apparently the *Burza* had no such fears, for a blast of smoke and flame erupted from her guns.

"Damn!" Sorenson said. He waited, gritting his teeth, for the four projectiles.

Two exploded well over the submarine and almost halfway to the *O'Leary*. Two smaller splashes indicated ricochets, caused by the low trajectory of the projectiles that bounced off the slightly inclined surfaces of the swells and did not not explode.

Sorenson held his breath. Aft there were two clangs but no explosions. He yelled to the man on the annunciators, "All ahead flank!"

He turned to Chief Bellows. "Tell the son of a bitch to stop firing. His ricochets are hitting us."

Bellows spewed Polish over the TBS.

Another salvo left the *Burza*, but there were no ricochets, and one of the projectiles hit the hull of the submarine.

The *O'Leary* pulled ahead so that Steiner could fire. The first salvo straddled the submarine. An orange flame spouted from the deck forward of the conning tower. Before the next salvo arrived, a hatch in the submarine's deck opened, and several men scrambled out to man the deck gun.

Another salvo from the *Burza* scattered the gun crew of the submarine. A hail of projectiles from the two destroyers raised sparks and spray. In a few minutes the submarine began to settle stern first. A few men from the gun crew leaped for the water.

Her bow lifted and she slid under for her last dive. Sorenson gave the order to cease fire and headed for the survivors. The *Burza* also closed.

As they slowed, Sorenson looked at Chief Bellows who was listening to a torrent of Polish over the TBS.

When the transmission stopped, Sorenson said, "What took you so long to give him that message?"

"Vell, I didn't know de verds for ricochet or son of a bitch."

"And why did it take so long for him to acknowledge?"

"He didn't know dem either."

The *O'Leary* closed the area where the submarine had gone down. The lookouts reported that it contained a lot of debris, a large patch of oil, some survivors, and some bodies of the gun crew.

Sorenson watched the *Burza* pick up most of the bodies and survivors.

The forecastle crew under Ensign Gerlach were able to snag a small grapnel hook in the life jacket ties of one survivor and pull him aboard. Gerlach ordered him taken to the well deck and watched as Fineman knelt over the German survivor and felt his carotid artery. Then Fineman motioned to Gerlach. Gerlach came over and knelt beside the survivor. He was dressed in an officer's uniform, but Gerlach could not recognize the insignia.

Fineman said, "He's trying to say something, but it's

in German. See if you can make it out. He hasn't got long to talk."

Gerlach put his ear to the young officer's mouth and listened. Then he said something in German in the officer's ear and listened again. After a few seconds he lifted his head and looked at Fineman.

Fineman felt the carotid artery again. "He's gone."

Gerlach got up and went up to the bridge. When he got there, Sorenson asked, "What did he say?"

Gerlach paused. "He asked if I was Jewish. I said no, but that the doctor was part Jewish. He asked me to ask the doctor to forgive his countrymen, particularly the young ones. They didn't all know what was going on. Then I told him not to worry, he'd be back there after the war was over. He said he didn't want to go back. It would be worse than after World War I, and he wanted to die. He did. I didn't think I should tell Doc."

Sorenson shook his head slowly. "Tell him."

Gerlach went back down to the well deck to talk to Fineman.

As he left, he heard Sorenson mutter, "The bastards. They all deserve to die."

     •   •   •

Fineman listened to Gerlach, sighed deeply, and then walked over to the young German officer and looked down at him.

The pharmacist's mate asked Fineman, "What shall I do with the body?"

"I'll go ask the executive officer," Fineman replied.

Sorenson was standing by the ladder looking down the ladder to the well deck, listening to the conversation below. Fineman went up and asked Sorenson, "What shall we do with the body?"

Fineman noticed that Sorenson was shaking and that his hands were tightly clenched.

Sorenson said, "Dump the bastard over the side so the sharks can eat him just like they ate our men."

Fineman shook his head. "Tex, you can't do that. Gerlach says he was different. He seemed to care, and he was brave enough to face certain death. He deserves a military funeral."

Sorenson took a deep breath, and his hands relaxed.

"All right. Have your pharmacist's mate get him ready, and we'll do it when we can."

Fineman said, "Thanks. In this cold we can keep him for several days."

    •   •   •

Sorenson walked forward to the pilothouse, still shaking. "All those German bastards deserve to die!"

Alvarado heard him, but didn't reply. Instead he said, "The *Burza* is speeding up and leaving the area."

Sorenson looked at the departing wake and said to MacIntosh, "Take station on his beam."

As they neared station, the TBS chattered again. Without being told Chief Bellows listened and then picked up the transmitter. "He say he sorry. If you want to take two free shots at him, is okay. What I tell him?"

For a moment Sorenson was tempted to tell him yes, but he said. "Tell him no harm was done, and it was an honor to fight with a ship of the gallant Polish Navy in the cause of freedom."

Chief Bellows turned away and began to transmit. The tufts of his gray hair sticking out from under his cap fluttered rapidly as he shouted the words.

Sorenson leaned over and said in MacIntosh's ear, "When he's done, tell him he doesn't have to shout."

MacIntosh laughed. "I'll tell him, but I doubt if it will do any good. I think all chief boatswain's mates were born shouting."

Back came a flood of Polish. When it was over, Chief Bellows turned to Sorenson. "He say, tank you, and he want to buy you a beer when dey get to Norfolk."

They were back on station in an hour, and Sorenson went below to inspect the damage. On the top of the refrigerator two shipfitters were struggling to keep from falling off while replacing some piping to the refrigeration unit. Durham was trying to supervise them from below.

Sorenson said, "What do you think, Bull?"

"I think we can fix the piping that was carried away by one of the ricochets and it will hold unless the ship rolls so much that the shipfitters can't make good joints. But we only have enough freon to fill the system part way. All the old freon escaped. That means the temperature in this box won't be very cold, but it won't need to be. It's almost freezing outside."

"What about the stuff inside?"

"There's only butter, bacon, eggs, and a little beef."

"Let's eat well while we can."

Durham laughed. "Why not. When we run out you'll see how we ate out in Java."

Sorenson went aft to the after deckhouse that housed the head, washroom, a small torpedo workshop, and a small emergency radio room.

Sorenson stuck his head in the port forward doorway. Two feet inside was a hole exactly the shape and size of a projectile in profile. Gerlach was looking at it. He turned to Sorenson. "A perfect outline. The projectile was tumbling, and it hit just as you see it."

Sorenson said, "We're lucky it didn't explode."

"No, it wouldn't. The fuze is armed by set-back at firing, and goes off on negative set-back when it hits something that slows it down. There wasn't enough slowing, either when it ricocheted from the wave front or when it hit us at an angle."

"What else did it do?"

Gerlach pointed to the amidships bulkhead. "It tore a hole there before it went out the outer bulkhead butt first. Fortunately it missed the gun cabling coming down from above and a guy sitting on a head seat. I'm not sure he'll ever come in here again. On the other hand, the chair he would have been sitting in, in emergency radio, is a shambles."

Sorenson said, "Overall, I guess we were lucky."

Sorenson went back up to the bridge and climbed into the Captain's chair. He noticed that the seas were beginning to moderate.

MacIntosh said, "The escort commander has just ordered the Canadian corvettes to fuel."

"Good."

Sorenson turned to the messenger. "Please find Morales and ask him to send me up some lunch." Sorenson yearned for something besides a few sandwiches, his only food for the last four days. What sleep he had snatched had been in the bridge chair. His legs trembled like pieces of small rope, and his head pulsed.

Before Morales arrived Sorenson was asleep.

• • •

Later that day all escorts but *Dianthus* and a Canadian corvette fueled. She reported that she did not think she could fuel in the heavy seas and requested permission to proceed to St. Johns, Newfoundland.

"Can you make it?" asked the escort commander.

"I hope so. I'm going to use everything on board that will burn—paint mixer, mineral oil, and butter."

• • •

The next night began quietly with improving weather and a washed-out orange and pink sunset. Sorenson watched the horizon from the bridge chair as the *O'Leary* plodded west into the rays reflected from the wave fronts. He thought of seeing Ferren and hoped the tempo of operations would ease. He knew he was exhausted, and the crew moved about the decks like old men, heads and shoulders drooping.

He was shaken out of his reverie when the *Campbell* reported a radar contact to port and then a second contact. The escort commander not only sent *Campbell* to attack but added *Burza* and *Chilliwack*. Soon there were the booms of depth charge attacks as the group fell astern.

Campbell reported, "Third attack completed. Trying another. *Chilliwack* reports hedgehog hit."

Sorenson grinned when he heard the report. "Maybe the new weapons will help. Something has to, or we'll never beat these bastards."

Then *Trillium* reported a radar contact astern. "Go get it," the escort commander ordered.

Rosthern reported a sonar contact to starboard, and the *O'Leary* was ordered to join her in the attack. The commanding officer of *Rosthern* was senior, so Sorenson reported to him. "Circle while I attack," came from *Rosthern*, and Sorenson conned the *O'Leary* in a circle around the reported contact.

Sonar reported, "We have *Rosthern*'s contact. Probable submarine."

Now *Spencer* was the only escort left with the convoy,

and she reported a high frequency direction finding bearing ahead with a strong signal. "Firing starshells," she reported, and the *O'Leary*'s lookouts reported the bursts, but nothing was seen.

Jablonski said plaintively over the squawk box, "We can't keep up with the surface plot in here. It looks like a spider web. The convoy commodore is making emergency turns by whistle signals, and many of the merchantmen are not responding. Also, all of the escorts except *Spencer* have left their stations for attacks."

Sorenson said, "Thanks. Don't worry about it. Just keep track of *Rosthern* now or anyone who gets too close to us."

After the *O'Leary*'s third attack, Gerlach reported that well over half of the depth charges had been expended. "We'd better cut down to half-salvos," he said.

"Make it so," Sorenson answered, too tired to give the problem further thought.

The problem was solved temporarily when Steele reported that sonar had lost contact. *Rosthern* gave up and reported the loss to the escort commander.

Gradually the escorts either lost contact or stopped holding the U-boats down until the convoy was well past, and the escorts began to rejoin. By dawn the convoy had reformed, and the screen was intact. When morning general quarters was over, Bronte reported that no merchantmen had been sunk during the night.

Sorenson was so elated he spilled hot coffee on his L. L. Bean suit. "Hot damn!" he said. "For once we stopped them." Then he realized it would take more than one good night to win the battle in the Atlantic and that the latest wolf pack had not been as good as the Seawolf group.

•   •   •

During daylight Sorenson urged all the officers and men to rest, and by dusk they were ready again.

That night, just after sunset, the *Campbell* reported a sonar contact, and she and the *Burza* stayed with it for several attacks. Sorenson and Steiner, who had the deck, listened closely as the TBS sputtered messages between the *Campbell* and the *Burza*.

Sorenson laughed. "They must have gotten that good

English speaker out of his bunk. The *Burza* sounds just like the Britishers."

Steiner said, "It sounds like they're doing a good job."

The next report was of a submarine surfacing.

Sorenson said, "I hope the *Burza* looks down-range this time before she fires."

Gunfire echoed over the next TBS transmission as *Burza* warned, "Look out!"

Sorenson turned to Steiner. "Do you suppose the *Burza* has shot at him or rammed him?"

Steiner shrugged his shoulders, and they waited for the next transmission. When it came, the *Campbell* reported, "I have a large hole in my hull from his hydroplanes. I'll have to lie to and patch it."

Steiner said, "I guess that answers our question. The *Burza* doesn't have hydroplanes. The *Campbell* must have rammed the surfaced submarine."

Then *Burza* reported picking up several German survivors and said she would screen the *Campbell* while repairs were made.

Just after dark, *Rosthern*, on the port side of the screen, reported sonar contact. "Turning to attack," she said.

Seconds later *Trillium* in the next station reported two sonar contacts, and the escort commander ordered *Spencer* to take on one of them. The remaining escorts raced to fill the vacated stations, and the convoy commodore ordered an emergency turn away. Merchantman whistles carried over the water.

Bronte reported, "The merchantmen seem to have gotten the word. They're still in proper positions."

Sorenson checked his report by looking at the bridge PPI. "Looks good," he said, "but the screen's a mess."

By midnight the escorts returned without any claim of success, but no merchantmen had been lost.

"Mexican stand off," Sorenson muttered.

Just before dawn, the CIC reported, "Three surface contacts dead ahead, five miles."

Sorenson relayed the report to the escort commander and sounded general quarters.

Almost immediately the TBS blared, "Valiant, attack."

"Jesus!" Sorenson said. "All three?"

MacIntosh shook his head. "I recommend you take the nearest one."

The *O'Leary* left the screen at 17 knots, with the sonar pinging ahead and Steiner and his director crew searching the darkness.

A lookout shouted, "Submarine on the surface! Dead ahead! Two miles!"

Sorenson gave the order to open fire when ready and soon Steiner shouted, "Commence firing." A two-gun salvo crashed out. Sorenson followed the flight of the tracers, and splashes rose behind the dark silhouette.

"Great!" Sorenson yelled. "Pour it on!" On the second salvo a dull flash indicated a hit, but then the submarine submerged. Radar reported the other two contacts also had disappeared.

Steele reported, "Sonar contact. Probable submarine. Two six zero. Turning to port."

A minute later he added, "Speed 8 knots. He's fast."

Sorenson increased the lead to port to compensate for the submarine's maneuvers, and the range closed rapidly.

Then Steele reported, "Lost contact due to short range."

Sorenson waited patiently in the darkness, counting the seconds, until it was time to drop the depth charges. "Drop depth charges," he ordered.

Sorenson opened the range to make another attack. All of his weariness had receded, and he felt a renewed vigor.

Steele said, "We hear breaking-up noises."

Sorenson turned to his talker. "Ask gun four if they can see any debris."

"Too dark," the talker reported. "They can't see anything."

Steele came out to the open bridge. "I think he broke up before he went below the layer. He tried several Pillenwerfers, but Terrill wasn't fooled by them, thanks to our time at Londonderry. I think the submarine sank below the layer, rather than manuevered there."

Sorenson shook his head because they probably couldn't confirm the kill.

Steele brightened. "Maybe we'll get credit for sinking

it. It will depend on what intelligence the hot-shots ashore have."

Sorenson said, "I hope so. While we've been fooling around with this bastard, the convoy has steamed past. Jablonski, give me a course to rejoin. They need us back there."

As they settled on a course, there was a large explosion ahead.

Jablonski said, "Lost another one."

Sorenson said, "Watch it. You're getting as cynical as I was a few days ago. Those are human beings over there, not just fireworks."

Jablonski sighed. "Thanks for reminding me. I feel for them, but I can only feel so much."

"I understand. If we let it get to us, we can't do our jobs."

They were so far behind it was dawn before they could join the convoy. Before they could take station they were ordered out on a radio direction finder bearing. While they steamed on the bearing, a lookout called, "Raft on the starboard beam. Two miles."

Sorenson approached the raft, and when they were close enough for Alvarado to see it in detail through his telescope, the signalman shuddered and said, "Sir, I don't think you want to see this."

Sorenson said, "We have to take a look. We can't leave it there."

He brought the *O'Leary* alongside the raft, and as they closed, Sorenson could see what Alvarado meant. There were parts of the bodies of three men in tattered remnants of life jackets lashed to the raft. Sea gulls, pecking at the bodies, flew away as they approached.

"Jesus!" Sorenson said, "They don't have any legs."

MacIntosh said, "And not much else."

Sorenson choked down the sensations of nausea rising in his throat. "Machine guns, destroy the raft."

MacIntosh said, "Shouldn't we recover the bodies?"

"Good God, no. There are only small pieces left."

The machine guns chattered, and the raft flew into pieces. The parts of bodies sank slowly, but some of the remains of the raft still floated.

Sorenson said, "May their souls rest in peace. All ahead full."

• • •

That night two submarines attempted to penetrate the screen on the surface. The *O'Leary*'s radar caught both of them, but both U-boats submerged before they could be taken under fire. One fired a torpedo spread at the *Campbell*, but she was able to avoid it.

The second contact was assigned to the *O'Leary*. "Off we go, again," Sorenson said. By now the adrenalin generated earlier had worn off, and he felt completely drained.

Sonar reported a solid contact, and Sorenson remembered that they had only two half-salvos of depth charges left. He ordered a half-salvo dropped.

After Sorenson had opened the range, Steele reported, "Regained contact. Definite submarine. Still making five knots."

The data sounded good, so Sorenson dropped the last depth charges.

Steele came out to the pilothouse. "The best we can do now is drop boiler brick. Maybe a case of salmon."

Sorenson said, "We'll hold the bastard down until dawn."

When the horizon brightened, Sorenson said, "That's it. Let's rejoin." He turned the conn over to MacIntosh and ordered him to set condition III.

• • •

The next day they were well within the area of air search, and no other submarines challenged them. After morning general quarters, Durham and Fineman came up to the bridge to see Sorenson. Fineman said, "MacIntosh told me the situation will quiet down now that we're in range of air patrols. Can we bury the German officer today?"

Sorenson sighed. "We'll bury him at sea as soon as we can get ready. Please ask Chief Bellows to have him sewn up tightly in a piece of canvas with a projectile at his feet."

Sorenson turned to Alvarado. "I don't suppose we have a German flag aboard."

Alvarado shook his head. "No, but I can cover him

with two Zed flags. The colors in them are close to those in the German flag."

"Fine."

Fineman said, "What will you use for a service?"

"Service? This guy doesn't rate a service after what the Germans have been doing. What about all the men they've sent to the bottom without services and those poor guys on the raft?"

"It's our duty," Fineman said. "It's the right thing to do. Doing the right thing is what separates us from that bastard Hitler."

Sorenson rubbed his temples. "All right. You win. I'll have Gerlach read in German a short version of the funeral service from the Navy Prayer Book, and then I'll say a short prayer."

Fineman looked off into space.

Sorenson asked, "What's the matter?"

Fineman took a deep breath. "I'd like to read the prayer."

Sorenson looked at him closely. "I don't understand. I thought you had Jewish ancestors."

"I have. One of my grandfathers was Jewish, but I know very little about the Jewish religion or its rites. He taught me a few prayers.

"I'm sure you've heard of the way the Nazis persecuted the Jews in Germany on crystal night, and there are rumors that they are shipping huge numbers of Jews to concentration camps. This man must have known about crystal night."

Fineman said, "Not necessarily, and I can't blame that young boy for the mistakes of his elders. I have to assume he is innocent and that he joined the Navy early enough so that he may not have known what the Nazis were doing. My grandfather taught me to believe the best of my fellow men. Besides, I admired his courage. He knew he was going to face certain death when he went out on deck to take charge of his gun crew. Gerlach said he regretted what his country had done."

"What kind of prayer will you give?"

"It will be in English. It's entitled, 'Mercy and Forgiveness.' Something you'll have to think about some day."

• • •

An hour later Sorenson ordered the officers off watch and a few of the crew assembled on the well deck. From the signal bridge, he looked down at the preparations on the well deck. Chief Bellows had prepared the body, and the ends of Alvarado's signal flags were tucked under the mess table on which the body rested. The mess table was placed next to the bulwark. Even in the partial lee of the well deck bulwark, the flags whipped and bellied in the heavy wind, and Alvarado stood near by, keeping an eye on them.

When he could see all were assembled, Sorenson went down to the well deck. He said a few words. Then Gerlach read the service in German, stumbling now and then over the translation of some of the unfamiliar words.

Then Doctor Fineman stepped forward and gave his prayer. When he was finished he looked up and said, "Gnade uber alles."

Sorenson leaned over to Gerlach and whispered, "What does that mean?"

"Mercy above all."

Sorenson gestured to Chief Bellows, and four men picked up the inboard end of the table and tilted it so that the body would slide over the bulwark. Alvarado kept a hand on the signal flags so they would not follow the body.

There were a few moments of silence, and then they filed off the well deck.

Fineman said to Sorenson. "I'm glad I did that. I forgive him, but for Hitler and the rest of those Nazi bastards, may they burn in hell."

• • •

A few days later they were off New York, and two local escorts came out to take over the convoy. The *O'Leary* was directed to proceed to Norfolk independently, and Sorenson increased speed to the maximum possible with the fuel left.

As they started south, Sorenson noted that the air and water temperatures were still above freezing as they had been since they left Londonderry. He reached up and rubbed his face. It was sore and chapped, and there was still rime ice on his eyebrows. Then he felt the fur strip around the opening in his parka and realized that it was free of ice. No wonder, he thought, it's wolf fur, and ice and snow don't stick to wolf fur. Otherwise wolves couldn't survive in winter. Real wolves were just as tough as those damned Seawolves.

Then he had another thought. He'd send Renard off to get ski gloves for the topside crews, and even ski face masks. He reached for a cup of steaming coffee brought up to the bridge by Morales. Why ski masks? Why not ask Linda and Ferren to gather a group of wives and knit wool helmets?

The thought of Ferren and the fact that they would be together soon focused his thoughts, and he felt warm all over. In two days, they would be together, and he could forget the nightmare of the last three weeks. He took a deep breath and sipped the strong coffee.

• • •

Two days later they passed the familiar net entrance and steamed up the channel. As they passed the naval base, Sorenson looked at the line of large senior officers' quarters along the base and wondered idly if he would ever live in one of them.

His thoughts were interrupted by the appearance of Meredith and Fineman on the bridge.

Sorenson smiled at the Captain. "You look great, even if you are a little skinny. What will Linda say?"

Fineman said, "I hope she meets him at the door in a filmy nightgown and with a plate of hot biscuits in her hand. He needs a lot of personal attention."

Meredith laughed. "I'm so hungry I might just go for those biscuits first."

Sorenson asked Fineman, "When will he be ready for duty?"

"Right now."

Sorenson said, "Good. I'd like you to take your ship in to port. Do you relieve me?"

Meredith said, "Slow down, I'm still a little weak. I'll take command now, but you bring her in. You deserve to. You did a great job."

Chapter Twenty-seven

Because the first day in port was Sunday, Sorenson started liberty as soon as the ship was secured. Linda was at the brow waiting for Meredith. Sorenson called Ferren and told her that he had to take care of the crew and the ship before he could leave.

About one o'clock, Sorenson finished work and went across the pier to the telephone booths and called Ferren again. In fifteen minutes her red Ford barreled down the pier, and Sorenson was off.

Ferren looked at his face. "My God, who stepped on you?"

Sorenson laughed. "Old Jack Frost."

•   •   •

Dinner was good that evening, with thick filets and a large salad, but Sorenson noticed that Ferren seemed preoccupied.

After they moved to the couch, and Ferren put two cups of coffee on a small table, Sorenson noticed that she was wearing his engagement ring. "I'm glad to see you're wearing my ring tonight. Does this mean anything special?"

"It doesn't mean I want to marry you yet, but it does mean I love you."

He moved next to her on the couch and took her in his arms. From somewhere down near his chest, he heard Ferren say, "Tex, I can't hold out any longer. I'm yours if you want me."

For a moment he was unable to say anything, and she pulled back and smiled. "I don't think you heard me."

"Oh, I heard you all right. I just want to be sure you mean it."

She pulled him down to her and kissed him deeply. "Does that tell you something?"

He picked her up and carried her into the bedroom where he lowered her gently to the bed.

She said, "Let me turn these covers back. We've put too much time on top of them." She giggled. "And this time you can take your clothes off."

Sorenson sat down beside her and ran his fingers through her shining black hair. He thought he saw a hint of mistiness in her eyes, and he wondered if it was regret for the loss of her husband or the beginnings of passion for him. He remembered something Fineman had said about having to share her love with her former husband. He looked at her and decided it was not too high a price to pay.

She said, "You're thinking about something."

"You can read my mind, and that's what two married people should be able to do."

She frowned. "I said I was yours, and I always will be no matter what happens. But I told you I want to wait to get married until the war is over."

"We'll talk about that later."

He undressed her slowly. He had seen most of her at the beach, but still he was unprepared for the total effect, and he enjoyed each part of her body as he revealed it.

"Turn out the light and get in bed," she said.

He threw off his clothes and took her in his arms. He caressed her slowly at first and then with increasing passion. Her breasts thrust up at his chest, and she pulled him tightly against her.

They lay quietly after the first time, entwined in each others arms. The rest of the night was just as good, and they awoke just before dawn. Ferren turned to him and stroked his face. Then she sat up, turned on the light, and examined his face carefully. "I've got to fix this," she said.

She walked to the bathroom and came back with a

big jar of Noxzema. She crawled back into bed, crossed her legs, and pulled Sorenson's head into her lap.

"What are you doing?" Sorenson asked.

"Trying to bring your face back to the land of the living. Something has happened to it."

"Hours and hours of standing out on the open bridge wings in snow, sleet, rain, and flying ice."

She began to rub Noxzema over his face, gently massaging the sore areas.

Sorenson sighed. "That's wonderful."

She gently lifted his head and put it on his pillow. She settled herself beside him and kissed him carefully, wrinkling her nose at the strong odor of Noxzema. "This certainly smells like it should do some good."

He started to agree, but before he could open his mouth he fell asleep.

　　　　•　　　　　•　　　　　•

Sorenson awoke in the sunlit bedroom. He sat up. "Where am I?"

Ferren, snuggled against him, said, "Slow down, Buster, you're in good hands."

Sorenson relaxed. "Sorry, I haven't had much sleep lately."

Ferren examined his face closely. "I suggest you wash this goop off in the shower, but don't shave today. While you're in the shower, I'll fix you a Texas breakfast: Steak, eggs, and beans."

Sorenson returned to the *O'Leary* that afternoon and found a beaming Carmody waiting outside his stateroom.

Sorenson asked, "What's so special?"

"I got to the post office at 0800. All the good mail is on top. The first one is the best."

Sorenson picked up the mailgram and started to read it. It was a promotion list. Near the top was Meredith's name for promotion to commander.

"Hot damn!" Sorenson said. "He deserves it."

Carmody moved from one foot to the other. "Sure, but keep going."

Sorenson read down the list. Then he threw it up in the air.

Carmody caught it, grinned, and read off, "Alden P. Sorenson. Congratulations, Lieutenant Commander."

Sorenson was speechless, and it was some time before Carmody could get him to read down the list. Sorenson came to Steiner for promotion to full lieutenant, and Jablonski and Gerlach to lieutenant junior grade.

Carmody said, "One more. You didn't get to Chief Aronson. He's selected for ensign."

"Great. He'll make a good one. We'll arrange a promotion ceremony for all of us at 1500."

Meredith presided on the forecastle, with the crew aft around gun one. When he was finished, he left for the shipyard commander's office, where he had asked to be promoted by the shipyard commander, an old friend. When he came back, he was met at the brow by Sorenson and all of the officers. Sorenson had sent Renard to the uniform shop to buy a commander's cap with scrambled eggs on its bill.

When Meredith came up the brow, they proudly presented the cap to him. Meredith turned and pitched his old cap into the water alongside. As he put the new cap on, Sorenson said, "On behalf of all of us, congratulations, Commander."

.   .   .

The next day Ensign Steele came back from a visit to Antisubmarine Warfare Headquarters just in time for lunch. After he sat down, Meredith looked down the table at him. "What did you find out?"

"A lot," Steele said. "First, we got half-credit for the submarine we sunk with the *Burza*. Also, it looks like we'll get full credit for the second submarine we attacked south of Newfoundland."

Meredith said, "I suppose they had some intelligence to back that assessment."

"Yes, sir. It was a member of the Seawolf group, too."

"What else did you find out?" Meredith asked.

"In this yard period, we're going to get one of the new sonar range recorders. It works in conjunction with the sonar system, and it will help us analyze submarine courses and speeds. Now I won't have to bother Terrill on the sonar stack so much."

MacIntosh laughed. "I know he'll appreciate that. He says your voice is louder than the sonar."

Meredith put his soup spoon down. "What else?"

"Land-based aircraft coverage is expanding. Aircraft patrols now go out a thousand miles from Canada, Iceland, and Ireland. That means continuous coverage for convoys on the northern route."

Jablonski said, "Won't the wolf packs move south to work on the convoys bound from the United States to the Mediterranean?"

Steele's eyes sparkled. "Wait! We have an answer for that. The Navy is forming hunter-killer groups to patrol the Central Atlantic. The new groups will protect convoys, and find and kill milk cows—the large supply submarines, which don't carry much armament but carry extra fuel, torpedoes, and food. Now the wolf packs go south out of aircraft range to replenish in safety, but with the hunter-killer groups, they'll be at risk."

Meredith asked, "Will the hunter-killer groups use the escort carriers we operated with off Casablanca?"

"Yes, and we'll probably be assigned to the *Santee* group with some other old four-stackers for ASW screen and surface attack units. By the way, the escort carriers are now called CVEs."

"When do we leave?"

"They don't know yet. The *Santee* has to retrain its air group for antisubmarine warfare, and we have to complete our yard period. My guess is early June."

Meredith said, "We'll start a leave program. The shipyard says it will take at least a month to complete our repairs."

•   •   •

The next day Sorenson knocked on Meredith's door frame. Meredith said, "Come in." When he saw Sorenson's face, he asked, "What's wrong?"

Sorenson sat down and said, "Captain, did you give Bull permission to start liberty at 1300 for the engineering department?"

"Why, yes, shouldn't I have?"

"Yes if you wanted to, but he failed to clear it with me before he asked you."

"Hell, I thought he had. I should have asked him."

Sorenson stood up. "I'll take care of it by granting 1300 liberty to the rest of the crew, and I'll straighten Bull out. Sorry to have bothered you."

• • •

When Sorenson got back to his room, he sent for Durham. An hour later Durham came in his room without knocking. "What's the trouble? I'm in a hurry to go ashore. It's 1300."

Sorenson looked at him sternly. "Bull, you ignored the chain of command, and I don't like it."

"Aw, hell, what did I do?"

"You went to the Captain directly about 1300 liberty for your department."

"All of my fireroom crew and I were up until dawn cleaning boilers. I think we all deserve early liberty. Hell, I promised them all a free meal at the Oriental Tea House."

"I agree they all deserve early liberty, but the way to do it is to ask me. I would have agreed. But I have to think about the other departments, too. Many of them have worked long hours also. I would have given the whole crew early liberty. I've done it, but it's a little late. You've made me look like a dope."

"Aw, hell, it came out all right. Jack didn't mind."

"Yes, he did. He didn't like it either. You've got to learn to work through me. It's my job, and if you want it someday, you've got to learn how it works."

Durham's face got fiery red, but he controlled himself. "Well, I'm sorry. I'll try to do better."

• • •

Durham shaved, showered, and splashed on a double handful of aftershave. Just before leaving the ship, he stopped by Sorenson's room and knocked. Sorenson said, "Come in."

Durham swept in on a cloud of aftershave.

Sorenson coughed. "Jesus, Bull, Sonya will choke on that stuff."

"No, she won't. She likes it. After you've been in China a long time you appreciate good smells. There are a helluva lot of bad ones out there."

"What can I do for you?"

"I'd like permission to go ashore."

Sorenson grinned. "Sure. Thanks for remembering to ask."

Durham laughed. "No hard feelings?"

"No. We need to get along."

Durham walked out to the gate, flagged a taxi, and offered an extra five to the driver to hurry. The driver earned it, and in a few minutes Durham was bounding up the stairs to Sonya's apartment.

This time Sonya ordered a catered dinner. While it was on the way, Durham and Sonya put away a whole bottle of White Horse Scotch and two trays of cheese snacks, now Durham's favorite.

By the time dinner was over, Durham looked at the dessert and said, "No cheese cake for me."

Sonya raised her eyebrows. "That wasn't the kind of cheese cake I had in mind."

This time, when they raced for the bed, Durham stopped to hang his trousers over a chair. Sonya laughed. "Why are you doing that now?"

Durham shrugged. "It's my best uniform."

"You'd think we were married."

"Not yet. Maybe some day."

It was as good as it had been the first time, and Durham said as he lay back beside Sonya, "Maybe I ought to think about reserving you permanently."

Sonya sighed. "You sailors sure get up a full head of steam at sea. I'm not sure I could keep up with you every night."

•   •   •

Sorenson insisted that Meredith take the first leave period so the Captain could recover his health. Linda promised to send him back at his normal weight.

Sorenson spent his evenings with Ferren and his weekends flying.

At the beginning of Sorenson's leave period, he was able to get two train reservations to Texas, and Ferren took time off to go with him. After a long and tiring trip, they arrived at Sorenville. Sorenson's brother met them at the tiny station. Ed was a larger version of Tex, but his legs were bowed more, and his skin was a leathery brown.

The next week Sorenson showed Ferren much that was new to her. She told him she loved horses, but she had a problem sitting down after her first day in the saddle. At night they made love in a large feather bed.

During the day, they covered as much of the ranch as they could, but after the fourth day, Ferren said, "I'll never be able to get to see it all. By the way, don't you have any flowers here?"

Sorenson laughed. "No, but we have plenty of mesquite. I'll show you something a little greener tomorrow."

The next day Ed rode with them to one corner of the ranch. Across it ran a small river, flanked by a large stretch of green grass. Ed led them along the river, and from a slight rise, they stopped under a tree and looked along the slender valley.

"I love this," Ferren said.

Ed nodded. "So do I. Someday I want to bring a skilled farmer in here to raise corn and hay for feeding our cattle in the winter and for fattening. We could double our profits if we didn't have to buy feed."

Sorenson let Ferren try some of the chili that night at a ranch hands' barbecue given for them. She managed to get it down, but that night she said, "Never again. It's filet mignon for me."

They returned by train, brown and fit, and Sorenson hardly noticed the discomfort of the train as they talked about the future.

Chapter Twenty-eight

The first week in April in the shipyard was frantic. The *O'Leary* was not scheduled to sail immediately, but the yard had other ships waiting, and the *O'Leary* was required to move to the Norfolk Naval Base.

Meredith inspected the last job to be completed, the amidships deck house. Steiner could not test the roller path of the 4-inch gun until they were out in the open where he could see the horizon, but Meredith was fairly sure the roller path had not been disturbed. The lesser jobs, such as the bent yardarm, the refrigeration unit, and the after deckhouse, had long since been completed. Durham had also reported cleaning all boilers and repairing all steam leaks.

Meredith asked him, "How long will these repairs keep us going?"

Durham shook his head. "Who knows? You used to be the chief engineer. You know she's old and hasn't yet been given a proper overhaul. All we're doing is putting on bandages. Someday she'll just fall apart."

"You have my sympathy. I tried to keep her running for over two years. Then I turned her over to you. I know you weren't glad to take over."

"I'll keep trying, but don't be surprised at anything that happens."

Several of the most experienced hands had been ordered to new construction. Chief Aronson, now Ensign Aronson, had been detached with regret after a rousing departure party by the chiefs, and he was bound for a new destroyer. Meredith knew the ship would miss him, but the Navy was growing, and Aronson was needed.

Meredith turned the conn over to Gerlach to move the ship over to a new berth at the naval base. After they were secured, barges came alongside with fuel and provisions.

•   •   •

Another barge brought new style depth charges. Steele and Gerlach went aboard the barge to inspect them. Steele patted the rounded nose of one of the tear-drop shaped charges, which had small fins in the rear. Narrow rings circled the middle and the outsides of the fins so that the charges could be rolled easily on their sides.

"What was wrong with the old ones?" Gerlach asked.

Steele said, "The old depth charges often tumbled end over end after hitting the water. Then they sank at an uneven and slow rate. These sink in a straight line and go down twice as fast. That means we can wait longer before dropping them, and the submarine has less time to maneuver and therefore less chance of evading."

Gerlach said, "I guess I understand this end of the system all right. Now let's go up to the CIC so you can explain the newly installed sonar range recorder to me. I understand it makes your job a lot easier."

In the CIC, Steele uncovered a metal box, shaped like a cash register, installed next to the sonar console. Its face was a piece of glass and its sides were about 16 by 18 inches.

Underneath the glass Steele pointed out a roll of chemically treated paper. Steele turned the recorder on. "The sonar isn't going now, but you can see that this paper is fed under the glass at a steady rate. A small metal bug under it starts at one side of the paper at the same time the sonar pings. The ping means a sonar signal is going out toward the target. When it comes back, you hear the result. This little bug moves across the paper in synchronism with the sonar signal, and makes a visual mark when there's an echo. Am I clear?"

Gerlach said, "I get it. You have a record of what you heard. Also you can measure the rate of change in the range by the slant of the successive marks. A change in the slant tells you the sub has changed course."

"Right, if our course and speed are steady. It gives someone who doesn't happen to have excellent pitch discrimination a chance to evaluate a contact with his eyes instead of with his ears."

Terrill, the first class sonarman, who had been listening, laughed. "When we got the sonar I was a radioman. I played the clarinet, so it was decided I would become a sonarman."

Steele said, "I think in those days they thought a musician would make a good sonarman."

Gerlach asked, "Did it help?"

Terrill said, "All I did to play the clarinet was press the keys. What they needed were singers who knew pitch. A sonarman has to judge change of pitch, or doppler. Mister Steele judges doppler better than I do, and he can't play a note. I think he must be a good singer."

Steele laughed. "I sing pretty well, specially the Whiffenpoof Song. Terrill is as good as our other sonarman, and he's been at it a long time so that he makes very sound judgements. I just help a little."

Gerlach said, "I like all this, and I'd like to go to sonar school. But if I had my choice, I'd rather be the gunnery officer."

"You will be," Steele said. "But keep your hand in here. We may need you."

     •   •   •

They spent two months acting as plane guard for the *Santee* as she re-trained her aviators for antisubmarine warfare. The F4F fighters practiced strafing towed spars that simulated surfaced submarines. The TBFs, normally torpedo planes, practiced dropping 500-pound depth charges and the new homing torpedo. Called FIDO, the torpedo could be dropped in the vicinity of a submarine and would then seek and destroy it with a direct hit. The SBDs dive bombers could dive bomb, bomb horizontally, or strafe with machine guns.

After elementary training in the Chesapeake Bay, the *Santee* headed out to sea off Virginia Beach, where the aircraft would fire live ammunition and dummy depth charges and torpedoes.

By early June they were ready, and Sorenson spent his last night in port with Ferren, not knowing when he would return.

Chapter Twenty-nine

On the morning of June 13, the *Santee* stood out of the net entrance followed by the *O'Leary* and preceded by three other four-stackers, the *Bainbridge*, *Overton*, and *MacLeish*.

The *O'Leary* was assigned to take station as plane guard 500 yards astern and slightly on the quarter of the *Santee*, and the other destroyers formed a screen ahead.

Almost as soon as she was clear of the net vessel, the *Santee* began launching aircraft. Sorenson stood next to Meredith on the bridge wing, watching F4Fs roar off the flight deck. A flight of three TBFs waddled off behind them, sinking slightly as they cleared the bow, and then clawing their way aloft. Finally, two SBD dive bombers brought up the rear.

Sorenson shook his head. "I'd like to be flying one of those F4F Wildcats, but the SBDs and the fat TBF Avengers leave me cold."

Meredith said, "The *Santee* is big for a CVE. She's about 6,000 tons, about 600 feet long, and makes 18 knots. The *Santee*'s extra speed and length should help her operate her aircraft."

"I understand she was a fleet tanker and still retains a lot of her fuel carrying ability. She has the lower hull lines of a tanker, rather than the lines of a merchant ship, which most of the other CVEs were. I think she'll be easier to fuel from in heavy weather."

Meredith said, "You're our expert in heavy weather fueling. I'll be depending on you."

Sorenson shook his head. "It's nice of you to say so, but I'll never forget that tanker when we banged up our side. I thought I'd be squashed behind the pelorus."

As soon as the aircraft were on station, Sorenson went below to inspect the lashings on the boats and other equipment. He felt a pang of disappointment, as he realized that during the last Atlantic crossing he had been in command, and now he was only the exec. Even the gold lieutenant commander's oak leaves on his collar didn't console him.

Renard met him as he went down the hatch toward the wardroom. "Mister Sorenson, you have three months pay on the books. You haven't drawn any money. Don't you want to be paid some of it next pay day?"

"I don't think so. I'd just spend it."

Renard looked puzzled. "Maybe it isn't any of my business, but is Mrs. Holderman rich?"

"No, why?"

"One of you is getting money from somewhere. I'd like to get in on the deal."

*   *   *

The next day Sorenson watched as they met convoy UGS-10, a seventy-ship formation bound for Casablanca. The *Santee* group maneuvered in the vicinity of the convoy, changing course to head into the wind to launch and recover aircraft on a four hour cycle.

Sorenson stepped into the CIC and watched Jablonski plot the daily search patterns on the status board in the CIC. As Jablonski raised his arm to get at the top of the status board, the back-lighting from the board glinted off of his rimless glasses and relieved the shadows in his angular face.

Sorenson, studying the pattern Jablonski was plotting on the status board, said, "It looks like our aircraft are trying to prevent U-boats from waiting on the surface ahead of the convoy."

Jablonski measured the distances. "Yes, as far out as possible. These late-afternoon searches are designed to keep the U-boats down. Of course some won't be detected and will surface at night. The only sure way to counter them is to put escorts out well ahead and use their surface search radars."

Sorenson said, "Makes sense, but we don't have that many escorts."

$\bullet$ $\bullet$ $\bullet$

One afternoon Sorenson stopped by the CIC where Jablonski had the chart showing the proposed track from Norfolk to Casablanca. They bent over it, studying the areas they would pass through.

Jablonski said, "Our track curves down about six hundred miles to the south. The German high command is setting up a barrier known as Group *Trutz*. I have it plotted here. It will have about fifteen submarines in it, and they will be in three north-south lines, with the individual submarines about twenty miles apart. The subs will be outside aircraft range from Bermuda. Their job will be to intercept east-west convoys like ours."

Steele came over and looked at the plot. He whistled. "A hell of a barrier. We must have broken the German code again to know that much about it."

Sorenson said, "It depends on how you look at it. I think it's a great opportunity for our hunter-killer group. A regular shooting gallery."

"For them or us?" Jablonski asked.

"Good question," Sorenson said.

The next day, MacIntosh brought another dispatch to Sorenson. "Our convoy has been diverted south to avoid the *Trutz* line."

"Maybe we should detach these hunter-killer groups from the convoys and go after the subs," Sorenson said. "That's the only way we are going to beat those guys."

"Don't be too eager," Jablonski said.

$\bullet$ $\bullet$ $\bullet$

The voyage continued uneventfully with good weather and enough wind to make take-offs and landings easy. Sorenson watched with interest as the ungainly TBFs and the speedy F4Fs plunked down on the *Santee's* small deck. There were only a few minor casualties because the prevailing winds were steady at 15 knots. All aircraft had been stored below so that aircraft not catching wires could take off again. Sorenson watched one

TBF blow a tire and bang its prop into the deck. Another took several wave-offs before it could catch a wire and almost ran out of fuel. "Amateurs," Sorenson muttered. "Damned kids!"

On June 30, a *Santee* aircraft, after taking off at dawn, reported a possible submarine submerging 15 miles ahead. The *O'Leary* was sent out to investigate. Sorenson and Meredith put their uniform caps inside the pilothouse and enjoyed the rush of warm salt air. Sorenson leaned against the 40 knots of relative wind and watched the wind whip through Meredith's long black hair. Meredith's mustache stood straight back along his cheeks. Sorenson felt his shorter hair ruffling in the wind, and he squinted a little to keep his eyes from watering. Sorenson raised a hand and tested the wind. "Must be like the Pacific," he shouted against the wind.

Meredith nodded. "It should be. We're clear down to twenty-two degrees north latitude and it's late June."

Meredith raised his binoculars and searched ahead. Sorenson went up on the fire control platform to get a better view ahead. In minutes an excited lookout reported, "Smoke flare ahead!"

Sorenson searched the area and decided that the thin wisp of smoke was coming from a smoke flare dropped earlier by the searching aircraft. It was almost out, but as they neared the area, a spreading circle of green dye outlined the contact area.

The bright sunlight almost blinded Steele as he stepped out on the bridge wing. "Captain, we don't have any contact. He's long gone. I recommend that we start an expanding square search."

"Concur."

Steele returned to the darkened CIC as they turned to the first leg after passing through the green dye. On the third turn, Terrill called from the sonar stack, "I've got him!"

Steele flipped the switch on the squawk box. "Sonar contact!"

The contact reverberated clearly on the CIC speaker as Terrill scanned across it, but something about it intrigued Steele. He used the squawk box and asked Meredith to come inside the CIC.

They listened for a few minutes. Then Steele grinned. "Captain, do you know what it is?"

"It isn't a submarine, although the contact is solid and moving slowly. Could it be a whale?"

"Almost correct. It could be a whale, but it's two whales. Can you hear them talking?"

Steele reached across Terrill and turned up the speaker. Faint squealing sounds filled the room. The effect was eerie. Meredith cocked his head to it for several minutes. Then he straightened up. "I guess we ought to pull the drapes and give them some privacy."

.   .   .

On the fire control platform, Sorenson sat on the forward edge of the raised director platform and opened his shirt. The *O'Leary* turned in a wide arc and headed downwind toward the distant *Santee*. The apparent breeze, now lessened by the 10 knot tail wind, was a pleasant 10 knots over the deck, and Sorenson let it riffle through his open shirt. Then he took off his shirt and let the sun warm his aching back. For a moment he felt like he was back on the beach in Norfolk with Ferren.

The sea was almost a Pacific blue, and he began to think about what he had heard of the *O'Leary*'s days in the Pacific. The battles against the onrushing Japanese must have been harrowing considering the overwhelming odds with no air defense. The *O'Leary*'s luck had held, but would it last much longer?

He lay back on the wooden grating of the fire control platform and breathed deeply. Then he tried to think about more pleasant things, and his mind returned to Ferren and the days they had enjoyed in Norfolk. The memories, pleasant as they were, blurred, and the next thing he knew, the director trainer was shaking him. "Mister Sorenson, Morales says they are about to close the pantry. Better go down below if you want some lunch."

Sorenson rose reluctantly and stretched. "Thanks," he said. Just ahead the *Santee* turned into the wind, and the *O'Leary* slipped into a screening station as he went down the ladder to the wardroom.

.   .   .

On the third of July the convoy arrived off Casablanca, and the *Santee* group entered the harbor, now cleared and enlarged. Sorenson sent the crew off on well-earned liberty. The next morning he walked around the ship on his regular inspection. All was well, with men sweeping and chipping paint, until he got to the forecastle. Behind gun one a group of men surrounded Kendrick. Kendrick was sawing a wooden wheel spoke held against the top of an upturned bucket. Sorenson watched him for a few minutes. When Kendrick finished the cut, he handed the small piece to one of the bystanders and said, "Next! Only a dollar an inch."

"Two inches," said the next man in line.

Sorenson got a little closer. On the deck next to Kendrick were a dozen wooden wheel spokes and a wheel hub. He said, "Kendrick, what the hell is going on?"

The small crowd opened to let him in, and Kendrick stood up, grinning. "Well, sir, me and Carmody wanted to see the French gun we shot up the last time we were here. We hired a taxi and went out on the road to Fedala. We didn't think we'd find it, but a spare twenty slipped to a local hot shot led us to it. It was still lying on its side in the bushes. Of course the locals had stripped all the metal off of it, but I guess they didn't have any use for the old wooden wheels. For another twenty, an old gaffer cut the wheels into pieces, and here they are. Would you like a free sample?"

"I don't think so. But aren't you taking advantage of your shipmates charging that much?"

"Hell no, sir. Twenty bucks for the cab, twenty for the finder, and another twenty for the guy who cut it up. We'll be lucky to break even. Ask Carmody. He's keeping the books."

•   •   •

Two days later they got underway and stood out of the harbor, followed by forty empty ships, which were to form a convoy back to the States.

Chapter Thirty

As Casablanca faded behind them, Meredith called Sorenson, Steele, and MacIntosh into CIC for a conference. When they had assembled, he began to brief them on the last-minute pre-sail conference he had attended aboard the *Santee*.

"Intelligence knows that the *Trutz* line has been abandoned and the U-boats from it moved to an area south of the Azores. More importantly, our carrier group will leave this convoy on the 12th and search for those subs south of the Azores."

"Now we go after the bastards," Sorenson said.

"We've chased the Seawolves out of their dens," Meredith said. "From now on, there will be at least two hunter-killer groups in the mid-Atlantic at all times."

"Which other carrier group will operate with us?" Steele asked.

Meredith said, "The *Core*, with *Bulmer*, *Badger*, and *Barker* as escorts. Those of us who survived Java will remember the *Bulmer* and *Barker*. It will be good to see them again."

MacIntosh asked, "Where will we go at the end of the cruise?"

"Back to Norfolk."

MacIntosh brightened. "If you've got to go to war, this is the way to do it."

•   •   •

On the morning of the 12th, *Santee* and her escorts left the convoy and headed north toward the Azores. The first two days were routine, as the *Santee* launched a series of air searches that covered the maximum area.

On the third day of searching, Steele listened to the aircraft frequency as a surfaced submarine was found by a Wildcat-Avenger team, the common names for the F4F and TBF. The Wildcat fighter quickly strafed the submarine, which made an emergency dive. The Avenger dropped one of the new homing torpedoes called FIDO for the first time in operational use. The pilot described its run over the medium frequency circuit. "The damned thing hit with a helluva splash!" he said in an excited tone. "I thought it had sunk, but I looked around the area, and sure enough, it was nosing around in circles just like a dog closing in on a fireplug. When it acquired the target, I could see it going deep. Then all hell broke loose, and there was oil and spare parts all over the ocean. We've got a great weapon."

Steele grinned, and said to Terrill, "Even allowing for an excited pilot, sounds like FIDO will make a great difference in ASW warfare."

MacIntosh was more sober. "The last intelligence summary said the Germans were about to deploy an acoustic homing torpedo of their own. That means we'll have to figure a way to counter it."

Steele shook his head. "I'm sure we will, but in the meantime the best defense will be to sink the U-boats before they can fire at us."

The next day Steele listened again as a pilot made a FIDO drop. "My God," the pilot yelled. "This thing works just like Freddy said it did. We got a hit the easy way. Just dropped the damned thing and watched it do the work. I thought it sank, but I guess it was just going after the Kraut. The explosion was down deep, and it took a few minutes for the oil to come up. What a hell of a weapon!"

•   •   •

That night, the *Santee* reported a surface radar contact. Meredith started to ask Bronte, who had the surface search radar watch, why the *O'Leary* hadn't picked up the contact, but then he remembered that the *Santee*'s radar was higher and therefore had a greater range. The *Santee* sent the *O'Leary* out to investigate.

Meredith said, "Sound general quarters. I have the conn. All ahead flank."

Soon the *O'Leary*'s radar acquired the target. Meredith ordered CIC to give the fire control director the approximate range and bearing by telephone. Unlike the newer destroyers, the *O'Leary* had no way to transfer directly a surface radar bearing and range to the fire control director.

Meredith pulled at the ends of his mustache, hoping Steiner would acquire the target visually, but nothing happened, and he knew he would have to illuminate either with starshells or the large searchlight.

At three thousand yards, Meredith chose the searchlight and gave the order to illuminate and to commence firing as soon as possible. The big light flashed on, swept a narrow arc, and caught the submarine hull broadside to. Men on the conning tower seemed to be surprised, trying to shield their eyes from the glaring beam. They scrambled below. Spray jetted out of the vents along the hull.

The director pointed and trainer shouted, "On target!"

Then Steiner bellowed, "Commence firing! Commence firing!"

The submarine was slightly on the port bow, as Meredith had planned, so that the waist gun on that side could bear on the submarine. The after gun could not quite make it without endangering the ship.

A two-gun salvo went out, the projectile from the waist gun swooshing by the bridge wing. Meredith followed the tracers, and just after the projectiles landed, a second salvo crashed out, and Meredith followed the tracers again.

The first landed over, but the second raised a double spout of water around the submarine's hull.

"Down one double oh!" Steiner spotted, and the next salvo boomed.

The fourth salvo raised sparks from the submarine's after deck, and Steiner shouted, "Rapid fire!"

"Great!" Meredith shouted. "Give it to them!"

Salvos poured out as fast as the gun crews could load,

and a projectile hit directly at the base of the conning tower, sending pieces of the superstructure flying. The pieces were caught in the searchlight's beam, fluttering like giant moths.

Before another projectile could hit, the submarine slid rapidly below the protective surface, obviously crash diving.

"Cease firing!" Meredith ordered reluctantly. "Out searchlight."

From the fire control platform Meredith could hear Steiner relaying his order, and the searchlight beam went out.

The sudden darkness, after the brilliant beam of the searchlight and the flashing of the guns, was so complete that Meredith realized he had lost his night vision. He knew he would have to rely on the surface search radar until his eyes returned to normal, and he was glad that Bronte was operating the console.

Then sonar reported, "Sonar contact! Definite submarine! Bearing zero six five! Range one oh double oh!"

Meredith ordered, "Standby to attack. Shallow pattern. I'm heading for it at 17 knots."

Steele's voice came over the speaker. "She's going down fast, but she's noisy. Sounds like metal flapping."

After the depth charges hammered the water, Meredith brought the O'Leary around to open the range for another attack.

With the excitement of the gunfire and the first attack wearing off, Meredith attacked deliberately with depth charges set on medium.

Steele reported, "Lost contact due to short range. We lost it at a longer range than before, so she must be going deeper. I don't know whether she's doing it deliberately or whether she's heavily damaged. Recommend set depth charges on deep."

Meredith said, "It's too late to set the depth charges on deep this run. We'll have to drop this load set on medium."

The attack seemed good, but there was no change in the submarine's situation. Meredith came around for another attack and gave the order, "Set depth charges on deep." He thought about Gerlach and his men scurrying about on the crowded after deck and fantail in the dark, trying to keep up with the changing settings and Meredith grinned, wondering if the men had been able to keep out of Gerlach's way.

Meredith brought his mind back to the present and began the approach.

•   •   •

Sorenson, in the CIC, watched Steele operate the new sonar range recorder. He noted that the delay timetable for the new tear drop charges had been reduced. "You like the new depth charges?" he asked.

Steele said, "You bet! We have more time to compensate for the sub's last-minute maneuvers. He hears the shortened intervals between pings, and he knows we're getting close to the drop point. Then, when he thinks we're there, he changes course or speed or both."

"Couldn't you keep your scale on long range?"

"Sure, but we'd make less pings and have less information to go on. It's a trade-off."

Sorenson watched the traces on the sonar range recorder march down the paper. The range rate decreased and the bearing began to drift left. He was able to follow Steele's reasoning when Steele reported, "Target is changing course to his port. Recommend delay an extra five seconds before drop, and decrease lead by five degrees."

Meredith acknowledged, and Sorenson could hear him giving the orders.

Then they lost contact because of short range, and Sorenson noticed that the wait before they dropped was noticeably shorter than with the old depth charges. When the order was given to drop, Sorenson listened carefully as the depth charges sank and exploded astern. Then, for the first time, he heard the awful sound of a submarine breaking up at extreme depth. First, there was a tearing of metal as the parts of the superstructure came away from the pressure hull. Then came the dull sound of an implosion as the hull collapsed inward. Sorenson knew that fifty German souls were within seconds of death, some by severe trauma, and others by drowning or asphyxiation. The men in the CIC were silent as the terrible sounds died away.

Funny, Sorenson thought, none of them seems to show any exaltation, and I certainly don't feel any. What a hell of a way to die, even if it is quick. I wouldn't wish this kind of death on anybody, even those German bastards. Then he remembered how many merchant seamen had been killed without warning, and he realized dying or burning in a fiery explosion was worse than the quick death of the German sailors, and he felt better.

Steele was the first to recover. He pulled down the transmit lever on the squawk box. "We just heard the submarine break up, Captain, no further contact. Recommend we rejoin."

Sorenson heard cheering as the word of success swept over the ship. Maybe they wouldn't be cheering if they had heard what I heard, he thought.

Sorenson leaned on the DRT as the annunciators clanged in the pilothouse. The blowers whined as the *O'Leary* heeled in its turn. Then he went out on the bridge to get some fresh air and to fight off nausea. He thought that this was a poor way to fight a war, when you couldn't see your enemy, much as you hated them. Surface action he understood, but the remoteness and impersonalness of the undersea kill haunted him.

*   *   *

The next week was without contacts, but on June 24, west of Madeira, an Avenger-Wildcat team found a submarine on the surface. The Avenger launched a FIDO. After the torpedo failed to acquire the target, the Avenger dropped its 500 pound depth charge. There was no way to tell what the results were. The pilot reported, "I made a normal drop and the fish started up and went down okay. Don't know what happened after that."

Steele shook his head. "Maybe we were being too confident about FIDO. Nothing works all the time."

*   *   *

A week later, after no further contacts, the *Santee* group shadowed a west-bound convoy of empty merchantmen in mid-ocean. The lure of the convoy helped, and on the next day, an Avenger-Wildcat team sighted two submarines on the surface. Meredith and Sorenson rushed to the CIC to listen to the aircraft.

A pilot radioed, "One is a milk cow. It's the kind intelligence said can also carry mines. It was getting ready to fuel the other. The Wildcat is strafing both of them to keep the gun crews below."

Then he said, "Damn! Both of them are submerging. I'm attacking the big one first, and it gets the FIDO."

The voice on the radio was drowned out by a loud explosion. After a few seconds the voice came back in.

"Good God!" the pilot shouted. "There must be a volcano down there. The whole ocean erupted!"

Steele said, "I think he was right that the milk cow had mines aboard, and the FIDO explosion set them off. That would be a lot of TNT."

•   •   •

The *Santee* group was now west of the German U-boat area, and they continued west toward Norfolk, providing protection for the convoy as they went.

On August 6, Sorenson sighted the net vessel, and the *O'Leary* began the familiar transit up the channel following astern of the *Santee*. Sorenson felt proud to be part of a new team that might eventually turn the tide against the U-boats, and he was deeply satisfied. Then he realized that the Germans hadn't used their own homing torpedo yet, and he felt a pang of apprehension.

Chapter Thirty-one

As usual, Sorenson waited to call Ferren until Carmody had the mail opened. When Carmody came up to Sorenson's room there was a long, slim box on top of the huge pile of mail he put on Sorenson's desk.

Carmody said, "This is personal so I didn't open it. It says 'Cartier's' on the return address. I think it's a jeweler in New York. Do you know what this is?"

"Probably a free sample. Let me have it." Sorenson stuck the box in his pocket. "If that's all, the rest of the mail can wait until tomorrow. I'm going ashore, and you do the same."

 •   •   •

Ferren was waiting for him, and when she opened the door, he could smell steak on the stove. He kissed her deeply, and took her into the living room.

"Do you want a beer?"

"Two." He finished the first in seconds.

Ferren watched him. "What's the hurry?"

"It's summer, and I'm thirsty. Also hungry for you."

He pulled out the box he had received in the mail and handed it to her. "This is a bracelet for you to show you how much I appreciate your thoughtfulness in giving your first pendant to Linda."

She opened it slowly, held it up to the light, and looked at it. "It isn't glass," she said, "and the diamonds are twice as big as those on the pendant you gave me."

"Put it on."

She did, and held her wrist up to the light. "It's a little big, but then I'm getting used to Texans. Now I have a surprise for you—a dinner party at the Meredith's tomorrow. The four of us, the MacIntoshs, Steiners, and Chuck Renard, David Fineman, and their dates."

They went into the tiny dining room to eat. Ferren had candles on the table, and in the light of the candles Sorenson noticed a glow in Ferren's face.

"Are you all right?" he asked.

"Never better," she said, "and I'm glad to see that your face didn't take another beating."

"Almost like being on the beach out there at sea. We went south, and there were days when I could sunbathe."

"Did you like working with the carrier group?"

"Yes. I think we hold the key to the antisubmarine war in the Atlantic if the Jerries don't come up with some new weapon. The combination of the destroyer and the ASW carrier and her aircraft may do the job. We did a lot of damage, and I think the Germans are retreating from the Central Atlantic to waters nearer home. When we can clean them out of places like the Bay of Biscay, we'll be on the way to final victory in the Atlantic."

"What's so important about the Bay of Biscay?"

"It's next to Spain and Portugal, and both are neutral. The German U-boats leave from French ports, transit the Bay, or circle it in neutral waters, and intercept convoys bound from Great Britain to the Mediterranean. It is also a short route to the Mid-Atlantic and the Caribbean and the coast of the United States. It's too far for ASW patrol aircraft from Great Britain to cover, although they are beginning to use very long-range aircraft to get there."

Ferren said, "Enough of the war. I've been waiting for you all day, and I'd like to go to bed." She raised her eyebrows. "There was a time when you wouldn't have spent all this time eating and talking."

•   •   •

At the Meredith's party Sorenson's tensions of the past month slowly subsided as two beers and Linda's beef stroganoff nourished his mind and body. "Sonya's recipe," Linda announced.

After dinner, they moved to the living room. As Ferren sat down, the new bracelet slid down from under her sleeve. Meredith noticed it. He took her arm and looked at the bracelet closely. Then he whistled. "This isn't glass. Neither was the pendant."

Meredith turned and looked at Sorenson. "Let's sit down and discuss a few things."

Meredith picked up his drink and took a deep swallow. "First, I had Linda's pendant appraised, and it's worth over a thousand dollars. This bracelet must be worth three thousand."

"No," Sorenson said. "You're exaggerating."

"Not much."

Renard smiled knowingly. "And what about those L. L. Bean suits?"

Sorenson looked at him and cleared his throat, but Meredith interrupted him.

"Don't say anything, Tex. The jig is up. Ferren has been telling Linda about your ranch and the thousands of steers on it. She says you both rode for three days and never came to any of the ranch boundaries. With the shortage of beef these days, you and your brother must be millionaires."

"Well," Sorenson began, "I . . ."

"Don't say anything. I can guess the rest."

Renard sat up straighter. "Jeez. How many millions?"

Sorenson didn't answer. Ferren took his hand. "There isn't anything wrong with having a little money if you spend it wisely. Admit it. You're a rich naval officer."

Sorenson took a deep breath, "All right, but all of you have to promise me this won't go outside this room."

They all promised, Renard somewhat reluctantly.

Sorenson looked at Renard. "We'll need some one to be business manager of our ranch if it gets any bigger, but he'll have to be a man who can keep a promise and keep his mouth shut. Are you interested? After the war, of course."

Renard's head bobbed. "Oh, yes. I'd like to learn about cattle. I know accounting and finance."

"There's more than that to it. You'll have to learn to fly and to ride a horse."

"Fly?"

"Yes, the bank in Sorenville is fifty miles from the nearest large town. We can't let cash lie around in a small bank, and I don't think you'd want to ride a horse that far. The trip in a pick-up truck is long and rough."

"Bandits?"

"No, we just don't want to lose the interest we could earn on the money."

Ferren said, "I've already learned to fly. That's the way I'll go shopping."

.   .   .

Meredith attended a number of sessions aboard the *Santee* designed to improve the cooperation between the carrier's aircraft and the escorts. The commanding officer of the *Santee* cited an intelligence warning that many larger U-Boats had been equipped with heavy antiaircraft machine guns. With this heavy armament they had been instructed to stay on the surface and engage attacking aircraft.

"Seawolves," Meredith said. "We know all about them. Maybe two destroyers should be sent out as soon as a contact is found to assist the aircraft. The aircraft could circle outside machine gun range to encourage the submarine to stay on the surface until the surface attack unit arrived."

The air group commander nodded, but said that the submarine change of tactics was because of the success of FIDO. He thought that the submarines were trying to keep the aircraft outside of FIDO's short range. He suggested adding another fighter to the search elements to suppress fire so that the Avengers could get in closer to drop their FIDOs.

Both suggestions were adopted before the conference ended.

.   .   .

Meredith left the conference confident that the hunterkiller group would improve, but as he drove back to the *O'Leary* there was a feeling of apprehension he couldn't quite quantify. What would happen when the Germans put more large Seawolves out to sea? One of them could almost face down a four-stacker. The commanding officer of the *Santee* had agreed to send out two destroyers on a contact, but how often could he? And a Seawolf's eight 20-millimeter guns could keep even three aircraft at bay. Add to that the acoustic torpedo, and the Seawolf would be a tough opponent for two four-stackers and three aircraft and maybe overwhelming for just one four-stacker.

He resolved to speak to the Captain of the *Santee* again about using two destroyers for a surface attack unit. Maybe the answer was to provide four escorts to the group instead of three. When he almost ran through a red light he decided to worry about the problem later, but he was still apprehensive.

That night he dreamed he was running across a prairie with a light rifle in his hands and being chased by a pack of wolves. He stumbled, and he could feel teeth tearing at his legs. Then he was aware that Linda was shaking him. "Wake up," she said. "What's wrong?"

He sighed and rubbed his calf. "Thank God it's just a cramp."

•   •   •

On July 24th they got orders to be ready to leave two days later for Bermuda and eventually the Central Atlantic and Casablanca.

Chapter Thirty-two

When the *Santee* group got underway, the *Greer* was substituted for the *Bainbridge* in the escort group, and the *MacLeish* was detached, leaving them with only three destroyers. Meredith grimaced. "There go our two-ship surface attack units."

Sorenson nodded. "I don't like the idea. There may be trouble using only one ship."

On the trip to Bermuda, most of the crew spent off-watch hours sun-bathing, but with their life jackets nearby. Chief Bellows made the rounds of the topsides checking up on them. Once when he passed by, Bronte muttered to Carmody, lying next to him. "He's acting like an old lady! We don't need to be checked on."

Carmody rolled over. "Yes, we do, or at least some of us do. I heard Mister Sorenson tell Chief Bellows that he spotted two men without life jackets yesterday. Chief Bellows is cruising around because Mister Sorenson told him to."

"I guess that's okay, then. Mister Sorenson always tries to do right by us."

The stop in Bermuda was just for fueling. After they got underway heavy rain closed in, making flight operations impossible. At dawn the third day the weather cleared, and *Santee* began launching aircraft. Sorenson stood on the bridge wing, watching with interest. Occasionally he used body English when a pilot came in off the normal flight path. He turned to Meredith. "The pilots are hoping to get rid of two days of rust. Even a short time away from flying can cause accidents."

Meredith laughed. "Tex, I know how much you miss flying. Do you think you can be happy in the surface Navy?"

Sorenson watched a final aircraft land. "I'm not sure, but I've qualified for a private pilot's license in Norfolk. I can fly all I want. I expect to keep a couple of aircraft on the ranch in Texas."

"Did you take Ferren up while you were flying in Norfolk?"

"We flew in the mornings and went to the beach in the afternoons. She's about to qualify for her private pilot's license."

Meredith grinned. "Bull says the beach you recommended to him was so isolated he and Sonya didn't wear bathing suits."

Sorenson said, "They weren't really necessary. Would you like to go with us sometime?"

Meredith pursed his lips. "Ah, maybe you could just tell us where it is. Linda's a little too modest."

Sorenson grinned. "We wore ours, too. Bull is in another league."

•   •   •

On the fourth day out, a *Santee* aircraft team reported a contact ahead. The *Overton* was sent to investigate. Soon the pilot reported the contact submerging and that depth charges had been dropped.

Meredith and Sorenson listened in the CIC. A sudden transmission squawked over the TBS. A second team searching on the beam of the formation had made a contact at 25 miles. The *Santee* directed the *O'Leary* to investigate. Meredith gave the necessary orders to Gerlach, and they swung around and speeded up.

Meredith said, "We agreed at the conference to try to send out two-ship surface attack units, but you can't do it very well with only three escorts when we have two contacts. One has to stay with the carrier."

Thirty minutes later lookouts spotted three aircraft on the horizon. Two Wildcats were diving and firing their guns. The submarine was trying to fight off the aircraft rather than submerge. Tracers streaked past the diving Wildcats. When the Avenger tried to attack, it broke off in the face of heavy fire. On a second attack a trail of smoke blossomed from the Avenger's wing root, and it limped toward the charging *O'Leary*. The submarine, freed of the threat of a FIDO drop, submerged quickly. The crippled Avenger circled the *O'Leary* once and then dipped into the water, tail first. It bounced twice and then settled. The pilot climbed out on the wing and moved aft where he struggled to get the canopy open.

Alvarado, following the actions on the Avenger, shouted, "The pilot is having trouble and is waving at us."

Meredith raised his binoculars and looked at the Avenger. He wasted no time. "Mister Gerlach, I have the conn. Go down to the forecastle and take charge. We'll have to abandon the sub and come alongside the aircraft. The pilot can't seem to get the two crewmen out."

Sorenson said, "You're taking a chance with the submarine."

"I know, but I think she's just trying to get away, and this may mean two lives. Tell Steele to keep a sharp sonar search, and if he gets a contact I'll take off."

The *O'Leary* swung to head for the Avenger, and Meredith maneuvered to come just upwind of the floating aircraft. He stopped the engines when the aircraft was slightly off the bow and backed them when it was abreast the forecastle. At the same time he tried to keep the *O'Leary* pointed in the direction of the last sighting of the submarine so that the ship would be the smallest possible target. The ship shuddered to a halt with the Avenger bobbing near the side. Two men with lines attached to their waists and small bolt cutters and metal shears hanging from their life jackets jumped over the side. They swam to the Avenger and climbed up a slanted wing. The two men and the pilot bent over the after canopy and worked over the sliding mechanism.

Meredith drummed his fingers against the bridge railing. Had he made a mistake? Was the submarine getting into a firing position? He turned to Alvarado. "Keep a sharp lookout toward the last position of the submarine." Then he shouted into the pilothouse. "Tell sonar to search ahead."

Alvarado screwed his eye tightly to his telescope and muttered, "Come on! Come on!"

Suddenly the canopy broke loose, and the men aft were helped out. But before they could be taken aboard, Alvarado shouted, "Torpedo wake! One point on the port bow!"

Steiner leaned over the fire control platform rail. "I see the wake. Recommend back emergency full."

Meredith heard him. He couldn't see the wake, but he trusted Steiner. "Back emergency full!" he yelled.

Alvarado pointed it out to Sorenson. Sorenson searched as the ship began to shudder. "I see it! Steady as you go."

From Sonar came an excited voice, "Torpedo launched dead ahead!"

Meredith shouted, "Rudder amidships!" He waited anxiously. Then he could see the straight wake of small bubbles coming toward the position where they had been, and he let out the breath he was holding. The torpedo passed close to the Avenger, almost exactly through their previous position.

Meredith shouted, "All ahead standard! Turns for seventeen knots! Sonar search thirty degrees on each bow!"

Almost immediately Terrill got a sonar contact. Steele's voice informed the bridge, "Bearing one two eight. Range two oh double oh."

Sorenson shook his head. "The guys on the Avenger can wait. Luckily the water isn't too cold for a swim if the aircraft goes down."

Steele reported, "Range one one double oh."

Then the range closed rapidly. Meredith was looking ahead watching the bubbles of the torpedo wake dissipate. Steele said, "Lost contact due to short range."

In a few seconds the depth charges went off. Nothing came up, and Meredith made a second attack also without results. Steele said, "We lost him, and I think he's below the layer."

Sorenson looked anxiously back toward the Avenger, now barely afloat. "Captain, I recommend we close the Avenger and get the men aboard."

Meredith said, "I agree. Let's go. All ahead flank."

Just a ship length short of the Avenger, Meredith backed full, and the *O'Leary* shuddered to a halt near the aircraft. The crew and its rescuers slid down the wing, swam over to the side, and climbed up the cargo net rigged by Chief Bellows.

Meredith gave orders for the machine guns to sink the wallowing Avenger, and they were off at flank speed.

•   •   •

Sorenson, with the situation under control, now had time to leave the bridge, and he went down to the wardroom. The pilot was stretched out on the wardroom table, and Fineman was listening to his chest with a stethoscope.

"How is he?" Sorenson asked.

Before Fineman could answer, the pilot whooped, "Tex, you old bastard! Good to see you!"

"It's Buster Benson! Are you all right?"

"Sure. Maybe a cracked rib."

Fineman said, "I don't think so. Just a bruise. You can get up."

"Give him some brandy," Sorenson said. "Doc, this is Buster Benson. A pretty good pilot. We were in the same company together at the Naval Academy."

"And at Pensacola in flight training until you got tossed out just as we were about to finish advanced training and get our wings."

"A long story, but come up to the bridge and meet the captain."

Sorenson took Benson up to the bridge and introduced him to Meredith. Benson asked to stay on the bridge while they closed the *Santee* to transfer the aviators by highline.

Sorenson and Benson watched the *Santee* come over the horizon. Sorenson said, "That flight deck doesn't look very big. I made all my landings in advanced training on a full-sized carrier deck, and even it looked mighty small."

"It's not bad once you get used to it. As I remember it, you were pretty good. I don't think you'd have any trouble after a few landings."

Sorenson smiled. "I'd like to try it sometime."

"Are you serious? If you are, I'll check you out when we're ashore in Norfolk. When we're in port we always move ashore to the Oceana Naval Air Station. And I'll ask our skipper to give you a try. We really need pilots these days. We're building carriers by the dozens, and we can't train pilots fast enough. We're grabbing every live body we can salvage. You'd be a natural."

"Yeah, but I had some trouble with Lieutenant Somerville over a little flat hatting."

"So what. These Avengers fly at low altitudes all the time. Somerville was shot down and lost at Midway. He didn't fly his torpedo plane low enough. Our skipper used to run flight training before he took over the *Santee*, and he can fix anything. Just let me know if you want to try for it."

Just ahead the *Santee* turned into the wind. As the *O'Leary* rounded up astern of her, wave tops slapped the side of the carrier and bounced upwards. The *O'Leary* began her approach, Meredith at the conn, and Sorenson noticed that Benson had a sheen of perspiration on his face. His hands clasped and unclasped, and he cleared his throat rapidly. Benson said to Sorenson under his breath, "Jesus! Look at those waves banging in there. They could give me an enema I don't need. Tex, will I be safe?"

"Sure. We do this all the time. The waves are small today."

The swells between the ships got bigger as the *O'Leary* came abreast of the transfer point and closed in. Wave tops swirled noisily in the gap and met occasionally, sending gouts of white water up the sides of the ships.

"I don't feel so good," Benson said. "I wouldn't do what you do for twice flight pay."

Sorenson laughed. "Just keep your eyes closed. Most of us watching you land on that small flight deck say the same thing, but I'd still like to try it some time."

Sorenson went down to the well deck to see Benson off. He turned to Fineman. "Do you have any bottles of brandy in your pocket?"

"Sure. A couple I didn't dispense in the wardroom."

"Give another to Benson. This is one time when a man rates a brandy before the hardship, not after."

Even with the brandy, Sorenson noted that Benson shut his eyes and gripped the arms of the boatswain's chair with white-knuckled hands.

Sorenson went up to the bridge during the transfer and stood behind Meredith. Over the *Santee* he could hear the familiar bellow of aircraft engines running up, and he became lost in thought. He wanted to fly again, but he liked destroyers, too. Was flying in the Navy possible? Benson had been optimistic.

There was a pull at his elbow, and he turned to find Alvarado offering him a mug of signal bridge coffee. Sorenson sighed. He knew he would have a difficult time leaving destroyers and men like Alvarado. The fact that Alvarado had offered him the mug, when he could just as easily have sent down to the wardroom for a fancy cup, meant that the crew had accepted him as one of them.

He tried to thank Alvarado, but the aircraft engines drowned out the words. He grinned and nodded instead, and Alvarado grinned in return.

• • •

The rest of the passage was quiet. One morning Renard brought a decoded dispatch up to Meredith and Sorenson. Sorenson read it, and said, "Intelligence thinks most of the German U-boats are no longer passing north of Great Britain to the Atlantic and are using the neutral waters of Spain and Portugal and the Bay of Biscay for transit and as sanctuaries."

Meredith said, "That doesn't make them any less dangerous. We'll just have to go after them."

They moored at Casablanca on August 29 and left for Norfolk three days later. The trip back was unusually quiet without a single contact, and when the *O'Leary* steamed in to Norfolk, Sorenson felt the ASW battle in the Atlantic was turning. The only trouble was that the further back the Germans were pushed the tougher they would be. If the hunter-killer group went into the Bay of Biscay, the Germans would have the advantage of their own air cover.

• • •

They moored at the naval base, and Sorenson found Ferren overjoyed by his safe return. Two days later he drove his Buick to the Oceana Naval Air Station. He flew in an Avenger with his friend Buster Benson for two mornings, and on the third day returned for breakfast in the wardroom.

Meredith strolled in late and sat down for a cup of coffee. "What are you doing here? I thought you'd be out flying again."

Sorenson shook his head. "I think I've had enough. I checked out okay except for refresher carrier landings, and I called on the skipper of the *Santee*. He was optimistic and said all I have to do is sign up."

"Are you going back to flying?"

"Maybe I enjoyed what flying we did, but it got a little old."

"Are you having second thoughts about being a Navy pilot?"

"I realize now I like the freedom of flying, but Navy flying, particularly over land, isn't very free. It took us an hour to file a flight plan and give the aircraft a preflight inspection."

"That's one reason why the Navy has such a good safety record," Meredith said.

"I liked the way we flew out at the civilian airfield below Oceana. We were safe, but not as detail happy. I could fly the way I liked and not worry about the aircraft so much. That Avenger cockpit is full of dials, lights, and controls. Too many. More than a ship has."

"You've got to make up your mind soon."

"I know. I'm still on the fence. I think I could qualify quickly and go to a carrier in a few weeks. But I feel a lot better now that I have a civilian license and can afford to fly when ever I want to."

"Sounds like some day you can own your own air force."

"I'll make up my mind soon. I'll do it when we get back to Norfolk."

•   •   •

The next day Carmody brought a thick mailgram up to Sorenson and laid it on his desk with a grin. "More promotions?" Sorenson asked.

"Two; Ensigns Steele and Jablonski are now jay gees. When do you want to make it official?"

"This afternoon. I'll take care of it with the Captain."

    •   •   •

For Sorenson the stay in Norfolk slipped by pleasantly with the Blue October days he remembered from the year before. He and Ferren spent several days on the beach, walking for miles, dodging patches of kelp and low-flying pelicans. The stay ended too soon, and the *Santee* group sailed in mid-October for Casablanca, shepherding a large convoy bound for the Mediterranean. No submarines attacked, and Sorenson was convinced that the German submarines had lost their grip on another piece of the Atlantic.

The *Santee* group arrived in Casablanca on October 13th and left hurriedly the next day.

Sorenson asked MacIntosh, "Do you know why we left so fast?"

"No," MacIntosh said, his Scottish accent still evident. "But there was a rumor on the *Santee* that we were going to meet one of our new battleships."

Four days out of Casablanca, the *Santee* aircraft began to provide aircover for the battleship *Iowa*. Once, when flight operations took them near the *Iowa*, Alvarado reported that he could see a civilian in a flowing boat cloak sitting in a chair on the machine-gun deck just below the bridge.

Meredith turned to Sorenson. "Do you suppose that's who I think it is?"

Sorenson said, "President Roosevelt was over here somewhere."

Two days after joining the *Iowa*, the *Santee* group was detached and sent to the Bay of Biscay for ASW operations.

On the bridge, Sorenson showed Steele the dispatch after Meredith read it.

Steele wrinkled his brow. "Now we get in the big leagues with the big U-boats. That's where they've been transiting. Now it will be a showdown. Either we get these damned Seawolves, or . . ."

". . . they get us," Sorenson finished.

Chapter Thirty-three

It took the *Santee* three days to approach the Bay of Biscay. The *O'Leary* fueled from the *Santee*, and Sorenson inspected the ship to insure that she was secured for heavy seas. As the group steamed north, the temperature dropped 10 degrees each day, and the days shortened appreciably.

Sorenson, shivering on the bridge, called Renard up to see him. Renard came up, blowing on his hands. "Damn! It's cold up here!"

Sorenson smiled. "Glad to hear you've learned to swear properly."

Renard shivered, his light skin growing even paler. "It doesn't help much."

Sorenson said, "It will have to do. Please re-issue the L. L. Bean cold-weather clothing."

The suits created a sensation on the weather decks of the carrier when they came alongside to fuel again two days later. Alvarado, after semaphoring back and forth with his signalmen friends on the carrier signal bridge, reported, "They didn't say a damn thing about the suits. I think they wished they had some. One guy said it gets cold as hell in the Bay of Biscay."

Sorenson, standing nearby, grinned. He figured that the growing panoply of flags, figures, and hashmarks on the side of the *O'Leary*'s bridge would impress the young sailors who might want to make a remark about an *O'Leary* sailor wearing a pink fur-lined parka with zippers on the side of the trousers.

On the fourth day, just 200 miles from the edge of the Bay of Biscay, *Santee* aircraft began to run aircraft searches over the bay.

In the CIC Sorenson said to Jablonski, "Lay out the charts we'll need."

"They're here, starting with the area around Land's End, at the southern tip of England. From below Land's End the charts run east to the coast of France and then south to Spain and Portugal. I also have charts from Cape Finisterre south to Cape St. Vincent at the southwestern tip of Portugal."

MacIntosh and Steele had just come in CIC to join them. Jablonski pointed out the 100 fathom curve paralleling the coasts of Spain and Portugal. "It's fairly close to the shore," he said, "and German submarines can have plenty of depth and still be in neutral waters transiting from their bases at Bayonne, Bordeaux, and La Pallice."

Steele said, "From Portugal, it's a short trip to the mid-Atlantic."

Jablonski nodded. "If we could deny these southern ports to the Nazis, they would have to go north around the British Isles and then south for hundreds of miles to get to the South and Central Atlantic."

Sorenson said, "MacIntosh, show us where the Allied ASW aircraft patrols operate from."

MacIntosh pointed to airfields near Land's End. "Long-range British aircraft operate from here. Also fifty American Catalina amphibians. Catalinas are big and clumsy, but they can fly all day, and they pack a wallop of four depth charges carried under their wings, or two FIDOs. I've visited the area, and the weather is foul. Aircraft can get in and out only about sixty percent of the time."

Meredith asked, "Are the Germans trying to shoot these patrols down?"

"Yes. They're using JU88s and a few other types. The Catalinas will have trouble with them, even if the JU88s aren't fighters. They can out-maneuver our patrol aircraft and have a heavy armament. They'll have Heinkel 111s carrying torpedoes looking for us."

MacIntosh went on. "Intelligence thinks the German submarines will try to stay on the surface and fight against our aircraft. Most of their present subs have two machine guns, as well as a four-point-one inch deck gun. Now we know the Germans have just completed the first two attack versions of a new class that has the big deck gun and eight heavy machine guns. It's almost half again the size of the U-boats we've seen, well over twelve hundred tons."

"Jesus!" Sorenson said. "Those are the Seawolf class we've been waiting for. They're the ones that could give us a good fight."

Meredith pulled at his mustache. "Intelligence has been speculating about these before, but now they seem to be a fact. Our aircraft spotted some of the variations, such as the minelayer and the supply submarine, and said they seemed huge. We'll have to approach the Seawolves at an angle so that at least two or three of our four-inch guns will bear. If we approach too sharply, only the one forward twenty-millimeter gun will bear. That's why I suggested that two destroyers be sent out as a surface attack unit."

"Sorenson scratched his head, ruffling his blond hair. "Yes, and what if we have two contacts at once?"

"It'll be one to one for sure," Meredith said.

.   .   .

Early the next morning, Sorenson stopped in the CIC after morning general quarters and listened to the air control circuit. He could hear several allied aircraft talking on the medium frequency radio, which had a range of about a hundred miles, instead of the line-of-sight range of the higher frequency TBS.

"Got the bloody bastard!" said an excited British voice.

"Look out!" shouted another voice. "There's a JU88 right behind you!"

"Balls!" said the first pilot. "Ring up the chaps at air-sea rescue. I don't think I can hold this blighter up much longer."

As they steamed closer, Sorenson could hear more

chatter on the radio. He asked MacIntosh to call Meredith into the CIC. When Meredith came in, Sorenson said, "Listen to this. I think these voices are American. Two search aircraft found a pair of U-boats on the surface headed west. The Germans didn't submerge."

"Dammit!" said a voice with a Boston accent. "Don't these Jerries know who we are?"

"Just who the hell are we?" said a second voice. "Personally I'm one scared chicken. These guys have more armament than we do."

Jablonski, also listening in, said, "This is a tougher league than we've been in."

Meredith nodded. "In close contact, a U-boat's machine guns could wipe out our gun crews."

Steele shook his head. "That's not all. Intelligence says they're working on new weapons. A new acoustic homing torpedo. They've only built a few so far, but just one or two could put us out of business."

"Christ," muttered Sorenson. "Speaking of business, I hoped this ASW business might get easier. Now it's worse."

•   •   •

The next morning the *Santee* group began a sweep 200 miles off the coast of France, sending aircraft as far as land. On the second patrol, a Wildcat-Avenger team sighted a pair of JU88s, and the Wildcat left in hot pursuit. In seconds he reported, "Got both the bastards!"

The team returned in triumph to buzz the *Santee* before landing.

Meredith said, "I'll bet the JU88s radioed that there were carrier aircraft in the Bay. Maybe that will help keep the German aircraft away."

"Maybe," Sorenson said, "but they have fighters, too, and more than we have."

•   •   •

That night the *O'Leary* was sent to investigate a radio direction finder bearing. About 10 miles out, Bronte reported a large surface radar contact, and Meredith sent the crew to general quarters. When the *O'Leary* had closed to 2,000 yards, Meredith ordered the searchlight shutters opened. The beam found a large U-boat, bigger than they had ever seen before. Meredith could see a large white U and the last of three numbers, 86. The first number was rusted over.

Steiner quickly opened fire, and at least two projectiles hit nearby before the U-Boat submerged, running at high speed to the south.

Jablonski recommended a course to intercept, but sonar had trouble gaining contact. Steele came out to the bridge. "Captain, maybe the sub headed south to throw us off and then reversed course to the north."

"Good thinking," Meredith said. "Jablonski, give us a course to search to the north."

In ten minutes sonar found him, running north at 10 knots, and Meredith delivered an attack using a medium depth setting. Nothing happened, and Meredith opened to make another attack. Again no results. Steele came out again. "Captain, he's pretty good. Twice he's used perfect evasive tactics. Let's try him again."

Twice more they tried without producing any evidence of damage, and then Steele said, "We can't pick him up any more. I think he headed for the disturbed water from the previous attacks and then went below the layer."

Meredith was disappointed, but after they had completed an hour of an expanding square search, he agreed to return to the formation.

"That Seawolf was pretty good," Sorenson said. "Now we know the number of one of them."

Steele said, "Let's hope it's the only one of the attack version they have in commission."

•   •   •

Meredith settled in his chair to rest while they returned to the formation, but he had hardly leaned back when he noticed that the ship had slowed. Meredith looked at the bridge talker, who had a hand pressed to one of his earpieces and his mouth open slightly as he seemed to be concentrating on the message coming over the telephone. His eyes were slightly glassy. Meredith said, "What's wrong down there?"

The talker tried a few words but stumbled to a halt with a perplexed look.

Meredith picked up the handset to main engine control. "Bull, what the hell's going on down there?"

Meredith listened intently for a few minutes and then turned to Sorenson. "Bull says all those depth charge attacks have loosened boiler brick in boilers two and three. Some have fallen out. Also he's had to shut down one shaft because it wiped a bearing."

Sorenson shook his head. "What can he do?"

"We can only make fifteen knots until at least one boiler is fixed and the bearing is re-babbitted or replaced. First, we have to tell the *Santee*." He grabbed the TBS transmitter and transmitted a casualty report.

The *Santee* replied, "I'll close you. Inform me as soon as possible how long you will be limited in speed."

Meredith didn't have to ask Durham. "Six hours," he replied.

Sorenson asked, "What has to be done?"

"The boilers have to cool so that men can get in the fire boxes to repair the brick. Bull has locked the shaft with the wiped bearing, and inserting a new bearing should only take an hour or so. But even with two shafts, we're limited to the power of one boiler."

Sorenson shook his head. "If number one boiler goes, we'll have to be towed."

"Right, but I think it will hold. It's farther forward in the ship and didn't get as much shock."

Meredith and Sorenson watched the horizon glumly as the hours slid by. Finally Meredith sighed. "The *Santee* doesn't seem to be in any hurry to get near us."

"I can see why," Sorenson said. "We aren't any good to her like this, and she's probably conducting flight operations."

"Damn!" Meredith said. "We're lucky this didn't happen when we were trying to catch up with a convoy."

"Yeah. Most of our overhauls were quick and dirty. This old girl is in bad shape."

Just before the *Santee* arrived, Meredith saw the talker grab his earpiece again, and he picked up the telephone. As he listened his facial muscles relaxed. "Bull says one boiler is back on the line and the bearing was fixed."

Meredith grabbed the TBS transmitter to report the good news to the *Santee*.

•   •   •

Two days later, the *O'Leary* had another assignment, this time with a contact found and attacked by a Wildcat-Avenger team, which failed to drive it down and could not get close enough to use FIDO. The Wildcat reported, "He's got eight large machine guns, and he can keep most of them on me all the time. When I attack I have to point my nose at him. It ain't fair. I can see an 86 on his conning tower."

Sorenson said, "That damned Seawolf is going to keep coming until he gets by us."

The *Greer* and *O'Leary* were assigned as a surface attack unit with Meredith in command. They raced out at thirty knots in a line abreast. As they neared the contact, the submarine must have sighted the ships because the Avenger reported that it had submerged and that a FIDO failed to hit.

Meredith headed for the smoke pot dropped by the Avenger and the *O'Leary* gained contact on the first sweep. Meredith made the first attack, and sonar reported that they heard slight bubbling noises. The aircraft reported a little oil welling up, but no other debris.

"Tell the *Greer* to attack," Meredith ordered, "while we get into position." He went into the CIC to look at the record on the sonar range recorder. Steele pointed out the part just before they had passed over the submarine. "It looks pretty good. I think we hurt him a little. He makes a helluva big contact."

"He should. He's a helluva big boat."

When Meredith returned to the bridge, the *Greer* was dropping depth charges. There was no other evidence of damage or sinking reported by the circling aircraft, and Meredith began another attack. This one brought a little more oil to the surface, and from the direction of the slight slick, the submarine had obviously changed course to the east.

Jablonski came out. "He's heading for the Spanish coast," he said. "At his speed we've got an hour to finish him off."

The submarine increased speed to 10 knots, obviously not worried about his batteries, and they kept after him. At this high speed and with frequent course changes, he was harder to attack, and the *Greer* expended three more patterns of depth charges. Even a new Wildcat-Avenger team failed to sink him. The submarine was apparently too deep for FIDO, and the large depth charge carried by the Avenger was not accurate enough at these depths and high submarine speeds. The time lost while the aircraft were making their attacks was enough for the submarine to enter Spanish waters. Jablonski, carefully keeping a surface plot, recommended that the attacks be stopped.

Meredith shook his head in frustration. "He'll fix his leaks and try again."

The trip back to the *Santee* was gloomy. The two ships had wasted six full patterns of depth charges with nothing to show for it but a few patchs of oil, and now the *O'Leary* had only two sets of depth charges left. Meredith sent word to Gerlach to use half salvos of depth charges in future attacks.

      •   •   •

Dawn the next day brought a red sky in the east. Meredith, lounging in his chair at general quarters, seemed to Sorenson to be apprehensive. His face was sallow, and the muscles in his jaw alternately sagged and clenched. Sorenson, watching him, felt apprehensive, too. There was something about the atmosphere that bothered Sorenson. He walked around to the back of the bridge structure and opened the door to the small box that housed the barometer and thermometer. The barometer was down to 29.50 inches, a whole half-inch below normal, and the weather should have been deteriorating, yet the weather was stable. He shook his head, and went below for a quick breakfast. Fineman was just finishing his toast and black coffee.

Sorenson sat down and ordered eggs and bacon. "Doc, do you believe in predestination?"

"No, but my psychiatric hackles rise when some one asks a loaded question like that. What's the trouble?"

"I feel like the Captain said he felt in Asia when a typhoon was heading for them. I looked at the barometer, and it was way down, but the weather reports are for normal weather."

Fineman stirred his black coffee even though it had

no sugar in it. "Maybe so, but that doesn't have anything to do with predestination. Do you mean you think this is supposed to be a bad day, so it will be?"

"Something like that. I just know I'm uneasy."

"Maybe it's just that big U-boat out there."

Sorenson shrugged. "That's enough to worry anybody."

After breakfast they both went up to the bridge. Meredith was in the CIC, listening to the aircraft circuits. Sorenson looked at the radar. "Where's the *Greer*?"

Meredith answered, "She was sent out on a contact."

"Any results?"

"No. It was pretty far out."

Meredith sat back in his chair and stretched. Sorenson wondered how long Meredith could cope with the strain of command, but then he realized that all of the officers and men were showing signs of fatigue. Maybe strain and not the falling barometer was causing his own feelings of apprehension.

Then the TBS chattered. Sorenson listened carefully. A Wildcat-Avenger team had located a surfaced submarine.

Sorenson said, "My money's on us to go out ... alone."

Fineman said, "What are you worried about? Can't we cope with a single submarine? We've done it several times before."

Sorenson said, "Sure, but there's going to be something more this time. I just feel it. Maybe big 86, the Seawolf, is waiting for us."

They went to general quarters and speeded up to 30 knots. For a half-hour they raced along through the small swells, spray occasionally breaking over the bow, soaking the 4-inch gun crew. Meredith ordered them to go back to the well deck until contact was made.

A lookout shouted, "Aircraft circling, dead ahead!"

Then the surface search radar picked up the periscope shears, and soon the submarine hull appeared on the horizon. Meredith ordered the crew of gun one out on the forecastle, and soon Steiner had the guns loaded and ready. They began firing at long range, about 10,000 years. The submarine refused to dive, all the time shooting at the circling aircraft. It was a big submarine, big enough to be a Seawolf.

"Jesus!" said Sorenson, who had come out of CIC and was examining the submarine through his binoculars. "That thing is bigger than we are. In addition to its deck gun, I can see a quadruple and two twin 20-millimeter machine guns."

Sorenson recommended to Meredith that he keep the *O'Leary* headed slightly to the side of a direct approach course so that gun two on the amidships deck house could bear. As the range closed, the shells from gun two got closer and closer to the bridge and blasted by the wing. Sorenson knew a cut-out cam would prevent the gun from firing into the bridge, but he moved all personnel to the opposite wing as a precaution.

At 6,000 yards, the submarine began firing its deck gun at the *O'Leary*. The first shell landed 20 yards short, amazingly close for a first shot. Sorenson was relieved when Meredith began to zigzag enough to throw off the aim of the submarine. This made it difficult to fire either waist gun on the amidships deckhouse, or the after gun, and with this handicap, Sorenson realized that the odds were almost even.

As they closed, one of the lookouts reported the telltale 86 on the conning tower.

Sorenson lowered his binoculars. "Right. It's the Seawolf."

Then a flash erupted on the forecastle, blinding Sorenson. The concussion drove air into his ears and squeezed his chest. Acrid gases burned his nose. He blinked his eyes, and his vision came back. He looked down at gun one. A lucky hit had exploded at the base of the gun. Part of the force of the explosion had been absorbed by the metal shield, but several of the crew were lying on deck, mixed with empty brass shell casings and a few live rounds. Sorenson cursed as he saw arms and legs at odd angles. The odds had shifted.

Stretcher-bearers from the amidships ammunition passing party ran forward and carried away men who couldn't walk. Kendrick, the gun captain of gun one, was not injured, and Meredith ordered one of the crews of the waist guns brought forward to replace the crew of gun one. The elevation controls had been damaged, making it difficult to follow the computer's orders, but the gun was able to fire at a slow rate.

From CIC, MacIntosh reported that the aircraft had not been able to penetrate the fire of the submarine's antiaircraft guns and had not released any of their weapons.

Steiner reported, "The Avenger has holes in its wings and is leaking fuel. We can see it returning to the carrier escorted by one of the Wildcats."

Sorenson turned to acknowledge the report. Before he could say anything to the talker, a burst of yellow light seared his eyes, and a strong concussion, nearer this time, drove the air from his lungs and knocked him to the deck. Shrapnel shattered into minute pieces the heavy bridge ports of tempered glass and blasted holes in the foreward bulkhead of the bridge. More shrapnel clanged off the inside bulkhead. Smoke and flying glass filled the air, and hundreds of small glass particles clattered against the after bulkhead of the bridge.

Momentarily stunned, Sorenson looked up from the deck and coughed as smoke and flakes of paint and debris swirled across the pilothouse. Holes in the forward bulkhead were as large as his fist. Sorenson stood up, the glass particles underfoot crunching like heavy sand. Meredith was down, sprawled nearby. There was blood on his legs, and a gash on his head bled just below the edge of his helmet.

Sorenson limped over and shook Meredith gently. "Are you all right?"

Meredith was losing consciousness, but he whispered weakly, "No. You'll have to take over."

Meredith's eyes closed, and Sorenson straightened up. He could barely hear Meredith, but he knew what he had said. Alvarado, at the helm, was still steering in spite of blood running down his face. He couldn't talk, but he looked at Sorenson and held up his thumb.

Several men were lying on the gratings. Jablonski was clutching his chest, but still on his feet.

In the strange silence that followed the detonation of the last projectile, Steele, still in the CIC, reported over the squawk box, "She's taking in ballast. I think she's submerging!"

Sorenson tried to ignore the men lying on the gratings and looked out the holes in the bulkhead where the ports had been. The Seawolf was submerging, and Sorenson was undecided as to what to do. On one hand, he wanted her to stay on the surface so they could exact revenge he could see by blasting her with gunfire, but on the other hand, he knew they would have a better chance if she went down and they could use their depth charges. Then he remembered they only had two more patterns of depth charges, and he would have to use them wisely.

He turned his attention to the chaos on the bridge. Stretcher bearers carried the unconscious Meredith below, his legs and arms limp. Jablonski had slumped to the deck, and he was being taken below. The bridge talker was wounded, and stretcher bearers were taking off his headset as they eased him onto a stretcher.

Sorenson grabbed the phone and put them on, leaving one ear uncovered so he could hear the squawk box and TBS. He said, "Gerlach, only six charges on the next pattern."

Gerlach's voice sounded very faint, and at first Sorenson couldn't understand him. Sorenson thumped his ears. He realized his hearing had been impaired by the blast, but he could hear enough on the second try to make out that Gerlach had acknowledged his order.

Sorenson limped over to the squawk box, the broken glass grating under his feet. He pulled down the handle to the transmitter. "Steele, I have command and the conn. Let me know when you pick him up. We'll attack right away."

"Aye, aye, sir," came Steele's deep tones.

Contact was made soon, and Sorenson altered course to head for it. Steele pronounced it firm and very big.

The first drop was a shallow pattern, and Steele said it was a good attack, but Sorenson hoped he could do better, and opened for another. Sorenson still had difficulty hearing, and the damage to his ears made him dizzy. He held on to the bridge chair, steadied himself, and concentrated on the recommendations from Steele.

The next attack seemed better, and Steele said, "Sounds good."

Then Steele's voice became more animated. "She's hurt badly! Blowing ballast! Look out!"

Sorenson opened out to a thousand yards and ordered Steiner to keep his guns trained on the last bearing of the contact.

Steele said over the squawk box, "I told the *Santee* the U-boat was surfacing. They're loading two SBDs with bombs, but they won't be here for thirty minutes."

Sorenson said, "They'll be too late. This will be over one way or another before they can get here."

The Seawolf broached, bow high, and came up with a rush, green water and foam spouting from her vents. Within seconds her gun crews scrambled out hatches and manned her guns. Sorenson opened out to 2,000 yards to decrease the effectiveness of the U-boat's machine guns and to take advantage of the *O'Leary*'s three 4-inchers.

The *O'Leary*'s 4-inch guns boomed. Steiner was punishing her, but the area around the guns and their crews remained untouched. An explosion rocked the base of the conning tower, and many rounds ricocheted off of the thick pressure hull. The *O'Leary*'s 20-millimeter guns aft chattered, and some of the sub's gun crews fell, but they were replaced by other men from below.

Sorenson cursed. The *O'Leary* couldn't seem to inflict killing blows and the submarine kept on firing, both with her deck gun and the six 20-millimeter guns that would bear. Machine-gun projectiles raked the *O'Leary*'s topside, even at 2,000 yards. The hail of fire destroyed equipment and wounded many of her gun crews. Only gun one, with her crew partially shielded by the steel spray shield, was able to keep firing.

A 4.1-inch projectile blasted the *O'Leary* amidships, and steam jetted out the starboard side from one of the firerooms. Sorenson was still wearing the telephone headset when a frantic report came up from main control. "After engine room doesn't answer!"

Then Sorenson had an idea, and he wondered why he hadn't thought of it before. Torpedoes!

"Fire torpedoes!" he ordered. MacIntosh, aft on the

bridge behind the torpedo director, had not been wounded, and he repeated the order over his telephones.

Then he cursed. "Nobody answers!" he shouted. "I'm going aft."

Sorenson heard his feet clattering down the ladder. He knew MacIntosh would have to climb up on the mount and train it on the submarine using a big hand wheel. There would not be time to change any of the settings on the individual torpedoes, and MacIntosh would have to use what he found. He watched anxiously for a few seconds as the mount slowly swiveled out until it was pointed at the U-boat. Sorenson knew MacIntosh would now have to climb down off the mount and go to its rear to fire the torpedoes by hand. The three torpedoes in the port mount chuffed out, fell heavily into the water, and began their run. Sorenson and Steele watched anxiously, as the three wakes diverged slightly in their pre-set spread. One would miss ahead and one astern. The middle torpedo arrowed toward the Seawolf. Sorenson clutched the bulwark as the wake reached the submarine. Then . . . nothing. The torpedo had probably passed under the submarine.

Sorenson cursed and glared at the U-boat. The Seawolf wallowed in the swells and did not move. Sorenson thought she must have lost motive power and steering, and he was glad they were on her beam so that she could not fire torpedoes.

Machine gun projectiles rattled off the forward bridge structure, but most of them were stopped by the armor plate. Steiner reported machine gun hits near the director and that it was out of commission and most of the director crew wounded. Now the only weapons left were gun one firing in local control with great difficulty, and two 20-millimeter machine guns banging away aft. The crews of the other 4-inch guns had been decimated by the U-boat's machine-gun fire, but occasionally those left at the after guns managed to get out a round. There were three more torpedoes left, but they were on the other side. Sorenson would have to turn the O'Leary to unmask them, and when he did so he would have to stop the after 4-inch guns from firing and try to survive the gunfire still coming from the Seawolf. After the failure of the first three torpedoes, Sorenson had no confidence in the remaining three.

For a moment Sorenson thought about opening the range and waiting for the SBDs or another destroyer to arrive, but then he thought that the Seawolf might regain her mobility and escape. If she did, she might sink more American ships. He thought about all the merchant seamen they had seen die at the hands of German submarines, and he knew he had to sink the Seawolf, even if he had to risk the *O'Leary*.

Sorenson knew he had one certain weapon left, and he decided to use it. "Left full rudder, Alvarado, ram the bastard!"

Alvarado grinned through the blood coursing down his face and spun the wheel with one good arm.

Then one of the lookouts above, still unhurt, shouted, "The sub has just fired a torpedo!"

Sorenson was surprised, because they were on the submarine's beam, and he doubted that a normal torpedo could turn enough so that it could hit them.

The remaining fireroom was furnishing enough steam to keep one propeller turning, and the *O'Leary* seemed to Sorenson to be flying, but they were still over a thousand yards away. He felt they couldn't miss, and it would be soon!

The submarine's 4.1-inch gun swiveled to follow the *O'Leary*, and Sorenson felt he was looking down its muzzle. A German sailor shoved a round home. Sorenson swallowed. The muzzle belched smoke and flame.

The blast of the oncoming shell drove Sorenson to the deck. The thin armor plate around the pilothouse took part of the blow, but pieces of the projectile penetrated it. Sorenson felt a sudden pain in his leg and then numbness. There were several gashes on his face, and he felt blood coursing down his cheeks. He pulled himself up, using the remaining pieces of the crushed bridge chair. The squawk box had been blown off its stand, its insides hanging out like twisted spaghetti. The bridge instruments were destroyed, but the wheel was still intact. Alvarado was down again, but Sorenson watched him stagger up and lean on the wheel. Sorenson found the strength to depress the telephone transmitter button and pass the word. "Stand by to ram!"

Steele came flying out of the bridge and into the pilot-house. "Jesus! There's an acoustic torpedo after us! Terrill heard it on the sonar and lost it in the stern baffles!"

"Oh, God!" Sorenson said. "Look aft!"

Steele spun around and ran out to the starboard wing. "Damn! It must be one of their new acoustic homers, and it's climbing right up our wake! Hold on tight!"

Sorenson staggered upright and limped to the wing where he leaned against the bulwark.

The torpedo explosion hammered Sorenson and lifted him from the deck. A giant geyser rose around the fantail, and the *O'Leary*, aft of the after deckhouse, simply disappeared.

The *O'Leary*'s momentum kept her going for a brief period. Then she swung slowly to port and stopped, rolling sluggishly in the swells.

Sorenson looked over at the submarine. It was now on the *O'Leary*'s starboard beam at about a thousand yards, still wallowing in the seas. He could see more men climbing out of her hatches to man the guns. Sorenson looked aft. The starboard torpedo mount was trained out and they were far enough away for the torpedos to arm themselves.

He turned to Steele, but a red mist came down over his eyes and he started to slump to the deck. Steele ran over and caught him. He breathed deeply, and the mist lifted. "Go aft and tell MacIntosh to fire torpedoes."

But before Steele could leave, Sorenson heard the familiar sound of torpedo impulse charges firing, and he knew MacIntosh had done what he thought was best without waiting for orders.

Another projectile from the submarine exploded aft, but Sorenson didn't react. He had done all he could.

Sorenson clutched the bulwark and watched the three torpedo wakes. Instead of diverging, as they would in a normal speed, they were all headed straight for the Seawolf. Sorenson felt a surge of admiration for MacIntosh. He must have been able to remove the off-set from the torpedoes and fire them all directly at the Seawolf.

Now all they had to worry about was the depth mechanisms. Sorenson remembered Meredith's stories about how poorly they had performed off Java. He gritted his teeth trying to stay conscious and blinked to keep the blood out of his eyes.

Then the trails of bubbles reached the giant submarine, and Sorenson held his breath. For a moment nothing happened, and he sagged against the bulwark.

Then a towering mountain of white and black spray covered the Seawolf, and a gigantic concussion shook the *O'Leary*. Sorenson guessed that at least two torpedoes had hit. The huge hull heaved upwards and slowly rolled over on its side. Sorenson could see the crippled rudder and propeller and knew why she had not been able to move. A few bodies slipped down into the sea.

As the red mist crept up again, he watched the Seawolf slide below the surface. There were voices over the telephone he was still wearing. The forward repair party reported that flooding was uncontrollable. A faint voice from main control said, "All steam is gone."

With his last strength, he pushed the transmitter down and said, "Abandon ship." His hands slipped off the bloody bridge bulwark, and he sagged slowly to the deck.

•   •   •

When the mist went away again, Sorenson realized he was lying on the well deck of a destroyer. For a few minutes he thought it was the *O'Leary*. Then he saw the word *Greer* stenciled on a man's life jacket, and he realized it couldn't be the *O'Leary*.

As he got stronger, he lifted his head as much as he could, and he could see Meredith stretched out next to him. Nearby Doc Fineman bent over a man on deck. Farther away were more figures, lying on deck in blood-stained cold weather parkas.

Then Sorenson saw Fineman looking at him, and Fineman came over, followed by Carmody, his arm in a sling.

Sorenson licked his dry lips. "I told you it was going to be a bad day."

Fineman felt Sorenson's pulse. "Not so bad for you. You're going to make it. We'll take the Captain down below to patch him up. Then it'll be your turn."

Sorenson felt weaker. "Please, can't you do something up here?"

"Maybe we can wait to fix you until we get you over to the carrier, but not the Captain. He's bleeding. Besides, he's unconscious."

"Bad?"

"No. We'll save him."

"You aren't kidding about me, are you? If you are, I'd like it straight."

"No, you'll have a lot of pain until we get your leg fixed up, but you'll ride a horse again."

"Nothing vital is involved?"

Fineman grinned. "No, you'll do all that, too."

"What happened to the ship?"

"She stayed afloat after the Seawolf went down. Then she seemed to settle down in the water and for a few minutes we thought she might survive. But soon we could tell that she wasn't going to make it, so Chief Bellows and Gerlach got all the rafts over. The second Wildcat was out of ammunition, but it stayed with us and must have reported what happened, because the *Greer* arrived in a half-hour. The *O'Leary* wouldn't go down, but it was just a matter of time. The *Greer* had to put a torpedo in her before she'd give up."

Sorenson thought of the many times the *O'Leary* had sunk or destroyed Japanese and German aircraft, ships, and submarines and even a French artillery piece. Her luck had finally run out, but no enemy had managed to sink her. It had taken an American weapon to put her under.

Fineman went on. "When the *Greer* arrived, we put the wounded in life rafts and just stepped off into the water. They had us aboard in a few minutes. The torpedo explosion aft had blown her colors off, but Steele had hoisted another set of colors on her foremast. Her colors, still flying, were the last we saw of her. She went down on an even keel, a lady to the end."

"How did our crew make out?"

"Carmody is still taking muster. Chief Bellows is helping him."

"Is he all right?"

"Yes and no. He still has his cap, but he lost his dental plates."

Chief Bellows came over and looked down at Sorenson. "Ha-ss ha-da ha-leg?" he asked.

Sorenson tried to grin, but the pain was too much. "Okay, Chief, take care of our men."

Fineman said, "Alvarado is gone. So is Kendrick. There are many others not accounted for yet."

"Where is Bronte?"

Carmody, still standing nearby anxiously, said, "He's over there, sitting by Alvarado's body. He won't say anything except he keeps muttering, 'I didn't mean it. She's a great ship.' Sir, I've got a list of the crew. I thought we'd need it when we got back to port. You'll have to write letters and all."

"Thanks, Carmody. Where's Mister Steele?"

"He's helping with the first aid. Do you want to see him?"

"Whenever he has a break."

Steele came over in a few minutes. He looked down at Sorenson. "Sir, I had the honor of commanding the *O'Leary* for a few minutes. Not as long as you did, but I'm proud to have done it." He thought for a few seconds. "And Mister Durham did too."

Sorenson asked, "Where is he?"

Steele took a deep breath. "He went down with her. When you collapsed, I called down and told him he was in command. He laughed, but he sounded very weak. I asked him if he was all right, and he said he thought he'd last for a few minutes more and for me to keep the conn. Then the phone went out, and I couldn't get a messenger down there. The hatches were jammed and the engine room was a shambles, so I took command."

"Thanks," Sorenson said. "Go back to what you were doing, and we'll talk some more later. You did a great job, and I intend to see that you're recognized for it."

Sorenson thought about Alvarado. He hated losing him. Alvarado had gone out the way he would have wanted to, fighting to the last. Sorenson was glad

Alvarado would never know the *O'Leary* was gone. She had been his home, and he would never have been happy without her.

Durham, too, had gone out fighting, and with a laugh at the end. He sighed as he thought of telling Sonya, and he wished that he had gotten to know Durham better. Then the pain grew. Sorenson groaned in spite of gritting his teeth until they hurt.

Fineman bent over him. He pulled out a morphine syrette and stuck it in Sorenson's leg.

"Jesus, Doc. You did that right through my pants. Aren't you afraid of infection?"

"No time to worry. You're too mean for germs. I'm going to leave you now. I have to take care of some other patients. You'll be going over to the *Santee* by highline soon."

Sorenson watched Fineman's figure disappear from his field of vision and thought about all that Fineman had done for him. Now he had given him another example of mercy, the mercy of morphine. He looked up at the familiar area of the well deck around him and remembered the burial ceremony for the German Naval officer. What was Fineman's prayer titled? Something about mercy. "Gnade Uber Alles." Mercy above all, Gerlach had translated. He wondered if he could ever feel merciful toward the Germans, and he knew he would have to think more about it. Somehow not feeling mercy had been gnawing at his soul, and he knew he had to change. It was hurting him more than it was hurting the Germans.

He lowered his head to the steel deck. Hard as it was, he welcomed it. But the pain was still intense, and he knew the morphine hadn't taken effect yet. He pulled a piece of his parka hood around so that he could get it in his mouth and clamped his teeth on it to resist the spreading and increasing pain. It wasn't enough, but it kept him from crying out until the morphine could take over.

He could hear the sound of aircraft engines on the carrier mixing with the whine of the blowers just aft of the *Greer*'s well deck. The sounds seemed to be competing for his attention, and he remembered he would have to make a choice soon between aviation and destroyers. Then he thought about the last few minutes when he had been in command of the *O'Leary*. He remembered how well the officers and men had performed ... Steele, MacIntosh, Bronte, Alvarado, Kendrick ... they had responded to his leadership, and he could not desert them.

He took a deep breath to fight off the pain. Suddenly he knew there wasn't any real choice. There never had been one. He was a destroyer sailor. Deep down he had been one for a long time, and he would always be one.

He let out his breath and allowed the pain to wash over him. He couldn't fight it any more, and the morphine still didn't help. He groaned as four men lifted him carefully off the deck and put him in a stretcher. They carried him up to the forecastle and rigged his stretcher for securing to the highline.

He was conscious of the rushing water alongside, but then he faded out again and he was riding his horse on the ranch with his wife beside him. He was barely conscious of the stretcher floating in space, and he knew he would live to be home with Ferren soon.

Chapter Thirty-four

Sorenson shifted in his rickety wooden chair to ease the pain in his leg. His battered wooden desk was in front of a window looking out on a parking lot at the Norfolk Naval Base. Rain spotted the window and bounced off the tops of the cars lined up in the lot below.

Carmody, at an adjacent desk, said, "Mister Sorenson, I've got most of these letters ready. Can I leave a little early this afternoon?"

"Sure. Another date with your girlfriend?"

"Yes. This will be a big one. I'm going to ask her to marry me."

Steele, wearing his new lieutenant junior grade stripes, was sitting at a nearby desk. "Do you think her parents will say yes?"

"I hope so. I think Lieutenant Commander Sorenson convinced them that I was civilized, even if I was a sailor."

Steele grinned. "And from Texas?"

Carmody said patiently, "Even that. He told them I would be a leading citizen of Texas some day."

Sorenson said, "Before you go, let me check a few items with you. First, I need several extra copies of my orders."

"On your desk. I think you'll like being skipper of a destroyer, even if it isn't brand new. Can you use a good yeoman?"

"Certainly. I'll get you ordered there as soon as I take

over. Did you call Mrs. Atkinson to make an appointment for me to see her?"

Steele interrupted. "I did, and I want to go with you. I know better than anyone how Bull died."

Carmody asked, "Anything I don't know about?"

"Maybe. I learned from an engineer who was one of the last out of the forward engine room that Mister Durham stayed until everyone else was out. Then it was too late for him to make it."

Sorenson sighed. "Sonya will miss him, and so will I. The medal he'll be receiving posthumously won't help much."

"Anything else?" Carmody asked.

"Yes, how about Bronte?"

"He got his orders to advanced radar school. He's also been recommended for a commission."

"Get me his address. I want to get him transferred to my ship."

Sorenson looked at a list on his desk. "How about Mister Gerlach?"

"On leave. Also Mister Jablonski and Mister MacIntosh are still in the hospital."

"And Chief Bellows?"

"Got a new set of dentures and orders to another destroyer."

Steele said, "Speaking of the hospital, when they let you out, how was Captain Meredith?"

"Better. He's going to the Naval Academy to teach. Maybe he'll move to Texas when he's through with the Navy."

Carmody cleared his throat. "I hope you haven't forgotten about me."

Sorenson laughed. "No. I need you on my ship. After the war, my brother may want to invest in some wildcatting. We'll see if we can find some 'awl' together."

The door to the temporary office opened and Renard came in, slapping his rain coat. Sorenson turned and watched him get out of his rain gear. "Everything okay?"

Renard shook his head. "Damned bureaucracy! I've got most of the pay accounts re-constructed, but the supply depot wants to know who's going to pay for the last shipment of medicinal brandy. It seems we exceeded our quarterly allotment."

Sorenson laughed. "Tell them to refer it to Mrs. Holderman. But they'll have to hurry. She won't be there long."

Renard's eyebrows shot up. "Where's she going?"

"To California with me. We're getting married as soon as we get there."

Steele asked, "Who's going to be your best man?"

"Doc Fineman."

"What's he going to be doing on the west coast?"

"He's traveling, and then he's going to my ship."

Steele said, "Lucky guy."

Sorenson said, "So are you, unless you don't want to go."

Steele brightened. "I'll be there."

Sorenson got up slowly. "Carmody, I'm leaving. We'll finish these letters tomorrow. Mrs. Holderman is coming for me." He adjusted his crutches and clumped over to the door. Carmody opened it and followed him outside. Ferren was waiting for him in the red Ford.

Carmody helped Sorenson into the right hand seat and put his crutches in the back seat. "Hi, Mrs. Holderman."

Ferren smiled and waved her hand.

Sorenson said, "How would you like this car for a wedding present?"

Carmody's mouth dropped. "But, sir, you couldn't do that."

Sorenson looked at Ferren and she nodded. "Oh, yes I could. We don't need two cars."

Ferren took a deep breath. "Right. We're going to be one family from now on."

•   •   •

Two weeks later Sorenson and Ferren drove up in the green Buick to the *O'Leary*'s office. The back seat was filled with baggage. Sorenson got out, limping slightly without his crutches.

"Why are we stopping here?" Ferren asked. "I thought you said everyone had been detached."

"They have, but I want to make sure Carmody left the

office in good order. He's not the neatest person in the world."

They stopped in front of the door. On it was a rectangular cardboard sign on which was crudely lettered, 'U.S.S. O'Leary—DD 200.' Below the lettering, someone had added 'Mabuhay.' The door was unlocked, and Sorenson pushed it open. They stepped inside, and Sorenson looked around the room. The floor had been swept and the desks and chairs were neatly lined up. Sorenson's eyes examined the room and stopped at Carmody's desk. Next to it was a waste basket filled with crumpled pieces of paper. A few pieces had spilled over to the floor.

Sorenson laughed. "Just like Carmody, but a little better than his office used to be." Sorenson walked over to the waste basket, picked up the papers, and stuffed them down in the waste basket.

"Let's go," he said. "It's a long way to San Francisco."

They walked out of the office and closed the door. Ferren looked at the sign. "What does *Mabuhay* mean?"

"Morales used to try to translate it for me. It's a Tagalog word, the language of most Filipinos. Their language is as exotic and interesting as their country. He said it means 'Good luck,' and 'Goodbye,' and 'Well done.' "

"All of them?"

"Yes. Take your pick."

"I'll take 'Well done.' "

Sorenson pulled out the thumb tacks holding the sign to the door and threw them in a nearby trash can. As he started to crumple the sign, Ferren put her hand on his arm. "You ought to keep that. It will always remind you of the *O'Leary*, and it's the only thing left of her."

"You're right." He folded the sign neatly and put it in his inside coat pocket. "Hundreds of men who served with her will always remember her fondly, even if she was old, cranky, and uncomfortable."

Ferren sighed. "And we'll remember those who went down with her."

They went back to the car, and Sorenson helped Ferren in. As he started to get in the driver's seat, he looked back at the office door. A discolored rectangle marked the area where the sign had been. Tomorrow, he thought, there will be a new sign there, and life will go on. As he stooped to get in the car, the folded sign in his pocket jabbed at his chest. He straightened for a moment and looked back at the door. *"Mabuhay,"* he said softly.

Afterword

Pursuit of the Seawolf is an historical novel based on several actual convoys and on Operation Torch, the landings in Northwest Africa. The events are portrayed as accurately as possible. The *Burza* incident is fictional.

The *O'Leary* is a fictional ship with a fictional crew. She has been added to the actual events in such a manner as not to disturb the historical accuracy of the events.

The German Navy did not officially name the large type IX U-boat the Seawolf class, but this name was used unofficially by the members of the German Navy and by the American and British Navies.

Only a few Seawolves were commissioned by the end of the war. After the war, several Seawolves were found in the German shipyards being outfitted with various combinations of armament. Some had two 4.1-inch guns and four 20-millimeter machine guns and others had a single 4.1-inch gun and a quadruple and two twin 20-millimeter machine guns. Although designed to be 1,250 tons, they were actually several hundred tons heavier. All were being fitted to carry acoustic homing torpedoes.

ABOUT THE AUTHOR

Vice Admiral William P. Mack served as an officer in the Asiatic Fleet as well as in the Atlantic during World War II. He became the first non-aviator commander of the U.S. Seventh Fleet in Vietnam, and later served as Superintendent of the U.S. Naval Academy until retiring in 1975. Vice Admiral Mack is the co-author of SOUTH TO JAVA, which was a Book-of-the-Month Club Selection, as well as three professional books: COMMAND AT SEA, THE NAVAL OFFICER'S GUIDE, and NAVAL CUSTOMS, TRADITIONS AND USAGE. He was awarded the Alfred Thayer Mahan prize for literary excellence by the Navy League in 1981.

Join the Allies on the Road to Victory
BANTAM WAR BOOKS

The history of man in flight...
THE BANTAM AIR AND SPACE SERIES

The Bantam Air and Space Series is dedicated to the men and women who brought about this, the era of flight—the century in which mankind not only learned to soar the skies, but has journeyed out into the blank void of space.